Trapped Under Ice

by

M.J. Schiller

DEDICATION

To my husband, who has always had more faith in me than I have in myself, who has always supported me one hundred percent, even though his analytical outlook on life is so different from my more creative view. For twenty-seven years he has been my best friend and the hero in all my stories. Without him, they would never have existed. My love always and forever.

PROLOGUE

C had Evans tried to play his heart out on stage, but he could never quite seem to leave it there. After his band, Trapped Under Ice, performed its second encore, he exited the floor, guitar in hand, soaked in sweat and exhausted. Once backstage, he handed his instrument to a roadie. He took the towel the kid offered with a nod, mopping his face, mustache, and goatee. He then lifted his curly, dirty-blond hair and rubbed the towel back and forth behind his neck, the friction making the cotton feel rough against his skin. He finally pressed it against his eyes for a minute with a sigh, letting it black out the world.

Sometimes the music helped, and Chad would be able to relax with the guys after a show. Sometimes, like tonight, he became even more keyed up. Only tonight seemed different from the rest. The feelings were sharper, like glass in his gut. Maybe he had reached his breaking point. A man could only take so much. And tonight, he felt like either the rage he felt inside would finally rip him apart, or things would change in some other way. He still held out enough hope to imagine there was some other way out of this, and enough dread to fear there was not.

Chad heard the rest of the band members approaching behind him and shook himself out of his thoughts. "Good job, guys," he threw over his shoulder to the three men entering the backstage area behind him. In contrast, the trio, his brother included, though equally tired, seemed pleased with the evening. They were now high-fiving each other with smiles on their sweat-glistening faces.

Chad listened to their banter as he opened the cooler resting at his feet in the eaves and reached into its icy interior for a brew. He twisted the bottle top off and dropped it carelessly on the stage next to a dozen others. He kept apart from his fellow band members, knowing he needed some time for the alcohol to do its work and relax his ragged nerves. Nodding to his body-guard, Pete, who stood off in the shadows, he sidled out a stage door.

Chad and Pete had come to a sort of unspoken agreement at times like this. Chad needed his space, and the older man had learned to give it to him—although Pete often told the singer it was "against 'The Unofficial Bodyguard's Code of Operation.'" Yet, it would appear after their five years together, Pete had come to know which fights he could win, and which were better left unfought, as he stepped aside without a word to let Chad pass.

Chad entered one of the hallways circling St. Louis's Edward Jones Dome to escape for a few minutes. By himself in the hall, he paced like a man on death row awaiting the final hour. He forced himself to stop his back-and-forth movements to take a long pull on his beer. He leaned against a wall. The beer felt good on his scratchy throat. He knew it was dangerous to sing as all out as he did—blown vocal chords were a singer's worst nightmare—but he could never sing anything halfway, so he was just waiting for the day his voice would finally give out.

It was cooler and not as close in the hall. Backstage was always stuffy, no matter how well-ventilated a venue was, mostly due to the fog from the smoke machine. The smoke remained after the show and never quite dissi-pated. Instead, it rose to the ceiling and swirled there like a malevolent, gray storm cloud.

Chad stretched long legs out in front of him, crossing his feet and plant-ing one heel of his boots against the toe of the other. His butt and shoulder blades were made comfortably cold where they touched the cinder block wall behind him. He closed his eyes and exhaled jaggedly, wishing to God he could lose the rage that had maintained a stranglehold on him for so long.

The amplifiers were still ringing in his ears as he relived the chords in his mind, so he almost missed the screaming. But just as he lifted his head and tried to place where the noise was coming from, a girl came tearing around the corner. He judged her to be about fifteen or sixteen, with soft brown hair falling just to her shoulders. She pulled up short and Chad could tell in her blink of surprise the girl recognized him. She only hesitated for an instant before running over.

"My m-mom," she gasped. Chad grabbed the teen by the shoulders to steady her as she tried to suck enough air into her lungs to make herself audible. The stark look of fear in her eyes told him this was no joke. "These guys attacked us—"

Chad interrupted her. "Go inside those doors and ask for Pete." He took off running in the direction the girl came from, yelling over his shoulder, "Tell him I need help!"

CHAPTER ONE

Beth turned her head to peer at Cassie's profile with a smile. How had her daughter known this concert was just what she needed? When she discovered the tickets—which the sixteen-year-old had tucked into the branches of their little Christmas tree a week ago—she was touched. Cassie was industrious enough to save money from her first job to purchase them as an early Christmas present for them both. As a barista at their local coffee shop, Beth wondered just how many cappuccinos were poured for customers in order to be able to afford them. Trapped Under Ice was one of the hottest bands going, not to mention her latest obsession, so she was absolutely thrilled about seeing them play.

Now here she was, screaming wildly as one of her favorite songs started. Beth began singing along with the crowd, asking herself for the hundredth time if it was appropriate for a thirty-seven-year-old mom to love a hard rock band whose lyrics were, sometimes, well...questionable. Shaking her head with a laugh, Beth decided, if she enjoyed it, what was the harm?

Beth glanced at Cassie as she bopped along beside her, face aglow with first-concert euphoria. She sent up a silent prayer, thanking God for the night. All they had suffered through in the past didn't matter right now. Tonight, they were just two girls having fun.

Too soon, the concert was over. After the second encore, mother and daughter followed the crowd down the staircase.

"I hope you didn't blow your vocal chords singing," Cassie teased. "You've got that big solo tomorrow."

"Nah, I'll be fine. All I need is a good night's sleep."

"On the contrary," a deep, male voice stated from behind them. "What you need is a night out on the town."

Beth turned to see if the man was addressing her. Evidently, he was, because his male companion added, "What do you say, ladies? We're so wound up from the concert. Maybe some dancing would help us settle down a little."

The first man who spoke was tall and good-looking, with dark hair and a beard. He reminded Beth of the lumberjack-looking man on paper towel packages. The second man was thinner and balding, dressed in a khaki jacket and jeans.

Beth smiled. "No thank you. We really do need to go back to the hotel to get some sleep. We have a choral thing tomorrow to attend."

"Oh, come on now," the dark-haired man insisted. "It's barely eleven o'clock."

"Yes, but that's late enough for us." They reached the bottom of the stairs, and Beth took Cassie's arm and steered her to the left. "Thanks anyway," she stated without turning back.

"Mom." Cassie giggled. "Those guys were hitting on you."

"Oh, come on. Don't be silly."

"I'm not. I'm serious."

Beth subtly changed the subject. "Cas, I want to thank you for the concert tickets. This was fantastic. I never dreamed I would be able to see Trapped Under Ice." She put an arm around her daughter and gave her a squeeze, then whispered to Cassie confidentially, "Weren't they awesome?"

"Yeah. They were."

They laughed, enjoying the opportunity to act more like friends than mother and daughter. The pair chitchatted down the hallway, comparing notes on what songs they thought the group did best and which songs they wished the band had played, but didn't.

Spotting a women's restroom, Cassie asked, "Hey, can we use the bathroom before we leave?"

"Good idea." Beth laughed. "I knew those sodas would come back to haunt us."

As the two joined a line stretching deep into the hallway, Beth noticed the men who spoke to them earlier standing back at a short distance. When they saw her peering in their direction, they glanced away. It seemed as if they were trying to look casual. An alarm bell began sounding in Beth's ears. *Are those guys following us?* After a few minutes she chastised herself, *you're just* being a Nervous Nelly. But to test her theory, she asked Cassie, "Why don't we go down farther and see if we can find a bathroom with a shorter line."

As they proceeded down the hall, Beth peeked over her shoulder. The men fell into step behind them. Beth searched for one of the security guards who seemed to be so prevalent when they first had entered the building. Seeing none, she picked up her pace.

"Geez, Mom," Cassie joked, "I didn't know you had to go so badly."

Beth whispered, not wanting to be overheard. "I don't, Cas. I think those two guys we talked to before are following us. Don't look. Let's duck back inside the stadium."

Beth took the next staircase to the interior of the building. They came out among the seats on the west side of the stage. She rapidly descended the interior steps, leading Cassie behind her, and finally exiting on a lower level of the building.

"Are they still following us?"

Beth scanned the area. The hallway was deserted. "I don't think so."

"Well, can we use the bathroom, now? I really need to go."

"Of course, honey." Beth made a mental note to head in the opposite direction when they came out. In trying to lose their pursuers, they had traveled closer to the backstage area and needed to get back into a more heavily populated area of the building.

"No line here," Cassie commented unnecessarily.

Beth entered the outer door behind her, and then waited for her daughter a few minutes, checking her hair in the large mirror. "I guess I better try to go, too," she murmured and stepped into the stall next to Cassie's. She heard a toilet flush and Cassie exited. A second later, water splashed into the sink.

"Hey, what are you doing in here?" Cassie's voice was shaky.

Beth froze at the sound of the low male voice answering her. "As if you didn't know." She could hear two men chuckle, the sound a haunting echo in the empty room.

Fumbling with the lock on the door, Beth rushed out of the stall, belt still undone, hanging loosely from the loops of her jeans. The larger man stood about fifteen feet to her left. The other was positioned inches away from Cassie, leering and reaching to touch her hair. They must have come in separate doors to make sure the women were trapped. He pulled a knife out of his pocket and held it casually in one hand. Cassie clutched the edge of the sink behind her, face pale.

In the few seconds it took to cross the five feet to Cassie's attacker, a half-dozen voices exploded in Beth's head. Her self-defense teacher instructed her, "If you're being attacked by a man, use his size to your advantage." She heard her grandfather's voice, a man who boxed in the Army, "Pop 'em in both ears at the same time. It will explode their eardrums." She remembered a time when she and her late husband, Paul, were goofing around and she accidentally hit him below the belt. "You've got a man totally in your control when you do that," he stated, grimacing.

But all these voices were drowned out by a sort of primal scream raging inside of her. She took in Cassie's eyes, wide with terror, and was transported to a time when Cassie was about four years old and the neighbor's black lab was jumping up on her. Beth did what she had done then; she let instinct take over.

Not even aware of what she was doing, Beth grabbed the man's head and, for a split second, saw his expression of surprise before she slammed it down onto the edge of the sink. He slid to the floor without a sound. She stood for a beat, stunned by her actions. Catching a movement to her left, she grabbed Cassie's arm and pulled her around the slumped figure of her attacker and toward the door to their right.

The pair made it out the door before she felt a hand clutch the back of her jacket. She shrugged it off as fast as she could. Cassie turned back just as the man's finger raked through and grabbed the back of her hair. Unable to help herself, Beth screamed in pain.

As the bearded man jerked Beth back, she pushed her daughter forward. Struggling against him, she shouted, "Run, Cassie, run."

Cassie turned and froze.

The man's forearm crossed Beth's throat now, but she still managed to look her daughter in the eyes and somehow scream, "Dammit, Cas. Get out of here."

The curse word was like a slap in the face. Beth rarely cursed in front of Cassie, and never at her. Cassie stumbled backward a few feet and then turned to run.

CASSIE RAN ALMOST BLINDLY. Inside her head a single scream of terror rang, knocking out all reason. She didn't know if it was the sound of her own voice she heard or her mother's as the man ripped off Beth's jacket and clawed at her hair. Cassie's legs pounded over concrete—propelled up and down like pistons in an engine—though she was sure her mind had not ordered them to. She sobbed once. Why wasn't somebody coming to help?

She fought to not break down, knowing she needed to keep it together in order to get help. Lungs burning and her eyes stinging with tears, she turned a corner and saw the tall figure dressed in black leaning against the wall. She wanted to give in to the desire to fall apart, to rush into someone's arms and find comfort, but she knew her mom was somewhere trying to fight off an assailant.

When Cassie pulled up, the lack of noise made it apparent she must have been screaming. Exactly what she called out, she couldn't remember, but as she got closer to the man, who pushed away from the wall and stood in front of her, she recognized him. Her oxygen-deprived brain scrambled to make sense. "My m-mom..." She couldn't get enough force behind her words. He braced her shoulders, and she gulped in some air. "These men attacked us—"

Before she could finish what she was saying, the man in black took off, shouting at her to find someone named Pete. Cassie stood for a second, collecting her scattered thoughts, and then stumbled forward a few feet, bursting through the doorway he indicated without knocking. The area was dark, but immediately a big, balding man—wearing a T-shirt with a black leather vest—rose from a stool and walked toward her.

"You'll have to leave, Miss," he muttered with a sigh, but not unkindly. "They'll be no autographs tonight."

"P-Pete?" she gasped.

He raised a hand to Cassie's shoulder to escort her out of the area but stopped, staring at her quizzically. "How do you know my name?"

Cassie's mind reeled. He sent her...a name most people knew...a name every girl knew...it should be there in her mouth. Chad Evans.

"Chad. Chad needs you. These men attacked—"

But Cassie found she was speaking to a metal door closing behind the large frame of the man named Pete.

CHAPTER TWO

As Chad ran, scenes from his childhood flashed in front of his eyes unbidden. He tried to tell himself this woman's attack had nothing to do with his past, but the same adrenaline was surging through his system now as it had in his youth. He had the same sweaty tongue, the same hammering of his heart shooting blood through his system, the same sick feeling in the pit of his stomach.

Chad tried to clear his head of the vision, but all at once memories crashed into reality as he skidded around a corner and made out a pair of figures up ahead. A large man sat on top of a woman who seemed to be struggling with him even as the man brutally punched her. Without even breaking stride, he rushed forward to tackle the man and the two rolled several feet beyond the woman.

Coming up on top, Chad gained an instant advantage over his opponent due to the man's complete surprise. The added strength of the blinding fury compelled his fists to pound the other man over and over again as the lines between cramped childhood apartment and echoing stadium hallway began to blur.

Somewhere in his mind he could hear the woman screaming at him to stop, but it was as if her voice were coming at him from across the years, blended with his mother's. While in truth, the woman had somehow managed to crawl over to within feet of him. He stopped, realizing the body beneath him was no longer moving. The red, murderous haze clouding his vision rolled back. His lungs seared with each intake of breath as he tried to focus on bringing his heart rate down.

BETH LAY STUNNED FOR a minute, unsure of what had just happened, and dizzy from being banged into the concrete repeatedly. She turned her battered head to see a tall figure in a black T-shirt and jeans wailing on the man who hit her. She lifted onto one elbow. Her vision was blurry, focus coming in and out.

It took her some time to figure out what was going on. For a minute or two, she watched the man's arms coming up and down, reminding her of the dunking bird she got as a child at a Stuckey's. The image of the comical yellow toy bird wearing a red top hat as it bobbed into a glass of water was a jarring contrast to what she was really witnessing. Then, she realized her attacker had lost consciousness, but the flurry of fists didn't stop. She rose, teetering, and stumbled over to where the two lay, falling to her knees.

"That's enough!"

The fists stopped their pummeling and the man on top turned his head to look at her, panting from exertion. For a minute, he seemed surprised to see her there.

"Chad!" a voice cried from down the hall. Beth turned to see a third man enter and run to their side.

Her eyes spun from the newcomer back to the man who had rescued her, still straddling the figure lying prone, out cold. Of course. It was Chad Evans, the lead singer of Trapped Under Ice. As she watched, he sat back on his haunches, breathing hard.

"It's okay, Pete," he finally told the older gentleman who had called out to him. The singer turned to her. "Are you all right?"

She peered at him. His brown eyes were soft with concern. For a minute, he reminded her of Paul. Beth always thought of brown eyes as flat and uninteresting before she met her husband. Yet Paul's eyes time and again demonstrated an ability to make her melt. She saw her husband again in these eyes.

"I-I'm fine," she stuttered, unnerved by his gaze.

"Can I help you, Miss?" The older man offered his hand and lifted her to her feet.

Chad rose, too. He looked down at the man between his boots, seeming to understand all at once that he was responsible for his bloodied chin and mouth.

"Looks like you did a number on him," Pete grumbled.

"Y-yeah," he responded, his unease with the fact evident.

Cassie appeared from out of nowhere and rushed into her arms.

"Oh, Cas." Beth clutched her daughter, struggling to contain her emotions. The fear she kept at bay, the horrible thought the men would hurt Cassie, surged through her like the crowd flooding through the open doors of a department store on Black Friday, only with less warning. She could feel her muscles shaking and allowed the tears to stream unabashedly down her face; she had no strength left to fight it.

CHAD STOOD OFF TO ONE side, feeling awkward. He had gotten into many fights before, some he had no doubt even started, mostly in the bars where the band played before they were booked into stadiums. And while he usually came out on top, Chad generally felt miserable afterward, as he did now.

His eyes were drawn to the pair of women who were the focus of the group, for others were arriving on the scene, too. The teen, who had found him in the hallway and had asked for help, stood hugging the woman the man had attacked, both obviously relieved to see each other in one piece.

While Chad watched, the woman with the unstoppable eyes glanced up and caught his. "Thank you," she mouthed silently.

He nodded in what he hoped was a casual style, but his heart cartwheeled in his chest. Out of habit he checked for a wedding ring, but her hands were bare. Was she single, or just one of those women who didn't like to wear jewelry on her hands? Then, he felt a wave of guilt. The woman had just been beaten and he was checking her out. What was wrong with him? Still, there was something about her...

He noticed, behind the women, Pete was filling in his brother, David, and Dante, who was his best friend and bandmate, Roger's bodyguard. David crossed to him.

"You okay, bro?" His lips were tight as he scanned Chad's face and searched for signs of injury elsewhere.

Noting David's expression, he realized he had been clenching and un-clenching his hands for some minutes now. "I'm fine, Davy." He laid a hand on the shorter man's shoulder.

David grabbed him up in a bear hug. Chad smiled, though a little em-barrassed. His brother released his grip but stood with an arm around Chad for a minute. He reached out his hand to the pair of women still huddled to-gether in the middle of the group. "Hi, I'm David Evans."

The ordinariness of his act helped to settle the mother down. She shook his hand. "Yes, I know." She smiled. She had one of those smiles that filled a room. "Beth Donovan...and this is my daughter, Cassandra."

"Cassie," the teen corrected, giving her mom a try-not-to-humiliate-me look and seeming to bounce back momentarily from her fright. She, too, ap-peared to be taken in by the sense of normalcy being reestablished.

Four uniformed security guards interrupted them, appearing from around the corner. Pete and Dante walked up to greet them. "This guy as-saulted these women," Pete explained, gesturing first to the man at their feet, who was coming around, and then back to Cassie and Beth.

"And there's another one in the bathroom," Beth added. "I think he may need some medical care." Her tone was remorseful, forehead creased with worry.

Chad gawked at her in surprise. How did this five-foot-two mother and her slightly taller daughter dispatch with a second assailant?

The oldest of the four guards, who appeared to be in charge, approached Beth. "It looks as if you could use a little medical attention yourself."

Beth seemed uncomfortable with all the attention drawn to her, her blush still visible despite the redness of her injuries. "I'm okay," she affirmed. She looked beyond the guard to David before her gaze finally rested on Chad, who stood with his hands in pockets next to his brother.

"Well, how about a beer, at least?" Roger queried, having entered with Keith a few minutes before. Chad guessed his friend was trying to ease the tension.

Beth sighed. "Now, that sounds pretty good." She looked at the guard for permission. He hesitated.

"Sure. We'll get the information from these two gentlemen—" he indi-cated Pete and Dante "—and if we need anything else, we'll come get you."

"And you'll make sure they are taken to a hospital?" Beth insisted.

"Yes, ma'am," he responded, raising his eyebrows. She exhaled, her face relaxing more, and then turned to follow Roger.

"Right this way, ladies." The bassist swept his arm wide and bowed, throwing Chad a wink over his shoulder.

CHAPTER THREE

When they entered the backstage area, a woman came rushing over to Roger. She had short, brown hair with one long strand of pink hanging from the side, and she wore an eclectic outfit consisting of a black and white horizontally striped, long-sleeved T-shirt that scooped low over her abundant breasts, and a short black skirt that looked like a tutu. The girl had an enormous black and white polka-dotted bow in her hair and hot-pink tights on under the skirt. Beth immediately thought of Cyndi Lauper.

"Are you okay, babe?" the woman asked Roger anxiously, hanging on him.

"I'm fine. I'm fine," Roger muttered, sounding a little annoyed. "Chad here took care of all the bad guys for us."

"Chad?" The woman turned her gaze on the singer.

"I just took care of one," Chad reminded him.

"Oh yeah. I stand corrected." Roger handed Beth the beer he had retrieved for her, studying her. He opened his mouth to question her further, but the woman at his side interrupted.

"Hi, I'm Michelle. Are you sure you two are okay? Boy, if it were me, I'd still be shaking in my boots."

Beth noted doing that wouldn't be too difficult in the high-heeled, thigh-high, black boots the woman was sporting. "Well, I may not be shaking on the outside, but..." Beth took a drink of her beer, grateful for its numbing relief. She raised her eyebrows and nodded to indicate she was indeed shaking on the inside.

"Roger, get her water or something," Michelle ordered, indicating Cassie. "What do you want, hon?"

"Water is fine," Cassie replied, somewhat subdued now.

"Let me show you gals to a restroom so you can get cleaned up," Michelle offered, leading them farther into the shadows. The rest of the group trouped after them.

Michelle opened a door on what appeared to be a large rec room, except for the mirrored vanities lining one wall, like the cliché dressing room. She opened a second inner door as the men fanned out around the room behind them, and the three women entered a spacious bathroom.

Beth glanced at her reflection in the mirror. Lovely, she thought wryly, the light seeming to accent every mark on her face left by the blows she received.

"Yeah, you're a piece of work. Let me get you a washcloth." Michelle rummaged around and came up with a hand towel, getting it damp and handing it to Beth. Beth touched it to her lip with as little pressure as possible but still sucked in her breath in pain.

"I'm Roger's wife, by the way," Michelle emphasized, giving Beth a slightly challenging look in the mirror before turning to Cassie. "And how are you doing, darlin'?"

Cassie was splashing water on her face at the sink next to Beth. She still looked pale but seemed to be regaining her equilibrium little by little.

IN THE OUTER ROOM, Chad was pacing again, half placing blame for the attack on himself. *It's little wonder something like this happened,* he fumed silently. *I mean, my music is pretty violent at times. It can't be any great wonder it draws violent people.*

He quickly downed his second bottle of beer and was well into his third when the women reentered the main room. Roger was giving a comical play-by-play of the fight without ever seeing any of it. Chad, half-sitting, half-leaning against some sound equipment on the far side of the room, couldn't help but grin at his antics. He knew it was just Roger's way of trying to make everything okay. He had a knack for that, he reflected.

Chad stood with a guilty start at the sound of the trios' entrance. Roger was about to go into another reenactment of a bar brawl he and Chad were in, when he warned him with a slight shake of the head. Switching gears, Roger launched into an amusing tirade about his mother-in-law, who Michelle halfheartedly tried to defend.

Chad's eyes casually strayed to Beth's face. She found a seat on one of the couches, taking everything in and sipping beer. It appeared as though she had straightened her hair and wiped the blood from her mouth. She looked much calmer. Watching her eyes dart from speaker to speaker, he decided she was even more beautiful than he had thought. He wondered how to determine for certain whether she was single or not.

Cassie sat without speaking on the floor in front of Beth as she stroked the teen's hair absentmindedly. He noticed, with a feeling of discomfort, her hands still trembled slightly. From time to time, she pressed the cold beer bottle to her cut lip and occasionally to the back of her head. He was about to offer her the ice wrapped in a towel lying next to him, given to him to ease his knuckles, but Roger asked him to clarify part of a story, and he lost track of his line of thought.

BETH EXHALED AS HER mind now had the time to sort through what took place throughout the evening. She went over each tortuous minute with her assailant and always came back to her overwhelming sense of relief that someone came to their rescue. After a few minutes, however, she recognized she wasn't contributing much to the conversation. She again blocked out thoughts of the attack to tune in to what was being said.

The group seemed to be comparing notes on their performance. As she listened, Beth tried to wrap her mind around the fact she was sitting in the midst of the mega-band Trapped Under Ice. What an odd turn of events.

From her position in a chair opposite the couch Roger, Michelle, and David occupied, she could easily observe everyone in the band. Her attention was first drawn to the most animated speaker, Roger. The bassist stood about five-eleven, built stocky, with short, brown hair and an open, expressive face. He looked like your typical kid brother, but with a touch of the devil in him.

"I screwed up on 'Second Time Around.' I thought we were on the third verse when we were only on the second."

"Oh, honey. You were fantastic. As usual," Michelle cooed, planting a hungry kiss on him.

The others seemed at ease with her display of affection.

"What about me?" David teased from his position to Michelle's right on the couch. He puckered up. "Wasn't I fantastic, too?"

Keith, the youngest of the four band members at maybe twenty-one or twenty-two, did not intend to be left out of the action. He leaned over Roger from his perch on the arm of the couch, opposite David. "Yeah, and I bet you never heard drums like that before, eh?" In torn jeans, with a double-pierced ear and hair containing at least a half-dozen styling products, he looked the part of the drummer. He and David made loud kissing noises as they tried to embrace the couple.

"Get the hell out of here." Roger chuckled, swatting at them.

They bantered comfortably, obviously a group more like family to each other than friends. It set Beth at ease to be in such a warm environment, to be in the midst of people who seemed to care a great deal for each other.

"What did you think, Beth?" Roger interjected.

"Me? Well, I'm hardly an expert."

"Nonsense. You are the expert. You're our audience. So what did you think?" Before she could answer, Roger added, "Be brutally honest, but kind."

She laughed. "Okay. I honestly thought you sounded great. The stage set up was impressive, the best I've ever seen, and I loved the way Chad interacted with the crowd. I've been to concerts where the band sounded exactly like they did on the radio, but had no real connection with the audience, and they weren't nearly as fun. But..."

"But what?" Roger prompted, sitting up straighter.

She felt all eyes on her. Here was her opportunity. "You didn't play 'I Just Had to Have You Last Night.' I love that song."

He smiled, appearing relieved the criticism was mild. "Yeah. I love it, too, but I feel like something's missing. We may have to rework it."

She glanced in Chad's direction. "But I thought—"

Roger anticipated her confusion. "Chad writes the music and sings the music and plays lead guitar and all, but I'm the real brains behind this operation. I decide what we play and what we don't. While Pretty Boy's off doing interviews and such, I'm back here slaving away, making the real magic happen."

There was a general uproar with his statement and Roger was pelted with couch pillows.

She again raised her eyes to scope out Chad. The singer was shaking his head in amusement and laughing quietly, but was standing apart from the others, behind the couch, almost lurking in the shadows like some specter. She witnessed his love for his brother and for Roger, yet he kept himself at a distance. As she tried to figure out the famous rocker, she couldn't help but admire his long legs, which were crossed at the ankles, and the well-defined biceps of his arms folded across his chest. Though she had never really considered anyone's hands before, even the length of his fingers she found indescribably beautiful as they curled loosely around his arms. He wore a leather cord around his wrist, Beth noted, and several silver rings on his fingers. She wondered idly if they ever interfered with his guitar playing. She realized the singer's gaze had shifted to her and was forced to pretend she was supremely interested in what Roger was saying.

"Mom, I'm sorry. I'm falling asleep."

She started at the sound of her daughter's voice. "No, I'm sorry, babe. We'll go." She stood and helped Cassie to her feet. "I want to thank you all so much for your help," she said to the group, looking at each one. "Especially you, Chad," she ended awkwardly. Should she call him by his first name? They hadn't even been introduced, but somehow Mr. Evans seemed wrong.

He started to step up, but Roger spoke for the group. Coming forward, he took both of Beth's hands in his for a minute. "We're just so sorry this happened to you. Both of you," he added, reaching out to touch Cassie's arm.

"Thank you."

She gave Chad one more wistful glance over her shoulder before turning to leave.

JUST AS THEY MOVED to the door, it opened. Chad noticed Beth jumped a little, but it was only Pete and Dante returning.

"I'm sorry, ma'am. I didn't mean to frighten you," Pete began. "The police came and escorted the—" he cleared his throat "—men," the bodyguard asserted as if he would have chosen another word to describe them, "to the hospital, as you wanted, miss, but there didn't seem to be any serious injuries."

Chad noticed his own sense of relief was mirrored in Beth's face.

"They said with the lateness of the hour and such, you could just come down to the police department tomorrow. They left their card." Pete handed her the card, adding, "We can walk you out to your car if you are ready to go."

"Yes. We're exhausted and we actually have our own 'gig' of sorts tomorrow."

"We're singing in a Christmas concert at the Old Cathedral. Mom's got a big solo."

"Oh, Cas. They don't want to hear about that," Beth commented, blushing. "Thank you again." She shook Roger's hand, and then goodbyes were exchanged all around. When she took Chad's hand, she turned it over to examine his knuckles and then looked up at him with concern. "I hope it won't hurt your guitar playing."

"Nah." He waved off the idea, but a glimpse at his knuckles caused him to flashback to the horror he saw in her eyes when she watched him flailing away at a senseless man like some sort of savage. He withdrew his hand as if it were somehow tainted, then instantly regretted doing so. She peered at him, her brows furrowed for a second and a frown of concentration on her face.

Chad didn't know what came over him earlier. But yet, he did. The things always eating away at his insides just came to the surface for a minute. Beth turned to leave, and on impulse, he reached for her arm. When she turned back around, he asked, "Would you mind if I called you tomorrow to check on you? To see how you're feeling?"

"I'm sure I'll be fine. But if you want to...we're at the Daltry Inn down by the riverfront."

"Isn't that the one right by the Arch?"

"Yes, that's the one. It's very close to here."

"What time will you be up?"

"The concert's not until two, but with going to the police station...nine, at the very latest. But you probably sleep in way past then."

"No, it's all right. I'll call you."

"Who are you kiddin'?" Roger snorted. "You never see him before noon. I don't even think he knows how to set the alarm on his phone."

Chad shot him a dark look but continued. "Do you mind if I walk you out, too?" He could feel, rather than see, Roger getting ready to make another smartass comment over his shoulder, so he quickly planted an elbow in his ribcage.

Beth appeared to catch the movement and gazed at the pair with a quizzical expression before responding. "Of course."

The group proceeded out the door with Chad trailing behind.

As the door closed, he heard Keith query, "Do you think they'll sue us?" Turning back, Chad saw the rest of the group looking at Keith balefully. "What? You all were thinking the same thing. You just didn't have the balls to say it."

Michelle picked up a pillow from the couch and threw it at him.

AS PETE HELD THE OUTER door open for the women, he started in on Chad. "What? Now you takin' over all my duties for me? Ya gotta walk 'em out, too?"

"Don't worry about me taking over your job, Pete," he replied ruefully as he rubbed his hands, stepping out of doors.

It was a common argument for the two. He'd resisted having a bodyguard from the start. It took David a long time to convince him that with extreme fans comes an increased element of danger and a need for professional protection. Chad felt like it was a blow to his ego for a big guy like him to hire a bodyguard. After all, he did have well-muscled arms from his guitar playing and from lugging the heavy amplifiers before they made it big. But when Trapped Under Ice's first album went platinum in 2001, Pete was able to sell him on the idea of personal protection by explaining it was the star's job to concentrate on music while the bodyguard focused on the musician's safety.

"Yeah. And how about that?" Pete continued, grabbing Chad's arm and holding his hand up in the parking lot's lights. "Ya bust your hand, who's gonna play your guitar? Dante, here?" They chuckled. But Pete's face turned serious. "I mean it, man. Why didn't you call me?"

"There wasn't any time," Chad argued. "And I did send Cassie in to get you."

"Yeah, yeah. But it's my job to keep you safe from the crazed fans who attack you."

"But this wasn't a crazed fan attacking me, Pete. If it were, I would have waited for you to come out and save me," he added with a healthy dose of sarcasm.

"Everybody's a smartass," Pete mumbled under his breath.

But the suggestion of the mad fan made Chad wonder. "So, Beth, were you chaperoning Cassie here to the concert?"

"Oh no," Cassie interrupted. "I bought the tickets for my mom as an early Christmas present. Mom is a huge fan, right, Mom? I don't think her music phone will play anything but Trapped Under Ice."

"Is that so?" He couldn't help the grin.

Pete and Dante were now involved in their own conversation, ignoring the three ahead of them. The group reached Beth's small, sporty sedan, alone in the parking lot, and the bodyguards hung back.

Chad spotted a copy of their newest CD on the dashboard and pointed to it. "Ah, I see."

Beth looked embarrassed, but she admitted, "When I've had a long day, I like to turn the music up and sing really loud."

"She's nearly made me deaf," Cassie teased.

"Really?" He crossed his hands over his chest and eyed Beth with humor, but sensing her discomfort, he changed the subject. "Couldn't find a better parking space than this?" he joked, indicating the distance to the stadium with a sweep of his hand.

"Somebody was running late." Beth gestured in Cassie's direction and pressed the remote entry key to pop the locks. "Couldn't decide whether to wear her hair up or down."

"Mom!" Cassie censured with all the general teenagerness she could gather. She walked around to the far side of the car to get into the passenger's seat.

He opened the car door for Beth. She hesitated before getting in.

"Thank you for everything."

He nodded, unsure of how to respond. "I'll call you at nine."

She gazed at him for a minute with those arresting eyes of hers, as if she had something to say. He stood, his fingers wrapped over the top of the doorframe, but she seemed to change her mind and climbed into the car seat. He closed the door carefully, then stepped back as she started the engine.

BETH WAS ABOUT TO TELL the singer he didn't need to call, but then realized she wanted him to. After all, she reasoned, who wouldn't want to hear Chad Evans's voice in the morning? She laughed to herself and adjusted the rearview mirror. She caught sight of him in the glass, trailing Pete and Dante as they walked back toward the stadium, his head down. She noticed, for the first time, he was only wearing a T-shirt. Even though the December evening was mild, he still must have been freezing. As she watched, he turned to glance back one last time before her car left the parking lot. That was the image she was left with as she fell asleep.

A FEW MINUTES AFTER nine, the red light on the phone lit up, the ringing ultra-loud in the still room. Beth fumbled with the receiver and tried to sound as if she'd been up rather than lying there hitting the snooze button.

"Hello?" Chad's voice was husky as if he had just woken up, too. She bet Roger was right about him not knowing how to set an alarm on his phone.

"Good morning."

"Hi. I just wanted to see how you were doing this morning?"

She tried to sit, but her aching head forced her back down. "I'm fine," she lied.

"Are you sure? You don't sound fine?"

Was it that obvious? "My head hurts a little, but I'm sure it's nothing an aspirin won't solve."

"We should have taken you to the hospital last night and had you checked out."

It occurred to her that maybe he wasn't really worried about her well-being; maybe he was worried about a lawsuit. She tried to tell herself she didn't know the man at all; she was fooled into thinking she knew him by what may or may not be revealed in his lyrics or in magazine articles. Whatever she felt about Chad Evans, it was driven more by lust and imagination than by anything real.

"Honestly, I'm fine."

"Okay," he conceded, sounding unconvinced. "If you're interested, I could leave tickets for you at the will call window for Saturday night's show?"

She thought about it. Another bid to ward off a lawsuit? She drummed her fingers on the mattress. What did she care? Free tickets were free tickets, and after how much she enjoyed last night's show, how could she resist? They planned on going home Saturday morning, but why not extend the visit another day? She knew Cassie wouldn't mind. "Sure. That would be great."

CHAD TRIED TO FIGURE out why he had called her. Why he had set an alarm to get up—so out of character for him—and call a woman he hardly knew. All he understood was her face, her eyes, swam before him all night. She was not like the women he was usually with, or more accurately, the girls. She had a self-confidence he found attractive, and at the same time, he sensed a vulnerability he was also drawn to. Like his frequent one-night stands, he could tell she was into him, but she still had enough self-respect not to throw herself at him. She was witty and smart without having the edge those qualities sometimes gave people; her intelligence was tempered with a certain sweetness.

And all this you gathered from spending less than an hour with her in the same room, huh? It couldn't just be that she was gorgeous, now could it?

Yet he knew there had to be some other reason he couldn't get her out of his head.

"So," he added subtly, "should I leave a ticket for your husband, too, or is he not a Trapped Under Ice fan?"

There was an awkward silence for several seconds, and he was about to kick himself for being such a bonehead until she spoke quietly. "I don't know if you would say Paul was exactly a fan...but he grew to like you guys over time. He passed away three years ago."

"Oh, Beth. I'm so sorry. I shouldn't have asked—"

"No, no. In three years a person should..." She didn't complete her thought. There was a strained silence while she presumably sought to control her emotions and Chad continued to berate himself. "Anyway," she continued with what sounded like forced cheerfulness, "we'd love tickets."

"Okay. And I want you to know, security will be heightened around here—" he had thought about this all night "—and I could have Pete pick you up and drive you if you'd like."

"That won't be necessary."

"Okay, if you're sure. Maybe I'll see you Saturday then."

Beth said goodbye and hung up the phone, staring at the ceiling. She almost jumped out of her skin when Cassie asked from the adjacent bed, "Was that Chad Evans?"

"I thought you were asleep." Beth tried to still her heart and after a moment was able to reply evenly, "As a matter of fact, it was."

Cassie sat up on one elbow. "Listen to you, all cool, calm, and collected. You'd think you'd been rubbing elbows with the rich and famous all your life. Like you're not absolutely thrilled Chad Evans just called you."

Beth giggled from her bed and launched a pillow in Cas's direction. "You just be quiet, you."

CHAPTER FOUR

The trip to the police station did not turn out to be nearly the ordeal Beth thought it would be. In fact, the officers were so efficient she and Cassie were in and out of there in less than thirty minutes. This gave the pair ample time for a relaxed lunch at Ted and Nancy's, a restaurant in their hotel, before their preconcert practice. They changed after lunch and headed to the Old Cathedral, located just across the street.

The weather had turned decidedly colder overnight. Beth could feel the wind as it swirled around her legs and under her dress. She was actually glad for the choir robe she carried, as it offered some additional protection from it. As they waited at the stoplight, big, fat snowflakes began to fall from the sky.

"Boy, if that doesn't make it feel like Christmas, I don't know what will."

"You're right," Cassie responded. The snow began falling thicker and faster.

Beth giggled as they hurried across the street. "It's like being in your own personal snow globe." She looked up and let the flakes pepper her hair and eyelashes. As she lowered her head, she took in the view of the Old Cathedral as it was nestled at the foot of the world-famous Gateway Arch. It was even more breathtaking than she remembered. In the midst of towering skyscrapers, it seemed to be in a time warp. Built around 1831, it had all the charm of a bygone era. Like something stolen right out of a lithograph, she thought.

Nudged by Cassie, she pulled her hood up against the cold and hurried forward.

"Brrrr." Cassie shivered as the two stood stomping their high heels in the foyer of the church. Her voice echoed against the walls hollowly.

When Beth followed her through the heavy outer doors, the heady smell of pine boughs greeted her like an old friend. As they walked through the second set of doors, she lowered her hood and gazed around in wonder. The whole basilica was festooned with live wreaths, garland, and bright red bows. Unlike other churches, the windows were clear glass but were no less majestic. The walls were a cream color with pale blue panels, and the pewter light fixtures had an organic theme, decorated with either flowers or leaves. Instead of a three-dimensional cross, a huge mural of the Crucifixion was painted behind the otherwise unadorned altar.

"Right this way, ladies," the older man who ran the choir called to them grumpily.

Beth tore her eyes from the architecture and hustled to take her place, along with a few other stragglers, as the organist began.

Two hours later, the church was packed as she stood to do her solo. Ordinarily she would have been petrified, but it helped she was singing one of her favorite carols, "Mary, Did You Know?" She squeezed her eyes together and began to sing, praying she wouldn't end up crying like she always did when she listened to the lyrics. While she sang, the room was stilled. People stopped shifting in their crowded seats, coughs were hushed, and the only thing that seemed to exist for those few moments was her voice. Many of the listeners seemed moved by her singing, and as the last note hung in the air, she opened her eyes and let them travel across the room until they stopped abruptly at a figure she recognized.

Chad stood leaning against a column in the back, appearing mesmerized by her singing. She was so stunned to see him that she almost swallowed the last note, but she hung on and gratefully stepped back into her place among the others when the song was finished. The applause hadn't abated when she turned back around to face the audience, and when she again searched, she saw him clapping with the others. He wore tan pants and a dark brown leather jacket. Snow still glistened in his hair and on his shoulders, so he must have stepped in just in time to hear her song. She was thankful she did not spot Chad beforehand, or the butterflies in her stomach would have been ten times worse.

When the concert was over, she shook hands in haste with the people around her, then rushed to hang up her choir robe as the crusty old choir leader directed. Cassie, who also seemed to have spied Chad, offered to carry it for her. Beth headed down the long aisle to where the singer still stood at the back of the church. He let the others file past him and waited for her behind the last row.

She smiled up at him. "You came."

He cleared his throat. "Yes. I wanted to see for myself how you were doing. How's the bump on your head?"

She reached up to rub it without thinking as she responded. "It's much bet—" She furrowed her brow. "How did you know I had a bump on my head? Did Cassie say something?"

"No, no. I noticed you holding your beer bottle against it last night, and wincing. May I?"

Before she could answer, he reached over and felt the back of her head. His nearness flustered her. He smelt fresh, like the outdoors. For a guy with big hands, his touch was surprisingly gentle.

His eyebrows came together. "Ooh. It's still pretty big."

"It's actually gone down quite a bit."

"Are you sure you shouldn't have a doctor look at that?"

"Yeah. It's just a bump. I never lost consciousness or threw up, so it's not a concussion."

He laughed. "You speak as if you know from experience."

"Well, ten plus years with an athletic girl like Cassie, and you're bound to pick up a few things in the E.R. Speaking of which—" she turned and spotted her daughter "—here comes my little angel now."

Cassie sauntered toward them with a giggling teenaged girl on either side of her. "See, I told you it was Chad Evans."

"Hi, ladies."

While one of the girls continued to say, "Oh my gosh. Oh my gosh," over and over again, the second asked him to autograph her program.

A smile rose to Beth's lips, until she wondered, is that what I look like?

Cassie interrupted her thoughts. "Mom, Jean's parents asked if I would like to go ice-skating at Forest Park with a group of girls, and then go out for pizza and a late show. Can I?" Cassie peered at her with the eyes that scored her permission for such things on many an occasion as she handed Beth both choir robes.

"Well, I guess so."

"I'm sure you could come, too. Although I'm not sure if there's enough room in their van..."

"Oh, Cas, I don't think I should be going anywhere close to a pair of ice skates with this bump on my head. But you go ahead. I'll be fine. I'll just relax and read, or something."

"Thanks, Mom." She blew Beth a kiss, halfway down the aisle with her friends already.

"Well, goodbye, then." She laughed, knowing her daughter was well out of hearing range. She turned back to Chad. "I'm sorry about that."

"No, no. It's okay."

"So—" she turned to leave the church with him "—are you staying near here? I promise not to tell any of them," she added, gesturing to the gaggle of girls with Cassie.

His lips turned up at the corners. "No, actually. We're out in Chesterfield."

"Chesterfield? That's a long haul from the stadium."

"Yeah. That's kind of the point, I guess. To keep the 'crazed fans' from finding us."

"Oh, but now you've gone and told me, and as we established last night, I'm a crazed fan," she joked. "So, where is Pete lurking?"

"Well, he and I have sort of an agreement. Sometimes I need my space, and he respects that, so he's taking the day off."

She nodded. "Which way did you park?"

"I didn't actually," he replied vaguely.

"Then how did you get down here?" As they started to cross the street, a driver honked his horn and gestured to another driver in a very unflattering way.

"Well, I didn't want to bring the tour bus down here in all this mess." He indicated the traffic. "So, I took a cab."

She stopped walking to gaze up at him in astonishment. "You took a cab here from Chesterfield?"

"Yeah."

"Well, gosh, that's a long way. Why don't you let me take you back? Do you have any shopping to do or anything?"

"No, I just came down to check on you and hear you sing, which was incredible by the way."

"Well, thank you," she responded, dropping her eyes and feeling the heat rush to her cheeks. "So, I'll take you back, but do you have time for me to just go in and change quickly?"

Chad opened the door to The Drury for her. "Sure. Take all the time you need."

Fifteen minutes later, he was seated on a couch in front of the lobby fireplace, his long legs spread wide, elbows on his knees, and hands folded when she came down in jeans and a sweater.

"Are you ready?" She smiled.

"Sure. But I was thinking, how about you and me grabbing a bite to eat? Are you hungry?"

"I'm starved," she confessed. She was too anxious about her solo earlier to eat much.

"Good. How about Ted and Nancy's?"

Chad seemed pleased about the idea, which he obviously got from some pamphlets lying on the table in front of him. She couldn't bring herself to tell him she'd eaten there for lunch.

"Sounds great."

BETH NOTICED THAT THE waitress appeared to be studying the pair as she handed them the menus.

"My name's Stacy," she said, drawing her words out. "Can I get a drink for you?"

She smiled. "I'll have an amaretto sour, please."

"Do you have Bud Light on tap?"

"Yes, sir, we do," the waitress replied in that same slow, contemplative way.

"That's what I'll have, please." He exchanged a glance with Beth.

The woman seemed to come out of her stupor. "I'll be right back."

Beth giggled. "You must get that a lot."

"Ahh, I don't know," he returned, seeming a little self-conscious. "Most people wouldn't recognize me dressed like this."

When he hung up their coats earlier, Beth saw he was wearing a light-weight black sweater with the tan pants, and although it was quite a different look from his usual black T-shirt and ripped jeans, she was sure she would recognize him anywhere. The rocker's sweater fit him well and accentuated his muscular chest, and once again she found herself asking how she came to be sitting across the dinner table from Chad Evans.

They looked at the menus and made small talk until the waitress returned with drinks and took their dinner order. In her wake, she left an awkward silence. For the first time, the pair was alone with no ready subject for conversation. They both took a sip of their drinks to stall for time.

"Your drink all right?"

"Good, good." She nodded.

"Good," he repeated, seeming at a loss as to where to go next. He exhaled with a laugh. "You know, I don't know anything about you, other than your name is Beth, you have a daughter named Cassie, and you're one hell of a singer."

"Ah...well..." Again she was unnerved by the praise.

"You're staying at this hotel, so you're not from here. Where do you live?"

"Bloomington, Illinois." When he stared at her blankly, she added, "It's about halfway between here and Chicago."

He nodded. "What's it like?"

"Well...it's a college town. In fact, we have the little-known distinction of being the only city with a university at either end of the same street," she threw in, remembering seeing that in a paper Cassie did for social studies.

"I see," he replied, bemused. "And what do you do in this fair city? I mean," he backpedaled, "do you work outside of the home?"

"Ah, so politically correct. Yes, as a matter of fact, I'm a lunch lady."

The singer looked for a minute like he was going to spit out his drink, but he swallowed hurriedly and laughed.

"What?" Beth retorted, pretending to be hurt. "You've got something against lunch ladies, I suppose?"

"No, no," he insisted. "It's just...you don't look like any lunch lady I ever had."

She took a long drink and considered his words. Was there a compliment in there somewhere?

"So how did you land this lunch lady gig?"

Now it was Beth's turn to laugh at his choice of the word "gig." "Well, in truth it wasn't all that difficult. I just showed up for the interview, they told me what the hours were, how much the position paid, and what it entailed, then asked me if I wanted the job. So, hearing what glamorous duties I was to have and what a fabulous paycheck I would be bringing home, I, of course, took it." He laughed. "No, really, I love my job. I love working with kids. I can come home and take a nap every afternoon before Cas gets home from school. What's not to like?"

"Well, when you put it that way..."

"Not to mention, sometimes I get to bring home leftover sloppy joe meat."

"It gets better and better. Sign me up."

"Oh yeah. 'Cause this whole rock star thing can't compare to the wonderful benefits I just described. Tell me the truth, it was the sloppy joe meat that really sold you, wasn't it?"

They both laughed again, noticing they were drawing attention from the other diners.

"Okay. So you're a lunch lady, you've lived in Bloomington, Illinois, all of your life—"

"Actually, I'm originally from here."

"St. Louis?"

She nodded. "I've lived in a few other places, but this is what I would consider my hometown."

"Then how did you wind up in Bloomington?"

She took another long drink before continuing. "My husband, Paul, got a job at Illinois Insurance as an actuary. Its corporate headquarters is in Bloomington. We met at the University of Missouri-Columbia, got married while still in college, and moved to Bloomington right after graduation." She felt the smile fade from her face. Chad seemed relieved when the food arrived.

"And you," she declared between bites, jabbing her fork in his direction as she ticked off points, "you are from a little town outside of Albany, New York. You, your brother, and Roger started Trapped Under Ice as a cover band...and then you got tired of playing everyone else's music and started writing your own."

He raised his eyebrows. "Should I be scared now?"

She leaned forward and whispered, "Terrified," with a smile, and then looked down to cut her steak. They ate for a few minutes in silence. She turned shy. "Chad, I have to tell you, this is a weird experience for me. I don't remember the last time I ate with someone who has three platinum albums hanging on his wall at home—"

"Actually, on the tour bus."

Her lips slid upward into a grin. "On the tour bus," she amended. He made it all seem so normal somehow. "And I know you probably get tired of talking about your life, so...I don't know if I should ask you things or—"

"Beth," he interrupted, placing his hand over hers on the table for a second, "you can ask me anything you want."

"Hmm..." She smiled wickedly for a minute, seeming to make him just a bit nervous. She took another drink, watching him over the rim of her glass as she stretched the moment out, wanting to make him sweat a little. Then, she settled for an easy question. "Tell me what it's like on the road."

"It's not bad," he commented. "We have two tour buses. One for Roger and David and their wives, and sometimes David's kids, the other for me and Keith. We call the first bus 'The Married Bus,' and our bus is called 'The Fun Bus.'"

"I don't think I want to know why." She glanced away.

"No. Let me amend my previous statement by saying there are some things you may not want to ask about."

"Ah." She could only imagine. The bus probably saw a lot of action. A rock star, right...they had a girl in every city. She wondered if she were becoming that girl. Then, she wondered if she even cared.

As he continued to talk, she analyzed him, putting his various pieces together and pulling them apart to study them. He had an amazing ease about him...being with him wasn't what she imagined sitting with a mega rock star would be like. It was more like sitting down to dinner with one of the janitors from work. Their conversations were so comfortable she might as well be talking to one of her girlfriends back home.

And his smile, the way he moved, everything about him, spoke of a natural sex appeal. She was sure it was something he possessed as a ten-year-old, but at the time it would have been seen as an adorable smoothness. And again, as a teen, it would have made him every high school cheerleader's dream. At that age, she was almost sure he would have strutted, proud of his newfound talent, but now she imagined it was so much a part of him he didn't even have to think about it anymore.

The waitress reappeared to take their dishes. "Coffee? Or maybe, dessert?" They both shook their heads. "Then I'll get you the bill. I hope you don't mind," she added tentatively, "but...aren't you Beth Donovan?"

"Why, yes." Beth felt her heart leap. Was there some type of emergency phone call from Cassie?

"Well, I was just wondering, if it wouldn't be too much to ask..." She pulled something from her apron pocket. "Would you mind signing my copy of Amber Waves of Grain?"

"No, of course not," Beth responded, taking her pen.

"I recognized you from your picture on the jacket. I just love your books."

"Thank you, that's nice to hear." While she was signing, the waitress looked at Chad. "Are you famous, too?"

He laughed. "No, no. I'm nobody."

Beth handed the book back, barely able to suppress a giggle.

The waitress took the book, beaming and hugging it to her chest, excited about her prize. "Thanks a lot. I'll be right back with your bill."

Chad peered at Beth with his eyebrows raised and a smile playing across his lips.

"Okay, so I also write from time to time. Just trashy romance novels. No big deal."

"Well, she seemed to think it was a big deal."

CHAD SHOOK HIS HEAD a little. She was incredible. Fun, sexy, caring...his heart beat a little faster. Something was happening here, something exciting, and maybe a little frightening. He'd never cared to learn much about the other women he was with. Oh, he'd be interested if they shared, but she was the first one he really wanted to know things about, and he suddenly wanted to know it all, know her all.

"Well, she's young. And," the writer/lunch lady leaned forward and whispered as the waitress walked toward them, "she's going to be kicking herself when she finds out she missed getting Chad Evans's autograph." They sat back and the waitress set the check down in between them. They both slapped a hand on it.

"No way," Beth protested. "This is on me. A small way to thank you for what you did last night. And for hanging around with me tonight."

"Tonight has been my pleasure. And you owe me nothing."

"Chad, please, I'd like to do this."

He heard Roger's voice inside his head. "Always insist on picking up the check when you're out with a hot girl, that way they are indebted to you." He gazed into her pretty blue-green eyes, "bedroom eyes" Roger called them last night when Chad borrowed the alarm clock. Aw...Roger's a jerk, anyway. What does he know?

He sighed. "I'll let you pay on one condition."

She nodded.

"You let me pick up the tab next time."

He relinquished the check and stood to get their coats while she finished paying. He held her ski jacket open and slipped it over her shoulders, resting his hands there briefly before bending down to whisper in her ear, "Thank you for dinner." On a whim, he spun her around. "Do you want to come to practice with me? It will be pretty boring, but maybe afterward we could catch a drink or something."

She hesitated. "Well...Cassie will be out all evening." She seemed to make a decision. "I'd like that."

"Good."

He chuckled as he held the door open.

Beth looked up. "What?"

"I can't believe she had the book right there and everything."

CHAPTER FIVE

C had watched Beth on the floor of the stadium in front of him. He loved how she was into his music. She danced and sang and clapped wildly after every song. She even got Michelle into it. She was dancing alongside Beth and hooting and hollering with her after each song; it had been a while since she had done that. And it was obvious Beth hadn't overstated her devotion to the band. She seemed to know all of the lyrics, even to some of their more obscure songs.

After about their fifth song, Roger, who had been watching the girls the whole time as well, called out. "Why don't you just come up here and sing with us, Beth? Chad told me you could sing."

She looked at Chad and he shrugged with a smile. Roger stepped forward and reached his hand down. "Come on," he urged softly. She glanced at Chad again, biting her lip.

He laughed. "Well, come on. You know you want to."

"But you guys are practicing..."

"We know these songs backward and forward, darlin'. You'd only be saving us from our eternal boredom," David spoke up. Keith nodded.

Uncertain, she placed her hand in Roger's. She glanced back, but Michelle had disappeared. He walked her a few steps to the right where temporary stairs had been set up by the stagehands.

Chad stood with his guitar and patted the stool beside him. She had to hop to get up on it. "What do you want to sing?"

"Well, what were you going to sing next?"

"'I Just Had to Have You Last Night.'"

"I love that one."

"Is there any you don't love?" Roger laughed. "Wait, don't answer that."

He and Chad began strumming the opening chords, and Keith picked up the drum line. Sensing her nervousness, Chad sang the first line with the gravelly voice that made their sound so famous. Beth knew the only way she could get through this was to concentrate on Chad. Gazing into his eyes, she boldly sang the next few lines. His grin grew wider as he took the next part. They continued back and forth, singing the chorus together.

Feeling braver, she turned to look at Roger with her next lines. He smiled and shouted, "Well allll right!" into the microphone.

With the final crashing notes, she bounded off the stool in excitement, jumping up and down.

"It's like the music surges right through you," she screamed, barely able to control herself. "That was amazing."

"No, sweetheart," Roger asserted, sauntering over to her and giving her a kiss on the cheek. "You were amazing."

David left his keyboards and high-fived her, and Keith nodded, adding his, "You kicked ass!" to the reviews.

"What did I tell you?" Chad gave her a hug as best as he could with a guitar between them.

"Why don't we call it a night," Roger suggested. "We nailed those first songs, and we need to save Chad's voice for tomorrow."

Everyone agreed wholeheartedly.

Michelle appeared from somewhere in the wings. "You promised you'd take me dancing, Roger."

Roger threw his arm around her, still full of the cheer a good practice brought on. "She's such a little dictator." He buried his head in her hair and started playing around, kissing her neck while she squirmed.

Chad turned to Beth. "Do you know any place to dance?"

"I haven't lived here in eight or nine years. You used to be able to dance onboard 'The Admiral,' only I think it's called 'The President' now. It's a big boat they restored. It's moored down by the Arch, but that was years ago. I'm not sure if they have any dancing these days."

"Let's go check it out," Michelle wheedled.

Roger now stood behind his wife, his hands around her waist. "What do you say, you two? Want to put on your dancing shoes?"

Chad turned to her, his eyes soft. "What do you say, Beth?"

"Well, I don't know for sure if there'll be any dancing, but I'm willing to check it out. It's only a few blocks from here."

He smiled. "I guess we're in." He swung his guitar up and set it in the stand next to him.

"David? Keith?"

"Cheri's got a headache, and besides, I'm beat. But thanks."

Keith answered with an air of mystery. "I've got other plans."

"Well, I guess it's a double-date then," Roger announced affably.

Chad grabbed Beth's hand and gave it a squeeze.

THE TWO COUPLES PILED into Beth's sedan. Within minutes, Roger and Michelle were going at it in the backseat.

"Newlyweds," Chad announced, looking embarrassed. "Can't get enough of each other." He sighed, looking out the window. Beth laughed to herself.

Navigating the one-way streets, she took them down to the levee, parking on the uneven cobblestones that slanted down to the river.

"Whoa!" Michelle cried out. "Don't you feel like the car's gonna tip over?"

Beth laughed. "A little bit."

They got out of the car carefully. She took stock of her surroundings for the first time. "Oh no."

They all stood staring at "The Casino Queen," its blaring lights announcing the new name for "The President."

"I forgot. They turned it into a riverboat casino." She turned to the three behind her with a look of disappointment, an apology on her lips, when someone called out in the darkness.

"Hey, there. What are you kids up to?"

Squinting, they could just make out the figure of an older man, sitting on a post near the water, evidently taking a break from walking the tiny dog that was busy wrapping his leash around the man's feet.

Roger spoke for the group. "We were just looking for a place to dance, but we see now 'The Admiral' or 'The President' or whatever was turned into a casino."

"Oh yeah. Done that years ago. It's a shame. Beautiful boat in its day." He started walking away then turned back. "If you want to go dancing, son, there's 'The Mississippi Queen.' She's moored up yonder." He pointed down the shoreline.

The four turned their heads as one to see the most spectacular riverboat imaginable. Lights illuminated five decks of the pristine-white "Mississippi Queen." Even in the dark they could make out the twin black smokestacks and the fabulous, large red paddle attached to the stern.

Roger said it for all of them. "Holy shit."

"Yeah, baby!" Michelle screamed, jumping up and down, nearly turning an ankle on the irregular cobblestones. "Come on." She took off, pulling him behind her. They soon put several yards between them and their friends.

Chad peered at Beth sideways with a grin on his face and wordlessly held out his hand. She smiled and placed her hand in his, meandering up the levee with him. Neither of them spoke; they just allowed themselves to enjoy the magic of the evening, and the closeness they were beginning to feel.

All too soon, they caught up with the newlyweds, who stood agog in the boat's lights, taken in by its splendor. Beth noticed a limo pulling up on the street above the parking lot that led to the water's edge. A man in an expensive-looking tuxedo helped a woman in a flowing gown out of the car. They walked down a runway and onto the ship like royalty.

She leaned into Chad. "I think we may be a tad underdressed," she whispered.

Bending close, he murmured, "I don't care, do you?"

She gazed into his eyes, the streetlights twinkling playfully in their depths, and knew, in that moment, she cared about nothing less. She shook her head.

"Good." His voice was nearly a growl.

Roger and Michelle were already ahead. A man in a doorman-type uniform appeared ready to turn them away. Taking in Roger's T-shirt and jeans, and Michelle's trademark thigh-high boots, red leather miniskirt, and the pigtails bouncing from the crown of her head, pink streak and all, he hesitated. But then, he seemed to decide their green spent as well as anybody else's, took their money, shrugged, and let them pass. Beth reached for some money she had stuck in her pocket.

"Nah-ah-ah," Chad chastised. "You told me I could pick up the next tab." She bowed her assent and he paid their admission. He slid his arm around her shoulders as they passed through the archway and onto the ship.

In front of them was a large stage with a full band playing "Moon River." Poinsettias lined the stage, and couples swayed gracefully on the floor in front of it, most in full-length gowns and tuxes. Cloth-covered tables lined the dance floor, the light from the candles on their surface sparkling off the silver trays men carried amid the guests and off the tall champagne flutes they bolstered. The light twinkle from the necks of bejeweled ladies who wore their hair up in sleek buns, adorned with more jewels, and off their husbands' conspicuously large cufflinks. As they were taking this in, the band finished its song and announced a brief break while the captain readied his crew for departure.

"Oh, Michelle," Beth breathed apologetically. "I'm sure this isn't what you meant when you said you wanted to go dancing."

"Nonsense," she cried. "I've never seen anything so beautiful in my life. Hey, there's a table." She and Roger grabbed champagne glasses from a passing tray and made a beeline for one of the few unoccupied tables. Chad and a relieved Beth followed suit, claiming flutes from the next passing tray and threading their way through the tables behind their friends.

By the time they reached Roger and Michelle, they were fully ensconced at the table. As Chad pulled up a chair next to them, Roger buffeted him lightly in the ear.

"Oww. What was that for?"

"For not telling us what a great singer Beth was before."

"I didn't have time—"

"I know, but you should have told me anyway."

"You make about as much sense as those warning signs on auto visors that say 'Do Not Drive Vehicle While In Place.'"

"Hey, that's my line," Roger asserted, rapping him again, this time on the forehead.

"Hey, cut it out before I have to take you out on deck and show you who's—"

"Boys. Boys," Michelle scolded. She looked to Beth for sympathy. "You can't take these two clowns anywhere, especially someplace classy like this."

"Okay, we'll behave, we promise. Right, Chad?"

Before he could respond, Roger jabbed him again in the arm while Michelle was looking the other way.

"Ouch!" Chad cried out, rubbing his injury.

"Did you see that? Did you see that?" Michelle asked Beth.

She shrugged innocently.

"Oh, you're incorrigible, the lot of you."

Roger winked at Beth as they all chuckled.

"So, how long have you two knuckleheads known each other?" Beth queried.

The two who had attacked each other seconds before leaned toward one another conspiratorially. "So now we're 'knuckleheads.' I've known this bloke since I was a wee lad," Roger announced, grabbing Chad's head and giving him a Dutch rub. Chad escaped the headlock and moved farther away from the tormentor, rubbing his hair and laughing. "Ever since he beat the crap out of me and stole my milk money."

"You liar! It was you who beat the crap out of me and it wasn't because of any milk money. It was because of Susie McFarren."

"Oh, God. Here they go again with the whole Susie McFarren thing." Michelle moaned.

"Susie McFarren had the hots for me," Chad insisted.

"That's just 'cause you picked up her damn pencil every time she dropped it."

"Yeah, well that's what nice boys do."

"Nice boy, my ass. You were just trying to get a look up her dress."

"He was not!" Michelle cried out in pretend shock, defending him. "That's the champagne talking," she proclaimed, leaning into Beth but saying it loud enough so everyone else could hear, "it goes straight to his head. Anyway, Rog, that was your M.O., not Chad's."

"Oh yeah. You're right," he admitted, while seductively running a hand up under her miniskirt.

"Stop," she squealed, but she was putting up a weak fight as he began kissing her neck again.

Chad and Beth exchanged an amused look, which turned, after a few seconds, into something more serious. Beth was saved from finding out about the look by the band starting up. When she turned again to Chad, he was standing beside her chair, offering his hand. All of a sudden, she felt very conspicuous in her short boots, jeans, and turtleneck sweater.

She glanced around. "Are you sure we should—"

"You said you didn't mind," he reminded her.

Spending the better part of eighteen years with an ultra-conservative husband who would never think of setting foot inside the boat without the proper attire, she now felt oddly uncertain of what she did, or didn't mind. In the end, she stood up to join him on the dance floor.

She thought about her day, seeing him at the back of the church, laughing with him over dinner, singing with his band, and she began to unconsciously sway in rhythm with him. His hand felt so good on the center of her back. As he pulled her close and their bodies touched, she felt a tingle running up her spine. She asked herself again, "How did I get here?" Everything she was doing was so far from her normal lifestyle. Yet, somehow it felt so right. She laid her head on his chest, listening to his heartbeat and the soft, musical tapping of his tennis shoes on the dance floor.

Still, the voice in her head insisted, *you don't even know this guy. You've known him less than twenty-four hours and yet he has his hands around you, and all you want is more of him. He could be a psycho for all you know.* The final voice sounded more like Paul than her; he was always so cautious, but invariably wiser.

But I do know him, somehow, I do.

There's something there...a connection.

Oh, good Lord, I sound like a page out of one of my novels.

A few beats after everyone else on the dance floor, they realized the music was over. The older people smiled and nodded at them, perhaps recognizing in the younger couple a feeling they felt before. Some lucky few of those who looked on may even have still felt it as they danced with their loved one.

A jazzier song started, and the dance floor began to clear. Roger and Michelle sat huddled together at the table, oblivious to those around them.

"Want to go outside?" Beth asked.

"Sure."

The boat was underway, and they watched in silence as it passed through the glimmering reflection of The Arch in the water. Beth rested on the rail, and Chad stood behind her with his hands grasping the bar on either side of her. The wind blew their hair softly, and she shivered, regretting her decision to leave her coat in the car.

"Are you cold?" he asked, taking his hands from the rail to rub her arms.

His touch felt so good, she found herself leaning back against him and closing her eyes. How long had it been since she felt a man's touch? She turned to peek up at him. She had to know if he felt the same way she did.

Chad took his hands from her arms and placed his fingers behind her neck. She froze, unsure of what he was doing. He gently rubbed his thumbs across her mouth, his eyes taking in the delicate curve of her lips as he touched them. Then, his eyes lifted to hers, and she saw in them anguish and need and pain and...something more. He bent closer, inch by inch, tantalizing her as she craned her neck, rising up on her toes to reach him. His lips finally claimed hers with a rush.

His lips felt, ooh, so good, and she realized for the first time how wonderfully full they were. With a moan that filled them both, he kissed her more deeply, his tongue exploring her mouth, his hands sliding down to pull her closer. When he finally pulled away, she almost cried out in protest.

WHERE SHE WAS HEARING Paul's voice earlier, Chad now heard a harsher voice, his father's. *You're not good enough for this girl, Chad. She's outta your league. Find yourself one of your usual floozies. You need a little one-night action. You're incapable of true love. You'll wind up hurting her in the end.*

This was the thought that truly terrified him, but it was as if he couldn't help being drawn to her. There was something there he couldn't define.

"Beth, I..." He could find no words to speak to her. This was all so different for him. He had never felt a kiss like the one he had shared with her—one that pulled from the inside out, originating in his core, not igniting on the surface and finding its way down. He pulled her close again and she laid her head on his chest. He leaned down to rest his cheek on the top of her head and clasped it to his chest with one large hand. He wanted this woman in a way he wanted no other woman. But, for the first time in a long time, he was at a loss as to how to achieve what he needed.

As he tried to sort through the jumble of emotions interwoven in his head, he slowly became aware that the shoulders of the woman he was holding had begun to shake and tears were dampening his T-shirt.

"Beth. Beth. What did I do?" he queried, trying to lift her face. That voice in his head bounced out of the shadows, *you'll wind up hurting her in the end*, and then twirled off to some other deep recess of his mind.

"You didn't do anything," her muffled voice came from his chest, where she was trying to bury her face in her hands. "Dammit," she blurted out, pounding him suddenly in the chest. "What the hell is wrong with me?"

"Wrong with you? There's nothing wrong with you."

"Oh, so you often have women who break down sobbing when you kiss them?" she cried bitterly.

"No." He had to laugh. "This is a first."

She raised her head from his chest, the tears still shining on her cheeks, and began to laugh, too.

"OH, THERE YOU TWO ARE." Roger crossed the threshold onto the deck. Beth turned away from him, and although Chad's arms were around her, the bassist could tell he'd interrupted some sort of conversation. "I just thought you'd want to know, the band's playing one of our songs."

Chad and Beth started laughing. The idea of an orchestra playing Trapped Under Ice was absurd, and pretty soon the three of them were in hysterics.

Roger was glad to see her laugh. If she was crying, like he thought she was when he'd come out on deck, she needed the pick-me-up. She was a nice girl, and he really wished she weren't getting involved with Chad. Chad was his best friend, but he was also an emotional basket case, and that wasn't good for anyone.

CHAPTER SIX

T he rest of the evening was fairly uneventful. The threesome returned to the table and kept the conversation on a safe level, just the kind of easy banter they all expected with Roger along. After a while, Chad attempted to hold Beth's hand again, and she rubbed her thumb across his, putting him at ease. When they strolled back to the car, after telling the affable doorman good night, Roger and Michelle again walked ahead, leaving them alone, though Roger occasionally threw a look over his shoulder.

Chad's arm was around her, continuing to try to keep her warm as the temperature had dropped several degrees more. He loped along without speaking, not sure about how to start a conversation about what had happened. Beth, for her part, was also quiet—perhaps tired from the emotional turmoil she had gone through. As she walked, she began leaning more and more into him, sliding her arm around his waist and laying her head down for brief periods.

When they reached the car, Chad opened the door for her. Michelle and Roger had already climbed into the back. As he moved to go around to his side of the car, she pulled him back, kissing him sweetly before getting into her seat. With a sense of relief, he ambled around to the passenger's side, sliding in beside her. The car ride back was silent except for some soft music playing on the radio. Michelle dozed off and the champagne finally seemed to calm Roger.

IN THE GLOW FROM THE dashboard lights, Roger could see Chad and Beth's hands intertwined, resting between them on the middle console.

God help her.

AT ELEVEN O'CLOCK, they finally pulled into the bumpy dirt lane leading to the private property their tour buses were on. The buses were huge monstrosities, a sort of cross between a bus and RV, with collapsible stairs leading up to a small landing outside the doors. As they pulled up to the clearing housing them, Chad wondered again over the buses clearing the low-hanging branches edging the road.

Michelle woke with the jarring movement, and Roger leaned up, startling the two in the front seat, saying with a funny accent, "Now you know our secret location, ve vill haf to keell you, you know?" When the car rolled to a stop, the pair in the back got out, giving their thanks and goodbyes, and then climbed the steps into the light of a welcoming bus.

Chad and Beth stood by the car, watching the couple. Then, with the click of the door behind Michelle and Roger, they were left in dead silence. Chad leaned against the car. He reached out for Beth's hips and pulled her close as she turned around to face him.

"Stay," he spoke the single word softly.

"I can't," she murmured, toying with the zipper-pull on his coat. "I've got Cassie back at the hotel." It sounded like an excuse. He crooked a finger under her chin and gently lifted it. "I can't." Her whispered response was swallowed up in his kiss.

He hoped his kiss would persuade her to stay, but Beth pushed away from him and turned, stepping off a few feet as if to clear her head. She ripped a leaf from a nearby tree and stood shredding it in the moonlight.

"Where will you go after St. Louis?"

"Detroit, I think," he murmured.

She nodded her head but said nothing. Without warning, she turned on her heel and rushed toward him. "I've got to go," she barely got out, reaching for the car door handle. "I'm sure there are some girls...but I can't. I'm sorry."

He tried to make sense of her words, but the only thing he understood was that her voice was shaky and she wasn't making eye contact with him. Catching him off guard she quickly slid into the car's seat and closed the door behind her. He sat for a minute with his fists on top of the car's roof, peering

down through the glass at her, but she didn't look up. When the engine started, he backed up a few steps, and then she was gone.

He turned away from that last image of her. "Dammit!" He let the old,
comfortable rage fill him again. Striding forward, he kicked a tree's trunk,
forgetting he wore tennis shoes, not his boots. He swore again, this time
under his breath, remembering his friends were sleeping. He yanked on the
door of the bus, stormed in, and poured himself a scotch.

BETH WAS GRATEFUL FOR the long ride back to the hotel so she
could collect herself before Cassie saw her. Why was she so crazy emotional
tonight? She trudged tiredly down the narrow hall to her hotel room, surprised to find the lights off when she entered. She saw the lump she knew was
Cassie on the far bed. She followed the lone light into the bathroom where
she found a note on the hotel stationery.

Sorry I couldn't wait up, Mom.

Long day. Hope your date went

well.—Cas

She could see Cas's mischievous grin as she wrote the last line.

Beth glanced up to catch her reflection in the mirror. The makeup hiding
her bruises had worn off and her exhaustion made her skin paler, her few
wrinkles deeper. I look like hell. Thank goodness Cassie is asleep. She would
know I was upset in a heartbeat.

Leaving the relative comfort of the lighted bathroom, she crossed the
room to the sliding doors that led out to the balcony. She opened the curtains
a little bit to gaze at the moon. Her heart felt heavy. Eventually, she ventured
out onto the balcony. She was relieved Cassie hadn't stirred with the cold air
rushing in. She leaned against the high railing and gazed out across the Mississippi.

Why am I letting myself get so worked up over this? You'd think I was
thirteen again, or a little older, and hadn't gotten asked to prom. Only I did
get asked to the prom, sort of, but I couldn't bring myself to go. Being in
Chad's arms felt so good; it transported her to another time, another man's
arms. She loved Paul with her whole heart, and now, somehow, the good feel-

ing of being in the arms of a man got wrapped up in the anguish she felt when Paul died.

She paced back and forth in the small confines of her balcony, becoming angry.

What's wrong with me? Am I never going to love again? Am I too afraid to try?

With a sudden conviction, she reentered the bedroom and wrote Cassie a note. It read:

Be back shortly.—M

She could think of no reason for her to be out at this late hour, so she hoped if called upon, an inspired answer would come to her.

As Chad sat on the steps leading up to the bus's door nursing his scotch, he suddenly found himself framed in headlights.

Who the hell would be out this late? I thought Keith was in the bus.

He was in no mood for company; that was for sure.

He set his glass on the steps, raising a hand to shield his eyes. He squinted, peering into the darkness. As it got nearer, the car cut its lights, cut the engine, and rolled slowly to a stop. He got to his feet as she exited the car. Beth stood for a few seconds, messing around with her keys. Then, she ran to him, dropping them in the grass.

Without thinking, he pulled her off her feet and swallowed her in an embrace. He laid a cold cheek against her warm one and squeezed his eyes shut. "You came back," he spoke huskily into her ear.

"I had to," was her only reply.

They stood there like that for several minutes, not letting up on their embrace for fear of losing it. Finally, he set her down.

She peered up into his face. "I want to stay with you, Chad."

Normally, he wouldn't need to be asked twice, but he stood there frozen for a second or two.

Beth gazed at him, her brow furrowing. "Did I make a mistake?"

"Dammit!" he fumed, turning from her and kicking at the dirt. He stood with his hands on his hips, back to her, looking up at the stars as if, for all the world, he expected them to give him answers. He whirled and moved toward her. Her face was lit from the outdoor light of the other bus. He strode forward so purposefully that she took a step backward. "I have to know if you are sure. If this is not right for you..." He couldn't bring himself to say it.

"Chad—" she started to answer, but without warning he scooped her up in his arms.

"Okay, good enough for me." He kissed her as he carried her back to a second set of steps in the middle of the bus. Balancing her on one knee, he struggled with the door. He deposited her inside, climbed up behind her, and closed the door.

"Is Keith here?" she whispered.

"Yeah, his room's up there." Chad gestured to the front of the bus. "Mine's this way." He grabbed her hand and led her through the blackness, cursing under his breath every now and then as he tripped over something. Finally, he opened a door and reached in to flip a switch.

The room was flooded with light, and Beth stepped into a surprisingly nice bedroom. A king-sized bed with burgundy sheets sat in the middle of the room, unmade. To the left was a wet bar with a mirror behind it on the wall and a set of three lights hanging from the ceiling above it. On the right was a door she suspected led to a bathroom. As she turned around to see the rest of the room, he snuck past her and subtly tried to straighten the bed. To the left of the door they had just entered through was a large desk with cubbyholes built into the wall above it. Splayed across the desk were sheets of music and packages of guitar strings. To the right of the door was a large, ornately carved wardrobe, which she thought too pretty to hold the T-shirts and jeans she imagined it did contain.

Beth turned around, and Chad rose up on one elbow in a casual pose so she wouldn't see him fixing the bed. It was almost comical, but she kept herself from laughing, considering that when he had kissed her earlier that evening, she cried. If she were to laugh now, when she suspected they were about to make love, it might be a final blow to his ego.

She still had some doubts as to whether she should be there at all. She didn't need her teenaged daughter getting mixed signals about where she stood on casual sex, or even sex outside the bonds of marriage. But even though she knew Chad for little more than a day, to her there was nothing casual about what they were about to do. She knew he would be gone the day after tomorrow. This might be the only chance she had to be with him, and she needed to do something with these feelings she had for him, or she would regret it forever. To her amusement, she heard the chorus of their hit song, "I Just Had to Have You Last Night," running through her head. She strolled toward Chad, her eyes locked on his.

He flew up to sit on the edge of the bed. As she neared, he reached out and grabbed the back of her thighs, drawing her between his legs without ever breaking eye contact. He rubbed the back of her thighs, anxious, but letting her lead the way. She brought her hands up and brushed the hair back from his face, then brought them forward again to rest against the sides of his face. It felt so incredibly good; this was like nothing he had ever done before. And for a second, as much as he didn't want to, he stepped out of the moment.

This bedroom, this bed, on what they all referred to as "The Fun Bus," had seen its fair share of action. A song lyric ran through his head. He couldn't even remember what song it was from at the moment. "There ain't much you can do when they just lay it at your feet." Was it Seger? U2? It didn't matter. Oh yeah, Melissa Etheridge. It was true; he'd had his fair share of women, and then some. But they were always gone in the morning, leaving him feeling even emptier than before. He was involved in only one, what you might call, relationship.

Julie. A tall model he met in New York. He thought she was fantastic at first, but she ended up being like all the rest, just robbing him of his heart at a much slower rate. Still, there were parts of their time together he didn't regret, the times he deluded himself into thinking she actually cared for him. Within weeks the relationship subtly changed, and it took months of her being demanding and critical, and eventually belittling him at every turn, before he reclaimed himself and said enough. Although, as he recalled, he yelled it at her, exploding in a bid for self-preservation. He remembered her face, surprised at first then turning hard. She released a torrent of hateful words, but they no longer held any power over him. He was finished with his self-torture; despite what his father had told him, he deserved better than that.

He pulled himself back into the moment. With her thumbs, Beth was tracing the line of his eyebrows. He closed his eyes, exhaling all of the pain of the last hour and drinking in her touch like a much-needed tonic. Her hands moved to his lips, and she traced their outline with one finger, in what he thought was the most erotic movement he ever felt. He unconsciously sucked in his breath and opened his eyes. They continued to gaze at each other for a moment, the sexual tension mounting.

HIS HANDS SEDUCED, moving up the back of her thighs little by little and over the curve of her buttocks. This time it was Beth who closed her eyes and sucked in her breath in anticipation. She thought it would be strange with another man, that she would at least feel self-conscious about her body. But she knew her body was possibly in the best shape of her life—better perhaps than even in her college days, when her workouts were less feverish and intense, before she was chasing ghosts around the weight room and the track. She knew, without a doubt, her body would respond to him, as it already was.

Her sex life with Paul was always hot. Beth had longed for him so strongly and often, he had begged off at times, laughingly admitting to being too tired. At first, this hurt her feelings, but Paul showed her how much he wanted her when they did make love. She learned in time to be patient. She thought now about how much they learned from each other. They were just kids when they got married, too young she would tell Cassie, but they loved each other, and love made up for a lot. Their lovemaking started out experimentally; they were both each other's first partner, and what started out as clumsy fumbling, over the years became an art form of sorts. They became comfortable enough to try new things, became more giving over time, wanting to please the other person, losing the selfishness of youth.

Beth felt much the same now. As she gazed into Chad's eyes, she could see his brokenness, the unending pain he hid so poorly. She wanted to take it all away from him for one night, if he would only let her. Beth stroked his mustache and goatee. She thought she didn't like facial hair in the past, but on Chad it was extremely sexy. Everything about him was extremely sexy. She bent to kiss him, softly at first, but with increasing urgency. His hands slid underneath the back of her sweater, and he caressed her back and sides.

The skin-to-skin contact seemed to ignite them. She tugged on his shirt, and he drew away long enough to pull it off. She ran her hands across his broad chest and let them explore his well-shaped arms, their hardness, the way she could see each curve of each muscle. Even the thin leather strap across the bare skin of his wrist was enormously appealing. She shimmied her sweater off over her head.

The exposure of an exponentially larger quantity of skin almost unraveled him. Chad laid his hand flat against her skin, just below her shoulder. He could feel her heart beating against it, could hear her quick breathing in his ears. He brought his other hand up, and with both hands followed the straps of her black, lacy bra. He slipped a tip of a finger under the straps, studying her every curve. Seriousness stole over him as her chest rose and fell beneath his hands.

Chad brought them down across her flat stomach, past the belly button, and then out to the sides. Beth's jeans were loose enough for his hands to slip under the denim and explore the curve of her hips. He brought them around to her backside, feeling her cool flesh there. Right when she would anticipate him pulling her closer, he extended his arms instead, giving him room to bring his head down to kiss her stomach. He moved up, inch by terrible inch, drawing each second of their lovemaking out. He felt her quiver with excitement and felt a momentary desire to make it last until she begged him to satisfy her, but he knew he couldn't last that long.

BETH THOUGHT SHE WOULD implode or explode or be shattered in some way if she couldn't feel him in her. She didn't know who taught his mouth to work that way, and right now, she didn't care. As Chad traveled across her stomach, she could feel her insides turn to jelly. The way his lips and tongue felt, and the soft brush of his goatee as he moved up...Beth couldn't take it anymore. She gently pushed him away and unbuttoned her jeans, wriggling out of them. He stood at the same time, moving to the side of the bed and switching the lamp off. He almost knocked it over in his hurry but steadied it before reaching down to take off the rest of his clothes.

In the moonlight, Chad could see her crawling up the bed, looking every bit like some kind of leopardess. He slid into bed just as she reached him. He froze, transfixed by her movements as she caressed each calf. She continued to move up until she was lying on top of him. She stilled herself, and all that could be heard in the darkness was the sound of their simultaneous breathing. He could see her eyes in the light from the windows, intensely liquid with desire.

AS BETH GAZED DOWN into his beautiful face, she could see his ache for her etched into every line of his brow. She could see it in his eyes, how much he needed her to love him. Chad reached up behind her neck and pulled her to him strongly, covering her mouth with his, and she could feel the power of his need. With one swift motion he flipped her over, his hands already tugging at her lacy panties. She lifted her hips enough for him to slide them down and off one foot, and she kicked them onto the floor with her other. Before she could even bring her foot back in place he was within her. She could see him shake his hair out of his face as he began to rock his hips rhythmically back and forth.

Beth moved her hands to his buttocks, feeling the motion and synchronizing her movements to his. She began to moan, the sensations he created rolling over her in liquid waves. Her lips rested against the skin of his shoulder, parted as she arched, her arms clamped tightly around him.

CHAD COULD SEE HER face contort, and then finally relax into a smile of supreme pleasure as her body released her from its sweet agony. He slowed till he was hardly moving, letting her feel each muscle relax, then he began the movement again, this time driving into her with each fall of his hips. Chad buried his face in her neck and his teeth found flesh.

BETH LISTENED TO THE signals his body gave, concentrating on her timing, their pulses pounding forward, until they both found pleasure together, collapsed, and slid into the tingling warmth, delivered at last from the strength of their desires. They clung to each other, sealed together in sweat, catching their breath.

Chad smoothed damp tendrils away from her face and kissed Beth over and over again before moving away. He flipped onto the pillow next to her, wrist resting on his forehead, a smile of contentment on his face. Happily, she ducked under his arm, resting her head on his chest. He brought his arm down around her and rubbed her, the motion incredibly soothing in the twilight of their lovemaking. Even this position made her feel too distant from him, so she squirmed closer, wrapping a leg over Chad's and stretching an arm across his chest to his shoulder. Tired from their exertion and the drama before it, they fell asleep.

BETH STIRRED. HOW LONG had she been sleeping? Had it been twenty minutes? Forty? She lifted her head from Chad's chest and squinted at the clock. 3 a.m. She could only hope Cassie was sleeping soundly. Chad stretched beside her and inhaled deeply.

"I have to go." Beth's voice was as heavy as her heart.

He hadn't thought of this. He hadn't, in fact, thought of anything beyond his desire for her. She shifted and he moved his arm. Chad sat up on an elbow, trying to wrap his mind around the fact she was, once again, leaving him. He saw her silhouetted outline as she sat at the edge of the bed, and he longed to pull her back into bed with him, to make love to her all over again. Beth was fishing around on the floor for something, her panties. She stood and went to the end of the bed, pulling her jeans on, and finally, the sweater slipped over her head.

Chad pulled up to a sitting position. When she came around to his side of the bed, he could see her lips were tight, brow creased, and shoulders slumped. "Beth—"

Beth covered his words up with her mouth, one hand on the side of his face. Her kiss held the bitterness of goodbye. She rested her forehead against his, and he could see her shoulders shaking silently. Chad couldn't understand why she was so upset. His hand trailed down her arm as she turned to go, trying to stop her.

When Beth reached the door, he called to her again, but the only response he got was the sound of the door closing, followed by the sound of the outside door, followed by her car engine starting, followed by silence. Chad sat in his bed with his head in his hands, trying to make sense out of what had just happened, but becoming more confused by the instant.

CHAPTER SEVEN

When Beth returned to the hotel room, she found Cassie still asleep. Without bothering to take her clothes off, she climbed into bed, first leaving a note telling her daughter she wasn't feeling well and asking to let her sleep in as late as possible.

And it wasn't a lie. She wasn't feeling good. No matter how hard she tried, her mind tortured her with images of Chad: singing with him on stage, dancing onboard "The Mississippi Queen," and every second they shared inside his bedroom. She ran fingers over her lips, remembering his kiss. She was glad she made love to him but knew she could not go back to him. She would want to leave in the morning rather than prolong their goodbye. It was enough to say goodbye now; a second night would kill her. She fell asleep shortly before Cassie woke up.

When she rose, she told Cassie she still wasn't feeling well, and they would have to skip the concert and return home. She couldn't bear to see Chad again, even if it was only on stage. On the drive back to Bloomington she was unusually quiet and distracted. Twice she went to switch lanes, forgetting to look in her side-view mirror, and received a loud honk and a shake of the fist.

"Mom, are you okay?" Cassie asked.

"Hmm...?"

"Mom, did something happen with Chad?"

Beth started, her eyes darting to Cassie and then back to the road. "No, Cassie. No. What could have possibly happened with Chad? I'm just...not feeling well, is all."

Cassie frowned. The look said she wasn't buying what her mom was trying to sell. Luckily, she seemed to decide it was better not to push as they continued the ride in silence.

Still, weeks went by, and Beth continued to live in the same sort of fog. She'd sit down to the computer to write and get up hours later, having added nothing to her latest book. After several wasted afternoons, she decided to keep the laptop closed for a while, until inspiration hit her. Blessed with another mild winter day, she decided to go for a speed walk to try to clear her head.

No matter how fast she walked, her problems seemed to keep pace. For some unknown reason, she flashed back to a Christmas before Cassie was born.

BETH'S FAMILY RENTED out a bed and breakfast in Pennsylvania for the weekend. She and Paul were looking forward to the getaway, because after a year of trying to get pregnant, they discovered she was experiencing some fertility problems. Her eggs were maturing, but not being released properly, so they started a course of daily shots. After months of disappointments, they were putting their hopes in the doctors. However, the heartbreak of all the ups and downs they experienced as they waited for their family to grow took its toll on them both.

Lugging bags up the stairs of their B&B, they found their bedroom, high above the others. With an irregularly sloped ceiling and a canopied bed, she thought it was charming.

"Oh, Paul. This is fantastic."

She was lying on the bed, soaking in the atmosphere, when Paul sat beside her. "I have a surprise for you."

"Oh yeah?" she answered, her voice honeyed-seduction.

"Not that," he responded, tapping her lip once, "although I might take you up on that later. Sit up."

"Okay."

"Close your eyes. Okay...now open them."

Lying on the bed was a candy bar.

"Did you get this at the gas station? That's so sweet. You know that's my favorite." She kissed him.

"Is there anything else?"

"Huh?" she said, already opening her candy bar. She looked back down on the bed. Nestled in the quilt where the chocolate had been, a diamond/sapphire anniversary band lay in the folds. "Oh my gosh, Paul!" she squealed. "I can't believe it."

He laughed. "Well, try it on."

"It's beautiful." She started crying. "I've got to show Dana." She flew out of the room, running down the stairs to find her little sister.

She heard him mutter as she reached the next floor. "How about that? I get a kiss for a candy bar, and she runs out on me for a ring. Go figure." The sound of his laughter followed.

THEN, LIKE A TWIST in some horror movie, Beth was transported to another time.

"IS THIS MRS. PAUL DONOVAN?"

A chill ran up her spine. Paul was away on a business trip. "Y-yes."

Then, the hesitation. "Mrs. Donovan, I'm calling from the Aurora Sinai Medical Center in Milwaukee, Wisconsin." Beth felt her knees starting to buckle. "Your husband was in a serious car accident..." The rest she barely heard. "His injuries were extensive...we used every measure available to us..."

A CAR HORN BLEW. SHE had come to a complete halt in the entrance to a convenience store parking lot. She scurried out of the way as the beat-up Beetle pulled into the parking lot. It had begun to snow again. She closed her eyes and lifted her head to the sky, wondering how it was a drunk driver was able to rob her of the man she loved with her whole heart. She trudged the rest of the way home, numb from more than the cold.

BETH PICKED UP THE phone and was pleasantly surprised to hear the voice of her best friend, Cali.

"Hey, babe. I think it's time for a girls' night. You up for it?"

She wasn't up for it, but Cali was so fun. Maybe she could help her get out of this funk.

"Sure. Where do you want to go?"

"Why don't you come over here?"

"Okay," Beth responded, surprised. Invites to Cali's were few and far between. "What should I bring?"

"Nothin'. Just your sweet self."

Even more unusual. "Who else is coming?"

"I'm not sure yet," Cali replied in a vague way. "Seven o'clock, then?"

"I'll be there."

The appointed time rolled around, and she arrived on Cali's doorstep a little late, having lost track of time. No other cars were around, but it wasn't unheard of for their other lunch lady friends to be late.

Right as she rang the doorbell, a high-pitched beeping began to issue from the inside of the house. After several seconds, Cali opened the door waving a towel. "The smoke detector went off!" she screamed, the explanation unnecessary as smoke billowed out the front door the minute she opened it.

"Cooking again?" Beth quipped with a wink.

"Very funny, smartass." Cali coughed, grabbing her by the arm. "Now get in here and start fanning."

She grinned, shaking her head at her friend's unending string of failed attempts at domesticity. Cali was a thirty-four-year-old divorcee, a professed man-hater, whose ex-husband cheated on her even as she labored delivering their stillborn child. Not only that, but the louse did it with a woman who Cali considered at the time to be her best friend.

She was the girl you would pick out in a crowd—bottled-blond, bodacious, and not afraid to spend outrageous amounts of money on the latest fashion. She was rarely serious, the ultimate party girl, but in addition, a loving and caring friend. Cali also had a knack for telling people in no uncertain terms exactly how she felt about things—a trait people either admired or hated.

Beth put down her infamous Mexican dip, a bag of chips balanced on top, as she grabbed the proffered kitchen towel and started waving at the smoke. Cali, though tall, was jumping up and down whacking the smoke alarm with the end of her towel. Beth started laughing and coughing. "Only you."

"Shut up." Her friend laughed back, snapping her towel at Beth with unerring accuracy.

"Ouch!" she squealed, coughing again. "How can a girl who's incapable of filling her own gas tank have such good aim?" she added, flicking her towel, but missing. Cali would drive out of her way to the one full-service gas station in town.

With a loud scraping noise, the cover of the smoke alarm fell off, held suspended by some wires, but at least the incessant buzzing had finally stopped. The girls stood panting from their exertion, bent over double, alternately coughing and laughing. They both straightened up, wiping tears from their eyes. Cali threw an arm over Beth's shoulder, leading her into the kitchen.

"You are so not telling anyone about this."

"What's in it for me?"

"Do I have to get the towel out again?"

Beth held up her hands in a sign of surrender. "No, no. Mum's the word. I promise." She ambled over to the oven. "So," she said, peering into the still-smoking pan on the oven, "what was this going to be?" She grinned, raising her eyebrows mischievously.

"Cheese dip."

"Uh-huh." She attempted to stir the charred remains in the saucepan, the pot spinning around and around, the spoon fused to the bottom. "Girlfriend, I think this pan is toast. There's no way you're getting this clean."

"Clean 'em? Why clean 'em? I just throw them away."

Beth laughed. People who didn't know Cali would think she was just kidding, but she knew it was likely to be true. She often wondered how her friend did it on a lunch lady's salary, though she knew her ex was paying out the wazoo for his affair. Beth stole a chip out of the bag Cali had just opened. "So, who else is coming?"

"It's just us tonight," Cali replied. "Irish cream?"

"Sure, sounds good." She was suddenly suspicious. "Just us?"

"Yeah," her friend returned defensively. "I haven't had a chance to talk to you for a while."

"Yeah, we've been on break a whole week."

"Well, we never get a chance to talk at work."

"Are you kidding? That's all we do."

"Good point. But I mean, really talk. Girl to girl."

Beth leaned back against the counter, her hands crossed in front. "About what?"

"Oh, you know...things," Cali replied with a vague wave of the hand. "So, how was your trip to St. Louis?"

"The trip I took weeks ago?" She accepted her glass of Irish cream, her suspicions growing stronger. "The one I already told you about?" She followed Cali into her posh living room.

"You only told me in monosyllabic terms: 'Fine. Good. All right. Super...'"

"Okay, I get it. I get it. What do you want to know?"

"Gee, I don't know. Like...what did you do there?"

Like snapshots falling from a photo album, she saw images of Chad. She got up from the white couch and strolled over to the window, watching the snow fall and swirl around the patio in playful little gusts. She winced and downed her Irish cream in one gulp.

"Could I get some more?" she asked, hoping to stall for time by going to the kitchen.

Cali, prepared for her subterfuge, lifted the big, brown bottle without saying a word.

"Oh, thanks."

"How was the concert?" Cali prodded.

"Great. Fantastic, in fact," she answered truthfully. She decided right away not to talk about the attack that happened afterward; no need to give Cali any more man-fodder.

Cali set her glass down on the coffee table with a loud rap, leaning forward with her hands on her knees to give her a come-clean look. Beth swallowed some more, the creamy drink stung as it went down, but warmed her.

"I met Chad Evans," she exhaled in a rush, emboldened by the alcohol.

"Really?" Cali picked up her drink and ran a finger around the rim casually. "What was he like?" She studied her friend's face.

Beth turned to gaze out the window again but still saw Cali reading her face in the glass's reflection. "He was...he was...great."

"'Great. Fantastic,'" Cali imitated her friend. "I'm needing more syllables here, girl."

All of a sudden, a light turned on. "Did Cassie tell you something? Is that why I'm over here tonight by myself?" Her anger gained momentum. "You wanted to grill me about St. Louis?" she spat out, fury coming upon her like a storm.

Cali rose from the couch. "Now, no need to get yourself into a huff. We've all noticed you haven't been yourself lately. And if that little rock star bastard had anything to do with it, I want to know."

"He's not like that!" Beth nearly screamed.

Cali raised her hands defensively. "Whoa! Okay. Obviously struck a chord." She eyed Beth, silent for a moment. "Now we're getting somewhere. That was definitely more than one syllable. So, what was he like?" she repeated in a more subdued tone, returning to her place on the couch and patting the cushion beside her.

Beth sighed, coming over to sit beside her friend. "It's hard to explain."

"You meet one of the world's biggest rock stars, and that's all you can give me? Cassie said he came to hear you sing."

"So, Cassie did call you."

Cali shrugged. "She was concerned."

She sighed. "He came to hear me sing. We had dinner. I sang with his band, we went dancing...and then I slept with him," she ended, her voice flat.

"Whoo! My girl got it on with a rock star."

"It wasn't like that," she snapped. "It wasn't like that at all." She got up and started pacing in front of the couch.

"I've never seen you so reticent. Dragging stuff out of you tonight is like trying—" she glanced out the window "—like trying to drag a sled over the Iditarod without snow."

"Ooh. Million-dollar word, 'reticent.'"

"Thanks." Cali smiled. "I pull them out every once in a while."

"And nice metaphor with the Iditarod and all."

"Yes, I guess hanging out with you is rubbing off on me. So, girl-with-all-the-words, give me a couple."

Beth exhaled and came to plop beside her friend again. "I guess it's a lot harder when you're not describing things in make-believe world. He-e-e-e was different. He was nice to Cas, and I've never laughed so hard in my life, outside of being with you," she added before Cali could pounce on her.

"Go on."

"Well, there was an unmistakable physical attraction. I mean, whoo! Red hot. I mean *red hot*. As my mom would say, 'One cool drink of water.' When we went dancing—"

"That's when he made his move?"

"Yeah. I guess you could say that." She smiled, remembering. "He kissed me, then I cried."

"You cried?"

She nodded.

"That bad a kisser?"

"Not hardly. I just, I don't know. I'm a nut, I guess."

Cali sat back, appearing to chew on this information for a minute. "Then he asked you to come back to his place?"

"No, I was giving him a ride out to his tour bus—"

"You did it on the tour bus? Way to go." She held up her hand for a high-five. Beth laughed but slapped her hand.

"You are not telling anyone about this."

"Hell, no. Not when you've got the whole cheese dip thing to hold over my head."

"And don't you forget it," Beth teased.

"And the sex was...?"

"Good girls don't kiss and tell." She paused. "But it was incredible."

"Ooh, I'm so jealous. And afterward..."

"I left."

"That's it? You just left?"

"Well, I had Cas back at the hotel and..."

"And what?"

"And he's a rock star. I'm sure he has a different woman every night. It was meaningless."

"From what you're saying, it doesn't sound like that." Beth remained silent. Cali reached over and touched her hand. "Why did you cry when he kissed you?"

She felt tears welling up. "Because I really liked him. I know I sound like an idiot. I hardly know the man. But...it's hard to describe..." She tried to rein in her emotions. "And I guess I was, sort of...afraid."

"Afraid?"

"Being with another man terrifies me."

Cali thought about this. "Or is it loving another man that really scares you?"

"Maybe. I went through hell when I lost Paul. I'm not sure I could do that again." She sighed loudly. "So that's why I've been like I've been lately. I think I need to be medicated."

"Well, I told you that a long time ago." Cali laughed. "Seriously, hon, I'm sorry this hurts."

She hopped to her feet again, agitated. "This sounds like a conversation you should be having with a teenaged daughter, not a grown woman."

"Hey. Love's hell at any age. I know that."

"Well—" Beth blew her nose on a tissue she had retrieved from her purse "—now that you have your information, Miss Inquisitor, do you mind if I bail on you? I'm exhausted."

"Sure. Go home and get some sleep." Cali walked her friend to the door. She shook her head as they passed through the hall. "Just like a man. Love 'em and leave 'em. I hope he gets what he deserves."

Beth brushed the comment off. "Well, I don't know..." She stopped under the disabled smoke alarm, looking up. "You'll have Patrick look at that?" Patrick was the cute, single guy who lived next door. He was always ready to do a favor for Cali.

"You betcha." Cali winked.

Beth hugged her. "Thanks for listen to me ramble on."

"That's what I'm here for. Drive safely," she added, eyeing the snow.

Cali hugged her then closed the door on the cold. Beth hurried to her car and started her engine, rubbing her hands even though she wore gloves. She glanced back at the house, noting her friend still watched through the window. She smiled and shook her head. Maybe Cali couldn't cook worth a damn, but she was right about this. What she had with Chad was one night, one very special night, but it was over. She needed to forget him and move on. Starting tomorrow, they'd see a new Beth. She'd get back to her day job and her writing, and there would be no more mooning over Chad Evans. She took a deep breath and pulled out of the driveway to head home.

CHAPTER EIGHT

C had woke up alone and unhappy. Even his friends who knew him as perpetually out-of-sorts noticed a difference, but no one was brave enough to ask him what was bothering him. They chalked it up to writer's block. He was supposed to be working on a new album, but he'd sit at his desk and all he could think about was Beth. He tried to channel his feelings into a song about her, as he did in the past with his problems, but he'd start and quit, then start and quit again. These songwriting sessions usually ended with the loud sounds of him breaking something, or on good days, with a flurry of curse words.

However, after weeks of breaking things, getting in fights, and getting stinking drunk, they'd all had enough. Chad was making everybody miserable, Roger realized, and something needed to be done.

Chad cursed after forgetting the words to the group's first big song, "Out of Touch." Practices hadn't been going well, and this one was no exception.

"I'm done," Keith finally announced, laying down his drumsticks.

"Keith—"

"No, Roger. I've had it! You call me when Chad here decides to quit being such an asshole." He stormed off the stage without looking back.

Everyone stared at him, but Chad only picked up the beer bottle by his feet and took a swig. David glanced at Roger. Roger nodded at him, and David followed in Keith's wake. He glanced over his shoulder then waited in the footlights to see what would happen.

Chad turned to peer at Roger. "So, aren't you going? Surely you must think I'm an ass, too?"

Roger set down his guitar, contemplating. "I think you've been acting like an ass, yes. What the hell's gotten into you?" Chad ignored him and took off his guitar, moving to put it in its stand. "You've been on a slow burn since...St. Louis." A sudden look of recognition crossed his face. "Since Beth." Chad's eyes flitted to him, but he said nothing. "That's it, isn't it?" He saw his words were hitting the mark and decided to try another tactic. "You slept with her didn't you? What? Was she that good?"

"Shut up, Roger." Chad moved closer, his jaw clenched.

"A little hot mama like her must have been a good screw, huh, Chad?"

"Shut up!" He stepped up and pushed his friend, anger written in blazing lines across his face, but Roger didn't back down.

"So where did you do her? In some seedy hotel room, or maybe in the dressing room? Or maybe you didn't take a lot of time with it, just gave her a little poke backstage—"

Chad launched himself at Roger, taking him into a stool and a cymbal stand. David came running from backstage.

"Chad! Stop!"

It took all David had in him to pull his bigger brother off Roger after the three scrambled around on the floor for a little while. Finally, Chad got up, shook David off, and turned around, marching away and standing with his back to them.

Roger got up wiping blood from his mouth onto the back of a hand but wearing a huge grin. "You love her, don't you? The impenetrable Chad Evans fell in love. And let me guess, you haven't talked to her since, have you? *Have you?*"

"I don't have her number," he mumbled.

Roger moved forward and clapped a hand on his shoulder. "Well, guess what, buddy? There's this new thing called the Internet. I could probably get you her number and find out what she ate for dinner last night. Let's go back to the bus."

"Nah, man. I don't know if she even wants to talk to me."

"Now, that's the ten-million-dollar question, isn't it? But there's only one way to find out the answer. Come on." Roger left the stage, and David followed, throwing Chad a backward glance. The big man hadn't moved. He stood studying a guitar pick, turning it over in his hand. David shook his head and walked off.

WHEN CHAD ENTERED THE bus, Roger sat at a table with his laptop open. Michelle stood behind him, leaning over the bassist to read what was on the screen. But when Chad saw her, she slid away. Keith sat on an L-shaped couch, his back in the corner, one leg bent, one leg stretched out, tapping a set of drumsticks together, not making eye contact, but obviously still peeved. David stood by the window, appearing somewhat nervous.

"What the hell is this?" Chad questioned. "A freaking intervention?"

"What was the name of her hometown? Bloomburg or Blooming City..."

"Huh? It was Bloomington, you moron."

"I'll let that pass since you've already beaten the crap out of me once today."

"And you don't want me to have to do it twice?"

"Exactly." Roger typed. "Indiana or Illinois?"

Chad scanned the rest of the group again, all of whom were eyeing him now. "Illinois," he replied slowly.

"And what was her last name again?"

"Donovan."

"That's right, Donovan." Roger paused. "There's four Beth Donovans in Bloomington."

"Four?" He crossed to look at the screen. "In a little city like Bloomington?"

Roger handed him the phone. "Start dialing."

He started punching in the first number. He turned around. Keith looked much happier now and swung his feet off the couch to lean in so he could listen better. The others were similarly posed. "A little privacy?" Chad growled. They all tried to look busy. He shook his head and turned around. On the second number he reached her.

WHEN BETH PICKED UP the receiver she was shocked to hear Chad's voice.

"Beth?"

Her heart caught in her throat. She thought it would be a friend or neighbor wishing her a happy New Year. The sound of his deep, gravelly voice filled her. She hadn't been able to play any of his music after leaving St. Louis. She shut her eyes, struggling to find her voice. She had moved on, she had. And now, just the sound of his voice, and she was right back to that night on the riverboat.

"Beth? Are you there?"

"Chad," she managed to get out.

SHE RECOGNIZED HIS voice; that was a good sign, Chad thought.

"How are you?" she asked, her voice small.

He sighed, rubbing his eyes. "I've been better." Someone sniggered and Chad turned around to give them all a menacing look. "How are you?"

"The same," she admitted.

Chad turned away from Roger's prying eyes, leaning his clenched fist on the window. "I want to come to see you. No, I need to come see you," he blurted out.

There was a long silence. "Oh, God, Chad," her words came in torrents, as if the floodgate of her heart was shattered. "I've been so miserable. I can't stop thinking about—"

"I know," he stated simply.

"When can you get away?"

"I'm in Alberta now. We've got a couple of days of travel ahead of us, but...let's see, we've got a show in Milwaukee Thursday night, one in Chicago Friday. I've got to sing the national anthem at the Black Hawks' game Saturday afternoon. Then, I'm off until Monday. I could come down on Saturday, after the anthem."

"I don't want to wait that long. Could you leave tickets for me for Friday night's show?"

"They've been waiting at will call in every city since St. Louis, just in case," he admitted.

"Great! Oh...wait!" She moaned.

"What?"

"I really can't. Ugh! I forgot that Cassie has a tournament game on Friday. And then her friend, Jessica, is coming home with her after the game to spend the weekend with us. Her parents are going to Galena for their anniversary. I promised them I'd take care of her. I can't break that promise and I can't leave two sixteen-year-olds home alone."

Chad thought fast. "Come Saturday then. Bring the girls. I'll get rooms for all of you. We can spend the rest of the weekend together." He held his breath.

"I don't know. I'd have to ask Jessica's parents, and I'm not sure that they'd approve of her spending the weekend with a rock star."

"I'm not just a rock star," he said desperately. "I'm a guy, Chad Evans."

"It's not just that. They don't know you—"

"Come on, Beth! Say you'll at least ask."

"Ask them if it would be okay if I took their daughter, and my daughter, on a date?"

He sighed. "Ah, when you say it like that, it sounds bad."

"That's what it is, isn't it?" she insisted.

"Yes, but...we'll have separate rooms."

She hesitated. "We'd have to behave ourselves."

Chad saw a glimmer of light. "I can do that!"

"I'm not sure I can," she murmured.

He shifted, parts of his body becoming awake. "I want to see you."

Her voice brightened. "I'll ask."

"Good!" He sighed. "So maybe I'll see you in just a few days then. Call me tomorrow, if you can."

"I will." She paused. "I'm really glad you called."

He smiled. "Me, too."

He held on to the receiver for several seconds after she hung up. He turned to his friends with a huge grin on his face. "She's going to try to come to Chicago."

They all whooped and offered various phrases expressing their relief.

"Thank God!"

"Maybe now there'll be some scotch left for the rest of us."

"Yeah, and we can get through a set without Chad 'accidentally' breaking something."

"Ahh, shuddup," he returned with a smile, but he knew, in their own twisted way, they were all happy for him.

CHAPTER NINE

As Beth pulled into the circular drive her jaw dropped. The girls in the backseat gasped.

"What is this place?" Jessica whispered in awe.

She glanced at the paper beside her, double-checking to make sure they were in the right place. "The St. Ives-Augusta, I guess."

"Holy shit!"

Beth frowned, though still staring out the window. "Cassandra Marie! Watch the language, please."

Jessica giggled.

"Sorry," Cassie mumbled.

In the rearview mirror, she caught her daughter elbowing Jess. They were both unbuckled now and breathing down her neck to get a look out the front.

She drove her late-model sedan slowly to better take in the sight, hunching over the steering wheel to look up through the windshield at the massive building that arced with the sweep of the drive. A wide, circular stone staircase curved up on either side of a long terrace in front of the brick structure. It was impressive.

"Holy shit!" she mouthed, careful to not let the girls catch her, eyes wide as she took in the architecture. She suddenly became aware of a man in a long wool coat at the edge of the roadway. She jerked and stopped abruptly for fear of hitting him. Where had he come from?

"Oh, man!" She glanced over at the seat beside her where a half-eaten bag of popcorn sat.

"What, Mom?"

"Valet parking." Beth shoved the popcorn bag at Cassie. "Hide this."

Cassie and Jessica passed it around like a hot potato for a minute, squealing in alarm and laughing at the same time. They fumbled the bag and spilled some kernels before they hurriedly stowed it under a seat.

Beth thrust the sheet of directions in the mini trashcan between the front seats, keeping her eyes on the attendant as he passed in front of the car. At the last minute, she spotted a soda can in the cup holder and launched it over the seat. Cassie, though surprised, caught it, dropping the can to the floor and kicking it under the seat in front of her in one smooth move. Beth scrambled to grab mittens and a scarf off the passenger seat just as the man reached her door and attempted to open it for her.

"Oh!" She looked up at him with a smile while searching for the door handle for the unlock button. "Sorry," she said through the glass. Her fingers finally located the button, and it popped up, startling her with its loudness. The attendant swept the door open, and she brushed at the flecks of popcorn on her black coat, straightening her shoulders and trying to appear somewhat sophisticated. "Hello."

The man tipped his hat with a smile, flashing brilliantly white teeth as he stood back for her to pass. Beth got out of the car. Hearing a shout, she glanced up. Chad was hustling down the staircase on the right, dressed only in a Blackhawks jersey and jeans, despite the threat of snow in the air and broadcasted warnings throughout most of Illinois. Her smile grew wider. He slipped on the slick stairs but grabbed the railing to right himself as he came around the corner toward her.

Catching the move, the attendant warned, "Careful, sir."

Chad reached their side. "Uhh...yeah. Thanks, James," he said under his breath, though smiling at Beth. "I was trying to play it cool in front of the ladies. Thanks for blowing my cover."

The attendant laughed.

"Hey!" Chad said softly, bending down to kiss Beth's cheek. "How was your trip?"

"Good. Good." Beth smiled then turned to watch as James reached inside of her car and removed the keys, which she had left in the ignition. He strode purposefully to the rear of the car as the girls tumbled out on opposite sides.

"Hey, Cassie."

Cassie gave a short wave. "Hey, Chad."

He turned toward the passenger side of the car. "And you must be Jessica." He extended his hand, and she placed her colorful, mittened hand in his.

"Nice to meet you, Mr. Evans."

He pumped it. "Hey now, it's Chad, okay?"

The teen smiled brightly. "Sure."

He started. "James, what are you doing?" He moved toward the trunk.

The attendant answered, without looking up, as Chad came around the corner. "Getting the luggage, sir."

"I can handle the luggage." He looked into the trunk, glanced at the three small bags on the ground, and then back into the trunk. "This is all?"

"Yes," Beth replied with a smile.

He checked the bags again, and peered back into the trunk, as if confused.

"We're only here for one night," she reminded him.

"I know. It just seems like there should be more." When Beth just stared, he added, "I mean...three women..."

She frowned and placed her hands on hips.

James bent in and said in a low voice, loud enough for all to hear, "If I were you, sir, I'd just pick up the luggage and go."

"Good idea!" Chad bent and slung two of the bags over one shoulder and extended the handle on the third to pull it behind him.

"Sure you don't need any help?"

"I can handle it, James. Get lost. You're not getting any more tips."

Beth laughed. Was he trying to impress her with his show of chivalry? Despite his words, she saw Chad slip a bill into the attendant's hand before shutting the trunk. He moved forward, the two duffle bags hanging at his side bumping together and bouncing against his hip. He smiled brightly, his eyes on hers.

He was halfway up the side of the car when James called out, "It would be easier to hold the lady's hand, sir, if you were less encumbered."

He stopped, as if considering. The attendant swooped in, plucking one of the bags from his shoulder and grabbing the handle of the suitcase. Then, he gave Chad a little push in Beth's direction.

She grabbed his now free hand. Chad smiled. "Anyone ever tell you you're brilliant, James?"

"Yes, sir." James handed the keys off to another attendant who had arrived on the scene and proceeded around the car. "Have you ladies ever been to the St. Ives-Augusta before?"

"No. Does it show?" Cassie joked.

Beth tuned out their conversation, slipping her hand out of Chad's and through his arm so that she could draw closer. "Are you trying to impress me?"

He kept looking ahead, but she saw the corner of his lip rise. "Depends." He turned his head to look at her. "Is it working?"

She laughed and gave his arm a squeeze, surprised by how good it felt to be with him again.

"Hey, hey! How are ya, Gorgeous?" Roger called out when they entered the lobby. He got up from the couch, where he was sitting in front of a roaring fire with his arm around Michelle. Keith and Pete sat on the couch opposite, leaning forward as if they had just been engaged in a story.

"Oh, did I tell you that they would be here, too?" Chad asked dryly.

Roger took Beth by the shoulders, hip-checking Chad out of the way to give her a kiss on the cheek. "And, Cassie. How are ya, hon?"

"Good. And how are you?"

"Pretty good. You know. Slumming it here at the St. Ives."

"Yeah." Cassie laughed.

Roger turned to Jessica. "And who is this lovely, young lady?"

Jessica blushed.

"This is my friend, Jessica Matthews."

He shook her hand gallantly. "Nice to meet you, Jessica." He held his arms out wide. "Welcome."

"Are you done?" Chad asked.

Roger nodded. "Pretty much."

"I'm going to get these guys settled in. If that's all right with you?"

"Fine," Roger said with largess, returning to the group on the couches. They waved and said hello, but didn't get up.

"He's such a ham," Chad mumbled, rolling his eyes.

They followed James down a long, carpeted hallway to the end where a large window revealed that the dreaded snow had begun to fall.

"It's started," James commented before turning to open the door. Everyone stood and watched silently as the flakes floated down.

The doors to the room were set at an angle to the hall. There were paned glass French doors with shades on the other side, which were closed. James unlocked them and let them fall open into the room, standing back so that the others could enter. Beth and Chad walked in with the girls on their tails.

"Wow!" Cassie exclaimed.

"Yeah, it's pretty nice," Chad conceded.

A wide, high-ceilinged room spread out before them. To the right, three large plush couches formed a u-shaped conversation area in front of a massive fireplace. To the left, light shone in through French doors and the semicircular windows above them. The off-white blinds on the doors seemed to let the light in, while still blocking intruding eyes from the terrace beyond. A large dining table dominated that side of the room, a state-of-the-art, full-sized kitchen to the left of it. Chad gestured to a hallway off the living room.

"The bedrooms are down there. You girls can have the two on the end or share one, if you'd prefer."

"First dibs!" Cassie called and the two tore off in that direction.

As their laughter faded, it became oddly quiet. Chad cleared his throat. "And your room is also this way."

He escorted Beth to the first door, opening it on a large bedroom with a king-sized bed, which was recessed into the wall a bit and on a raised platform. The lighting and the décor screamed classy. He set her suitcase on a luggage stand and it was immediately dwarfed by the massive room. She took a few steps tentatively forward.

"The bathroom is over here." He crossed to the far corner of the room and reached in to switch on a light. She walked slowly in his direction and peered in without venturing further. On the right, a small waterfall poured from the wall into an enormous sunken tub. Thick towels hung from rings, and flowering plants were nestled in alcoves around the tub. The rest of the room was as spacious as Cassie's bedroom at home.

Beth felt Chad looking at her, and she lifted her head to find his eyes locked on her with a burning strength that almost took her breath away. She stepped back, reaching around to grab the doorframe to steady herself. He inhaled shallowly, licking his lips but remaining silent. She was intensely aware that this was the first time that the two of them had been alone together since she left his bed in St. Louis. She glanced away, feeling awkward.

"I'll let you get unpacked or freshen up or whatever, and wait for you outside," he said, and was gone before she could comment.

Beth stood frozen in the doorway for several seconds, thinking about the look on his face. Finally, she forced herself to move, crossing slowly to the bed. She stepped up on the platform and ran a hand along the russet and chocolate colored silky comforter. Spinning, she sat as if testing the mattress, bouncing a few times with her hands on the edge. She fell back, staring at the ceiling. What was she doing here? She didn't belong in a place like this, with someone like him. She closed her eyes, concentrating on just breathing in and out. After a time, she slowly turned her head to the side and opened her eyes, almost imagining him there beside her. So strong was the feeling, she reached out, again passing her hand over the place where he belonged, warming the surface with his heat. She squeezed her eyes shut. This was going to be so hard.

CHAD CROSSED TO THE couch and plopped down. His hands slid up his face as he bent over, the fingers threading into his hair, palms on his temples. What the hell was he doing? All morning, he had been second-guessing himself, nervous to the extreme, tapping on stuff constantly like he was the drummer instead of Keith. His insides felt tighter than they had before his first big stadium concert. Why had he invited her there, a woman he barely knew? And better yet, why had she agreed to come? He had pretty much convinced himself that it was a mistake when her car pulled in.

When his eyes first landed on her as she got out of the car, his heart had literally leapt in his chest. A shot of pure joy unlike any he had felt before spurted through him. It was like that burst of adrenaline that had filled him at that same first big concert about halfway through his first set, when he realized that this was where he belonged, this was what he was made for.

He slid down, laying his head on the back of the couch and staring at the ceiling, hands falling to his sides. In her bedroom, he had been filled with a need for her so consuming he had to leave, or he would have peeled her clothes off there and then. He didn't even need to make love to her, just feel her beside him, her skin against his, so comforting. He laughed. This was just beyond him.

Hearing her door open, he sprang up to a seated position, deciding at the last minute to stretch his arms along the back of the couch in what he hoped looked like a relaxed position.

He turned, trying to keep his voice calm and even. "Hey! You all settled in?"

"Pretty much." She came around the couch, but hung back, her hands behind her. She looked as uncomfortable as he felt.

He patted the seat beside him. "Come here." He wanted to comfort her about as much as he wanted her comfort. She strolled over and sat. He turned toward her a little. He gestured with his head. "The girls are playing ping-pong in the game room."

"Game room?" She turned and noticed for the first time a recessed bar to the left of the door they had entered through. To the right of that was a carpeted stairway leading down. From the opening a distinct sound rose. A ping-pong ball was being paddled and bouncing across a table rhythmically.

"Uh-huh. There's a ping-pong table, a pool table, darts, and a hot tub. They wanted to go into the hot tub, but I said they'd have to ask you. I thought you might want to catch something to eat first."

She smiled, seeming to loosen up a fraction. "I am starved!"

He put his palms on his knees and got ready to stand. "Let's eat then."

She put a hand on his arm to stop him from rising.

"Why did you switch hotels?

He wasn't ready for this. "Huh?"

"Why did you switch hotels? When you first called, we were staying at a low-budget place. Why did you switch?"

He wasn't about to tell her the real reason. "This place is a little...quieter. Not as many people in and out. I didn't want to be interrupted by fans. I wanted you all to myself." He reached over to play with her hair. It was true. He hadn't wanted a lot of commotion with fans. Their time together was short; he wanted to make the most of it. But that wasn't the only reason.

"Okay," she said slowly. She brought her eyes up to his and the mesmerizing green-blue had his head spinning. "I just want to be sure that you weren't trying to impress me or something, because that is so not necessary."

"Impress you? Not really," he answered honestly, letting the back of his hand trail down the side of her face. "I did want to spoil you a little."

Her lips slid into a smile. "I'm good with that."

He chuckled and sat straighter. "Speaking of which, I wasn't sure what you'd want to do today, so..." He pulled a handful of different sized tickets out of his shirt pocket, fanning them out in his hand. "I've got tickets to a show, to a museum, and to the Blackhawks' game, just in case you wanted to hang around after the anthem."

She studied his face. He tried to keep it neutral and not give away which would be his choice. She plucked the Blackhawks tickets out of his hand. "I love hockey."

His eyebrows rose. "Really?" He couldn't hide his pleasure.

"Yes. My dad used to always take me to the Blues games when I was little. We'd park across the highway and cross over a pedestrian walkway that spanned it. It was terrifying with all of those cars whizzing by underneath, but my dad would hold my hand, and I would feel safe." Her face grew softer with the memory. "He used to answer my questions so patiently, about offsides and high-sticking..." She laughed. "Actually, I remember once—I must have had a lot of questions that night, because my dad handed me a legal pad—why he had a legal pad with him, I don't know. Probably to collect stats, he was a statistician—and he told me to write down all of my questions and he'd answer them during breaks in play."

Chad smiled, leaning forward to take her hand. "That's a nice story."

"Did your dad ever take you to hockey games?"

"Our house was pretty much a hockey game every night," he said, a bitter taste in his mouth.

"What do you mean by that?"

He looked up, shifting his weight. How did that slip out? "Nothing. It's just, growing up so close to Canada, hockey was just what you did." He hoped she would let it drop. Standing, he reached for her hands and pulled her to her feet. "Now, how 'bout we get some of that food?"

"Sounds good."

Dodged a bullet.

He turned from her and exhaled, crossing to the stairs. He stuck his head down a little and hollered, "Hey, girls! Ready for some grub?"

There was a general hubbub followed by pounding of feet on the stairs.

"I'd say they're ready," he joked.

CHAPTER TEN

They headed out, but as he was locking the door behind them, Chad heard a voice calling his name. He turned, inwardly cringing a little, as he was expecting a fan. A Latino man with a blue bandana wrapped around his head stood behind him, his arm around a girl in a maid's uniform.

"Manny! Manny Juarez! What the hell are you doing here, man?" Chad swallowed the short, squat man up in a hug.

"Hey. I didn't know if you'd recognize me."

Chad kept an arm around the shorter man's shoulders. "Not recognize an ugly mug like that? Of course, I recognize you. You haven't changed a bit."

"Heh, heh. But you have. Big man on campus."

"I always was the big man on campus," he boasted.

Manny turned to address Beth. "Don't let him fool you. He was so scrawny when we were growing up that we worried that the breeze would sweep him into a bad neighborhood."

"Who are you kidding? There weren't any neighborhoods worse than ours."

Manny slapped his arm, chuckling until he started to cough. "No kidding. You got that right." He stood back a little as if to appraise Chad. "You've put a little meat on now, though." He jabbed Chad in the ribs, then turned to the woman beside him, who had been smiling and nodding throughout their conversation. "You remember my cousin, Rosy?"

"This is Rosalita? Little Rosalita?" Chad remembered her as perpetually thirteen. He was pretty sure she had a crush on him back then. She continued to nod and smile. He looked at Manny. "Still doesn't speak any English?"

Manny shrugged. "Not much."

"Uhh...bonito volver...a veros, Rosalita." He looked at Manny.

"Not bad. Little rusty, are you?"

He ignored the remark.

"Tambien," she responded, still nodding her head like a bobble doll.

Chad turned to Manny. "So, you never answered my question. What are you doing here? Down for a visit?"

"Nah, man. I live here now. Lost my job at the supermercado. Old man Sanders, he got all crabby after you left. Made us clock in and out for lunch. I think he was just looking for an excuse to fire me. Couldn't afford to pay me no more. So, I live here with Rosy. She's alone, too, so, you know, why pay two rents? I got a job as a night janitor at a school. St. Alvarez."

"What about your mom? She move down, too?"

"Nah, man. My mom died three years ago." Manny shook his head, shuffling his feet. "That emphysema is some nasty shit."

Chad clamped a hand on his shoulder. "Oh, sorry to hear that, Manny." He turned them a little and drew closer, pulling out his wallet. "Listen, why don't you let me help you."

"Nah, man. I don't need it!"

"Come on, now. I owe you. Remember that time you helped me haul my equipment in the rain? Those amplifiers were heavy, weren't they?"

"Damn straight, they were heavy." Manny laughed.

"Well, I never paid you for that." Chad began peeling off bills.

"Are you sure?

"Yeah, I'm sure." Chad continued to lay bills in his hands.

"Nah, man. This is too much."

"It's interest, Manny. I owe you interest on that."

"Well...okay. You're sure?"

"I'm sure. And hey, what are you doing later? I've got some extra tickets to the hockey game."

Manny's eyes brightened. "Oh yeah?"

"I'll leave them at the front desk for you. Game's at two. Need a ride?"

"Nah, man. I'm good."

"Still drivin' that old beater Buick?"

Manny laughed. "Nah. I got a new beater Buick now."

Chad laughed along with him. "Well, I've got to take these ladies to lunch."

"Ahh, the lunch is good here," Manny assured them.

"Good. 'Cause I'm starved," Beth asserted.

"Nice seeing you again, Manny."

"Yeah. You too, Chad. I'll see you later. At the game."

"Good. Adios, Rosalita."

"Si, adios."

Chad put his hand on the small of Beth's back so that he could lead her to the restaurant. "Sorry about that."

Beth looked up with a smile. "Don't be. He seemed like a nice man."

"Who, Manny? Manny's the best. I haven't seen him in...forever. I should have introduced you. I was just so surprised to see him." They continued walking for a few minutes in silence, Jessica and Cassie whispering to each other about something as they followed behind.

After a bit, Beth spoke up. "You're quiet."

"Hmm. Oh, sorry. I was just thinking about Mrs. Juarez. She was a nice woman. Used to make these one Mexican cookies with chocolate in the middle. Man, were those good." He chuckled. "I guess I must be hungry, too." But after a second or two, he continued. "She used to call me 'skinny chico blanco.' 'Come here, skinny chico blanco,' she'd say."

"She called you a skinny, white chick?"

He swatted her. "No! Chico is boy. Skinny, white boy."

"Oh." She shrugged. "Sorry, I took French."

God, she was beautiful like that, when she smiled, so carefree. "Ooh, la la."

She laughed and squeezed his hand.

And he was supposed to behave himself. This was going to be hard.

CHAPTER ELEVEN

It turned out that the lunch at the St. Ives was far better than even Manny had espoused.

When the homemade chips with your sandwich are to die for, you know you've had a good lunch, Beth mused.

Now, they were on their way to the stadium for the hockey game. The group, too big for even a taxi van, had split up. Chad insisted that she leave her car and not have to worry about finding the arena. They sat in the far back together, Cassie and Jessica in the seat in front of them, and Pete in front with the driver.

She glanced at Chad, who seemed to be listening to the girls' conversation with an amused smile on his lips. He took his arm from around her shoulder and sat forward, leaning on the chair in front of them.

"So, Cas, how long have you two known one another?"

The girls looked at each other. "Forever," Cassie supplied.

"Since second grade," Jessica corrected. "I started at St. Dominic's in second grade, and Cassie came up to me on the first day of school and asked if I wanted to be her friend."

"How sweet."

Cassie gave him a hard stare, although it looked like she was trying not to smile. "Are you teasing me?"

"No, no. Well, yes. But now that I think about it, it is kind of nice. I wish someone had been like that when I was growing up."

"Oh, like you weren't Mr. Popular," Cassie needled.

"I wasn't. Me and Davey—you know David, the quiet one in the band?" When Cas nodded, he continued. "We were kind of left out of everything."

"You were? Why?" This time Cassie seemed genuinely concerned.

Chad shrugged. "I don't know. We were closer than most brothers. I think they thought that was weird or something. And our parents passed away when we were young, which was also unusual—"

Cassie interrupted. "How old were you?" Both girls turned to listen now.

"I was thirteen. Davey, eleven."

"I was thirteen when my dad died, too."

"Yeah. That's rough. I'm sorry, Cas."

Beth noticed Jessica slipping her arm through Cassie's to comfort her and her heart tightened, but she remained silent.

"What about you, Jessica?" Chad asked. "Tell me about yourself."

"Oh, man." Jessica glanced at her friend, looking nervous. "Sounds like an interview question." Cassie nodded to encourage her. "My parents are both alive. And married. To each other. That's kind of unusual these days."

"No kidding." Chad sat back, stretching his arm around behind Beth's neck again. "What does your dad do?"

"He's an attorney at Illinois Insurance."

"Corporate attorney, cool. Must be a smart guy."

"He is. My mom's a lawyer, too."

"Wow. Brain trust. Brothers or sisters?"

"Just one. Zack. He's eleven. He's okay, I guess."

"They get along pretty well," Cassie agreed. "Except when Zack listens in on her phone conversations."

"Yeah, I know. Did I tell you about the other night when he..."

Chad relaxed back into his seat and Beth tuned out the rest of the conversation. He whispered in her ear, "Good kids." The warmth of his breath on her neck was inviting. She tried to distract herself from thinking about that by looking out the window.

"The snow has slowed down," she commented. "Maybe we won't get as much as they say."

"I don't know. I don't think I'd mind being snowed in with you," he answered with a sexy smile.

Recognizing something outside the window, Chad sat up and called out to Pete, who directed the cabbie to a service entrance to the United Center. Once inside, they were hustled to a luxury box and then Chad was whisked away. He looked back apologetically as he was led through the door. Before long, his voice was ringing out through the P.A. system. Though the national anthem would seem to be far from his regular thing, he did an outstanding job, and Beth was impressed. When he returned, they cuddled together in the seats at the front of the booth. Within the first five minutes of the game, a fight broke out. The three Bloomington women sprang to their feet, appalled and thrilled in equal measure.

"And here I thought you abhorred violence," Chad teased.

"I do," Beth insisted. "Just not at a hockey game."

He laughed. "Okay, I'm trying to work that one out..."

Soon after, Manny and Rosy arrived. Chad excused himself and got up to talk to them for a moment. Beth watched him throw back his head and laugh a couple of times when Manny said something. She enjoyed the opportunity to just watch him, apart from her. When he returned, he apologized.

"I'm sorry. I just haven't seen Manny in so long."

"That's okay," Beth began.

"No, it's not. I want to spend time with you. This was about us getting to know each other better. You have my full attention for the rest of the afternoon."

And she did.

When they filed out of the booth at the end of the game, Chad heard Cassie say to her mom in a low tone, her voice tense. "Mom, I need to go to the bathroom." Both women eyed the bathroom door warily.

"You can't wait?" Beth whispered back.

"I don't think so."

Chad realized that this would have been the first time since their attack that they had been in a stadium. He tightened his grip on Beth's shoulder, his eyes scanning the area by reflex. He leaned in. "I can try to find a more private bathroom for you, somewhere in the—"

"No," Beth said firmly. "We'll be fine. Come on, Cas. I'll go with you."

"I'm coming, too," Jess added, hurrying after them.

Chad watched them go in and felt his stomach do an odd dip as the doors closed behind them. It didn't help that Pete seemed to be unusually attentive beside him, eyes roaming everywhere even as he adapted a casual pose and leaned against a support column. Logic told Chad that the women were safe inside. It was a well-lit, crowded area... But still, he couldn't help that his heart was beating faster than normal, that his palms were sweaty, or that he was staring at the exit door like he was trying to melt it with his laser vision. He shifted his weight. His hands were in his pocket, and he glanced at Pete from time to time, wanting to ask him if he thought everything was okay, but knowing that was a stupid question. After a while, he couldn't hold it in any longer.

"Sure taking a while." He forced a smile, trying to play it off as a joke about men always waiting on women.

Pete shrugged and continued to let his gaze dart from face to face as people passed by. Chad checked out other men waiting for their dates or wives outside of the bathroom, trying to determine from their demeanor if there was anything suspicious about them. When Beth and the girls finally emerged from the exit, he exhaled loudly, causing Pete to look at him with an odd expression.

By the time they winded out through the crowd, it was approaching five. On the way home in the cab, Beth noticed that Chad was again looking out the window. The snow was floating lazily down, like dandelion fluff against the now dark sky.

"Let's go night-sledding," Chad suggested out of the blue.

"Night sledding? Is that anything like night swimming?" Beth joked.

"Yes, only fully clothed." He waited expectantly for an answer.

"You're serious?"

"Yeah. Come on, Beth. I know it's kind of crazy, but...I've never been sledding."

"Never?" Who's never been sledding at our age?

"I haven't." He looked out the window again and she watched his reflection in the window. "Not the kind of thing my father would have enjoyed."

His jaw was tense now, and his eyes had a faraway look. He seemed so unhappy, and she just wanted to change that. "Well..."

Cassie, sensing something was afoot, turned around. "What are you two discussing?" Jessica mimed her, both of them resting their chins on their hands on top of the backs of their seat.

Chad hesitated. His mouth was open as he looked at Beth sideways.

"Chad wants to go night sledding."

He sat straighter. "Manny mentioned that—"

Beth crossed her arms. "So, this is Manny's fault."

"—the St. Ives-Augusta is on a golf course. They rent sleds at the pro-shop, and he could get me the keys."

Beth frowned. "Is this legal?"

He grinned. "Pretty much."

"What do you say, Mom? Sounds like a flawless plan to me."

All eyes turned to her hopefully.

She hesitated. "Who am I to mess with flawless?"

CHAD SQUEEZED BETH'S mittened hand before they worked their way up the steep slope to the top of the hill. Railroad-tie steps helped, but the snow was packed pretty tightly between the steps sloping evenly from one icy tie to the next, so they had to hold on to the rope railing, which was supplied just for this reason. Beth was in the lead, while he followed with a short wooden toboggan in tow. Cassie and Roger struggled behind them, toting their finds, one with a plastic saucer, the other with a longer plastic sled. Jessica brought up the rear. Beth lost her footing and came down hard on one knee on a tie, but righted herself and continued to climb the grade slowly.

Chad started feeling bad about dragging Beth out on such a frigid night. The wind picked up and was blowing the snow, making it swirl around them. It whistled through the trees lining the hill to the left of the makeshift stairs. When she turned to him at the top of the hill, he could see her eyes smiling. They were the only things visible between the bottom of her hat and the scarf covering her mouth and nose. He stuck the end of the toboggan in the snow, grabbed her, and pulled her scarf down enough so he could give her a quick, spontaneous kiss. Their mingling breath warmed him briefly; the kiss warmed him even more. He smiled and pulled her scarf back up without saying a word. His eyes scoped out the hillside for the best route for the toboggan. The moon was shining brightly through the thin branches of the trees, so it was easy to find their way.

Strangely enough, he found himself thinking about his ex, Julie. By now Julie would have been pitching a royal bitch-fit, he was sure, telling him he was an idiot for choosing to do this. No, he corrected, she would have never come in the first place.

He pulled the toboggan out of the snow and set it down. "Are you ready?" He raised his eyebrows in mock-challenge. She was clapping her hands together to keep them warm, but he could see her cheeks rise in a smile, eyes dancing as she nodded. As usual, he thought she looked cute. A hat covered her whole head, except the hair sweeping across her forehead. Her cheeks, what he could see of them, were rosy, and somehow, those sexy eyes of hers were that much more gorgeous for being the only part of her face he could see. He held the toboggan as she climbed on in front. He sat, wrapping his long legs around her.

When he pulled his legs up, the toboggan lost its tentative grip on the snow and started nosing downhill. He tightened his arms around her. The thrill of the speed and the feeling of totally abandoning himself to the moment filled him. Beth's scream of delight as they whizzed over the snow harmonized with his deep laughter.

At the last minute, he realized that he would have to stop the sled before they passed through some scrawny trees and ended up in the creek. The abrupt stop turned into a colossal wipeout, Beth being thrown off first as the toboggan swung around one-hundred-eighty degrees before stopping.

Chad sat, laughing, then turned to see her sprawled out in the snow behind him. He crawled over. Looking down, he could see her face was covered in the snow kicked up when they tried to stop.

Oh, man. Now she's really gonna be pissed.

But she was chuckling and sputtering, trying to get the snow out of her mouth and using the back of her mittens to wipe away the snow covering her eyes. He roared with laughter again, and covered her with his long body, bending in for another kiss. The feel of the cold snow around her lips combined with the warmth of her mouth turned him on, and he pressed against her even more.

A shout of, "Knock it off, you two. You're going to melt all the snow!" broke the stillness, and they turned their heads to catch Roger calling to them with his hands used as a megaphone. He followed this pronouncement up with a shout of "GERONIMO!" and then ran forward a few steps and belly-flopped onto the saucer at the top of the hill. He steered himself deftly to where they still lay in the snow, coming so close that Chad had to roll them out of the way to avoid a collision. He and Beth sprang to their feet and started pelting Roger with snowballs even before he could rise from his sled.

"Ahh!" he yelled, as one of Beth's luckier shots hit him in the back of the head. She froze; her hand over her mouth. Roger's eyes narrowed to slits. "You are so dead."

Beth took off running over the slippery surface as he bent to gather more snow into a ball. Before he could straighten up with his ammo, he was hit with a barrage of snow from Chad, who scampered off after Beth. Roger was left with a handful of the white stuff and no one to throw it at.

On the way back up, Chad led, warning Beth about particularly slippery spots. They saw Jessica whiz by on the saucer. When they reached the top, Cassie called out, "Chad, ride down with me."

Chad glanced at Beth, but she nudged him. "Go on. I'll wait."

SHE WATCHED AS THEY took off and felt her heart warm at the sight. However, she didn't have time to think about that as she heard a sound to her right. Roger had reached the top of the stairs. She took a defensive position.

He laughed, panting a little from the climb. "Truce."

She held out a hand and they shook on it.

He tilted his head in the direction of the hill. "Wanna go down?"

She hesitated.

"Come on. I won't make us crash like Mr. Reckless down there."

She agreed and they sped down the hill in the darkness. Roger brought the sled up to a neat stop short of the creek. "That was great," he was saying when a snowball hit Beth in the shoulder. "Okay, that's it. No more Mr. Nice Guy."

He and Beth gathered up snow and charged after their attackers who took shelter in the trees beyond the stairs. They chased the pair up the slope until Cassie and Chad made their getaway downhill on their toboggan. "Let's see if we can catch them," Roger yelled, and they piled onto the sled. Intent on catching the toboggan, he seemed to forget to regulate his speed.

Understanding their predicament first, Beth let out a scream of warning, and he was miraculously able to bring the sled up just short of the precipice over the creek bed. The two turned to each other, smiling in relief over their near miss, when suddenly the bank gave way, and they plunged with a splash into the creek. They came up gasping for air in the chilly water and then laughed as they sloshed their way over to the bank. Roger climbed out and offered his hand to Beth. She grinned and yanked, pulling him back in before scrambling up the bank. He came up again, spitting out water.

"That's my girl!" Roger hollered into the night.

Chad, Cassie, and Jessica, who had joined their ranks, came rushing up, barely suppressing their amusement. "Are you all right?" they managed to get out as Beth stood there dripping into the snow.

"Yeah, peachy," Beth returned. "Why don't you ask the speed demon here?" She pointed a thumb over her shoulder.

Roger joined them. "You were supposed to put the brakes on."

"Me?" She punched him in the arm. "You had your legs over mine."

"Ouch!"

She ignored him. "I guess my sledding is over. I didn't bring any extra mittens or hats or coats. You guys stay and have fun, and I'll get some hot chocolate going for you. I brought some in my suitcase."

"I'll come back with you," Chad offered.

"Oh no. I don't want you to have to quit on my account."

"But I want to spend time with you. And besides, I'm cold."

"We can hit the hot tub," Jessica blurted out.

"Yeah," Cassie seconded.

She laughed at their exuberance. "Okay. But let's get moving. I feel like a human icicle."

CHAPTER TWELVE

Beth was in front when they got back to the hotel suite. As if in slow motion, Chad watched from behind as she reached for the paper attached to the door by tape. He lunged to snatch it before she could. She turned to look at him with a question in her eyes.

"Uhh...sometimes fans leave some very...inappropriate notes." He exchanged a quick look with Roger.

She arched her eyebrows. "I see."

Chad hurried to open the door, holding it for her. "You ladies get out of those wet clothes and into something warm, and I'll be right with you." Beth studied him for a second then turned to the girls.

"Come on, girls." She followed them into the room. Chad closed the door behind them, sighing and spinning around to lean with his back against the door. He tore open the folded sheet of paper, ripping it a little in his hurry.

"Another one?" Roger commented, trying to read over his shoulder.

YOU ARE A LOSER, CHAD. YOU NEED TO STOP USING WOMEN AND TREATING THEM LIKE SHIT. I FOUND YOU HERE. I'LL FIND YOU AGAIN.

"Ooh. Sounds even madder than the last one."

"How'd they find us? I thought switching hotels would do the trick. There's got to be thousands of hotels in this city."

Roger shrugged. His brow creased. "You know, none of this started until you began seeing Beth."

"So?"

"So how much do you really know about her."

"It's not Beth, Roger. She wouldn't do this. Besides, she was with us, you idiot."

"She could have gotten someone else to put it there for her."

"It's not Beth."

"Ookay." Roger began to whistle in an annoying way as he unlocked the door to his suite across the hall that mirrored the suite Chad was in.

"I'm telling you, it's not her."

Roger got the door open, stepped through, then called through the crack as he closed it. "Whatever you say, buddy."

"Ignoramus," Chad mumbled. He turned to enter his room, shoving the note into his jeans pocket. No one was around, though he could hear noise from one of the girls' bedrooms. He rushed to his room, threw on some fresh clothes, and then came back to start the fire, hoping that James had supplied the wood he had asked for.

Minutes later, he fell on his tush in front of the hearth and watched his work come to life. Flames began to spring from the starter log James had provided, although he hadn't thought to ask for one. He stared at the fire, wondering again how his little "hideout" had been discovered. Who was mad at him enough to even try to find him in the first place? He pulled the note out of his pocket and read it again before tossing it on the flames. He backed up to the coffee table and looked on as the tongues of fire lick their way up the paper. It crumpled, turning up at the corners and in on itself. He was mesmerized by the red-hot glow and flickering movement of the fire.

"Why did you burn that?"

He jumped at the sound of Beth's voice. "Huh? I...needed some more kindling." He rose, noticing she held a box of hot chocolate mix in her hands. "I can't believe you brought your own."

She smiled, spinning on her heel to head into the kitchen. "I told you the other night on the phone that I almost can't sleep without it."

He followed her. "But you said you like Irish cream in it. I don't see any Irish cream."

She turned her head to look at him with a grin. "Too big to pack. I'll just have to do without."

"I think there might be some up in the cabinet."

"I doubt that," she said, but she opened one. She froze. Inside were a half-dozen boxes of different kinds of hot chocolate and several brown bottles. She set one on the counter and reached for another. She emptied the cabinet of bottles and then stood staring at the different brands of Irish cream. She turned around slowly.

"You did this."

He shrugged. "I couldn't have you losing sleep."

She sauntered over to where he leaned against the counter and he straightened, reaching out to touch her shoulders. She pressed against him, extending her arms to bring her hands to either side of his face. She pulled him down and gave him a long, sensual kiss.

"Thank you."

He cleared his throat for fear his voice would come out in an unmanly way, he was so affected by the kiss. "You're welcome." He wanted to pull her in again, but they heard the girls' voices and broke apart.

She smiled at him in a sexy little way. Her eyes twinkled, while calling out, "Girls, do you want some hot chocolate?"

"No, thank you, Mrs. D."

"No thanks, Mom. We're going down to get some good use out of that hot tub."

"Okay." She addressed Chad. "Why don't you go in by the fire and sit down and relax? I'll make us some hot chocolate."

By the time she came out, he had rearranged the furniture to make them as comfortable as possible. He moved the coffee table to one side and pulled one of the couches so that it was directly in front of the fire. He threw cushions on the floor and sat with his back against the couch. Beth placed the cups on the table near him and sat. Chad put his arm around her, and she snuggled into his chest. They sat quietly for several minutes.

"This is nice."

"Mmm," he agreed.

She sat up a little bit so that she could look at him. "This was a great day. Lunch, the hockey game, night sledding..."

"How fun could that have been? You ended up in the drink."

"That part I could have done without." She reached up to run a hand across his cheek. "But I liked watching you have fun. Even when you were talking to Manny. I was imagining the two of you as young kids."

He turned, thoughtfully gazing again into the fire. "You wouldn't have liked me back then."

"Why do you say that?"

"I was worse than I am now."

"Meaning?"

He gave a half-shrug, turning to look at her. "When Davy and I were on our own, I never knew where our next meal would come from, if we'd have electricity so that he would have light to do his homework by..." He reached up to move a piece of her hair back out of her face. "It made me uptight. Like an animal struggling to survive on a day-to-day basis. Not nearly the happy-go-lucky guy I am today."

She laughed. "Happy-go-lucky sounds more like Roger. You're...intense."

He raised his eyebrows. "Is that a good thing?"

The corners of her lips lifted, quivering slightly as she teased, "It can be."

"Hmm."

She tightened her arms around him, laying her head on his chest. They watched the wood in the fire glow orange-red. He squeezed her tighter.

"Do you miss your mom and dad?"

"My mom, some. My dad and I were never close."

She pulled back again, searching his face. "But you still miss him. He was your dad."

The vise that was always around his heart tightened for a few seconds until it was excruciating. How did she know? His muscles tensed. How could he miss someone who was unrelentingly cruel to them all, David and him and his mom? But the truth was, he did. Or at least he missed the idea of what a dad should be, the kind of man he had imagined his dad becoming half his childhood. A normal dad. One to play catch with, to talk with, to be with without fear of a mood swing making his jaw tense or his fists clench. The stab of pain he felt had a familiar taste to it. Like when you press an old bruise and the fresh pain reminds you of how you got it. He wanted to look away from her, to conceal what he always kept hidden, but he couldn't. He had lost himself in the depths of those eyes. And now he recalled another pain.

He straightened. "Beth." He looked down for a moment, collecting himself. "Why did you leave...when we were in St. Louis? Why did you leave my bed that night?"

Her face paled. He could tell that she was surprised by this. "Because..." She sat up now, drawing her knees in, their bodies no longer touching. "You're a rock star. You have a different girl every night, right? I thought it was...I don't know. I thought that you—"

"You thought you were one of those girls."

She nodded.

He frowned. "Did I do anything to make you feel that way?"

"I don't know."

"I went too fast."

She nodded. "Maybe."

He reached out and took her shoulders, turning her to face him. "Beth, with you it is different. It's been different from the start. I wanted to be with you...how can I explain this? I wanted a connection with you. Maybe I fell back on sex as a way to establish that connection. Maybe that's the only thing I know," he added, more to himself than to her. "All I know is that I missed you when you were gone. The fact that I thought of you at all made you different." He shut his mouth, afraid that she would disapprove even more of the shallow way he had been living his life. Maybe he had revealed too much. He rubbed up and down her arm. "I want to see where this can go, do you?"

Without hesitating, she nodded.

He exhaled. "Good!"

They sat quietly for several minutes, absorbed in their own thoughts.

"Chad?"

"Yes?"

"You know that kiss you gave me at the bottom of the hill?"

Where was this leading? "Uhh...yes?"

"That was some kiss."

His face felt suddenly hot, and not from the fire. "Oh." He wondered how he was to answer that, and then found himself saying, "That was only scratching the surface."

She pulled away a little to look at him with a wicked smile. "Really?"

"Yeah. The kids were there and all. What I really wanted to do was this."

He ran his hand along the base of her throat, sliding it up until he cupped her chin firmly. He leaned in, but didn't kiss her at first. Her pulse raced underneath his palm. Her smile changed to something more serious. Her lips parted, the heat of her breath warming his fingertips as she released one trembling breath. Her eyes trailed to his lips and then back up, locking on his. She seemed to be trying to anticipate what he would do next. He leaned in closer, tilting his head and just brushing his lips against hers. He pulled back and smiled. Her eyes widened as if to say, "No more?" Yes, there was going to be more. Definitely more.

He dipped back in to take his first real taste, his fingers sliding up into her hair. Her skin was so blessedly soft, hair so silky. He felt his blood begin to heat and pulsate in his veins. He took more, going deeper to taste more of her.

There was no hesitation in her reaction, no coyness. She wanted this kiss. She'd asked for it and now she would take it. Her hand slipped under his shirt, finding skin. He groaned. She slid down against the couch so that she was underneath him a little. One hand rested behind his neck, keeping him close, the other now just nipped below the waistline of his jeans in back. With one arm he braced himself on the floor so that he could stay above her. The other hand impatiently pushed the couch back a little so that she could lie down.

SOME PART OF HER KNEW that there were children downstairs. It just didn't care at the moment. She'd spent the last three years caring for Cassie alone, untouched and unloved by a man. She deserved a moment of selfish abandon, of letting it all go—the fears, the responsibilities, the aching loss. She wanted to shut out emotion and feel things carnally. She deserved this long, hot, lean mass of man sliding down along her body. Her core melted. But when he looked down on her, she knew that she could not do this with him without feeling something more, a sweet pain deep within. The body responded, oh yes. But so did the heart. She pulled him in again, her mouth opening wider. His tongue, oh, his tongue. It was between them, then in her. He was an amazing kisser.

Her hand dipped lower into his jeans, breezing over his tight tush and holding him just above his long legs. There was a flash of a memory of him above her in St. Louis, in her as she tried to match his rhythm. He began to kiss her neck, and she bit her bottom lip to keep from making a noise, screaming out his name, moaning, calling out to some deity, or begging for more. Her hand fell from his neck and found his chest. She could feel the definition underneath the lightweight cotton, but that wasn't enough. Shocked by her boldness, she yanked the tail of his shirt up to his armpits. The other hand came up along his hip, crossing his waist, moving over the soft hair of his stomach, to join in the exploration of his broad chest.

"I thought we had to behave," he breathed.

"I don't want to."

Her mouth came to his chest, kissing, and then she trailed her tongue across his skin until she met his nipple and sucked for a beat. As if it had given her an idea, she impatiently brought her hands to her blouse and unbuttoned enough to pull it open to her sides. In the firelight, she saw his eyes follow and his face become tight.

He brought his hands to her, tentatively at first, skimming along the edge of her bra. Then, perhaps sensing her hard nipples beneath the silky fabric, he tweaked them. This time she did let a little moan escape. She arched and he took his cue, bringing his mouth down to suck through the silk and lace of her bra. She loved the urgency in his move, like he couldn't wait to tug the fabric away; he just had to taste her. The thought thrilled her. His hand closed on her other breast, and he jerked the fabric aside and twirled his tongue around her nipple.

She squirmed, pushing her pelvis against his and finding him hard. "Mmm...yes. More." He lapped, his eyes closed, appearing to be totally into what he was doing.

They both sensed a noise and froze. The girls were tromping up the steps, chatting about something. In an instant, Chad and Beth were both sitting up.

"Oh shit! What was I thinking?" Beth whispered, panic making her voice hoarse.

Chad's shirt fell back into place when he rose, but Beth's required a little bit more work. She feverishly tried to button it, and he reached over to try to help. The girls were almost at the top of the stairs. She slapped at his hands.

When the girls came around the side of the couch, they found both adults in a seated position, a throw pillow in Chad's lap.

Cas smiled at them. "You moved the couch back. Was it too hot?"

Chad started to laugh but attempted to cover it with a cough. Beth reached over and squeezed his hand, harder than it appeared.

"Just, you know, needed more room." Her voice was higher than usual and pitchy.

Cassie's brow furrowed as she studied her mom. "Ookay. Well, we're headed to bed. The whole sledding thing wore us out. See you guys in the morning."

"Okay, honey. I think I'll do the same. See you in the morning. Night, Jess."

"Good night, Mrs. D. Chad."

Beth turned to Chad with a relieved smile, releasing the vice-like grip she had on his hand.

"Umm, Mom?"

When she turned back, Jessica was somewhere down the hall, swallowed up in the shadows. Cassie stood in the entrance.

"Yes?"

Cassie smiled and pointed to the middle of her chest, waving her hand up and down.

Confused, Beth looked down. She had missed a button.

"Uhh, oh. Thanks."

Cassie turned around and left without saying another word. Beth put her head down on Chad's shoulder.

"That was so embarrassing."

A second later, they heard a burst of laughter from the hallway.

"Go to sleep," Beth snapped. She buried her head in his shoulder again with a huff of frustration.

Chad tried to sooth her. "It's okay." He kissed her hair.

"No, it's not." She crossed her hands in front of her chest self-consciously. "And you keep those lips to yourself."

Chad withdrew his hands, holding them up in innocence and backing away, laughing. "Okay. Okay."

Beth frowned at him for several seconds, her shoulders tense, but then sighed. "I guess there's nothing I can do about it now. What's done is done." She moved to stand. Chad beat her to his feet and reached down to help her up the rest of the way. "I'm going to sleep now so that *you*—"she stabbed him in the chest with her finger with each word "*—won't tempt me anymore.*" To his credit, he didn't mention that she was the one that pulled her blouse open.

"Okay." He chuckled and she let her face relax into a smile.

He walked her to her door; his room was directly opposite. They stood, each with a hand on their doorknob.

"Good night, Beth," he said softly.

"Good night."

They entered their rooms and shut the doors, peering at each other through the cracks as they closed. Beth let out a frustrated scream.

"I need a long bath," she said out loud, though there was no one to hear her.

Half an hour later, she came to bed with wet hair. She had let herself slip under the water when reliving his kiss in her mind. Lying in bed, she thought about the fact that he was just yards away and had trouble sleeping.

IN THE MORNING, THEY enjoyed breakfast together in the hotel's dining room then came back to the room to play cards with the girls. The laugher and the ribbing reminded Beth of family times with Paul, putting puzzles together with Cassie or playing a game. It warmed her and pained her at the same time.

At one, Chad walked them out to their car, insisting again on carrying the luggage. Once everything was in the trunk and the girls were in their seats, it was time to say goodbye.

Beth opened her car door, but didn't climb in. Chad stood with his hand on top of the doorframe.

"Sure you can't stay longer?"

Beth grimaced. "We have to get back in time to shower and get ready for four o'clock Mass. We're already pushing it."

He reached out and ran his hand up and down her arm with a sigh. "It was worth a shot." He leaned his head into the car. "Bye, girls."

Cassie looked up from something she was showing Jessica. "See ya, Chad. Thanks for everything."

"No biggie. Good to see you again."

"Bye. It was nice meeting you," Jess added politely.

"It was a pleasure meeting you, Jess."

Chad looked at Beth. "I had a great weekend."

"Me, too." She smiled, then wrapped her arms around him.

"You'll call me tonight?"

She pulled back, but found she had a lump in her throat, so she just nodded and turned to get behind the wheel.

"Drive carefully," was his last instruction before closing the door. He stood back, sticking his hands in his jeans pockets, and watched them drive away.

CHAPTER THIRTEEN

Beth lay snuggled in her bed in an oversized T-shirt. Her laptop rested on her legs. Her fingers weren't flying over the keyboard, though, because she was on the phone with Chad. It was late, Cassie should have been in bed, but she was still taking her shower after studying for a big test with Jessica. "That's a deal breaker. I'm paying for half or I'm not coming."

"Beth, do you have any idea the disgusting amount of money I made last year just for singing?"

"Singing and shaking your bootie," she corrected.

She could tell by the way his voice warmed that he was smiling. "I do not shake my bootie."

"Oh yes, you do." She dropped her voice. She set her laptop aside and threw the covers off. "And it's very hot, by the way." She crept over to the door and listened for Cas. It seemed quiet.

Chad shifted gears. "You bet your sweet ass, it is."

She turned away from the door with a sly grin. "Oh," Beth returned coyly. "You think my ass is sweet?" She took a few steps toward the bed, her bare legs feeling chilled. What he said next had her stopping for a second.

His voice purred in the unique way that was totally Chad. "Baby, sweet doesn't even begin to describe your ass."

"Ooh!" She squealed in delight. Then, "Ooh. Cas. I th-thought you were in bed."

"Going there, just wanted to say good night. That wouldn't be Chad telling you that your ass is sweet, would it?"

Beth frowned. "Cassandra! Really!" But her giddiness took over. "Well, it's not your Aunt Cali." Both girls giggled.

"Beth, I'll let you tell Cassie good night. Roger is pounding on my door and evidently isn't buying that I'm not in here. I'll overnight the plane ticket tomorrow."

She hung up with Chad and gave Cassie a hug good night. As she crossed to return to her bed, she caught her reflection in the dresser's mirror. She was wearing one of Paul's old Mizzou shirts. The smile faded from her lips. She stared at her image, noting the sadness in her eyes, weighing her shoulders down. Slowly, she pulled the shirt off over her head. She folded it up and laid it on the dresser, smoothing it out with her hand. She turned away and crawled under the covers in just her bra and her underwear.

LATER THAT WEEK, BETH found herself winging her way to Kansas. Chad had arranged for a rental car for her so that she could drive to the stadium where they were playing. Roger was the first to see her backstage after the concert.

"Beth!" he shouted, spotting her down the hall. He enveloped her in a hug. "How are you?"

"Good. How was the show?"

"Awesome, as usual. How are you? How's Cassie doing?"

"We're both fine. Thanks for asking."

"Good. Now, I know you're not here just to be with my outrageously cute self, which I find highly disturbing, by the way. Chad's in our dressing room, down the hall, second door on the right, not the bigger one across the hall, Keith and David commandeered that," the bassist added with a frown. "But he may have already hopped in the shower. He didn't want you to see him all sweaty," he informed her with a teasing smile.

BETH ENTERED THE DRESSING room, which was smaller than the one in St. Louis. She could hear the shower running behind the bathroom door. She sat on a stool and waited impatiently for Chad to come out. After a few minutes, she thought idly, "I wonder if rock stars sing in the shower?" She crept forward to put her ear to the door, and when she did, it swung open. She hesitated for only a second, then snuck inside and closed the door behind her. There was no sound besides the running water from the other side of the curtain. She had a sudden urge. This relationship made her feel young and reckless. Dare I?

On a whim, she peeled her clothes off, and then as quietly as she could, slipped into the back of the shower. She slid her hands around Chad's waist, her body pressed against his. He leaned back against her, his body relaxing for a minute, and then turned around to kiss her.

"Hey."

She was surprised by his total lack of surprise. "I could be a crazed fan. Do you often have women in your shower?"

Chad bent to kiss her protests away. "I could see you in the mirror." Beth looked over his shoulder, through the crack between the curtain and the wall, and sure enough, the mirror offered a plain view of the rest of the bathroom.

"Well, all right then." She let her fingers slide up his wet back.

Chad pulled her farther into the shower so the water could warm her from head to toe. He brushed wet hair back from her face and just gazed at her for several seconds. "I missed you." His gravelly voice filled the space between shower wall and curtain, and he began to kiss her in earnest. "This could get dangerous," he added seductively.

She nipped at his bottom lip. "Yeah, well Danger is my middle name."

"Hmm...Beth Danger Donovan, interesting."

"Oh, shut up and kiss me, you fool."

"Yes, ma'am." He clutched her closer. "Thank goodness for handrails and nonskid mats, eh?"

The couple was spending some time rediscovering each other's bodies when there came a knock at the door.

"Chad? Chad? Have you seen Beth? I told her how to get here, but I wonder if she got lost?"

"Beth? Beth who?" Chad answered with a grin.

Beth slapped him on the chest. "Chad," Beth whispered urgently, "what are we going to do?"

He kissed her neck. "Well, I've got several ideas along those lines."

"Chad. Stop! He's going to know I'm in here."

"Well, darlin', what did you think he would think when he saw your wet hair?"

"Oh. I hadn't thought that far." She considered her options. "It'll dry in a half hour."

"So, we're going to stay in here for a half hour? Don't you think that will look a little suspicious?" he teased her.

She frowned. "You are getting way too much pleasure out of this."

"Actually, I was hoping for a little more..."

"Chad, stop." She giggled and squirmed in his arms.

"All right." He made an attempt at seriousness, thinking for a moment. "I'll get out and lure Roger away from here, offer to go and get a beer. Yeah, that'll work. Then, you sneak out and we act like you had to go back to your car for something."

Beth smiled at him. "Brilliant."

They got out of the tub and toweled off. As Chad slipped his jeans on over his long legs, Beth couldn't help admiring his physique again. She loved the way his legs seemed to go on forever and wished they were wrapped around her. Beth stopped him before he put his shirt on and brought her mouth to his without saying anything. He smiled at her, his hand gently cupping her chin as he pulled her in for another kiss, and then he slipped his shirt on and left the room.

Beth could hear the two men talking, and then the outer door closed behind them. She grabbed a blow-dryer and quickly dried her hair. Then, she set off down the hall in the direction of the most noise. She entered a small room with a couple of vending machines, a handful of chairs and tables, and a cooler, which she guessed supplied the beer the band members gathered around the small table were drinking. Roger leaned back in his chair with his foot on the cooler.

"Did you find what you were looking for?"

"Huh?"

"Chad said you had to go back because you left something in the car. Did you find it?"

"Oh yes. Yes. I left...my purse. But I've got it now." Beth tapped the purse draped over her shoulder as if to prove it.

"Yeah, but darlin', didn't you have that with you when I saw you in the hall earlier?"

"Oh yeah." She thought in haste. "That was the funny thing. I had it all along."

Roger leaned forward with his arms on his knees. "You're a terrible liar." He started snickering and Chad joined in.

Beth shot an accusatory look in his direction, but he just shrugged. "He heard us."

Roger added, "You better never play poker." This set them off in another peal of laughter.

She could feel the heat rise in her cheeks, which only served to make her madder. With a hard stare, she growled, "Get me a beer, asshole."

"Ooh. You're sexy when you're mad," he retorted, opening the cooler and handing her a bottle.

Chad grabbed Beth as she walked over and pulled her into his lap. "Just ignore him."

But Roger wasn't finished having fun. "So how did you get your hair dry so fast?"

She looked at him evenly. "Blow-dryer." She took a pull on her beer, never breaking eye contact.

Keith's figure suddenly filled the doorway. "He-ey. What's going on, dude?"

Roger eyed Beth mischievously. Chad shot him a warning glance, which he appeared to ignore. He waited a beat.

She slowly stood and sauntered over behind him, bending to whisper in his ear, "I have a beer and I know how to use it."

"M-mmm," Roger hummed, appearing thrilled at the sound of her voice so close to his ear. He craned his neck to peer up at her. "Wouldn't be the first time."

"Now, why doesn't that surprise me?"

He eyed her, seeming to gauge her level of seriousness, then turned to Keith with finality. "Nothing. Nothing's going on in here, man."

"I get it, dude..."

"What happens in the dressing room stays in the dressing room," they all said at once.

"That's cool, dude."

"You guys are scary," Beth commented with a shake of her head.

David stuck his head in the room. "Ready?"

"Yeah, dude."

"Let's go."

The guys stood and chugged what was left of their beers, the humor evaporating like a puddle on a sunny day. Chad grabbed his leather jacket off the back of his chair.

"Where are we going?" Beth asked him; it was difficult being the new girl in this fraternity they called a band.

"To the buses," Chad explained.

They headed down the hall as a group. Beth felt nervous about the shift in mood. The jibes and general goofing around seemed to diminish.

Pete stood at the door at the end of the hall. "Are you ready?" he asked in the same ominous tone, his hand on the metal bar that would open the door.

They all nodded. Chad slung his arm still holding the leather jacket over her shoulder, but he was staring at the door. She glanced around at the men to try to figure out why they were all of a sudden so solemn. Then, the door opened.

Despite the fact it was the middle of the night, light flooded the loading zone beyond the door. Dante and some other men stood on the opposite side of the door, some walking ahead of the group, most fanning out to the sides. But what accosted her more than the blaring light, which was making her blink, was the noise. Hundreds of fans, mostly young women, stood behind barricades on either side of them. The tour buses waited at the end of their route, and she couldn't help but be reminded of walking the gauntlet.

As her eyes adjusted to the bright lights, they were assaulted anew by the action of the crowd. Teenaged girls pushed and jostled to get a better view, most scantily clad despite the February weather. Her eyes ran over the made-up faces. Some were smoking cigarettes, some drinking beer, although she was certain most were underage. Her eyes fell on one girl in particular on the right who seemed more exuberant than even the wildly squealing girls surrounding her. She had long, curly, platinum-blond hair and wore a glittery, sequined tube-top over her ample bosom and a tight, leather miniskirt. Her makeup was picture-perfect.

She can't be any older than Cassie, Beth realized, shocked.

People screamed over each other so it was hard to make out their words, but occasionally Beth could pick out shouts of: "You rock, Trapped Under Ice," "You're hot, Roger," and "I love you, Chad!" She had the strangest sensation, as if she was wading forward in slow motion, then things sped up to double-time for an instant or two, returning quickly to the foggy, walking-through-peanut-butter/dream-sequence sort of feeling. There were cameras flashing and people jumped up and down. They even climbed on things to get a better view. It was as if her brain couldn't process the explosion of information her senses were telling her at the same time.

Chad turned to say something to her. His leather coat slipped out of his grasp and fell to the ground. Again, in slow motion, Beth saw Chad reaching to pick up his jacket. At the same time, she caught movement out of the corner of her eye. The girl she noticed earlier snuck past the wooden barriers and a guard who was looking the other way, his attention diverted momentarily by someone else. She crossed the twenty-or-so-feet of space in surprisingly few seconds in the high-heeled boots she was wearing and timed her lunge perfectly to avoid Pete's closing hands. She caught Chad just as he rose with his coat. She wrapped her arms around him and kissed him with all the passion her few seconds could afford. Chad stood limply, neither rejecting nor encouraging the behavior. Pete, who was usually very polite with intrusive fans, seemed irritated by being bested by the teen.

At the same time, a second fan broke free on the left. She got passed the initial guard, but Dante scooped her up before she could reach her target, who happened to be Roger. The girl screamed and lashed out, and a second guard moved over to assist him. "I love you, Roger!" the girl belted out hoarsely through her strained vocal chords. Her face was contorted with the rage, frustration, and passion she felt. As Beth watched, it appeared almost animal-like in its intensity. With a sense of horror she watched the two men grappling with Roger's admirer. Her already skimpy outfit got disarranged in her tussle, revealing more than she may have intended.

Roger seemed concerned about the safety of the struggling, thrashing girl, too, and called out, "Be careful, guys! Don't hurt her."

His attention to the girl seemed to freeze her for an instant. The two men took advantage of the moment and pushed her back toward the barrier.

"I love you, Roger!" she cried out again in desperation.

Roger waved a hand and smiled, but Beth heard him say under his breath, "I love you, too—psycho!"

Dante and his helper returned to the group after depositing their charge firmly behind the lines of security personnel. Beth overheard Dante saying, "Damn bitch bit me!"

And then she was scrambling up the steps and onto the bus.

CHAPTER FOURTEEN

The door closed behind them, shutting out the zoo they had just left. Everybody inside seemed to breathe a joint sigh of relief, except for Beth, who still stood, stunned, right inside the doorway. Keith headed to the fridge for the booze, Roger was wrapped around Michelle, and Dante was pulling his sleeve over his massive bicep to show Pete his war wounds. Beth became aware of Chad talking to her.

"You okay?"

She nodded numbly.

"I probably should have said something—" He broke off as David approached them, his hand around a pretty, young blonde's shoulder, his face beaming.

Beth noticed for the first time how different he was from Chad. He probably stood all of five-foot-nine and wore his hair closely cropped. There was a simplicity about him and innocence. While Chad's T-shirt and jeans screamed rock star, David's said he would be just as at home on a farm. The girl with him had a similar aura. Her sweet, freckled face was surrounded by long, straight, blond hair. She was shorter even than Beth, and Beth was not surprised to find her soft, melodic voice held a hint of country twang.

"You must be Beth," she stated in a most welcoming way, shaking her hand. "David's told me a lot about you." David's cheeks colored, but he nodded his agreement. "I'm Cheryl, his wife, but you can just call me Cheri."

"It's nice to meet you," Beth responded warmly, roused from her semi-stupor. The contrast between the events outside and this civilized, homey greeting was notable.

"Come in. Have a seat. We want to get to know you."

"Yah, Bethy." Roger patted the couch beside him on a semicircular, red sofa. "Come have a seat." Michelle sat curled up to him on the other side. "Keith, supply us, man."

Keith came over, managing three beer bottles in each hand, the long necks laced between his fingers. He distributed them to Roger, Michelle, Beth, Chad, and Cheri, keeping the last one for himself. "Sorry, dude, you're out of luck," he told David.

David socked him in the shoulder as he got up to get a drink, and Keith stole his seat by Cheri on a second couch facing the first. A round, low table took up most of the space left in the middle.

"First things first," Roger announced. "To a good show." Beer bottles were clinked all around, and there was a silence while everyone took a long chug on their beer. There was a loud noise outside, as if something slammed into the bus, and a cheer went up from those who were still gathered outside. The others seemed to take it in stride. Pete got up and pulled back a curtain a fraction to take a look.

"They've got it under control," he grumbled, then took his seat again—a stool pulled up to a kitchen counter. Beth wondered silently what "it" was.

"To Beth," Roger began again, raising his bottle. Beth looked nervously at the sparkle in his eyes and the grin on his face. "Who makes life with Chad so much easier to bare," he finished, winking at his best friend. The pun went right over the others' heads, but Chad and Beth chuckled as voices called out, "Hear. Hear."

Again, there was a loud noise, and the bus was rocked by some unknown force. Chad, who was about to take a drink, spilled beer down the front of his shirt.

"Damn," he said, sitting up.

"I'll get a towel," Beth offered from her position on the end. She headed into the little kitchen area.

"Anybody else got the munchies?" Cheryl called. Several voices added their assent, and she rose to check the cupboard. Beth stood at the sink, water running pointlessly down the drain, a dishtowel in her hand. She was looking out where the curtains were pulled apart above the sink, watching as some security guards were actually cuffing a pair of guys who evidently got into a fight. Blood was running down one's chin, and a cut was visible on the other's cheekbone.

"It's hard to get used to," Cheri commented, making Beth jump in surprise. "I guess we're all kind of immune to it by now, sadly enough." She put her arm around Beth in a friendly manner. "Come on. Help me dig up something to eat." They found a bag of snack mix and a bowl then returned to the living room together.

Chad looked up when the girls reentered, and Beth saw him exchange a look with Cheri. "Come here, babe," he murmured. He raised his arm so she could snuggle in beside him. "Forget about the towel. I'll dry." He kissed the top of her head and bent even lower to whisper in her ear. "Are you sure you're okay?"

She scooted closer and squeezed him, peering up and forcing herself to smile. "Fine." She raised her voice. "So, Cheri, I noticed you have a little bit of an accent, where are you from?"

"Why, right here in the beautiful state of Kansas," she answered proudly. "Atchison, Kansas, to be exact."

"Oh, Atchison. Isn't that where Benedictine is?"

"Yes. That's where David and I met."

"You went to school in Atchison?" Beth responded in surprise. "That's a long way from New York."

"That's because he was trying to get as far away from his big brother as possible," Chad joked wryly.

"That's not true," David interjected. He turned to Beth to explain. "I needed to grow up, to make it on my own. Ever since I could remember, Chad's been taking care of me. I love him for it, but it was time for me to do something for myself." He spoke with conviction on this point. "Even so, Chad sent me money whenever he could. Money he saved working in seedy dives before someone finally recognized his talent and signed him to a label. And eventually, I missed the bum too much, so I joined the band so I could tag along with him, like old times."

"Now—" Chad sat up "—David's selling himself short here. He's one hell of a guitarist and an even better artist. He designed all the cover work for our three albums," he added with a note of pride.

"Nah." David waved a hand to dismiss the idea, though looking both pleased and embarrassed.

"Oh, come on, honey. You are a fantastic artist." Cheri turned to Beth again. "You should see the portrait he painted of me and our three girls. It gives me chills."

"I'd love to see that some time. So, you guys have three little girls?"

"Yep," David affirmed, clearly a proud papa. Cheri rummaged through her purse and came up with a picture. David took it, pointing to the girls as he talked about them. "Samantha's six, Alexis is four, and Ce-Ce, our youngest, just turned two. Her real name's Cecelia, but we call her Ce-Ce. And she's a little spitfire, that one. Just like her momma."

"Oh my gosh. They're just gorgeous. This one's Samantha? She looks just like you," she commented to Cheri. "And your little Ce-Ce reminds me of you, David."

"Wish I had some baby pictures of him," Chad added with regret, "'cause you're right. She's the spittin' image of Davy when he was young."

"And Alex," Roger chimed in, "she's a smart little cookie, I'll tell you. I don't know how many times she's twisted my words around in knots and come out with the upper hand." They all laughed.

"That's just 'cause she has a soft spot for Uncle Roger." Cheri winked and they all chuckled again.

Roger leaned back. "Yes, I'd say those Evans boys are lucky in love." Michelle jabbed him in the ribs. "Oh, and me, too, of course, schnookie-wookie," he added belatedly, grabbing her and kissing her neck.

"Well, if you want to 'get lucky' tonight, you better be coming up with those compliments a hell of a lot quicker."

As the conversation continued, Beth found she was only half listening. She couldn't shake the image of the girl outside kissing Chad. She knew she was being stupid, but the whole thing was sort of shocking. Then, she started thinking, he could have any one of those girls out there...

"What do you say, Beth?"

"What? Oh, I'm sorry, Roger. What was the question?"

"We were just wondering if you were up for some cards."

"Sure, I love cards. What's the game?"

"I don't know. Hearts? Spades?"

"Either is fine with me."

They began a game of Spades. They played partners so Chad sat across from Beth, and Roger joined forces with Cheri while David and Michelle watched. Pete and Dante went outside, and Keith was catching up on emails on Roger's laptop. At first, Chad and Beth were dominating.

"That's my girl," Chad cried out after a particularly spectacular hand. Beth, having kicked off her shoes, ran her bare foot up Chad's long leg. They smiled at each other across the table.

Roger, catching the look passing between them, yelled, "Hey. No playing footsie under the table." He appealed to David and Michelle, "They're sending messages back and forth." Chad and Beth just smiled more broadly and dealt the next hand.

But after a while, Beth found her mind wandering again to what happened outside. It was obvious this wasn't an occasional thing; it must happen every time they played. He could have a different woman every night of the week, or probably even more if he wanted. Young, gorgeous women, willing to do anything to please him. How could she possibly compete with that? It's not like I didn't know he was a rock star, she chastised herself, but it's so different when you actually see them touching him, hear them crying out for him.

"Beth, it's your turn."

"Oh, I'm sorry." She couldn't remember what was played.

"Oh, dude. The ace is still out there." Even Keith, who just ambled by on his way to the kitchen, knew she misplayed.

"Oh, I'm sorry, Chad. I must be getting tired."

"I'm exhausted, too," Cheri admitted. "You wild boys are used to staying up to all hours of the night."

"I'm sorry, babe." Chad helped her out of her seat. "I should have known you were tired." He smiled in a way that told her he was not at all tired, or at least not interested in going straight to sleep. "Goodnight, everyone."

"We're going to sleep, too," Cheri announced, David's face displaying an identical grin to Chad's. "It was nice meeting you, Beth."

"Yeah," Roger added sourly, "even if you did beat our ass."

Michelle swatted him. "Don't be a sore loser. You're incorrigible, ya know that?"

Beth almost cringed when Chad opened the door to head to the other bus, but there was no one around except for Pete and Dante, who were smoking cigarettes. "Goodnight, Chad. Goodnight, Beth," they called out.

The couple walked in silence a few paces.

"Do you want my coat?" he offered. A stiff breeze had picked up.

"No, that's okay. All you've got is a T-shirt."

"Yeah—" he took it off "—but I'm hot anyway. Come on, the air will do me some good. Besides, we don't have far to go." He nodded in the direction of the second bus.

Beth pulled the jacket over her shoulders. It smelled good, like Chad. She glanced over her shoulder and could make out the glow of Pete's cigarette as he stood watching them until they were safely in the bus.

Once inside, she handed him the jacket. "Thanks."

"No problem. Are you hungry or anything? Need a drink?"

She shook her head. She glanced in the direction of Keith's end of the bus. Light poured out from under his bedroom door.

Chad put his hands on her shoulders. "He'll be up for hours. He's kind of obsessed with this computer game. Some kind of battle thing. I forget what it's called...but he'll be sure to tell you all about it tomorrow." He turned her, studying her. "Are you having second thoughts about staying here?" They decided over the phone she would stay with him on the bus. "Would you rather have me get you a hotel room for the night?" he asked tentatively.

"No. I want to be here with you."

Her answer seemed to convince him. He smiled. "Well then, are you ready to go to bed, or do you want to stay up and talk, or do something else?"

"I guess I'm ready for bed," she responded, still feeling as distracted as she had all night.

"Okay." He led the way into his bedroom, holding on to her hand behind him.

When they entered the room, she stood staring at the bed, which he had made for a change, anticipating her being there. How many women have been in here with him? She told herself it didn't matter, but she knew it was a lie.

Chad sat on the end of the bed and peered up at her. "Beth, what's wrong?"

She turned away from his soft eyes, irritated with herself. Pacing back and forth in agitation, she tried to find words to describe her feelings.

"It's just, that girl..."

"Oh, come on, Beth. You have to know it didn't mean anything. She practically jumped me."

"Yes, I'm aware of that," she retorted a little sharply. "I'm well-aware of that. I was right there. Not that that seemed to deter her."

"Beth, they're crazy. You saw the girl who went after Roger. And he's married. Listen—" He tried to pull her between his legs; she relented for a moment. "I would never let anyone hurt you."

She moved away from him again. "It's not that."

"Then what is it, Beth?"

"Ugh. Chad!" she shouted, exasperated, not wanting to reveal her insecurities to him. "It's just...you could have any one of those girls tonight. Any one of them. Screaming out your name, all those beautiful, young girls who would do anything to be where I am right now."

"Maybe, but I didn't want them. I wanted you."

"Well, then," she returned with a touch of bitterness, "you're an idiot."

"I've never tried to hide that fact from you," he stated simply.

Beth stopped in her tracks and stared at him. He smiled. He just had a way of erasing everything for her.

After a pause, a broad smile broke over her face. "I'm going to jump your bones now like you've never been jumped before."

Chad opened his arms wide with a grin. "Bring it on, woman."

She ran the few feet between them and leaped on the rocker. He caught her hips like a professional dancer doing a lift and rolled back with her, kissing as if on fire for her. After a minute, he rolled her over onto the bed and pulled away. "Wait, wait!" he muttered, panting.

"What?"

"I want you to know..." He slowed his breathing, regaining control. He pushed a stray hair out of her eyes. "I want you to know, I'm not doing this casually. Nothing about this is casual for me." He hesitated. "I've never felt, for any woman, the way I feel about you." As he verbalized it, his face changed, a look of wonder brightening his features as if sensing for the first time how true the words were. He bent to kiss her, taking her heart up with

each breath. Then, he made love to her unhurriedly, purposefully, each movement telling her she was the only woman on his mind.

CHAPTER FIFTEEN

Sunlight filtered into the bedroom and fell across the burgundy comforter Beth had pulled up to her shoulders. The sheets felt good against bare skin as she took in a deep breath and stretched like a lazy cat.

"Good morning."

To hear his beautiful, deep voice so close to her first thing in the morning was a huge turn on. She felt his hand that was under the covers touch her bare hip. "M-mmm. Good morning." She opened her eyes to see him on his side, leaning on his elbow. He bent to kiss her with tenderness.

"Did you sleep well?"

"Fantastic. But what about you? You shouldn't be up this early. Roger said you're never up before noon."

"I want to take advantage of every moment we have together." Chad pulled the covers off and swung his legs over the side of the bed. She took in his butt, waist, and broad shoulders as he pulled on his clothes, suddenly wanting him to come back to bed. Before she could suggest it, he asked, "How about a little road trip?"

"A road trip? Where?"

"Somewhere close," he came back with an air of mystery. "Did you bring any hiking shoes? If not, tennis shoes should be fine. Or we could go get you some hiking boots if you'd like."

"I'm sure tennis shoes will work."

He moved to the end of the bed and pulled on a fresh T-shirt. She sat up and brought her knees into her chest, wrapping her arms around her legs.

Chad turned and crawled back up the bed, putting one hand behind her neck and drawing her in for several quick kisses, which, nonetheless, left her feeling weak. He was such an incredible kisser. "How about you take a shower, and I'll make us some breakfast."

"You can cook?"

He hesitated. "Define 'cook.'"

She climbed out of bed, taking the sheet with her. "Kiss me again like that and I'll eat anything you put in front of me."

He didn't need a second invitation. After he drew back, she kept her eyes shut, savoring the moment. He took the opportunity to reach back and give her a slap on the behind. "Now, get in the shower!"

"Ouch. Okay, okay."

She took a nice steamy shower. As she was getting dressed, she could hear Chad whistling in the kitchen. She smiled and hurried to join him.

"Good timing." He set a plate of bacon, eggs, and toast down on each side of the table next to two small bowls of fresh strawberries, cantaloupe, and pineapple.

"Holy cow. This looks like a meal fit for a king."

"Too much?"

"Not at all. I'm starving." She sat and began to devour her food ravenously. "Oh gosh." She lowered her voice. "I hope I didn't wake Keith. I almost forgot he was here."

"Don't worry. These buses are pretty well soundproofed, so he couldn't hear you...now, or last night," he added with a wicked grin.

"Well, I guess we'll just have to try harder tonight," she retorted, leaning forward to kiss him.

He laughed. "You're naughty. I like that about you." He cleared their plates and set them in the sink. "I'll just take a quick shower and be right out," he stated, pulling his shirt off as he strolled out of the kitchen. She admired his muscular shoulders and arms.

She sighed. I am so lucky.

When Chad finished his shower and ambled into the bedroom, Beth was applying makeup in the mirror behind the bar. He thought she didn't need makeup, but had to admit, she looked pretty hot when she was finished.

Chad never felt so happy before. The closest he came was in his first days with Julie. But this was even sweeter, because now he knew this relationship wouldn't turn sour. He knew from experience what signs to recognize, and none of them were there with Beth.

The day was record-setting warm. It was supposed to get close to sixty-seven degrees and it was still February. He was pleased when he heard the forecast. It made what he was planning that much better. Pete waved good-bye as they crossed the parking lot to climb into the rental car. It felt oddly spring-like, and before they even hit the highway, Beth opened the sunroof to let in some air. Chad was thumbing through the playlist on her MP3 player as she was navigating traffic out of town. They were headed east, toward St. Louis, for a destination only he was aware of.

"So, Mystery Man, just where are we going?"

"Oh, just you wait and see."

"You're not going to tell me yet?"

"Just keep going east until I tell you to do something else."

"Hmm." She bit her lip and glanced at him, as if trying to read the destination in his features somehow.

He acted oblivious as he scanned the listings on the screen. "Neil Diamond?" He raised an eyebrow.

"Yeah." Seeming to feel an explanation was in order, she expounded. "When I was little, my parents got divorced and I had to kind of grow up fast to help raise my little sisters."

He nodded. He knew the feeling.

"So, I listened more to their music, you know? I guess I was the only kid into Neil Diamond and Elton John at that age. Most of my friends were more into Rush and Led Zeppelin."

He put a hand on her knee. "I was just teasing. I actually like a wide range of music, too." Noting she relaxed, he began going over her choices again. "You do have every album we've ever made."

"I think I'm making up for lost time. Going through my second adolescence."

He grunted. "Wonder what my excuse is then." He scrolled down. "Oh my gosh. Have you seen how much you've played these?"

"You can do that?" she said, trying to get a glimpse at the screen.

"Holy shit! I think you've played these more than I've sung them. Except for 'Night in Barbados.' What's wrong with 'Night in Barbados'?" he questioned with mock severity.

"It...just...reminds me too much...of things..." She checked her sideview mirror, avoiding eye contact, but he could still read the pain in her eyes.

She must have really loved him for the pain to be this fresh after so many years. He busily read through the songs, searching for one he would feel confident wouldn't make her sad. He pushed his selection, praying this song wouldn't have some secret significance, too. The first few notes of The Police's "Roxanne" filled the car.

"Ahh...good choice." She smiled, and he was rewarded for his efforts. They began to belt out the lyrics, but after a few verses she dropped out.

When Chad noticed, he stopped, too. "Hey, you quit on me."

"I just wanted to listen to your voice. You sound great on that song."

"I used to sing it when we were a cover band."

They continued to bask in the sunshine as the temperature rose and enjoyed the light air blowing their hair back as the car sped forward. They listened to most of the rest of the album, singing loudly and putting many miles behind them. Then, he scrolled up to Jimmy Buffet. After a rousing version of "Cheeseburger in Paradise," "Slow Boat to China" came on and he skipped it.

"Oh no. Go back. I love that song. I love how he set it on a cruise ship, and you can hear the people talking in the background."

He complied and listened to Beth as she sang the lyrics in her soulful voice. "That is pretty cool," he admitted.

"It makes me wish I knew how to soft shoe."

"It makes me wish I could get you on a slow boat to China," he teased.

As he took in her profile, he had a sudden urge. He leaned over and began to kiss her neck.

She moaned. "Chad. Are you trying to wreck us?"

"I'm sorry." He sighed. "I'll be good. So, what do you want to listen to now?"

"Umm...U-2, 'Sunday, Bloody Sunday.' They were my favorite band before I heard Trapped Under Ice."

"Ahh." He squinted at her sideways. "I suppose you had a thing for Bono, too?"

She nodded and giggled.

"You're kidding. He's like, sixty or something."

"Yeah, but he's still got it."

"Nah, you just dig his Irish accent. Admit it."

"Well, there is that."

"I've so got you figured out."

"No, no, wait. There's more to it than that. He's a humanitarian."

He snorted incredulously. "I knew you were going to go there."

"No, really. I think there's something special about a person who believes in the ability of one person to change the world."

"I do, too," he added seriously. "I'm a huge fan." He sat straighter. "Hey, get off at the next exit."

She squinted at the sign. "Sweet Springs. Just what's in Sweet Springs?"

"Nothing. I just thought I could drive for a while, if that's all right?"

"Sure."

They pulled into a gas station and Chad got out, leaving the car door open and strolling around to her side of the car. Beth stretched muscles tight from driving. He came over and grabbed her hips. He kissed her, and soon their kisses became increasingly urgent and out of control. He walked her back until she was against the car, pressing his body to hers.

We should stop this, she thought. People could be watching us. But the gas station was deserted. Chad searched for the skin at her waistline. The touch of his hands and the strength and desire with which he pulled her to him nearly drove her wild.

She couldn't be sure who it was that pulled away first. They just sat for several minutes with foreheads together, eyes closed, gathering themselves.

"My God. I could take you right now. Right now, in the middle of this dusty parking lot. Why didn't I just stay home with you and make love to you all day long?"

Beth didn't respond. She couldn't respond. The sound of his voice so close made her melt.

"I guess we better go," he finally said.

"Uhm-hum," she agreed, though reluctant.

He watched her all the way around to the other side of the car. Then, he put one foot on the running board and crossed his hands on the roof of the car with a goofy smile. She mirrored his posture for a minute, and without saying anything, they slid into their seats.

She giggled as he started the engine. "I hope we don't have to stop for gas down the road, or we may never make it to your secret destination."

He grinned and swung the car around, speeding out of the parking lot. "Whoo. This baby's got some zip."

She grabbed his hand. "May I say I'm absolutely loving this?"

"You may." He returned with a grin, obviously pleased with himself.

Farther down the road, she let a huge yawn escape.

"Beth, why don't you close your eyes for a while?"

"Oh no. I couldn't do that. You're the one who should be tired. You need someone to keep you awake."

"No, really. I'm fine. Just shut your eyes for a few minutes. You could cover up with the coat in the back."

Beth glanced at the down jacket on the rear seat. She reached over and pulled it up to the front, drawing it around her body and tucking it behind her shoulders. "Maybe for a minute."

With the sun warming her and the drone of the road, she dozed peacefully for several miles. It felt good to be taken care of. It was so terrifying after Paul died to be suddenly forced to make decisions on her own, and care for herself and Cassie. She felt comfortable letting him make the majority of the financial decisions in their marriage. But over time, she became more used to deciding things on her own, with input from her friends on most occasions. But, even the act of letting someone else drive was freeing.

She found her mind returning to the scene at the gas station. Her body luxuriated in the sensory memories washing over her—the first thrill when his searching hands left cloth behind and touched skin, the warmth and softness of his mouth, the feeling as if nothing else in the world mattered at that precise moment than that precise moment. It was a feeling Beth knew in the past.

SHE REMEMBERED A WEEKEND in college they had spent in her dorm room. Paul came over, knowing her roommate went home for the weekend. They pulled both twin mattresses onto the floor to make a sort of nest for their lovemaking. And being young, foolish, and in love, they spent the entire weekend held up in the room. Beth checked the halls whenever Paul needed to use the bathroom, as it was an all-girls' dorm. It was not unheard of for a boy to be present, but sneaking was half the fun. They slept in past the hours for breakfast in the cafeteria and fooled around through the hours for lunch. On weekends, the cafeteria closed for dinner and students had to find their meal elsewhere. So, at three o'clock, famished, they ventured out of the room, hiking across campus to the McDonald's. They pooled what little money they had together for a meal, then returned to the dorm to find Beth's roommate had returned from home earlier than they expected.

THAT WONDERFUL, HEADY feeling of being in your own private bubble together, of making love while the world went on without you, this was what Chad gave her for a second time, and she knew just how precious it was.

CHAPTER SIXTEEN

C had stole peeks at Beth as he drove, asleep on the seat next to him, a secret smile on her lips. He fantasized about kissing those lips again. He couldn't get enough of her. Her face looked so serene. And as he thought about it, he realized that was what she brought to his life, a sense of peace. In fact, she demanded nothing of him, asked nothing of him, and simply enjoyed whatever it was he had to offer in the relationship. His heart had ached for so long that he had grown immune to the pain. But now, with her near, he could almost forget about those horrors that haunted him without ceasing.

He saw the sign for their exit. Rocheport. It didn't sound like a nice place, but he knew she would like it. He looked over to see if she awoke with the change of speed, but her eyes remained closed. He turned down the rural route and drove about five miles before finally turning off on a short, bumpy side road.

Beth woke up as the car jostled over uneven pavement. She sat up and looked around to get a sense of where they were. They crossed a set of railroad tracks and then the car was moving along a concrete drive that dead-ended in a wall of vegetation. He pulled into a small parking lot to the left.

"We're here," he announced, smiling and turning off the engine.

She just smiled back at him. They got out of the car, and she turned slowly in a circle to examine her surroundings. The mass of greenery in front of them was either a scraggly bush or an overgrown patch of weeds, she couldn't tell which. Beyond Chad, on the other side of the car, was a concrete pathway leading who knows where into some farther foliage. Behind them was a small café, "Trails End," with a few picnic tables in front of it. There was an attached shop, which sold hiking paraphernalia. To the right, across the drive, was a second trail, or perhaps a continuation of the first, as it was located directly across the parking lot from it.

He watched her as she took in their setting. He expected a sense of let-down. They drove over two hours for this? But her face glowed as usual. They walked around and met at the back end of the car. He held both of her hands in his, still smiling. He waved toward the café where there was a sign in the window reading, "Bikes for Rent."

"Should we rent bikes?" he asked.

"Oh no. Let's walk. That way we can talk."

"Good idea." He gave her a quick kiss and turned to his left.

"Besides," she said, shading her eyes and blinking at the little roadside restaurant, "I don't think it's open. I think it's just seasonal. It may feel like May out here, but remember, it's still February."

"You're right," he agreed jovially. As she set off on the trail in front of them, he casually waved back at the window of the café where someone watched from within.

For several minutes they meandered along the path, which now consist-ed of loose rock. They held hands and Beth seemed perfectly content to stroll along at his side, with the twist of plant life on her right, and what now ap-peared to be wooded hillside on the left.

"So? Just where are we?"

"Rocheport."

"Rocheport? Did I sleep that long? We're almost to Columbia. That's where Paul and I went to school."

"Have you been here before?" Chad asked quickly.

"No. No. We always talked about coming, but we never made it. There are supposed to be some cute bed and breakfast places near here." She looked thoughtful. "But you probably aren't into the whole bed and breakfast thing, huh? Being a rock star and all."

"Actually, something like that sounds kind of good. Quiet, low key. I could use that sometimes."

"I love you," she blurted out effortlessly, bringing his hand, still interlaced with hers, to her mouth and kissing it.

She looked away, oblivious to the effect it had on him. The touch of Beth's lips set him on fire, but it was her words that undid him. She, of course, would have no way of knowing how few the times in his life were when someone spoke those words to him. His mom, once or twice. Julie, whenever she wanted something. His dad, never. He could count on his hands the number of times he heard those three little words. He heard Beth saying them to Cassie, and Cassie to her, so the words came easily to them; yet he had no doubt she meant them.

Up ahead, the pathway made a wide curve to the right, and they could see the wild barrier of shrubbery came to an end at the foot of the curve but could see nothing beyond it. The sound of water grew louder as they walked a few more yards, and then a breathtaking vista spread out before them. The mighty Missouri River, in all its grandeur, whisked past them, its current strong and swift. On the far side of the river, the bluffs rose skyward, and a singular hawk circled overhead.

"Oh, Chad." She stood, spellbound by the spectacular view. "It's awesome."

He stood behind her with his arms wrapped around her, and bent in to whisper, "I thought you'd like it." They stood that way for some time, transfixed by the beauty before them and happy to be sharing it with someone they loved. He leaned in again to speak to her, the current loud here in the open. "Should we keep walking?" She nodded, and they continued on, with his hand around her shoulder.

As they strolled, Beth chatted animatedly. "I forgot Rocheport was on the river. Can you believe those bluffs? Isn't this called the Katy Trail?"

He nodded. "Named after the MKT railroad: Missouri, Kansas, Texas. The trains were actually still running through here even a couple of decades ago. When they closed the line, the state of Missouri turned it into a walking trail. I think it's almost forty miles long, from St. Charles, just outside of St. Louis, all the way to Clinton."

"You've been here before, then?"

"Yes, a couple of years ago." Then, seeing the look of disappointment crossing her face, which she was trying to hide, he read her mind and added quickly, "But it was just with the guys—Roger, Dave, and Keith, oh, and Michelle and Cheri...and I think Pete and Dante tagged along, too."

"Oh," she said, seeming happier. "Look, Chad. There's a little waterfall in the cliff. The water runs underground and must feed into the river. Can you imagine what this must have looked like to Lewis and Clark? Totally unspoiled. It must have been extraordinary." She pointed out pretty flowers along the path, a cave, the hawk banking overhead, and was, in general, delighted by everything she saw.

Chad tried not to be too conspicuous about searching for the trail. Finally, he suggested, "Hey, look, Beth. It says this path goes up to the winery. Let's go up there. I'm sure it's closed, but it's bound to be a nice hike anyway."

They began to climb. The dirt path led up the cliffside and past huge boulders hidden among the tall trees covering the slope. The recent snows were completely melted, even in the shade, but it made the path slippery in spots. It smelled wonderfully of dried leaves and pine needles, and although they could no longer see it, they could still hear the river below. The sun dappled the ground as it fell through the pine branches and the elms and oaks, which still stubbornly held a leaf here and there.

As the pair climbed higher, the ascent became a little steeper. The hillside was shaded by the massive trunks of ancient oaks, but it did not give off an oppressive feeling. Instead, it felt ageless. The dark places, little nooks and crannies in the rocks, were not frightening, but seemed to invite the visitor to explore, as if they held some magical secrets just for guests. They were high enough now the sound of the Missouri was left below them. They finally broke out of the tree line and reached the top, finding themselves at the end of a gravel driveway. Signs indicated the winery was to the left, so he led her in that direction.

After a bit they came upon a second gravel driveway and followed it to a wooden A-frame building. He pointed out a blue jay to keep Beth from noticing a car parked off to one side of the road.

"Let's just go and check out the winery," he suggested.

"Do you think we should?"

"Why not? I don't see any no trespassing or private property signs." They scooted along the side of the house on the wooden deck, which led to the back.

The building itself was unremarkable, but when they came to the back, Beth let out a little squeal. "This is so cool."

At the rear of the building, the deck became terraced with a series of steps leading in all directions to little areas where bistro tables sat. It fanned out and became wider until it hit an open patch of grass at the edge of the cliff with a three-foot-tall wrought iron fence. A half-dozen picnic tables were situated in the grassy area.

Beth started hurrying down the steps in order to reach the edge where she was certain a spectacular view awaited when she heard an unfamiliar voice.

"Hey, Chad."

She turned to see Chad shaking hands with a man behind the bar jutting out from the back of the building. Huge chalkboards on the walls displayed the names and prices of numerous different kinds of wines behind him.

"What'll you have?"

"Oh, whatever your favorite is, Mark. Beth, what kind of wine do you prefer?"

She made her way back up the few stairs slowly. "A Riesling?" she answered, giving him a curious look.

The man behind the bar did not seem at all surprised the two hikers came by the winery on a February day. In fact, it seemed as if he were expecting them. He poured a glass of red wine and her Riesling and handed the glasses to Chad. "You can have a seat, and I'll bring the rest to your table."

Chad stepped down the few steps he climbed to reach the bar, enjoying her confused look.

"What...who...?" she sputtered.

"Don't you want to have a seat?" He gestured below, and that was when she spied the table, covered in a white tablecloth with a small, crystal vase holding three of the most beautiful roses she had ever seen. They were pale yellow, tinged with a dark pink at the edges of the petals.

"Chad..." For the first time in an hour, she was speechless.

"Come on." He handed her the glass of white wine and took her hand, leading the way down the steps. He placed his glass on the table and pulled out her chair. She sat, overcome for a moment. He sat beside her, looking like the cat that'd swallowed the pretty, yellow bird, and sipped his wine, waiting for her to speak.

"How did you do this?"

He answered, staring out over the vista without turning to her. "Mark's a Trapped Under Ice fan. Are you hungry?"

"Famished, actually," she admitted.

As if on cue, Mark came down the stairs with a large basket. "Is the wine all right?" He smiled, seeming to thoroughly enjoy his part in surprising her.

"It's fantastic," she responded, grinning at him and then letting her eyes rest on Chad's profile.

"Did you need anything else, Chad?"

He turned finally to look at her, raising his eyebrows as if to ask her if there were anything else she needed. She shook her head, and Mark left them, having set the basket on the table. He held her hand.

"You—" Her voice caught, and she looked away for a minute. "You did all this?"

"Well," he admitted, "Mark did most of the work. But yes, I called and asked him if he could set this up for us."

"This is the sweetest—" She got choked up again.

He leaned toward her. "I just wanted to make today special."

"It already was," she asserted, her eyes brimming with tears.

He kissed her and that was when he knew he didn't want this to ever end. He picked up his wine glass and raised it. Looking her in the eyes, he toasted, "To many more days like this." And he, too, became emotional for a minute. They clinked glasses and drank.

He set his wine back down and rubbed his hands together in anticipation of their feast. "Let's eat," he offered, pulling back the napkin covering the top of the basket. He withdrew a small cutting board and knife, a green apple, a roll of salami, a loaf of crusty French bread, and a chunk of creamy white cheese. He cut the apple, and they split their repast between them, drinking their wine while they relaxed.

When they were finished, Chad asked her if she wanted to get a closer look. Leading her down the rest of the stairs, their wine glasses in tow, they reached the edge of the parapet. They set their glasses down on one of the picnic tables nearby and approached the fence together. A light breeze kissed their faces as they drank in the landscape in front of them.

Just outside the fence, large golden grasses danced in the wind on the edge of the cliff, and one large, graceful tree spread its branches as if beckoning the viewer to take a further look. To the left, a picturesque railroad bridge spanned the river. To the right, they could see a barge working its way up-stream with the ever-present hawk now drifting below them.

Chad's arms encircled her, clasping the railing in each hand. She leaned into him, breathing. "Could this day be any more perfect?"

"I don't think so," he noted, their voices hushed in the stillness out of a sense of reverence. "Do you want to sit?"

They climbed up on the picnic table, so they could still have an unob-structed view of the river. Beth sat between Chad's long legs, as his feet rested on the bench, and once again leaned into his body. He kissed her neck from time to time but mostly enjoyed the quietude and her warmth.

"Beth," he asked softly, "why did you cry the first time I kissed you?" He felt her body go rigid. "You don't have to tell me if you're not ready."

"No. I want to tell you, but it's hard to explain. I don't want you to think I'm...Oh, God," she murmured, sitting up and putting her head in her hands.

Oh, man, this is SO not what I wanted to happen.

"Ugh," Beth cried out in frustration, jumping up and pacing in front of him. "I don't know why I cried. It's just, you were so nice and funny and—" she chuckled "—attractive. And you kissed me, and I cried." She stopped pac-ing and gazed up at Chad helplessly.

"I'm," he said slowly, "still not sure what I did wrong."

"You did nothing wrong." Beth pounded her hands on his knees. He jumped, surprised by her mini-explosion. "Can't you see? It's me, Chad. I was afraid."

"Afraid of me?" He recalled the horror on her face the first time he saw her. "Because of what I did to the guy who attacked you?"

"No," she uttered weakly. Looking down, Beth took a deep breath and closed her eyes. "Afraid of the things I was feeling when I was in your arms. Afraid because it reminded me of the way I felt with Paul. And..." She looked up, searching his eyes as if willing him to understand what she couldn't bring herself to say.

And suddenly, he knew. While this little dynamo he had come to love so much fought through much in her lifetime, this was the one thing she was afraid of, going back to a place where she had so much to lose. It must hurt like hell to think of losing it again. "Oh, Beth," he cried out, pulling her to him. "I pushed too much. You weren't ready—"

"No, Chad." She struggled to pull away from him. "It's not your fault. I've had three years to put this behind me—"

"Beth, this isn't something you can put behind you." He took her hand, looking down for a minute before continuing. "It stays with you." And as he said it, he wondered if he, too, would always be saddled with his past. "If this is going to work, we have to be honest with ourselves," he added as much to himself as to her.

She turned with her back to him, crossing to grip the railing and dropping her head. "And now I've ruined the perfect day you tried so hard to make for us."

He jumped up and went to her, leaning his back against the fence so he could get a good look at her face. "You didn't ruin anything. This was the perfect day. And I'm glad you told me what you did."

She slid her eyes to him, and then suddenly moved to hug him, burying her head in his chest. "Oh, God, Chad. I'm sorry."

"Shh-shh. There's nothing to be sorry for." He reached down and lifted Beth's chin to kiss her. Her lips curved up slightly. "There, that's better." Chad suddenly saw the time on his watch. "Oh shit. If we don't get moving, I'm going to be late for sound check. Roger goes totally ape if you're late to sound check." He grabbed her hand and started rushing up the stairs.

"Roger? He seems like Mr. Happy-Go-Lucky to me."

"He is," Chad admitted, "just so long as you're not late for sound check."

"You guys leaving so soon? You're welcome to stay as long as you want."

"No. Thanks a lot, Mark. Everything was great." He laid several large bills on the bar with a dozen or so concert tickets.

Mark shoved the money back across the bar. "The tickets are enough, Chad."

"No. Please take this. This meant a lot to us. I'm sorry we have to run off, but if we don't hustle, I'll be late for sound check."

"Shit, man. You'd better get going. You don't want to have to deal with Roger."

"You ain't kiddin'."

He and Beth hurried up the inclined drive. They reached the dirt path and scrambled down as fast as they dared. Belatedly, he thought, I should have asked Mark if he could drive us to our car. Chad decided not to climb back up. For all he knew, Mark had already left.

About a fourth of the way down, his feet hit a patch of loose rock, and he tried to backpedal as the ground crumbed away beneath his feet. Not able to react quickly enough, he slid off the side of the path into a deep ravine. After a few harried seconds, he was able to stop his drop by digging his heels into the soft mud and grabbing at some fledgling pine trees trying to grow in the shade of much grander trees.

"Chad!" Beth screamed, but just as she put her foot forward to climb down to help him, her own path broke away underneath her. Whether the snow eroded the base of the path or his mini-landslide stole away its last support, she careened down into the same pit he fell into, only where she was standing on the path, the trench along the side was much deeper and the ground beneath it much rockier. He saw her body falling through space and then heard her land with a sickening thud.

CHAPTER SEVENTEEN

"Beth! Beth!" Chad skittered along the slope, trying to manage a nearly uncontrollable slide. He could see her feet but not the upper half of her body because of the curves of the landscape. But when he came around the corner, he saw her sit up.

She moaned. "Man. Every part of me aches." She laughed.

"Did you hit your head, 'cause I'm not sure I'd be laughing after a fall like that?"

"I'm fine. But you look terrible." She giggled, reaching up to pull a leaf out of his hair.

"Oh my God. You scared the shit out of me!" His words came out angry, but then, just as quickly, his tone turned remorseful. "Are you sure you're okay?"

"I'm fine." She reached up to touch his arms. "Are you okay?"

"Yeah. Yeah. I'm fine." He sighed. "That was stupid of me to rush."

With his help, she got to her feet. She looked back up the side of the cliff. "Well, we got down here a lot faster."

"Yeah. The hard way." He tried to get his bearings. "Well, I think we'll be okay if we just keep heading downhill, toward the river." He checked her over again. "But maybe we should have you sit for a while."

"No, Chad. I'm okay, really."

"All right," he consented begrudgingly. "If you're sure. But this time, let's take it slow."

"Okay," she replied with a smile, reaching up again to rub some dried mud from his hair.

"You're crazy, ya know?"

"Yeah. I know." She stood on her toes to kiss him.

WHEN THEY GOT TO THE car, Beth could tell Chad was tired, so she offered to drive. After much debate over the wisdom of someone who had taken such a fall driving the vehicle, he finally relented, with Roger's fury in mind, and climbed in beside her. He fell asleep almost immediately.

It was more of a memory than a dream.

He was in the room he shared with his brother, David. Both of them were listening to the noises coming from the living room of their small house. David was crying. As Chad watched, his little brother hopped out of bed and ran to the door. Chad, whose bed was closer to the door, jumped in front of David and blocked the way, spreading his arms wide across the door. David buried his head in Chad's chest. Slowly, he brought his hands down around the younger boy's shaking shoulders.

Without warning, the door they were leaning on vibrated and at the same time they heard the nauseating sound of their mother's body hitting the wall during a break in the shouting. Furious, Chad yanked on the doorknob and entered the hall, keeping David in the room with one hand.

"Chad!" his mother screamed, her mouth already bloodied. "It's okay. Go back to bed."

His father's form towered over his mother, but the man didn't even look away from her in his drunken rage. Chad's stomach lurched involuntarily; he felt like he was going to be sick.

"Chad!" she screamed again, desperate now, tears in her eyes. "Go back to bed. Please."

"Ch-Chad?" David's trembling voice called.

He turned to stare into his brother's frightened eyes, the light from the hall seeping through the crack in the door to illuminate the boy's face. He glanced back at his mom, and wished, as he had on too many occasions, he could be big enough to stop his father...he could be brave enough to kill him. Swallowing his deep sense of shame and uselessness, he did the only thing left to him. He pushed his little brother back inside the bedroom and closed the door on the shouting. He peered down again into David's innocent face.

He was only seven, but he scooped David up, footy-pajamas and all, and placed the boy in his own bed. He climbed in behind his younger brother, and they turned on their sides, pulling the covers up over their heads. He put an arm over David, trying to block his little ears from hearing the sounds emanating from outside the bedroom. Sometime later, David's whimpering finally stopped, and he drifted off to sleep. But Chad lay awake, listening and praying, well into the night, wondering just what set his father off this time.

The second memory was as vivid as the first.

He was ten, asleep in his bed, when a loud sound jolted him awake. He lay for a second, eyes wide, heart pounding, and then, quickly, five more cracks rent the air. There could be no doubt now. Chad always feared someday he would kill her, and now it had happened.

He sat silently in the dark, tears running down his face. He had not been able to protect his mother, and he hoped now his father would come and kill him, too. Amazingly, David stayed asleep. And then, Chad heard her voice, a strange, almost inhuman wail, and his mind spun madly.

He didn't know how long it was before he heard the sirens. He went to the window and pulled back the thin, dingy curtains that did nothing to keep out the streetlights. Peering down from the third floor, he saw people gathered outside, talking and gazing up at their apartment. Two police cars sat at angles in the parking lot, their lights on. He could hear the police radios squawking loudly, but didn't understand what they were saying.

A lady saw him in the window. Her hand flew to her mouth, and she screamed something. A policeman, who was talking to the onlookers, barked something into his radio. Chad jumped back from the window, somehow thinking that the police were going to come for him. He heard the loud pounding on the stairs in the hall outside their apartment, then fists were banging on the door, telling them to open up. David woke up with a start, sitting up in his bed and looking around in confusion. Like a zombie, Chad left the room.

He could hear her crying in the kitchen even before he came to the doorway. "I'm so sorry," she repeated over and over again. He crossed into the path of light spilling from the kitchen, and saw her lying over his father, blood everywhere. He wondered, idly, if he would have to clean it up like so many times before. As he stood staring, a policeman cracked the frame of their door with his first try. David started crying.

Chad turned from the gory scene in the kitchen. He trudged down the hall to his bedroom door. "Let me in, Davy. It's me, Chad," he called dully.

The crying continued unabated. He stood on his tiptoes to reach the corner of a picture frame and tilted it to retrieve something from the top edge. It fell to the floor, and he bent to pick up a somewhat straightened paperclip. He scooped it up and walked over to the door to stick it into the hole in the knob. He pushed and popped the lock. As the door opened inward, Davy came barreling out and wrapped himself around Chad's legs. There was a bustle in the kitchen, and they turned to see two police officers escorting their mother, who was handcuffed and covered in blood, out of the room. She turned to stare at them with an expression that wrenched at his heart, but she didn't say a word.

Then, his mind remembered the second day; the two tragedies forever linked in his brain.

The phone had been ringing all morning. Chad decided, finally, to wake his aunt. After his mother killed his father and went to prison, his Auntie Mary had enough pity to sober up for the week it took to convince the court she would be a fit guardian. He begged his aunt, afraid the courts would split David and him up, and she relented, allowing the kids to come live in her apartment as long as they agreed to stay out of the way. She was no mother, after all.

This particular morning, she was passed out, nude, in her bedroom with a man Chad had never seen before. The man was also passed out, wearing only a T-shirt. He heard the answering machine through the bedroom door and knew there was an important message from the prison concerning his mother. The fifth time the phone rang he went in to try to wake her again.

"Wh-what the hell? Chad. What have I told you about waking me?" She hastily pulled a sheet over herself.

"But, Auntie Mary, there's a call from the prison. Something about Mom. You need to call them."

"The hell I do. Now get out of here." He didn't move. She opened one eye. She was not a heartless woman, so seeing the concerned expression on his face, she said, "Okay, if they call back, you can wake me."

David was watching cartoons, so Chad sat where he was beside his aunt's bed and stared at the phone. An hour later, it rang again. He shook his aunt, but she wouldn't wake. In desperation, he picked up the phone, trying to sound adult.

"Well, thank goodness somebody is there," the disembodied voice said, cut-off mid-message. "As I was saying, we are trying to contact the next of kin for a prisoner, a...Donna Jo Evans. It says here we're looking for a Chad Evans."

"Yes, I'm Chad."

His aunt stirred and again opened one eye, watching the boy.

"Good. Well, sir, I regret to inform you that Donna Jo Evans was killed this morning in a fight involving a number of inmates..." Chad didn't hear anything else. Tears running down his face, he simply dropped the phone.

HE WOKE WITH A JERK, startling Beth.

"Are you okay?" she asked, a hand over her heart.

"Yeah. I'm sorry. How far are we?"

"I think we've got about forty-five more minutes."

He looked at his watch. "We might make it," he remarked, grim-faced.

It had begun to rain half an hour before. He stared at the rain running down his window and listened to the sound of the windshield wipers as they kept their monotonous pace. Beth had turned on some quiet music, and he began, again, to drift back in time. Although it was years ago, he still remembered exactly how his aunt's face looked when she heard the news.

Seeing Chad's distraught face, his aunt picked up the phone, still dangling from the dresser, a disembodied voice still rattling on. She sat up in bed; the man next to her groaned and yanked on the covers.

"Hello? I'm Chad's aunt. Would you please tell me what you just told him? He's thirteen; I'm his guardian. Yes...oh, I see..." Her eyes grew wide as she looked at Chad. "Thank you...yes, I will."

That was the only time their aunt ever took them out for ice cream.

The next morning, she was gone, and she never returned.

Chad dropped out of school and started a job at a grocery store. Being tall for a thirteen-year-old, he was able to convince the manager he was old enough for the job. Every day he would pack up David's peanut butter sandwich, and every night he would help him with his homework. He had no friends, just Davy. And when Davy went to sleep at night, Chad's guitar would keep the older boy company. The guitar was the only thing his dad ever gave him, and to it he gave his misery.

One day, on the grocery store bulletin board, he saw a note about a band needing a guitar player. That was when he met Roger. And from that day on, Roger was his best friend.

The same Roger that was going to kick his ass if he didn't show up on time for sound check.

Finally, Beth pulled up to the stage door and they ran inside. Pete was standing at the door with a gloomy look on his face. "You'd better hurry. He's probably fit to be tied."

Beth and Chad literally ran on stage as they were about to begin.

"Why, look what the cat drug in?" Roger began, but then noticing their appearance, he added, "What the hell happened to you two?"

They stood panting, dripping wet, and muddy. "Hey, man, I'm sorry we're late."

"Well, I'm guessing we're lucky you even showed up, with Beth being here and all." He winked at Beth.

"Yeah. I..." Chad was dumbfounded by his nonchalance. A stagehand brought them towels. "Thanks."

"Well, come on. Strap your guitar on, buddy. Beth, you'll sing with us, won't you?"

"Are you kidding?" She accepted with a smile. "Are you sure?"

"Come over here. I've got a wireless mike for you. Besides, Chad's been hogging you all day." Roger slid his hand around her hip and gave her a squeeze. Beth glanced back at Chad in surprise. He shrugged with a smile on his face and began tuning up his guitar.

Roger was about to begin when he noticed someone approaching from the back of the auditorium. When he got into the footlights by Joey, their pyrotechnics manager, Roger recognized him as Stan Mikas, their promoter.

"Hey, Stan. What's up?"

"Hey, guys. Don't let me interrupt."

Roger played the first few chords of "I Just Had to Have You Last Night."

With a grin, he began singing the words to Beth.

You we're lookin' so good with your miniskirt on

I kept imagining you with your miniskirt off

I know it's been wrong for me to think of you
But lately it's just too damn tough.

BETH JOINED IN, SINGING and playing around with Roger. She
stroked his face, which he loved.

When you look at me that way
I don't know what to say
I love him, you know I do
But now with your come-ons, you just had to go
And make me want to have you."
They both sang the chorus.
And I just had to have you last night
You whispered my name as you turned out the light
And now that it's done, there's no setting it right
So, my best friend and I are in for a fight
'Cause I just had to have you last night.

CHAD TOOK THE NEXT verse, looking at Beth as he did.

You were lookin' so good with your blue jeans on
I was imagining you with your blue jeans off
I know sometimes I should keep my hands off you
But baby that's just too damn tough.

BETH WALKED SLOWLY, seductively toward Chad; for some reason, being with them on stage brought out a different side of her.

I KNOW WE'VE BEEN SEEIN' each other for awhile

But you still turn me on like you're turning a dial
I'm not thinking of him when I make love with you
But being with him, what else could I do?

ALL THREE SANG,
> And I just had to have you last night
> You whispered my name as you turned out the light
> And when I am with you everything feels so right
> So, baby, let's not go and get into a fight
> You know I just had to have you last night.

BETH STOOD BETWEEN the two as if torn. Roger got up, walking to-ward her as he sang,
> You're his I know; oh, God, do I know
> But when I try to leave, my feet are just too damned slow.

BETH RESPONDED,
> I want to do things I just shouldn't do
> And you know it's all 'cause of you.

NOT TO BE OUT DONE, Chad walked toward her, joining in with,
> When you walk by, my heart goes berserk
> And certain body parts just start to work.

AND THEY ALL THREE finished with,
> And I just had to have you last night
> You whispered my name as you turned out the light
> And now that we're done, there's no getting it right
> Because I just had to have you last night.

THE TRIO LAUGHED AND Beth gave them both a kiss on the cheek. Singular applause surprised them from the floor.

"I love it. When are you going to use it?"

"Tonight," Roger said.

"What?" Chad and Beth said in unison.

Roger sauntered to the edge of the stage and continued talking with Stan as if they weren't there.

"It gives the song a whole new angle."

"I agree. A whole new energy. It's hot. She's hot. What label do you sing with, hon?"

"Me?" Beth returned, stunned.

Chad smiled. "How long have you been thinking about this?" he asked Roger.

"Since St. Louis. What do you think?"

"Well, I think it's great, but..."

"And what about you, Beth? What would you think about doing this for real?"

"What do you mean?"

"Performing it live. Tonight, at the concert."

She laughed. When Roger didn't join in, she queried, "You're kidding, right?"

"I'm dead serious."

She looked at Chad. "Were you in on this?"

He lifted up his hands to express his innocence. "I swear I had nothing to do with it."

"Roger. Be serious. Do you know how many people are going to be in this auditorium tonight?"

"A little under twenty thousand."

"Exactly. Twenty-thousand people who came to hear Trapped Under Ice, not Beth Donovan, lunch lady."

"Lunch lady?" Stan repeated in surprise.

Roger ignored him. "Twenty-thousand people who came to be entertained, and Stan here says the three of us are very entertaining, right, Stan?"

"Very."

Beth laughed again. "You're crazy. I've never even performed before."

"What about the concert at the Old Cathedral in St. Louis?"

"A choir Christmas concert, that's hardly performing."

"It's not? Didn't you have a solo?"

"Yes. And I was terrified. And it was in front of...what...a hundred people at best?" She glanced at Chad for confirmation, but Roger rolled on.

"Well, I guess I was wrong about you," he said with an air of disappointment. He moved to put away his guitar. "When I met you backstage in St. Louis, I thought you were one gutsy lady."

Chad chuckled. "Man, you're good."

"That's different."

"It's all about facing your fears head on."

Roger had struck a chord. Beth had thought about this the whole way back from the winery. If she was going to try to make a go of things with Chad, she was going to have to let go of her fears. She hesitated.

Sensing a weakness, Roger struck. "Come on, Beth. You know this would be a dream come true. You can't pass this up. Besides, Chad and I will be right here. You'll just be singing to us like you did a few minutes ago."

"Only there will be about twenty thousand other people here."

He disregarded her remark. "It'll be fun. You know you want to. Besides, Chad has promised certain sexual favors if you do."

Chad took his cue and nodded his head vigorously with a silly grin.

"You two are a pair of morons, you know?"

"We know," they answered simultaneously.

Roger turned serious. "What do you say?"

Beth thought for a minute. She looked up and asked wickedly, "What sort of sexual favors?" They all laughed. "All right," she agreed before Roger could argue further, "I'm in."

Everyone whooped. Chad grabbed her and gave her a kiss. She pulled away. "But you damn well better have a shot for me before I go on stage."

"No problem," Roger countered. "We always have a shot before we go on stage."

CHAPTER EIGHTEEN

Beth stood at the bottom of a ramp leading up to the stage. Her whole body was shaking, and she thought there was a strong possibility she was going to throw up. She could hear the thunderous applause of the audience, a strange wave of noise, but she had not been able to enjoy the band's playing at all.

As they wound up the first set, she could hear Chad say, "We're going to take about a one-minute break, so make-out with your boyfriend or girlfriend or do whatever comes naturally, within legal limits. We'll be right back." The four came down the ramp together, accepting cold beers and waters from people in the wings.

"You ready, Beth?"

She paced at the end of the ramp, dressed in a black camisole and black silk shirt. She wore jeans and little boots Roger called her "rock and roll boots."

"I don't think that shot was such a good idea. I think I'm going to be sick."

"I'm pretty sure it wouldn't be the first time that happened at a rock concert," Roger remarked with a grin. She stared at him darkly. He turned to Chad. "She's all yours, man. I think I've done all I can."

"Yeah, thanks," he retorted. He grabbed Beth by the shoulders. "Babe, it's not too late to back out if you want to. You don't have to do this."

Roger looked at her with raised eyebrows. She took in all the expectant faces around her then stared back at Roger. "No. I'll do it."

Roger's face relaxed. "Good." They all got ready to go back on stage.

Chad took her hand and leaned in to say, "If you get scared, just look at me."

She smiled at him, the words giving her some comfort. Roger grabbed her other hand.

She spoke through gritted teeth. "I'll get you for this."

"I'm counting on it," he responded out of the corner of his mouth without looking at her.

They entered the stage with cameras popping in their faces and the applause actually sending out waves of vibration. The heat from the lights and pyros was unrepentantly intense. Beth peered out and the people looked like a sea, like one huge, undulating entity. She was glad for the shot. She was feeling a little fuzzy, but powerful, and she realized she just might be able to do this.

"Thank you," Chad shouted into the microphone. "We're going to do a little number for you," he continued slowly, adjusting his guitar into a comfortable position, "called 'I Just Had to Have You Last Night.'"

The monster that was the crowd roared, and she worried all those people who loved to hear Chad and Roger sing this might be a little miffed she was singing. But before her thoughts could get much further, Roger was singing to her. Gazing into his face for courage, she belted out her lines like a pro, draping her arm over him flirtatiously. He was eating it up. When Chad started his lines, she sauntered over to him and did the same thing. When they reached the chorus, they all faced the audience, and the applause was deafening.

They're actually enjoying this.

Whether from the alcohol or the lights or her own nervousness, all of a sudden she was nauseatingly hot. Roger sang his next lines, and she dramatically fanned herself as if his words turned her on, but with Chad's lines she actually peeled off her blouse, whipping the crowd into a frenzy. As planned, with each man's lines they got closer and closer to her until, with the last phrases, she was holding them apart with her hands, and then the lights went down. It came off beautifully. She bent and scooped her shirt up off the stage, and Roger covered his microphone with one hand.

"I told you, you could do it." He gave her a happy kiss. The audience cheered.

"Hey, where's mine?" Chad protested into his microphone. Beth strolled toward him. When she reached the singer, he grabbed her, swung her around, and dipped her, kissing her long and passionately, if not a bit awkwardly with a guitar between them.

"Now, wait a minute," Roger complained into his mike. Then added, "How come the lead singer always gets the girls?"

Beth came up laughing and hustled off stage, pleased with herself and relieved it was over.

"Beth Donovan," Chad announced to the crowd; they responded with even louder cheering.

At the bottom of the ramp, she was met by Cheri and Michelle. "Way to go girl!" they hollered, giving her high-fives.

"Here. We have one of these for you," Michelle added, handing her a second shot of tequila.

She downed it without a second's hesitation. "Smooth," she uttered with a strained voice. They all laughed. The music started so the conversation ended. Beth sat and watched Chad for the rest of the show, remembering what drew her to the singer in the first place. He sang with a passion, energy, and intensity which completely turned her on. When the show was finished and Chad came backstage, she grabbed him, pressing her lips to his with a new-found hunger.

She gazed at him, her eyes dancing. "I am so incredibly turned on right now."

"Umm...someone's had some more tequila."

"Just one more, and it wore off a while ago."

"Okay, if you say so." He held her tight, rubbing her back at the same time. The rock star kissed her again.

Roger, who had just come up for air himself after kissing Michelle, hollered, "Ahh, get a room, you two."

"Sounds like a good idea," Chad purred.

WALKING THE GAUNTLET to the buses wasn't quite as intense this time, though Chad noticed there seemed to be a lot more men present than usual. Had they come to see Beth? The idea didn't thrill him.

When the noise outside was shut behind the door to the bus, he asked, "Do you want another drink?"

"No. I'm fine," Beth hummed seductively.

"Me, too." Kissing her, he led her through the kitchen and into the bedroom, closing the door behind them. He stood facing her. Her back was toward the door, and he rubbed her shoulders. "Taking off your blouse—" he closed his eyes for a minute "—was a nice touch."

"Oh, that wasn't part of the act, at first. I was just too damned hot."

"I'll say." He jerked open her blouse, straining the buttons, and pulled it down to expose her shoulders. He began kissing her neck and shoulders, the combination of his tongue and facial hair again sending her into orbit. He finished unbuttoning the blouse and let it drop to the floor. He ran his hands over smooth shoulders and up and down her arms, feasting on the way her breasts looked in the low-cut camisole. Suddenly, he turned his little songstress around and pressed her against the door.

She leaned her cheek against the cool wood, moaning in pleasure as his hands ran across her breasts and down to her waist. He unbuckled her belt and slid her jeans and underwear off. Starting where he left the jeans on the floor, he worked his way up, first kissing her ankles, then her calves, her thighs, and her tush, where he lingered, and finally the small of her back.

Unable to bear it any longer, she turned around. Taking his face in her hands, she could see the want in his eyes, the need that was almost an ache. They never even made it to the bed, though it was just feet away. When they exhausted themselves, Chad pulled the pillows down, and the comforter, so they could just stay where they had made love.

He held her, brushing his fingertips along her arm. He spoke into the darkness hesitantly, "When do you have to leave?"

"Well, no later than eleven. But you don't have to get up—"

"Don't be ridiculous. I'm getting up."

"You'll go back to bed?"

"Probably." He shifted onto his side, wrapping her in his arms. "I don't want you to leave."

"I know. I don't want to leave either, but..." They both knew she had Cassie, and a job.

"This is harder for me than it is for you," Chad complained. "You have no idea what you do to me. You make me crazy." She filled a void inside him, and when she left, it ripped him apart anew.

"Chad..." she began, but she knew there was nothing to say. She could hardly bear to leave him, too. "I'll look at the tour dates. And you'll be done by June, right?"

"Yeah." He sighed. They both lay heavyhearted, knowing that with the sunrise tomorrow, a goodbye waited that neither of them wished to say.

BETH LAY WITH CHAD until nearly eleven, skipping a shower to have more time next to him. He walked her to the car without talking. When they reached it, Beth leaned against it. Chad rubbed her arms, looking off beyond to the horizon, trying to find the strength to let her leave. "You'll be safe?"

She nodded, slipping her arms around his waist and laying her head on his chest. He brought his arms around the woman he knew he would miss with every breath and laid his cheek on her head. The couple stood like that for several minutes, until she shifted and pulled her head away. He peered down at her, his brow furrowed. He brushed a hair from her face gently, and then bent to kiss her, long and deep. He thought about being with her like this at the gas station. But then, it had been the fever of passion. Now, it was the pain of goodbye. He finally stepped back and opened the car door for her. She slid into her seat, and he closed the door. She rolled down the window. "I'll call you tonight."

He simply nodded. She reached out and squeezed his hand, and he gave her a small smile. He stepped back and she drove away. Peeking back in her rearview mirror, she could see him striding in the direction of the buses, his hands shoved in his pockets, his head bent against the wind.

"YOU'RE QUIET TODAY," Beth's coworker, Peggy, commented. They were set up at opposite ends of long kitchen tables, working on preparing the day's lunch.

"That's just because she's exhausted from screwing her rock star boyfriend all weekend," Cali interjected as she scooped fruit.

"Cali!" Beth cried out reproachfully, waving the frozen chicken patty she had in her hand. "You know it's not all about that."

"So, you're saying you're not hot for his bod?"

"Well, I didn't say that," she returned, getting red in the face. Everyone laughed.

"Just ignore her," Linda asserted, indicating Cali. "But give us all the juicy details."

"Okay. When I got there Friday night—" She mentally deleted the scene in the shower, albeit doing a quick replay in her mind. "We—"she fast-forwarded through the scene on the way to the bus "—played some cards with Roger and David's wife, Cheri. Chad and I kicked their butts."

"And...?"

"And Saturday he wanted to go on a road trip to a secret location, which ended up being a winery on top of a cliff overlooking the Missouri River. It was beautiful."

"Just the two of you? No bodyguards or entourage?"

She sighed. "Just he and I. It was a gorgeous day, and when we hiked to the top, the owner had opened up just for us. He was a Trapped Under Ice fan."

"That sounds fantastic," Linda commented dreamily.

"It was. But let's talk about something else. This is just making me miss him more. Oh, but there's one more thing I have to tell you. At Saturday night's concert, I got to sing with Chad and Roger."

"What?" Linda set her scoop down.

Peggy's jaw dropped, but she managed to get out a, "You're kidding?"

"We've been here over an hour, and you just now inform us you got to go on stage and sing with one of the hottest bands in the country, probably in the world?" Cali queried caustically. "You just fail to mention it?"

"It was pretty cool."

"Beth, can I ask you something?" Peggy ventured.

"S-sure," she returned, uneasy about what might come.

"What's Roger like?"

She laughed. "He's...he's a male Cali."

"No way," Cali burst out.

They all laughed. "You're kidding?" Peggy said again.

"Nope. He's irreverent, says what's on his mind. He's funny, cute, and when you get right down to it, he's a great guy."

"Oh, he does sound like me."

"Yeah," joked Linda, "especially the irreverent part. Shh. The Boss Lady's coming."

"Girls, you don't have very much fruit cupped. Am I going to have to separate you two?" This was a common threat as Beth and Cali could be a handful at times.

"No, Boss Lady. We'll be good." Beth saluted comically, but when her boss turned around, Cali hit her square in the forehead with a grape. "Ouch!" she couldn't help but exclaim. The other girls burst out laughing and Cali tried to look innocent.

"Everything okay?" The Boss Lady raised her eyebrows.

"Yeah, fine," Beth returned, but when the B.L., as they sometimes referred to her, turned back around, Beth pointed to her eyes and to Cali, giving her the universal "I'm watching you," signal.

Linda and Peggy sniggered and the Boss Lady sighed. It was going to be one of those days.

CHAPTER NINETEEN

It was about a week before Chad was going to fly Beth out to New York City for the weekend, and she was getting excited.

"So, let me get this right," Cali was saying, "your daughter is going on a weekend retreat, and you're flying to New York to get laid. Anybody else see something wrong with this?"

"You think all we do is hop in bed together, don't you?"

"No. You break it up sometimes with a concert or two. But that's as good as sex for you anyway, isn't it?"

Beth flicked her with a dish towel. Luckily it was about time for the kids to come through the lunch line, so their conversation was cut short as Beth opened the serving window of the kitchen.

They had doled out lunch to the kindergarteners, and Beth was pulling out more food for the first graders when she heard Cali say under her breath, "Well, I'll be damned."

"Cal." Beth checked around for the Boss Lady. "You're gonna get us both in—" She stopped short, seeing finally what Cali was staring at. At the end of the lunch line was either a very tall first-grader in a black T-shirt instead of a uniform shirt, or Chad. "Well, I'll be damned," she whispered, her lips sliding into a huge smile.

Out of the corner of her eye, she saw Linda elbow Peggy, and they both stopped cleaning the equipment to check out the rock star. The freckled-faced little girl in front of Beth cleared her throat. "Oh. I'm sorry, sweetie." She handed the little girl a lunch tray. "Have a nice lunch." She resisted the urge to launch herself over the counter and tackle Chad in front of the kids. As she watched, she saw the little boy next to him craning his neck up to see Chad better.

"Hey," the boy asked now, "aren't you the guy from Trapped Under Ice?"

Chad bent his long legs, crouching until he was almost at eyelevel with the kid. He stuck out his hand. "Hi. I'm Chad Evans. What's your name?"

"Cool!" The first-grader's eyes lit up. "I'm Michae-Mike Sully. Who's he?" Michael whispered, pointing at Pete.

"Oh. That's just Pete. He's a good guy," Chad added, seeing the uncertain look on the boy's face.

Pete smiled uncomfortably at the kid. "I feel like we've entered the land of midgets," he grumbled.

Chad smiled glowingly at Beth, following his new friend in line at the same time.

"So, how comes you're here?" the boy inquired.

He bent down again. "Can you keep a secret?" Michael nodded solemnly. Chad whispered to him, "I have a thing for one of the lunch ladies."

"Which one?" Michael whispered loudly.

"Mrs. Donovan, the one passing out the trays."

"Good thing 'cause she's a nice one. Pretty, too," Michael added.

"Yeah, I think so, too." He smiled at her again. It felt so good to see her. "You're not going to hit on my girl now, are ya?"

"No, sir, Mr. Chad."

"Good. Let's shake on it." Michael soberly put his tiny hand into Chad's and gave it a sturdy shake. "Now, will you show me the ropes when we get up to the front?"

"Sure, Mr. Chad. I'd be happy to."

"Thanks. I like you, Mike Sully."

They reached the front of the line where a teacher's aide was checking off names. She was spellbound. "Wow. You're even taller in person."

"Y-yes." He was never quite sure about how to respond to some of the strange things people said to him. "Umm...in the office they said I could pay you for a lunch?"

She snapped out of her daze. "Oh yes." She started to mark something down but then looked up confused. "You're going to eat here?"

"That was the idea..." he responded, at a loss.

"Oh yes, of course. It's two dollars."

He handed her a five. "I'll just pay for my buddy here, too, then." He gestured over his shoulder with his thumb to indicate Pete, who nodded at her.

"Okay." She handed him back the change. "Now, you just go up there—"

"I'm showing him the ropes, Ms. Crenshaw," Michael announced proudly.

"Well. Are you? That's a good boy, Michael. Thank you."

Michael helped him to retrieve milk from the cooler, but as they got closer to where they would receive their trays, Chad had eyes only for Beth.

When he reached her, she was absolutely beaming. "What are you doing here?"

"Our concert was canceled. Isn't that great? I can stay tonight."

"Really?" she returned with equal enthusiasm. They just stared at each other for a moment, the line backing up.

"Why don't you just kiss him and get it over with?" Cali prompted.

Beth leaned over the counter and kissed him. His lips felt unbelievably good.

"Ahem. There are children present," said the Boss Lady, who was called from her office in a rush of excitement to see their celebrity guest.

"Oh." Chad glanced down at Michael, who was staring at him in wonder. "Sorry about that, Mike."

"Noo problemo, Mr. Chad," Michael responded with a grin.

Chad reached down to ruffle his hair.

"Well, you guys don't have to eat out there..." Beth started tentatively, looking at the Boss Lady.

"They can eat in my office."

"Just go through the door at that end." Beth pointed toward the corner of the room.

"Here, Beth, I'll take over for you," Peggy offered graciously.

"Thanks, Pegs," she whispered, "you're the best."

"He's cute." She giggled.

"I know. Hey, Pete." Beth gave the older man's arm a squeeze.

"Good to see you, Beth," he answered warmly.

She walked them back to the office, where the Boss Lady gave them their privacy.

"You're really going to eat cafeteria food?" Beth questioned.

"Is something wrong with it?"

"No. No. It's really quite good."

"Okay, then. I'm going to eat it."

She winced. "I've got to go help, but I'll come back."

"No, go. I understand."

"Okay." She left hurriedly but came back a few seconds later and grabbed the sides of his face to pull him in for a kiss. "I've missed you," she murmured with feeling. "Sorry about that, Pete," she apologized to the bodyguard who was busily eating his chicken patty.

He quickly swallowed his food. "No problem, Beth. Hey, this stuff is really good."

"I'm glad you like it." She gave Chad one final, lingering look before going back to work.

Beth stepped in and took over the dishwashing, which had begun to stack up in her absence. After he finished eating, Chad wandered out to observe the whirlwind of activity in the kitchen. As he watched, it seemed to him like a kind of ballet. Each of the girls was good at anticipating what the other needed. They moved in tandem in the small area. They read each other's minds much like he and Roger did on stage.

Twenty minutes later, hot, sweaty, and steamy, Beth glanced up to see Chad across the room, leaning against the wall with his long legs crossed in front of him, his arms crossed over his chest, and an amused smile on his lips.

"What?" she questioned, smiling and brushing a stray hair out of her face with the back of her hand.

"Nothing. Nothing. I'm just enjoying watching you."

She sprayed off another dish. "You're weird, you know?"

"Yes, I know." He looked up as Cali entered with an armload of dirty dishes. "Hey."

"Hey, yourself." She continued over to the dishwashing area and set her load down on the counter. "What's he doing?" she asked Beth, jerking her head in Chad's direction.

Beth looked at him for a moment. "Watching me do the dishes."

"That's weird."

"I know," he responded, overhearing their conversation as Beth said at the same time, "He knows."

"Geez," Cali said with a smile. "We're going to need the sprayer to hose you two down in a couple of minutes." She turned to walk away, and Beth aimed the sprayer at her back. She winked at Chad, who quickly removed himself from the line of fire.

"Hey!" Cali screamed when the spray of water hit her.

Beth put a hand to her mouth and gave her friend a wide-eyed, innocent look. "Oops!"

"That's enough, you two!" the Boss Lady called.

"She started it!" the girls yelled simultaneously.

"I tell you—" the Boss Lady looked to Chad for sympathy "—these two about give me fits."

"I can see that." He laughed. "I may have been distracting Beth," he confessed. "I'll just go back to the office and be a good boy now."

"Yeah. I'm watching you, Evans," Cali responded.

The boss rolled her eyes. "You just get out there and clean the steam table."

About fifteen minutes later, Peggy came back and grabbed the sprayer from Beth. "Get out of here."

"What? Oh no, Peggy. I can't—"

"We've got it under control. You guys don't get enough time with each other as it is. Now get out of here."

"I owe you big time." Beth gave her a big squeeze and then practically ran to the office. "I'm out of here," she announced to Chad, who sat in a rolling chair with his elbows on the desk and chin in his hands, wearing an extremely bored expression.

He looked up and a wide grin split his face. "Great!"

"Let me just hang up my apron." She entered a back storage room to hang her wet apron on a hook. Suddenly, she felt arms around her waist. Chad, who had followed her, couldn't resist a quick kiss. He found himself in a short, narrow hallway where dozens of colorful aprons hung on hooks behind the door.

He buried his face in her hair, breathing in her fragrance, mingled as it was with the smell of bleach and laundry detergent in the small laundry/storage room. She spun to face him, his hands grasping two of the hooks above her head.

"I missed you," he declared simply, pressing her up against the cinder block wall. Their lips found each other.

"Umm...I'm all wet," she murmured apologetically between kisses.

"I don't care." He moved his hand behind her head and pulled her into another kiss. All at once, the couple found themselves being smashed behind the door as someone entered the storage room.

"Ahem," Linda broadcasted loudly, coming in to retrieve some storage containers from a back shelf. They guiltily moved apart and gave Linda an awkward smile as she strolled out with an empty whipped cream container in hand, sliding Beth an amused look.

Beth grabbed Chad's hand as the door closed behind her. "Let's get out of here. Where's Pete?"

"He's out back smoking a cigarette."

"Okay." She grabbed her jacket and headed into the kitchen. All of the girls were gathered, no doubt discussing them. "Thank you, guys, so much." She gave them all a hug in turn.

Chad reached out to shake their hands. "Nice meeting you all."

Before they knew it, they were peeling out of the parking lot in Beth's car, Pete in the back.

"Whoo! This is great. I feel like I'm playing hooky. Where to?"

"Well, we can't check into the hotel yet...I thought I should get a hotel with Cassie and all..."

"Good idea. Well, do you want to go back to my place and I can get changed into some real clothes?" She was wearing an old T-shirt and jeans.

"Well, I don't mind what you have on, but if you want to."

"I'd like to at least get into something dry."

"I can't believe how hard you work. Some of those pans seem like they're really heavy."

"They are, but it's no harder than what you do on stage."

Chad reflected on this. It was quite a workout entertaining for two hours under the bright lights.

"Oh shit!" Beth cried.

"What?"

"Oh." She moaned. "I told a friend of mine I'd bartend for her tonight. She works as a teacher's aide at the school, but moonlights as a bartender at a place in a little town not far from here. She had carpal tunnel surgery and was worried about asking her boss for the time off, so I said I'd fill in for her. Oh, man-n-n."

"What do you know about bartending?"

"Nothing. But I figured, small town, I could hand out beers and pour the occasional shot of whiskey. And Kim gave me this." She picked up a book sitting on the console between their seats, handing it to him.

"'The Bartender's Little Black Book,'" he read. "I see. Well, lucky for you, I've partaken of most of the concoctions in this book, so I'd be happy to help you."

"Are you sure?" she asked doubtfully, pulling up to a red light.

Pete poked his head between them. "Let's see. Hang out with you, at a bar, where alcohol is readily accessible...doesn't seem like Chad's gig at all." He snorted sarcastically.

Chad shoved Pete's head back, at the same time saying, "I'll be with you and that's exactly where I want to be."

"I love you."

"Yeah, that's another thing," Pete began, sticking his head between them as before. "I don't get that." They both pushed him back and kissed.

CHAPTER TWENTY

The threesome pulled into the garage of a two-story house, much like the other houses in the neighborhood, except, perhaps, for its interesting roofline.

"I wasn't expecting you, so you might as well know now that neatness is not my strong point."

"Don't worry about me. You remember my bedroom."

"Yes. I was speaking more to Pete," she joked.

The men followed her into the house. Chad felt uneasy at first about entering what had been another man's home with Beth. But the interior of the house was all her, light and airy, while at the same time, warm, inviting, a little quirky, and pretty. Despite what she said, the house was not messy. It definitely had a lived-in air—a few things here and there left where they didn't belong—but that added to its charm and comfort. The floors were light wood, and there were a lot of windows whose shades were open to a view of a semi-wooded lot. Several Monet prints hung on the walls, and a large Tuscan countryside tapestry hung from a wrought iron bar above the couch. A brass fire hydrant and weathervane spoke to her more whimsical side, but the black accents everywhere gave it all a touch of class.

Chad took in his surroundings.

"This is great, Beth," Pete said. "I love the layout."

"Thanks. We looked at so many houses, which basically all had the same design...we wanted something a little different." She was watching Chad.

"The trees are nice, too," Pete added, peering out the window.

She gazed out wistfully. "Coming from Missouri, we missed the trees. I think this is the only neighborhood with mature trees in Central Illinois. You missed it, flying in, but the drive here, from just about anywhere, is mile after mile of flat farmland, not a hill or tree to be found." Chad remained silent, casually scanning some pictures over the fireplace. "You guys make yourselves at home and I'll change as quickly as I can. Can I get you anything to drink?"

"No, I'm good."

"Chad?"

"Huh? Oh, no thanks. I'm okay."

"All right, I'll be right back then." She gave him a quizzical look before heading up the stairs.

PETE'S FACE BECAME stern. "You need to tell her."

"Shh, Pete! She'll hear." Chad listened at the bottom of the stairs, holding a hand up, until he heard the water turn on. "I'm going to tell her."

"When? She deserves to know about these notes you keep getting. And the other day, when we found your guitar gutted."

"Don't remind me." He groaned.

"You know, she could be in danger, too."

"Don't you think I know that?" he snapped, and then realizing he'd been too loud, he moved over to listen at the stairs again. "I'm not going to let anything happen to her."

"You can't guarantee that."

He ran his hand through his hair and paced back and forth. "I just need more time. I really like her, and I don't want to scare her off."

Pete put a hand on his arm. "I know you like her, son. I like her, too. That's why I think you ought to tell her. And besides, you'd never forgive yourself if something happened to her."

"I'll tell her. I swear, man. I just need a little more time is all." He craned his neck toward the stairwell. "The shower's off. We need to stop talking about this."

"I'm not gonna wait forever. If you don't tell her soon, I will."

"Okay. I promise. I will."

Pete sighed, sitting on the couch, but Chad wandered over to the mantle. He took down a wrought iron picture frame containing a photo that had to be of Paul. He looked like the kind of guy you could throw a couple of beers back with. The image was of a handsome, boyish face, framing thick, dark hair and kind eyes. Chad picked up a smaller frame next to it displaying a black-and-white photograph of Beth and Paul and an infant Cassie. Paul was peering down at the baby, but Beth was gazing at him with a face clearly portraying the love she had for her husband. He set it down as if it held an electrical current.

"Hey, look at these," Pete called from the couch. "Cassie looks just the same as she did when she was a baby." He held a thick scrapbook in his hands with colorfully captioned pages and picture upon picture of Cassie.

The two men were still absorbed in examining it when Beth reappeared. She was putting an earring backing in as she glided in. She had done a good job of restoring her hair back to the style the steamy dish room stole and had put on a fresh layer of lip gloss.

"Oh, you're looking at those." She laughed.

Pete glanced up. "Yeah. Did you scrap these?"

"Yes. I haven't done any in a long while, but I used to like doing that."

"They're great."

"Thanks. So, do you guys want to go check in at the hotel or...?"

"Yeah. That might be good," Chad answered, closing the scrapbook and standing. "We left our bags at the front desk earlier, because they hadn't cleaned the rooms yet."

"Okay, where are you staying?"

"Actually—" the two men exchanged glances and chuckled "—we're staying in Normal."

"Oh yes. The twin cities. Bloomington/Normal, Illinois."

"Sure, Minneapolis/St. Paul ain't got nothing on you," Pete teased.

"And, we noticed...you're not a resident of Normal are you?"

"Yeah, well, normal's overrated. Let's get out of here."

As they sped down the main thoroughfare minutes later, she pointed out landmarks.

"This area of buildings on your right is called Corporate South. It's where most of Illinois Insurance computer analysts' work is done. And that building beyond it is the regional office building for Illinois Insurance."

Chad wondered if Paul worked here, or at the big, brown corporate office building they passed on the way to the school earlier in the day. As he stared off into space, he felt Beth's hand on his. "Are you okay?"

"Yeah," he responded, forcing a smile. "Just tired, I guess."

"Of course, you are. Maybe you should lie down for a while when we get back to the hotel room."

"Yeah," he repeated vaguely. "Maybe I should." He stared out the window again and became silent.

Pete stepped up and filled the void, asking all kinds of questions about the city, keeping Beth occupied until they got to the hotel.

She was relieved Chad grabbed her hand when walking from the car to the hotel lobby.

"Mrs. Donovan," the clerk behind the desk called.

"Why, Amy, I didn't know you worked here," Beth exclaimed, recognizing the cute blonde behind the counter as one of Cassie's classmates.

"I just started. It's with the work program, so I get out of school early." She whispered, "Is that him?"

Beth peeked over her shoulder to where Chad was leaning his hand against the mantle, staring into the depths of the fake fireplace. "Yes," she responded absentmindedly.

"Way to go, Mrs. D."

She realized, with embarrassment, what it must look like, checking into a hotel room in the middle of the day with her boyfriend.

As she stood at a loss for words, Pete came to her rescue. "I've got two rooms for Pete Harris, please?"

She strolled over and touched Chad's back. He was so absorbed in his thoughts, he jumped. "Is anything wrong, babe?"

He put a hand on either of her shoulders. "Nothing a few minutes alone with you wouldn't cure."

The corners of her lips lifted; she was glad to see the light back in his eyes. "Well, we'll just have to see what we can do about that."

When they got to their floor, Pete searched Chad's room. "You can never be too certain," the older man told Beth with a smile before heading to his room, which was connected to theirs.

Chad had already slipped into the room and flopped onto the bed. He lay with his eyes closed and arms folded under his head.

Maybe he is just exhausted. She stood, feeling awkward, inside the doorway. The room was spacious, with a king-sized bed, but fairly nondescript.

"Come here, babe," he murmured, raising his arm.

She crept up the bed next to him and laid her head on his chest. He rubbed her arm idly. After several minutes, she commented, "It's too bad you're so tired..."

Perhaps hearing something in her voice, he slit his eyes open and lifted his head off the pillow a little to look at her. "It is?"

"Yes." She sat up, walking her fingers up his chest. "'Cause I was thinking..."

"Yes?" he growled sexily.

"We never did finish our shower—"

Before she could complete the thought, he rolled out of bed and rushed into the bathroom. She smiled as she heard the water starting. When she entered the bathroom, she saw his clothes tossed haphazardly under the sink. She undressed slowly, building the anticipation, and climbed in behind him, grabbing him from behind, as she did in his dressing room. He turned to look at her, his hair dripping wet, the water running down his shoulders, his face serious. She began to kiss his chest. The combination of the feel of his skin and the warmth of the water running over her lips and into her mouth was tantalizing. They made love slowly, sensually. Whenever the water cooled, he would reach back and turn the temperature up, and the renewed warmth would rush over them, reawakening their urgency.

THEY HAD DINNER WITH Cassie at a nearby restaurant Pete checked out beforehand. There were a few stares and some whispering, but since Trapped Under Ice wasn't playing in town, most people chalked it up to a phenomenal resemblance. The mood was lighthearted, and Cassie seemed glad to see Chad again.

After dinner, Beth kissed Cassie goodbye, and she and her two male companions piled into the car for the short trip to Wapella.

Beth had visited the bar before with her lunch lady friends, so she knew the somewhat gruff owner, Chuck. He and everybody else in the place, most of whom seemed to be older farmers, gave Chad the once-over. They didn't often have long-haired strangers in the bar, but they left him and Pete alone.

She set at once to the task of washing glasses and cleaning behind the bar, and after a while, the owner seemed satisfied enough to go back to his office to do some paperwork.

Around eight-thirty, a large group of younger people strolled in, raising the volume about a hundred percent. They pounded quarters into a jukebox, which Chad commented earlier featured absolutely no Trapped Under Ice tunes. Country music was blaring, and by nine-thirty the group was well on its way to being liquored up. While Pete stopped at two, Chad pounded away the beers at a steady pace, eyeing his fellow bar mates with suspicion.

Beth was leaning across the bar, having a conversation with Chad, when a particularly loud customer whistled for her. Chad stared at him darkly as she sauntered down the length of the bar, taking her time, irritated at being summoned like some kind of dog.

"Yes, sir," she intoned icily. "What can I do for you?"

"Umm, baby, I'm guessing from your looks, a whole lot." His friends jeered. "Nah, I'm just kiddin'," he stated, backing off. "Where's Kim tonight?"

"She had carpal tunnel surgery today."

"Hum." He threw a knowing look at his companions. "I wonder what kind of repetitive motion she was doing." His group laughed again as he made an obscene gesture.

She chose to ignore his rudeness, figuring he was just trying to get her riled up. "Is there anything you needed?" she asked again tiredly.

"Yeah, babe. Get me a couple of shots of Wild Turkey."

Chad sat at the other end of the bar clenching and unclenching his fists, getting madder by the second over the way the jerk was treating Beth. She poured the customer his drinks and turned around to put his money in the cash register. As if in slow motion, Chad saw him stand on the foot rail of the bar and reach over to grab her ass.

Before anyone knew what was happening, he crossed the room, snatched one of the guy's friends by the back of the jacket, and tossed him out of the way. With his pals standing around in a tight circle, Chad pulled the guy off the bar, grabbed his shirt front, and reached back to deliver a punch to his face, full-force.

Beth turned around, ready to ream the guy out, only to see Chad come flying in from nowhere.

Pete, who had stepped across the street to get a pack of cigarettes, entered the bar just as Chad's elbow was pulled back to deliver the first blow. "Oh shit! Here we go again."

Beth scrambled to gather all the beer bottles off the bar so they could not be used as weapons, which infuriated several of the men now jumping Chad. She searched for Pete and saw him pushing his way through the crowd, yanking guy after guy out of the fray as he made his way over. She saw Chad's nose was already bloodied and one guy was holding his head back by his hair while another guy got ready to punch him. She launched herself across the bar and latched onto the assailant's arm, hoping at least her weight would slow the punch down. Just then, there was a loud shot. Everyone froze. Chuck was standing in the entrance to the back hall, holding what appeared to be a starter pistol, still smoking, over his head.

"What the hell is going on here?"

Chad and a number of others started yelling out accusations. Chuck waved his arms, still holding the gun.

"All right. All right. Enough! Beth, you and your asshole boyfriend need to get out of here."

The competitors stared at each other for a couple of seconds as if unwilling to quit, then there was the general noise of people releasing their hold on others and straightening their clothes. Chad's opponents smirked at him but seemed disappointed they weren't going to get a chance to do more damage to his face. For Chad's part, he appeared to be holding back on his anger with a strand of two-pound test line.

Beth slid, rather ungracefully, to the floor on her side of the bar. She grabbed her purse and jacket from a shelf and exited. As she passed Chuck, she murmured, "I'm so sorry, Chuck."

"That's okay, Beth," he mumbled, almost being kind. "It's not your fault," he added loud enough for Chad to hear, his eyes blazing. Pete was already escorting him out the front door. She slid past where people were picking up stools and broken glass.

"Do you want me to stay and pick up at least?"

Chuck looked past her, out the window where he could see Chad wildly gesturing at Pete as he paced back and forth. "I think you better just get out of here, Beth."

She turned around again, feeling the eyes of everyone on her. She skirted the small crowd trying to bring the guy who grabbed her back to consciousness.

When she stepped out into the parking lot, she could tell Pete and Chad were arguing. They stopped and stared at her, their breath turning to frost in the particularly cool March air. "Are you okay?" she asked Pete.

"Yeah. I'm all right," he replied brusquely, obviously still ticked at Chad for starting the fight.

She turned her eyes on Chad. He looked pretty messed up, and her heart went out to him. For a minute, she thought about going to him, but then anger washed over her in a wave. She spun on her heal and stormed off in the direction of the car.

"Beth..." she heard him say behind her, but she just got in the car and slammed the door shut.

"Don't you say anything," he warned Pete.

CHAPTER TWENTY-ONE

T hey got into the car, and for the first fifteen minutes of the trip, there was complete silence, except for the sound of Chad drumming on his knee. Pete vacillated between wanting the pending fight between them to start, so he could get his two-cents worth in with Chad, and praying it wouldn't, because he would feel uncomfortable being witness to it. But after a while, much to his relief, it seemed as if they had totally forgotten he was there.

Beth stared stonily out the front window. Chad gazed out the side window, with one knee bent, leaning against the door; his other leg was as straight as it could be in such confined quarters. He would occasionally glance over at her and appear as if he was going to say something, then seemed to think better of it and looked away. Finally, he caught her eye.

"Beth, the guy's hand was on your ass."

"I'm perfectly aware his hand was on my ass, seeing as it was my ass his hand was on," she sniped. Another several seconds of silence were punctuated by the sound of his fingers thumping up and down on his blue jeans. With a suddenness that jarred both men, she said, "I mean, didn't you think I could take care of myself? My God, I put a man in the hospital in St. Louis with a broken nose and a concussion. I'm perfectly capable of taking care of myself." In truth, the whole fight had her rattled. Besides what happened in St. Louis, she had never witnessed a fight before, let alone been a participant in one.

"Oh, okay, Beth," he muttered, letting a thread of sarcasm leak into his voice. "So, what exactly were you going to do?" he challenged.

"I guess we'll never know, because I didn't even have a chance to react."

Another uncomfortable silence ensued. She glanced sideways at him for a moment, and noticed his nose had started to bleed again. He became aware of it at the same time. "Here," she said, handing him some tissues from the middle console. After a few minutes, she added in a much softer tone, "Are you okay?"

"Yeah," he answered, the word laced with self-loathing. He bent his head back to try to stop the bleeding. "I'm sorry, Beth. It's just, when I saw him touching you, something exploded in me."

PETE FELT LIKE ADDING, "Something always explodes in you," but kept his mouth shut. He had asked himself many times why he stayed with the hot-headed rocker, and it always boiled down to the fact that beneath all of his bullshit, Chad was a good guy.

"THAT GUY GOT WHAT HE had coming," Chad added, with a little bit of the anger they saw earlier.

"Well, I'm not going to argue the point. But if we went around punching everybody who pissed us off, we'd all have broken noses and bruised knuckles. It doesn't solve anything."

"It made me feel better," he replied with a childlike air.

"Chad!" she spouted, exasperated.

"All right. All right. I let my temper get away with me, and I'm sorry. If I had it to do again, I would walk over and say something to him, let him take the first swing, then deck him."

She sighed. "I'm not sure we're getting anywhere here." But her initial fury had left her. They pulled into the hotel parking lot. "Has it stopped bleeding?"

He sniffed. "Yeah. I think so."

She turned to Pete apologetically. "Pete, are you sure you're all right?"

HE WANTED TO SAY WHEN he signed on he expected to protect Chad if someone attacked him, not defend him when he attacked somebody else, but gazing into her eyes, he just couldn't do it. So, even though he had a cut across one hand and he was pretty sure he pulled something in his left shoulder, he said, "I'm fine, Beth."

They made their way up to their adjoining rooms. Pete opened his door. "If there's anyone lurking in your room, I'm sure Chad can take care of them," he said with his last bit of resentment.

Chad reached out and touched his shoulder. "Hey man, I'm sorry."

Pete turned to him, his eyes blazing, but when he saw the hang-dog expression on Chad's face, he hesitated. They locked gazes for a minute, something passing between them, and then he opened his door and went inside without saying a word.

Maybe I should have said something; maybe I should have warned her. Pete sighed. *But when he looks at me that way and I see how lost he is, I just can't do it. It would be like kickin' a dog that continually peed on the carpet. It would only hurt him and probably serve no purpose.*

"She's his only hope," Pete said aloud to the empty room, "and he's going to blow it."

CHAD LEANED AGAINST the door with his eyes shut, breathing a deep sigh of relief. He sensed Pete's urge to tell Beth everything, every fight he'd been in, his DUI, all of the awful things the old Chad did. But now that he had her in his life, he wasn't going to stray down that path again.

Then, why the fight tonight?

He suddenly felt tired beyond bearing.

"Chad, are you okay?"

Yeah. Now that's the question, isn't it?

He could hear his father's voice inside his head like a repeating rifle. "I'm fine." He sighed in a way that indicated he was anything but. He stumbled over to the bed and fell into it.

She lumbered over, trancelike, and stood over him, saying at last, "I have to go."

His eyes popped open. "No. Not yet." He grabbed her hand and sat up at the end of the bed. "Come here," he pleaded, pulling her into his lap. "I'm so sorry, Beth. I should have let you handle it. I shouldn't have gone berserk. I was a complete and utter ass. Will you forgive me?"

She pushed the hair away from his face with her fingertips, sighing. "I already did. We all make mistakes, Chad."

A wave of relief washed over him; the grace Beth offered floored him. He reached behind her neck and craned his until their lips met. He drew her in, little by little, taking her under.

AS SHE FELT THE INITIAL slide of surrender, a resounding "yes" pulsed through her brain. Yes, I love him. Yes, I need him. His breath tasted pleasantly of beer as he twisted to lay her on the bed. He kissed her neck, his hand sliding down to touch the soft skin on her upper chest, and he started to unbutton her blouse.

"Please, don't go tonight," he breathed.

He made it all too easy to agree. His hand was underneath her shirt now, caressing her. She resisted, battling against the tide threatening to sweep her away. "I have to go."

HE COULDN'T SAY GOODBYE to her again. Not tonight. His hand traveled over the smooth skin of her waist, over jeans covering the front of her thigh. It stopped at her knee, and then moved to the back, moving slowly over the back of her thigh. He could feel her heat.

"OHH," SHE MOANED. "I have to go." She rolled away from him, nearly toppling off the other side of the bed, and stood. "I'm sorry." She fought to explain, to find the reason despite the blood rushing to her head. "It's just, Cassie's at an impressionable age and I don't want her to think it's okay—" he stood and crossed to her and put his hands on her hips "—I mean for people of her age—"

He moved a finger to her lips. "Sh-sh-sh. I understand." Having his finger there, it was as if he couldn't resist. He traced her lips, and she closed her eyes, hands freezing midway through buttoning her blouse. With a show of willpower, she took a large step backward. He moved toward her.

"Nah-ah-ah." She took another step back, knocking into the dresser. She smiled at him. "You stay over there."

He complied, though his face was tense with the ache to have her. She retrieved her jacket from on top of the dresser and slid it over her shoulders. He was at the door and had it opened a little. "Let me walk you out."

She hesitated. "Okay," she finally relented. She bit her lower lip. This was going to take every ounce of restraint she had.

THEY MEANDERED DOWN the hall together hand in hand. They entered the elevator, and Chad stared straight ahead until the doors closed. Then, he whipped around, pressing her against the back wall, kissing her with mind-numbing intensity. When the elevator came to a stop, he pulled away, leaving her breathless and wanting more. He smiled, knowing he affected her the same way she affected him.

When they got to the car, she leaned against her door for a minute with her head down. She was searching for words. "It was really nice having you here...getting to have the girls meet you..."

"Getting in a bar brawl."

"That I could have done without, but it's behind us." She peered up at him as if to memorize his face until the next time. "Thank you for coming. And thank you for surprising me."

Her smile cracked, lips showing an almost imperceptible quiver, and he could see tears in her eyes.

She swallowed. "These goodbyes get harder every time."

"I know, but we'll be together in less than a week in New York City."

Beth's eyes brightened. "That's right. I'd almost forgotten." They sat for a while without saying anything. She sighed. "Well, I guess I better go. If Cali catches me yawning tomorrow, I'll never hear the end of it. She already thinks all we do is have sex."

"Well, that's not true. We played cards once."

She swatted him on the arm. "Very funny." She got into the car. "See you in New York."

"See ya."

He watched her drive away, thinking it was far too often he sat watching her taillights fading into the distance.

BETH CAME OFF THE FLIGHT still flying high. A whole weekend together. She searched the crowd for his face, her heart already beating wildly in anticipation. She scanned the faces, so many people. Maybe he was late. A big, bass voice called out her name. She turned to see a heavy-set, African American man holding a sign with her name on it. He wore a suit and tie, and a little black hat over his graying hair. She couldn't help but feel a little disappointed; Chad said he would see her at the airport.

It'll be just a little while longer, that's all.

Beth crossed to the man, saying as cheerfully as she could, "Hi. I'm Beth Donovan."

The chauffeur took her bag out of her hand, bowed slightly, and extended his arm. "Right this way, Ms. Donovan."

She followed him as he weaved through the crowd and headed toward a pair of sliding glass doors leading to the outside, where a shiny, black limo awaited. The man passed through the doors and set the suitcase down on the sidewalk for a moment to open the door for her, tipping his hat as he did so.

"Thank you." She bent to get in. Suddenly, hands were around her hips, dragging her into the car. She laughed delightedly, "Hey," was all she got in before her mouth was covered with Chad's. He held her on his lap, kissing her, while the limo driver threw the bag into the back.

"It's so good to see you. I'm sorry I didn't come in. I just didn't want to deal with people when...I knew...I'd...be wanting...to kiss you this way." He punctuated each part of his sentence with a kiss.

"Umm, this is better," she agreed, smiling and kissing him back. Finally, she pulled away. "What are you wearing?" He had on a black button-down shirt with a wide collar and a handsomely tailored black suit.

"We've got a club opening tonight. Do you think you could find a dress in an hour?"

CHAD SAT UNEASILY IN a chair outside the dressing room of a high-class shop in the middle of downtown Manhattan. He nodded to an older lady who smiled at him as she returned a dress to a rack nearby, straightening out imagined wrinkles with her hand. He was the only male in the shop, and he was keenly aware of it. He leaned forward, arms resting on his knees, hands between his legs where he twiddled his thumbs. He glanced up at the sound of heels approaching. Beth was gliding toward him wearing an electric-blue strapless number that clung in all the right places.

He rose to his feet, laughing. "Holy shit!" She did a little spin for him. "Check, please?" he joked, his voice squeaking.

She laughed. "I take it you approve?"

"Oh, I more than approve."

"I don't know." She rotated again in front of a set of triple mirrors. "I'd definitely get sent home from school for wearing this," she murmured.

"And that's a bad thing?" he questioned with a growl, pulling her into his arms.

She slapped at his hands. "Hands off. We've got to get going, remember?"

"How mad do you think Roger would be if we, say, just didn't show up?"

"Furious, you little reprobate." She laughed again, disengaging herself from his arms.

"We'll take it." He handed the saleslady a card. "Do you need anything else?"

"Well, she picked out jewelry and shoes and a purse, so I think I'm good. I'm going to pay you back for this with my next check."

"Absolutely not. You wouldn't even need this if you weren't going to the opening with me."

A second saleslady was circling Beth, removing all of the tags with a small, sharp pair of scissors. "I think you're all ready, dear."

Fifteen minutes later, the limo pulled up outside of a new night club. "Just stay there," Chad said. "I'll get your door."

Beth's mouth dropped when she peered out of her window. People were crowded behind roped-off lines and a red carpet led to the club's entrance. Photographers held their cameras poised, ready to snap celebrities' pictures. Before she had time to even take it all in, the door opened and he offered his hand, smiling as he helped her out of the limo. Immediately, lightbulbs began flashing like fireflies on both sides of the carpet.

A reporter shoved a microphone in his face. "Chad, who's your lady friend?"

"This is my girlfriend, Beth Donovan. You may have heard her sing with Roger and me in Kansas City."

For a moment the concentration was taken off Chad as all heads turned to the newcomer. "Ms. Donovan. What's it like dating a rock star?"

"Oh—" she shot Chad a look "—it's full of surprises." His hand on her back, he rushed her down the rest of the carpet without having to field any more questions. They got inside a set of double doors. "Why didn't you tell me this was a red-carpet affair?"

He paused with his hand on the inner door. "Because I thought you might freak out like you're doing now. Believe me, this is the less painful method."

"Just remember, Evans, paybacks are hell." Under her breath, she muttered, "I need a drink."

He simply smiled and opened the next door. "I think I can accommodate you."

The lighting was low, but she could tell the club was already full of people who were milling around with drinks. Chad led her to the bar and found an empty stool for her while he ordered. The rocker handed her a glass of wine and held up his bottle of beer tentatively. "Are you really mad at me?"

She eyed him for a moment, giving him a chance to sweat a little, then clinked her wine glass with his bottle. "I guess I forgive you."

"Good."

Before he could say anything else, a familiar face appeared out of the crowd. "Chad." Stan Mikas clapped him on the shoulder with enthusiasm. "Hi. Beth, isn't it? Nice to see you again." He shook her hand amiably.

"Chad, can I steal you away from this lovely lady for just five minutes? There is someone I promised to introduce you to."

"Stan, can't it wait until Michelle and Roger get here? I don't want Beth to have to sit here alone."

"I'm fine, Chad. Go on."

"Are you sure?"

"I'll just sit here and sip my wine and try to catch my breath. We've been running since I got off the plane. I'll be here when you're finished."

He bent to kiss her. "I'll be right back."

The two men moved off through the crowd, Stan saying, "I don't blame you for not wanting to leave her. She's a knockout."

Chad glanced over his shoulder to where Beth sat alone. She was perched on a high stool, with one foot on the crossbar beneath. The other leg was crossed over the first, that foot bouncing to the beat of the music. With her heels on, her legs looked incredible. She somehow managed to get her short hair up (he would never understand how women did that), and a few wispy tendrils lay invitingly along her neck. No, he wouldn't be leaving her for long.

He did his duty and chatted for a few minutes with some execs from the record label and their wives. After exchanging pleasantries and answering a few questions, he excused himself to return to Beth. He could see her from across the room, sitting in the same position, foot still bouncing. He smiled and watched her as he weaved through the crowd, though his view was cut off from time to time by people crossing in front of him. That was why he didn't notice the woman approaching until the very last second.

"Julie." Her name sounded like a death knell as it came out of his mouth. He paled. He hadn't been expecting to see her here. His eyes shot to Beth at the bar. "What are you doing here?" he inquired darkly.

"Well, last time I looked, this place didn't say 'Chad's' outside," she huffed, her face a mask of haughtiness.

Chad studied her. Julie was even more emaciated than when they went out, and she was little more than a pencil then. She was nearly as tall as he was with her stilettos on, and she still wore her dark hair straight, cut above her shoulders. Her forehead looked even wider now that her face had thinned in-to nearly a point at her chin. She was still pretty, he guessed, in that she had high cheekbones and perfectly arched brows over her wide hazel eyes, but somehow he couldn't help thinking of an alien when he looked at her.

"I guess you heard." Julie shoved a gargantuan diamond ring in his face. "I'm getting married to Edward Julien."

Julien was a prominent New York City politician. Chad hadn't heard and he didn't care. Though, it amused him that soon her name would be Julie Julien.

"You look good," she continued appraisingly when he had nothing to say. "And I can see you've moved on with your life, too." She waved a hand in Beth's direction. "She's pretty." The model paused, running a finger around the rim of her glass while Chad stared at her coldly. Without prefix, she threw her arms around his neck, purring in his ear as she did so. "When she finally wises up and discovers what an ass you are, give me a call. I cheat on Edward all the time, and you were always good in bed." She gave him a squeeze and a kiss on the cheek then strutted away in the opposite direction. He watched her leave, wondering at how ballsy she could be for a woman.

When he turned his attention back to Beth, Chad saw a dark-haired man was leaning on the empty stool next to her and talking to her, his foot resting on the rung of the stool casually. As Chad got closer, he saw her laugh about something the stranger said, and he could feel the anger beginning to boil inside of him.

"I leave for a few minutes, and you just hit on my girl?" he snarled.

The guy threw up his hands in a gesture of innocence. Dwarfed by Chad, he sputtered, trying to convince him of his blamelessness.

"Chad," Beth cut in, "we were just trying to figure out how to get the bartender's attention."

The blood in his veins seemed to burn him from the inside out. "No offense, Beth, but you wouldn't know a guy was coming on to you if he came up to you and licked your palms."

The smaller man finally found his voice. "Dude, I was not hitting on your girlfriend, I swear."

The bartender appeared from out of the blue, saying, "I'm sorry. I wasn't trying to ignore you, it's just so busy. What can I get for you?"

Chad felt foolish. "I guess I'm sorry then. Your drinks are on me."

"Hey, man, no problem." As he passed Chad, he acknowledged in a low voice, "If I had a girl as hot as that, I'd run off any guys I could, too. But I wasn't hitting on her. She's way out of my league." The man left them in an uncomfortable silence. Chad leaned with his back against the bar, chugging his beer.

Beth tried to figure out what had just happened. Chad seemed fine when he left. She saw a woman approach him, and a strange expression crossed his face.

"Who was the girl you were talking to?"

Chad seemed surprised by her question, perhaps relieved she wasn't reaming him out for his actions. "Julie." He took another hit from his bottle. "We dated."

"You dated her?" Beth asked in surprise. The girl was gorgeous. She thought she recognized her. A model? A light dawned. "Wasn't she the model in that perfume ad?"

"That's the one," he muttered.

Beth fiddled with her cocktail napkin. "How long did you date?"

"Three or four months," he replied. He turned around and rested his forearms on the bar. "She's the one 'Jigsaw' is about."

"Jigsaw" was the song that launched them to stardom. A line went through her head: "You left me like a jigsaw puzzle, pieces spread across the floor/And I've lost the picture on the box now/so I can't put myself back together anymore." So, obviously this was someone who meant something to him at one time. After a bit, she inquired, her voice wavering slightly, "So, what did she say to you?"

"She said you were pretty. Then, she offered to sleep with me," he pronounced matter-of-factly. "Bartender, can I get another beer?"

Beth was so shocked she didn't know what to say. She stared at her wine glass, totally taken aback. They sat in silence until the bartender shuffled off. She couldn't help but feel insecure in this environment. Models, politicians, movie stars, and who was she? A lunch lady from the Midwest dressed up in a fancy dress.

"Do you still love her?"

He thought about this. "I'm not sure I ever did. I thought I did, for a while." Chad saw a shadow cross over her face. "But no, I don't love her. To tell you the truth, she makes me sick."

"But sometimes bitterness conceals feelings—"

"Beth," Chad interrupted, taking her hands and looking her in the eyes, "whatever feelings I may have had for that woman at one time, it has nothing to do with you and me."

"Okay." She sighed, unable to hide her relief. Chad hugged her and they held on to each other for a moment.

He drew apart with a wry expression on his face. "Now, are you going to dance with me, or what?"

IT HAD BEEN SO LONG since they'd been together—well, long enough—and she didn't want to let anything interfere with them having a good time tonight. Her lips lifted and she spun off her stool. "Lead the way."

Having cleared things between them, they relaxed and actually ended up having a blast on the dance floor. But after about twenty minutes, a song came on they didn't recognize.

"Argh. You can't dance to this trash," Chad muttered in disgust. "I need to run to the bathroom for a second, anyway."

"Okay, I'll go get us some more drinks. Meet me by the bar. You want a beer?" Chad nodded and they separated.

As she waited for the bartender to bring back the drinks, a young man approached her. "Excuse me. I hope I'm not being too much of a bother, but is that Chad Evans you're with?"

"What?" Beth yelled. "I'm sorry. I can't hear you above this music."

He moved closer to her so he could talk directly into her ear.

"Oh yes. It's Chad Evans."

"I'm a huge fan of Trapped Under Ice. Do you think he would give me his autograph?"

MEANWHILE, CHAD WAS returning from the bathroom. He saw a dark-haired man at the bar lean into Beth intimately.

The guy actually came back to hit on her. It wasn't enough he'd attempted it once, but as soon as he saw Beth alone, he came back to try again. Talk about ballsy.

Chad might have believed the guy's excuse the first time around, but he was not about to be made a fool of now. He tried to talk himself down from the ledge, but he went from zero to sixty in about two seconds. Without saying a word, he marched over to the guy and punched him in the face. A fraction of a second before contact, he had the sudden realization this was not the same guy as before.

Beth screamed as the guy fell into her. "Chad. Stop. He's just a fan wanting an autograph for God's sake." Her voice was shaking. "Oh my God, are you all right?"

"Yeah, yeah, I'm fine," the guy claimed, though he seemed to be trying to appear a lot tougher than he probably felt.

"Shit! I'm sorry, man."

The nightclub owner came over. "What's happening here?"

The fan was brushing himself off. "Nothing. It was just a misunderstanding is all," he avowed, peering at Chad.

The owner glanced at Chad, too. Recognition sparked in his eyes. "You're Chad Evans. A friend told me if you were going to be here tonight, I should get rubber stools. Now I know what he meant." He licked his lips. "Look, we don't want any trouble in here."

Stan bustled up to take charge of things. "There won't be any trouble. Chad was just about to take his lady friend here home, weren't you Chad?"

Chad studied Beth. He could see how upset she was, and he was kicking himself for having done it to her. Yes, their evening was definitely over.

Somehow Stan got the limo to drive up outside. He hustled them into the back, reassuring Chad he would take care of everything. He'd give the guy some tickets or some money or whatever it took, and the club owner, too. He would smooth things over.

CHAPTER TWENTY-TWO

It was a short, silent ride to the apartment Chad kept for whenever he was in town. When he tried to hold her hand, Beth brushed him off. He could see she was on a low simmer, getting closer to a boiling point with each block. When the door closed on his loft apartment, he made an attempt at conversation.

"Beth—"

"Don't say anything, Chad. Just don't say anything. I've got to think. I've got to get out of here for a second." She moved to the door. It got about two inches open before Chad slammed it shut again, his hands on either side of her to keep her from moving. Fire dancing in her eyes, Beth turned on him. "Dammit, Chad, let me out of—"

He kissed her.

She pulled away. "Chad, don't!" she spat angrily, but he kissed her again. She pushed on him. "Chad. Sex is not going to solve our problems." He moved his hands from the door to her back and pulled her into him. "Chad, please." Her voice was weak.

And that was the end of the argument.

BETH WOKE UP NAKED on the couch next to Chad, feeling guilty somehow for giving into him the night before. She extricated herself from his arms and scouted around for her bag, pulling out the clothes she planned for the day. She realized, with regret, she forgot to pack a second bra. Her eyes roamed over the items of clothing flung here and there, searching for the bra from the night before. She saw her dress, one stocking, her heels, and there it was, under Chad's left shoulder. Cursing fate, she pulled on the rest of her clothes. She would have to wait until he woke up.

The morning sun was pouring in the windows, and she crossed the apartment to gaze out at the new day dawning. After a while, she glanced back at him, crammed onto a sofa much shorter than he was. She felt the surge in her heart she went through whenever she observed him.

What am I doing? I'm living in a fantasy world here, sleeping with a rock star and...and what? Would this ever work between them? He on the road, she at home. And what about these fights he was starting? Did she really know what was driving him to do these things? Did she know him at all? After all, the first time they met, he was punching somebody. Maybe that should have been an omen. She sighed. But he did that to help me, so maybe it was a good omen.

Then, there were the other questions. Can I really love a man again? Maybe this is only an attraction, like Cali says, simply two people who are hot for each other. Her heart was muddled. Then why do the feelings I have for him terrify me so? She peered at him again, alone on the couch. Maybe I should just end this. We're so different, he and I. I should just save myself the pain. But the very thought made her feel sick and caused tears to come to her eyes.

How odd that, at a time like this, Beth's thoughts turned to Paul. It was then the tears really came, coursing down her cheeks. Oh, God, Paul. How I wish you were here sometimes. I counted on your advice so much. She started laughing through her tears, realizing how asinine it was for her to ask her late husband for advice on her new boyfriend. I'm freakin' losing my mind. She wiped furiously at her tears. Would Paul have liked Chad? Her immediate thought was, no. They were so different. But wouldn't he see the same things in Chad I do? How funny he is, and how sweet, when he's not punching things. And there was that unexplainable something, the pull he had on her heart. It was the age-old dilemma.

A line from a song drifted across her mind, The Clash singing, "Should I stay, or should I go, now," She knew she had a decision to make, and it wasn't going to be easy.

CHAD WOKE UP IN HIS apartment on the couch, naked and alone, covered only by a thin blanket. He lifted his head to hunt for Beth. She stood by the window wearing jeans and a soft, thin, yellow sweater. She was leaning against one of the brick walls surrounding the apartment, staring out one of the three large windows taking up most of the one outside wall. The sun shining in through the windows gave her an almost magical luminescence. She had one hand across her chest; the other arm was bent as she was chewing on her fingernails. He sat and regarded her for several seconds without speaking.

After a while, she felt his eyes and she turned her head. He could tell she had been crying. She trudged over to him, her arms crossed over her chest. That was when he could see she had no bra on.

Beth cleared her throat. "I need to get my...clothes. You're sitting on them."

Chad was amused by the fact she seemed embarrassed to say the word "bra" in front of him, especially after the wild sex they had the night before. He sat and handed her the bra, fighting the smirk that threatened to cross his face. She snatched the bra from his hand in irritation and spun away from him. She pulled her arms in through the sleeves and hitched her sweater up a little so she could put her bra on. He saw the silky skin of her back, the indent of her waist, and he wanted to drag her back to the couch and make love to her again. He fantasized briefly about it, replaying images from the night before, and then she was yanking the sweater down and he was back to the here and now.

She didn't turn. "I'm leaving now," she stated firmly. "I need to think."

Before he could say anything, she was out of the apartment. He jumped up. Realizing he was naked, he grabbed the blanket and wrapped it around his lower body before rushing out to the hall. She was waiting at the end of the corridor for the elevator. "Beth, you can't leave. For God's sake, this is New York. At least let me come with you."

She appeared torn for a minute. "No. I need to breathe. I can't breathe when I'm around you," she cried out, almost in a panic. "I need to breathe."

"I'll go with her," Pete put forth, stepping out of the adjacent apartment he stayed in whenever they were in town.

Chad's eyes swung from Pete to Beth and back to Pete again, unsure of what to do. "You'll take care of her?"

"That is the idea," he remarked gruffly, marching past him to take her elbow and escort her into the now open elevator.

The elevator closed and Chad could hear it descend to the lower floors. He stood for a minute in the hallway, wrapped in the blanket. Then, having nothing else to do, he turned and went back inside.

THEY RODE IN SILENCE for several minutes, Pete thinking about just what he would say to Chad if he got the chance. Though watching the crowd outside, he'd heard about the incident at the club. He thought about Chad's comment. 'You'll take care of her?'

Better than you do, you asshole.

The bodyguard noticed Beth's shoulders shaking and her hand covering her eyes. Poor thing. He handed her his handkerchief, adding a few more curse words to his imagined dialogue with the singer.

"Thanks." Beth seemed to regain control. The elevator came to a stop, but luckily no one was waiting to get on. "I'm sorry," she added, focusing briefly on his face. "I know how uncomfortable you must feel..."

"Now. Now." He hugged the diminutive woman, his larger arm cumbersome as he tried to slip it around her. Then, unsure of his next step, he simply patted Beth on the back, hoping she would find it comforting. "You have nothing to be sorry for."

Beth remained silent. The two left the apartment building and trudged up the street, the bodyguard holding her hand patiently. Beth stopped at the corner. "I don't know where I'm going," she came out with, her voice small.

"How about a cup of coffee," Pete suggested. "There's a place across the street, and I won't bother you. I'll give you all the space to breathe you need," he promised.

She gave him a quivery smile and stretched up on her tiptoes to give him a kiss on the cheek. Without saying another word, they trudged over to the coffeehouse directly across from Chad's apartment. They ordered and Beth moved to sit by the window.

"I'll just be over here if you need me," Pete offered, choosing a table at some distance from her. He was a patient man. He learned all about waiting as a bodyguard. He thought about his wife, whom he had lost to cancer before coming to work for Chad.

He would wait all day if he had to.

CHAD SAT IN HIS WINDOW seat, miserable. The upper floors of his apartment building overhung the street, so he did not see the pair leave, but he soon saw them crossing the street and entering the coffee shop next door. He stood, thinking about throwing some clothes on and going after her.

No. She said she needed to breathe.

He sat back down and waited.

About midmorning, she called. He dove across the couch and grabbed the phone off the end table before the second ring. He heard her voice on the other side. "Chad?"

"Are you breathing?"

She couldn't help but smile a little. "We need to talk. I'm at the coffeehouse across the street."

"I'll be right there."

He threw on a lightweight, brown sweater, one of the few things he owned that wasn't black, jeans, and tennis shoes. He glanced at his hair in the mirror. It would do. He brushed his teeth and left the apartment without even bothering to lock it.

When he entered, Beth rose from her chair. He knew she chose a neutral location so he couldn't lure her into bed again.

"Let's go for a walk," she said.

"Okay. There's a huge park near here."

"Just a second." She left his side and moved over to Pete's table. She bent and said a few words to him, then kissed a cheek and squeezed his hand before rejoining Chad.

"What did you say to him?"

She shrugged. "I just said thank you for being a friend." Chad nodded at him guiltily, but the older man just stared back.

They shuffled along in silence for a while. He moved to take her hand, and she didn't resist, nor did she respond. When they got to the park, she followed the path for a while, then spotted a pond through the trees and took off in its direction. Near the edge of the pond, she stopped, dropping his hand and gathering her thoughts.

"Chad," she began, "I love you." It was the first time the words were said in more than just a casual way. Her voice began to crack, and she swallowed, starting again. "You have to know how much I love you." She peered at him now for the first time, and he could see how torn up she was. "But I can't live with this." Her words gathered speed. "I grew up in a house where I was protected from things, some might say sheltered, and maybe it was wrong to raise me that way, but the point is, I can't stand violence. It makes me sick to think of people hurting other people. As stupid as it sounds, it scares me."

"That doesn't sound stupid. It's quite reasonable to be scared of violence."

"It's just, sometimes I don't even feel like I know you."

"You're the *only* person who knows me." Chad touched her face, his fingers grazing over the surface of her skin as if she were a china doll he was afraid to break but couldn't resist touching.

She seemed to lose her train of thought and turned from him, presumably to collect herself. There was a long silence.

"Beth, you're not scared of me, are you?"

She considered this.

"Beth, I would never, never lay a hand on a woman. Never!" he repeated vehemently.

"Okay," she asserted. "I believe you."

He breathed a sigh of relief.

"But that doesn't change things. I still can't live with all the fighting. I mean, that guy did nothing last night. *Nothing.*" She started to get upset remembering. "Chad, what got into you?"

He thought about telling her he was jealous. He thought about telling her Julie upset him, but Chad knew there was more to it than that.

There was a little concrete bench by the edge of the pond. He moved to sit on it, a lone bird hopping out of the way of his over-sized tennis shoes. Beth sat next to him. He stared out across the pond. "When David and I were growing up..." He took a deep breath.

How do you say a thing like this?

He grasped for the words to frame it, but there was no easy way to put it. "My old man..." He sighed. "He used to beat the shit out of my mom, almost every night. I mean he beat the crap out of her. And—" his face contorted in pain "—I wanted to stop him, but even though I was tall for my age, he was a big man. He would just push me into my room and jam something under the doorknob. All I could do was take care of David. So, I did." He paused, lost in a memory for a moment. "It was sick, the sound of it. We used to bury our heads in the pillows, but you could still hear it, feel the vibrations." He stopped abruptly, closing his eyes and shaking his head. After all these years, he could still hear it. He could still feel the fear, the anger, the hate, and the pain.

"That's awful." She put her arm around him. "I can't imagine any child..." She stopped. After several seconds had passed, she asked in a hollow tone, "Did he hit you and David?"

"He never hit David. He hit me every once in a while, but mostly he took it out on my mom. He had better weapons to use against us," he remembered, the rage showing on his face. "He used to tell us we'd amount to nothing. That we weren't good enough to lick his shoes. One time he tried to force me to lick his shoes, but I wouldn't," Chad declared with a kind of twisted pride. "He couldn't make me. He could hit me and kick me, but I wasn't about to lick that bastard's boots." He gazed out across the lake for a moment, trying to rein in his emotions.

"Then," Chad continued, "when I was ten, one night my mom blew my old man away." His chin shook for a minute, his eyes disbelieving. "And she just sat there crying over his body, screaming at him to forgive her. Forgive *her*. Aw, shit." He jumped up and paced back and forth in the grass.

He didn't want to remember this. He stopped, raising his eyes to hers. "Beth, I'm not making excuses for myself. I know what happened last night was my fault. But I just thought if I told you about this, it might help you to understand why I'm so...fucking fucked up." He ended with a note of exasperation. He stepped forward and kneeled in front of her in the grass. "But, Beth, I love you. I really do. And I want to change who I am, for you. But also for me. I'm tired of living this way. Tired of living with this white-hot rage burning a hole inside me. I know you don't have any reason to trust me—"

"Chad, I do trust you. This isn't who you are, this person who hits people and explodes at everything. That is not the man I fell in love with. I'll help you. We can do this. But only if you agree to see a therapist."

Chad climbed on the bench and drew her into his arms. "If that's what you think I should do, I'll do it." He rested a cheek on her head, and she could feel him shake as he tried to control his emotions. "Beth, I need you. Don't you ever leave me."

Her heart went out to him. It struck her to the core to witness him falling apart. The man, who always seemed so strong and in control to her, was now so weak and vulnerable. It was too horrible to contemplate what he and David had gone through together. She could see that frightened little boy in his eyes. She couldn't bear the thought of him going through that. As a child, he lost everything that ever mattered to him, except for David, and now anything that might take her away from him was a threat. It all made sense.

All of a sudden, they both felt a vibration between them. They were confused for a minute. "Oh, it's my phone." Chad drew it out of his pocket. "It's Roger. That's weird...I think I better answer it."

She nodded.

"Hey, Rog—I'm with Beth, why?" He paused, his face concerned. "What's wrong? Yeah, we're just a couple of blocks away. I'll be right over. Just stay there."

"What's going on?"

"I don't know. He's at my apartment and he sounds pretty upset. I'm sorry, Beth—"

"No, no. Let's go."

CHAPTER TWENTY-THREE

They marched briskly down the street without talking, Chad leading the way and holding Beth's hand. Waiting at a stoplight, he admitted nervously, "I've never heard Roger like this." Worry creased his face. "Outside of David, Roger is like the only family I have."

"I know." She squeezed his hand.

At the next intersection he was so distracted he almost raced out in front of a truck. She yanked him back onto the sidewalk just before a truck rolled past, blasting its horn.

They finally arrived at the apartment to find Roger waiting anxiously in the hall in a wrinkled suit, shifting his weight from foot to foot.

"Hey, Beth. How are you?"

"Good," she answered tentatively. "And you?"

Roger forced a smile. "I've been better."

"Why are you wearing a suit?" Chad asked bluntly.

"Uhh...this? I guess I never changed from the club last night. Beth, do you mind if I steal Chad for a few minutes?"

"No, of course not."

"Just go on in, babe. I think I left it open."

AS THE DOOR CLOSED behind her, she heard Chad ask, "What the hell is goin' on, Rog?"

Beth crossed to the window, but she could still hear their conversation through the walls. All she could make of Roger's voice was a low mumbling, but Chad's came in loud and clear and was punctuated with a lot of "You're kidding!" and phrases of a similar nature, interspersed with varied curse words.

"Are you sure?"

"Chad. Shit, man! Do I have to paint you a friggin' picture? They were naked, in our bed."

"Okay. Okay. I get it."

"And the worst thing about it is I'm paying the guy's salary. I'm freaking paying the guy to screw my wife."

Chad could see the logic had gone astray, but he hardly thought now was the time to point it out. "And who was it again?"

"Andre. You know, the really big African-American guy on the pyro crew with the shaved head."

"No, shit? I can't believe it."

"Neither could I. Michelle said she had a headache, so the limo driver took her back to the bus. I decided to cut out early to check on her, and there they were, man, right in my bed." The bassist seemed like he was still in shock.

"What happened then?"

"Well, the guy put his pants on in a hurry. I think I yelled and screamed and threw some things—and I don't know what Michelle was doing—and finally, I couldn't stand to look at them anymore and I went out in the living room." He laughed in disbelief. "Then, I heard Michelle tell him, 'I'll handle it,' like she was going to 'handle' me." He started pacing the hall, gesturing wildly. "Andre didn't want to leave. I guess he thought I was going to beat Michelle up or something. So, I told the motherfucker, 'I'm not gonna lay a hand on her. Believe me, I don't want to touch her ever again,' and he finally left."

"I can't believe it."

"Would you quit saying that?"

"I'm sorry, Rog. I guess I'm just so shocked." He placed a hand on his friend's shoulder. "I'm sorry, man."

"Yeah," he answered absentmindedly. "And then she told me it's been going on for three months. *Three months.* We haven't even been married a year yet."

"I know."

"Chad, I want to leave for New Jersey today. I don't want to be in New York anymore. I know we're not supposed to leave until later—"

"Hey, man, anything you need." He lowered his voice. "Where's Michelle?"

"She left, man. She just packed her bag and left. Said she wanted a divorce."

He took this new information in. "Listen—" he put his hands on Roger's shoulders "—you go next door and tell Pete we're leaving. Hopefully he's in his apartment. I'll get Beth."

"Oh yeah, Beth…"

"I'll get her a ticket out of New Jersey. No big deal."

"Thanks, Chad," he returned with what seemed like a sense of relief.

Chad entered the apartment feeling stunned. Beth crossed from the window with a question in her eyes. "He walked in on Michelle and another guy in the tour bus."

"Wh-what?" Her mouth hung open a beat. "Is he sure about what he saw?"

"O-oh yeah. He's sure."

"Oh."

"He wants to leave, get out of New York. I know we planned on doing some things together today—"

"No, Chad. Whatever he wants to do."

He pulled her into his arms. "Thanks, Beth. Thanks for understanding. And you'll come with us? I can get a ticket for you out of New Jersey—"

"You can do that? Yeah, I'll come with you."

"Good. I have a feeling I'm going to need you around."

Within an hour, the buses were loaded with the appropriate parties, and they were on their way to East Rutherford, New Jersey. Keith offered his room to Roger for the time being, so he wouldn't have to "return to the scene." Roger, for his part, was anesthetizing himself with a bottle of rum, the only thing they could find to drink on the bus.

"I feel like a friggin' pirate." He sat at a table with Chad and Beth, drinking straight from the bottle. He set it down on the table and turned his eyes to Beth. "Maybe I shouldn't have been on the road so much."

"Roger, don't you dare blame yourself. Michelle knew what she was getting into when she married you. And since she traveled with you anyway, it shouldn't have made much of a difference." She noticed the alcohol helped to calm him a little bit; in fact, he was beginning to appear sleepy. Concerned about the amount he had consumed already, she suggested he lie down for a while.

"You know, I think I will. I've been up all night. I'm beat." He swayed to his feet, putting his hands on the table to steady himself. "Thanks, you guys, for listening."

"Any time, bud," Chad answered for the two of them.

Roger turned to go but then swiveled back around to take the bottle with him. Once they heard Keith's door close, they began to talk in earnest.

"Man, poor guy."

"I can't believe Michelle. I always liked her. If she were here right now, I would throttle her."

Chad, who had his arm around her shoulders, lifted his hand to rub her hair. "And I thought I was the violent one." He bent in to steal a kiss. "I've wanted to do that for hours."

"I know. Me, too." She laid her head on his shoulder for a moment, again absorbed in thought. After a while, she shook herself. "Chad, would you mind if I took a shower? I feel all grubby."

"Sure, go ahead. I'll probably hop in after you."

A half hour later, Beth left the bathroom feeling refreshed. Chad lay sleeping on the bed, his shoes still on. She slipped his shoes off so he could be more comfortable. She would be leaving in a few hours, so she quietly packed her things. She took her duffle bag and grabbed her laptop and headed out to the living area. Being alone, in peace, Beth was able to crank out a large part of a chapter of her next book. When the bus came to a stop outside of the Izod Center, where Trapped was to play the next night, Chad woke up and came into the kitchen stretching.

"Working on your book?"

"Um-hum."

Just then, Roger stumbled out of the front bedroom, dropping a bottle in the doorway and leaving it there.

"Wh-what are ya doin' there, Bethy?"

"She's working on her next novel," Chad answered, retrieving the bottle of rum and holding it up with a surprised expression on his face to show her. It was completely empty.

Beth exchanged a worried look with Chad. Roger flopped onto the couch next to her. "What kinda novel?"

"Oh, just a trashy romance novel."

Roger raised his eyebrows comically. "Ahh."

Chad came around and sat on the other side of Beth. "I wouldn't say they were trashy." Something in the way he said it caused her to look at him.

"You've read my novels?"

"Just the first two, I'm halfway through the third. They're great."

"Oh my gosh. I can't believe you read them." She sat straighter. "I'm kind of embarrassed."

"There's no need to be," he responded, surprised. "I mean it. I really liked them. They're funny, but moving, full of action..."

"But it's nothing like what you do. The music you make, the lyrics you write."

"I disagree. They're just different mediums. We both write about people, and passions... It's actually very similar. That's why you like my music. It tells a story."

"And there's the fact she's hot for you," Roger interjected.

She laughed, squeezing Chad's thigh. "Yeah. There's that."

Roger reached up and felt her hair. He examined it drunkenly. "Your hair's wet. You took a shower. You look good wet."

"Uh...thank you." He began to slouch against her, and she pushed him up so he sat straighter. She turned to Chad and whispered, "We need coffee."

"And water or he'll have one hell of a headache."

"You speak as if from experience."

He only smiled in reply.

"There are some water bottles in the fridge."

"But we're out of coffee. I checked earlier. I'll go get some from one of the other buses. You want me to ask Pete to come in here?"

"No. I'll be fine. You'll be back in a minute."

"Okay," he said, and left.

Beth began packing up her laptop while talking to her friend. "Okay, it's just you and me now, Roger. I'm going to get you some water if you can sit up here by yourself."

"Of course, I can, B—" *hiccup* "—Beth. I'm not drunk." He did remove his weight from her, but his head wobbled back and forth as if it might roll off his shoulders and he had a goofy smile plastered on his face.

"Yeah. You're not drunk. Right." She set her laptop on the seat by the door with her bag, safely out of harm's way. Then, she got a bottle of water. Returning, she slid back onto the couch next to him. "Here you go. Drink this. It'll help you feel better."

"But I feel great," he countered, smiling even wider.

She handed the bottle to him. "You won't tomorrow if you don't drink this."

"Okay, Bethy. Anything for you. You know, you're a nice girl. Chad doesn't deserve you, you know? He can be a real asshole."

"Can't we all," she replied, encouraging him to take another drink of water.

"Ain't that the truth?" He laughed then became serious. "I mean it, Beth." He reached up to touch her hair. "You're really beautiful."

"Uh, Roger...what are you doing?" She leaned away from him.

Chad arrived with the coffee, but as he tried to juggle it and the doorknob at the same time, he accidentally spilled a little on his shoe. He did a little hot-dance as it seeped underneath the tongue and into his socks, spilling more. As he sat there inwardly cursing, the door swung open and he heard Beth scream, "Roger. Stop. Get off me! Mmm—" To his shock, he saw his best friend forcing a kiss on Beth, who was obviously trying to squirm away from him.

He set the coffee on the counter and rushed over to disengage Roger from Beth.

"Come on, Beth, don't you want me, too?" Roger said.

Chad put one hand on his collar, and with the other, he grabbed the waist of his friend's pants, jerking him to his feet.

Roger rounded on him, eyes blazing. He pushed Chad hard in the chest, which caused him to stumble backward a few feet. "Come on, you want a piece of me, Chad?"

Beth had fallen off the couch and was getting to her feet. She took in Chad's tight jaw and his eyes, which were shooting fire. But seeming to understand his friend was drunk, he put up his hands and took a deliberate step backward.

"Come on, Mr. Big Shot Rock Star, take your best shot." Roger swayed on his feet, fist clenched and raised. "No? I'm disappoint—"

He turned slightly as if to leave, then swung around and punched Chad right on the chin, snapping his head back. All three of them froze for a second in disbelief. Then, he ran at Chad and tackled him in the midsection, ramming him up against the counter, sending hot coffee flying everywhere. He pushed away and took another swing at him. Chad was able to dodge it, but he came to an end of his patience. He pushed Roger full-force against the opposite counter, scattering everything in close proximity.

"Chad. Chad! Stop! He's just drunk. He doesn't mean it. Pete!"

The two men were a fairly equal match. Chad was taller and had longer arms, but for Roger, being more compact had its advantages, too. What made him even more dangerous was the fact that he was drunk and overwrought.

Strangely, as Roger grappled with his best friend, the scene he walked in on earlier replayed in his mind—the sounds of pleasure he heard right before he opened the door. His wife, his Michelle, in the throes of passion with another man, in the bed they shared all of their married life. With a new fury, he pushed Chad back from the counter and swung with wild abandon, catching him high on the cheekbone.

BETH WATCHED IN HORROR as the two men threw each other around the bus. She was forced to dart out of the way as they came crashing into the wall where she had just been standing. She heard a noise outside and peeked out the window to see Pete and Dante running in their direction.

They must have heard me.

She turned back around just as Chad pulled back his arm to punch Roger. His elbow hit her hard, just below the nose. The blow sent her reeling backward, until she hit the back of the couch. She slid down to the floor, a hand automatically going to her face. She cried out in pain just as Pete and Dante charged in the door.

Chad and Roger quit struggling as they realized what happened to Beth. They released their hold on each other. "Oh, God, Beth. I'm so sorry—" Chad started to say.

"Get away from her, Chad! Haven't you done enough?" Pete yelled at him as the two bodyguards helped her to her feet.

"It was an accident—" she started to explain, but Pete would have none of it.

"Yeah, well 'accidents' seem to happen a lot around Chad. It's high time you and I had a talk. Come with me."

Alarmed and infuriated, Chad took a couple of steps toward Pete. "Let go of her. She doesn't have to go with you." He really looked at Beth for the first time and saw where a cut was opened right at the base of her nose, a larger area already swelling.

Pete released Beth's arm and stepped toward Chad until they were merely a foot apart, the singer still breathing hard from his fight with Roger. "I've had it with you, Chad. You're just a punk. You want to go a few rounds with me, I'll be happy to oblige you." The older man whipped off his jacket in order to free his arms up better.

Chad put his fists up, one of which was bleeding from a jagged cut he received from broken glass on the counter. The blood ran down his forearm.

"Chad!" Beth cried in near hysterics. "Stop this! I'm going with Pete. Come on, Pete." She was crying. "Please!"

Pete looked from her, back to Chad for a moment, his fists clenching and unclenching. Finally, he turned and picked up his jacket from where he threw it on the couch. He spun back as if having second thoughts and stepped up until he was inches from Chad's face. "You're just lucky she's here right now," he hissed, just loud enough for him to hear.

"Pete, *please.*"

"Okay, Beth. Have it your way." He snatched her bags off the couch and led her out the door. Dante took the chance to grab Roger's arm and pull him along, too. "You're coming with us."

The door slammed shut behind them, and Chad stood alone in the bus. The only sound was the water running into the sink unchecked from the faucet, which was turned on in the ruckus. Without a transition from a bus full of bodies being flung around and shouting, to complete quiet and stillness, his brain seemed stuck in gear. He sat for ten minutes in the same position, staring at the door and wondering how he managed to lose both his best friend and his girl at the same time. Slowly, he moved over to the sink and stuck his cut hand under the running water.

CHAPTER TWENTY-FOUR

Pete's days in the military as a drill sergeant took hold of him. He hustled Beth down the stairs of the bus. David and Stan were striding toward them.

"What happened?" David called out. "Beth, are you all right?"

Pete continued to hurry her in the direction of a white Cadillac sedan parked alongside the buses without saying anything in response.

"I'm fine," Beth called, looking over her shoulder at David.

Pete turned. "Give me your keys, Stan," he commanded.

"My keys?"

"Your keys. Throw them to me."

Stan hurriedly fished the keys out of his pocket and tossed them to Pete. He caught them in midair. He opened the passenger door for Beth. Once the door was closed, he told Stan, "I'll be back in about an hour." Without any further explanation to anyone, he got in, started the car's engine, and took off.

FOR SEVERAL MILES, they drove in silence, welcomed silence after the commotion of minutes before. Pete contemplated how best to impart the information to Beth he had to tell her, and Beth thought about Chad and the cut on his hand, still in shock.

"Beth, I know you are not gonna want to hear what I have to say...and as much as I hate to say it, you need to hear it. I know you're enamored of Chad—why, I can't fathom," he couldn't help but add. "But Chad is trouble. Trouble with a capital 'T'. In the relatively few years I have known him, he's gotten into at least a couple dozen fights, probably much more than that, but no one was exactly keeping a tally sheet."

Pete maneuvered deftly through traffic as he continued. "I thought, maybe, when you came around, things would be different. He would change. But he didn't and he never will." The bodyguard glanced over to gauge her reaction to his words. She stared straight ahead. He almost couldn't bring himself to bring the next blow, but knowing it was the only way, he forged on.

"But that's not all. Did he tell you he had a DUI?" Her head spun in his direction. "I didn't think so. He was a drunk driver. Fortunately, he only hit a brick wall when he crashed, but it just as easily could have been your husband." He left her with that thought, remaining silent.

When he turned onto the highway, Beth spoke up. "Pete, where are you taking me? My flight leaves in just a few hours."

"To the airport," he answered gruffly.

"But I didn't even get to say goodbye to Chad."

"Believe me, it's for the best. You need to go home to Cassie. You don't belong in this mess," he observed, his voice soft.

Beth stewed in her seat, glancing at the clock again. She threw the numbers around in her head. There wasn't time to go back. She sighed, looking out the window. Maybe it was best that they have some distance anyway. She needed to think things through.

PETE RETURNED THE CADILLAC to its parking space at the stadium. As he got out, Chad, who had been watching out the window of the bus, came running toward him. He craned his head to scout behind the big man, but seeing no one else get out, he asked flatly, "Where is she?"

"She's gone," Pete replied, unable to keep the note of self-satisfaction out of his voice.

Chad turned around and marched toward the bus, saying over his shoulder, "I'm calling a cab."

"It's too late. She's already gone," Pete yelled after him. Chad entered the bus. "I made sure of that," he added to himself.

CALI OPENED THE DOOR to find her best friend on her front stoop. Her shoulders were slumped, and her face was cut and swollen. "Shit, girl! What happened to you?" Cali threw her arm around Beth and pulled her inside.

Hours later, after Beth had told her story and had taken a second shower, she lay sleeping on the couch. She told Cali what had happened, but Cali saw it as tinted by her own past experience with men. She sat in a chair with her feet up on the coffee table, sipping coffee and watching Beth sleep. She told her it was an accident, but didn't they all say that?

She's too damn naïve. She wants to think everyone is like Paul, but they're not.

Paul and Beth were the exception to the rule—two people who loved each other with all their hearts, unselfishly, unendingly. She simply has no idea how rare that is. This Chad was a jerk, like all the rest, and all that could mean was heartache for her best friend.

The doorbell interrupted Cali's thoughts. She glanced over at Beth, but she hadn't stirred. Cali wondered who it could be; she wasn't expecting anyone. When she opened the door, Chad stood there in his signature black T-shirt and jeans, although there was a cold wind blowing his sleeves and it was easy to see the hair standing up on his arms. He had his hands jammed into his front pockets and stood there uncomfortably, shifting from foot to foot, a remorseful expression on his face.

"Hi, Cali," Chad began.

She stepped onto the porch, closing the door behind her. "What the hell did you come here for? To finish destroying her? And for that matter, how the hell did you know where I live?"

He sighed, looking down and scratching at some invisible dirt with his foot. "I asked for your address at the school. Told them I'd lost it, and I was supposed to send you some concert tickets."

"You just lied to them, and they believed you, just like you've been lying to Beth."

"I've never lied to Beth."

"No, you just conveniently forgot to tell her the truth about yourself. That you're a drunk and a thug and you slept with her just to get laid."

"That's not true!" he responded heatedly, reflexively taking a step forward.

Cali stepped up on the doorstep, grabbing the doorknob. "So, what? Are you going to hit me now, too? You just stay the hell away from her! She's a kind, sweet person and she deserves better than you." She slipped inside the door and quickly slammed it in Chad's face.

Beth was up and shuffling toward her. "Who was that?"

"Oh, just a neighbor wanting to borrow a cup of sugar."

"From you? Don't they know you can't bake?"

"Apparently not," Cali rejoined, glancing back over her shoulder as if expecting to find someone there. "How about a cup of hot chocolate? Come with me into the kitchen and talk to me while I make some."

Cali waited uneasily, worried Chad would bang on the door or make his presence known in some other way. She had to keep him from Beth.

CHAD STOOD ON THE PORCH, trying to figure out what his next move was. When Beth hadn't been home, he decided she must be at Cali's. The way she chewed him out, Beth must have told her what happened between them, and the way she was blocking the door like a mother bear told him Beth was inside. If he could only talk to her, explain himself. But what was he to do? Wait around like some stalker for her to come out? Bang on the door and call her name? No, that was the kind of behavior that got him into this mess in the first place. Confused and upset, he turned and climbed back into the cab he had hoped to send away.

On the plane back, Chad stared out the window, but it was nighttime and there was nothing to look at. Cali's voice was still ringing in his head.

What the hell did you come here for? To finish destroying her? You're a drunk and a thug and you slept with her just to get laid.

He had not slept with her to get laid; he knew that to be true. She captivated him from the start. She asked nothing of him, and somehow made the ache inside him go away. She had the power to pull him out of himself, out of the darkness, the misery, and the despair. He couldn't let that go.

But what about the other accusations? It was true he had hurt her on more than one occasion, despite his best intentions. The image of her cut and swelling face as she lay on the floor of the tour bus haunted him. He knew he didn't intend to hurt her, but like Pete said, 'accidents' seem to happen around him. And he heard his father's voice, the voice she made silent, telling him he was no good, he was worthless. The farther he got away from her, the louder the voices grew, until he finally asked the stewardess for a drink in an effort to silence them.

THE NEXT MORNING, CHAD didn't call, which was unusual. Beth expected him to phone because she could never be sure when he'd be available. She figured he was exhausted from all the turmoil of the last couple of days and must be sleeping in. She tried to reach him after work, but he never picked up. She left messages, but he never called back. By late that night, she had to believe that he was no longer interested in talking to her. She tried to wrap her mind around that, but something just didn't seem right.

Beth got up early because she'd offered to drive Cali to work while her car was in the shop. She checked her phone. No messages. As she drove to her friend's she wondered what she should do. She wanted to be a responsible parent, and bringing someone with a violent temperament into the home was not good for Cassie. But Cassie would be gone to college in just a few months. She knew that it was foolish to go into a relationship thinking you could change someone, but Chad had never really had the opportunity to change, no one to care enough about him to help him through it. She was sure that with a good therapist he could gain control over his temper. At least she needed to give him a chance. She was subdued on the drive to school.

As Beth began her day's work, the school secretary walked in. She and her friends greeted the older lady warmly. "Good morning, Barb."

"Good morning, ladies. I've got your lunch count here." She addressed Beth, "Oh, and I just have to tell you that your young man was so sweet when he stopped in the other day to get Cali's address. Were you able to spend your day off with him?"

"Huh? No," she said slowly. "No, he had to get back."

"Oh, that's a shame. Well, you all have a good day."

"You, too, Barb," the rest of the lunch ladies chorused.

Chad had been there...and he must have been at Cali's, too. That was who was at the door. He must have caught the very next flight out of New Jersey to talk to her. Cali entered from the back room, tying her apron strings behind her.

"Why didn't you tell me he was here?" Beth blurted out, her voice like the edge of a blade. The chitchat, which was the usual trademark of the kitchen, was noticeably lacking; all eyes were on Beth and Cali.

"Beth, he's no good for you."

"That is my decision to make."

"You were in no shape—"

"Cali!" Just when it seemed like she was going to explode, Beth sighed. "I know you were doing what you thought was best for me—" the fire returned to her voice with her final words "—but don't *ever* lie to me again."

"I'm sorry, Beth," she answered contritely. "I made a mistake."

"All right, then," Beth relented, but internally she worried about whether it was too late to fix the mistake.

After work, Beth drove Cali home. She parked in the driveway but left the engine running. "I need a favor."

"Anything," Cali offered, grateful for an opportunity to make up for lying to her. She took Beth's hands. "You know your friendship means everything to me. No one has ever been there for me like you have."

"I know, Cali."

"What can I do?"

"Cassie gets home from her retreat tonight. Can you stay with her?"

"You're going to see him."

"We have to talk."

Cali nodded. "I'll stay with Cas as long as you need me to."

"Thanks," Beth said, giving her a quick hug.

CALI WATCHED HER DRIVE away with deep regret. She's just going to get her heart broken. She shook her head and turned away from the window. She packed an overnight bag, so she'd be ready when Cassie got off the bus.

Beth had poor timing as Pete was just coming out for a smoke as her cab drove away.

"Beth, what are you doing here?" he stammered, clearly disappointed.

"I think you know."

"Believe me, you don't want to go in there. He's in worse shape than I've ever seen him before."

"Pete," she began, contemplating her words as she spoke, "I am very grateful for all you've done for me, and for Chad. But if you don't get out of my way, I'm gonna start calling out his name."

Pete was surprised by the amount of determination he heard in her voice. Realizing he'd done all he could, he stepped aside. But as Beth started to walk through the door, he put a hand on her arm. "Good luck," he murmured with sincerity. "If you need me, I'll be right outside this door, you got it?"

She put her hand on top of his and gave it a squeeze. "Thank you."

CHAPTER TWENTY-FIVE

It was immediately evident Chad had been on one hell of a drinking binge. Bottles lined the counters and tabletops and spilled out onto the floor from overflowing trash cans.

Beth surveyed the damage. "Good Lord!"

Then, her eyes fell upon Chad. When she came in, he was sitting on one of the couches with his head leaning back against the top of the cushion.

But as soon as he heard her voice, Chad's eyes flew open. A spark of hope flitted through them, and his face lightened for a second. He almost stood but seemed to change his mind halfway up and sat again. He tore his eyes from her and stared at his hands as he folded them on top of the table. "What are you doing here?" he asked coldly.

Startled by his tone, Beth hesitated. The words she was about to speak flew out of her mind as if spirited away on a sudden gust of wind. "I-I came—"

"YOU CAME TO MAKE THINGS up with me, huh?" Chad queried, his voice laced with sarcasm. "Well, it's too damned late." He knew he had to make the words hurt to drive her away for good.

She stumbled forward a step, appearing to fight to remain calm. "You don't mean that."

Grabbing on to the words Cali gave him, Chad threw out the lie, trying to make it sound as real as possible. "The hell I don't. Beth, don't you understand? You were nothing but a good lay to me from the start." He inwardly cringed at the sight of the pain he caused on her face, but he kept going, knowing it was the right thing to do, even if it was killing him. His mind spun, finding the words he needed. "But this whole relationship is just more trouble than it's worth. I could have any girl out there." He waved his hand at the window, but suddenly he remembered the conversation they had in his bedroom that night in Kansas City, and he faltered.

Beth also seemed to remember the conversation as she sprung on his line. "But you chose me."

Chad strove to regain his footing. "That was a mistake." He took another swig from his bottle to numb the darts of pain stabbing through him.

She sobbed, looking away from him, toward the ceiling, unable to continue staring into his emotionless eyes. "Why are you doing this? Why are you saying these things to me?"

Chad stared down at his hands again, trying to hide how difficult this was for him. Without warning, Beth sat across from him and laid her hands on his. The sight of her little hands covering his massive ones, along with the warmth and familiarity of her touch, was almost too much for him. He jumped up and swept his arm across the table, clearing all of the bottles onto the floor with a crash. "Get the hell out of here!" he roared. "I'm finished with you!" He turned around so she couldn't see the tears in his eyes or the way her touch affected him.

Outside the bus, Pete sprinted up the stairs. He had his hand on the doorknob when he heard Beth scream, "I'm not going anywhere!" He waited to see what would happen next.

"Turn around and look at me, Chad. If you're going to throw me out of here, you're going to do it looking into my eyes."

Chad drew in a shaky breath and tried to steel himself. He turned around, trying to muster as much antipathy as he could. "Beth, leave," he ordered, but the vehemence was gone. "Just—" His voice cracked, and his eyes darted away for an instant. "Just get out of here."

"Damn it, Chad! Why are you doing this to us?" she screamed, her voice nearing hysterics.

He didn't answer her. Her tenacity had him stymied. Why wouldn't she just leave?

She studied his face. "You're lying to me. You don't want me to leave."

His eyes flashed. "Yes, I do."

"Why?" she continued, her voice level now. "Tell me why, Chad. Tell me to my face."

"I just told you," he hissed, flabbergasted. "I don't want you around anymore. It was fun, but now it's over. It was nothing more than a roll in the hay. I'll have another woman in my bed before the concert is over tonight. Someone who will just do me and leave. That's what I want."

Her gaze was unflinching. "But I want you."

"Well, then you're an idiot!" he yelled, exasperated.

"I never tried to hide that from you," she countered.

A smile played on the edge of Chad's lips for a moment, and he almost caved in. Turning from her, he yelled, "Don't you get it? You mean nothing to me."

"Then why did you come to Bloomington? Cali didn't tell me, but I found out. If I mean nothing to you, then why did you come to see me?"

He tried to come up with an answer, but she had worn him down. "Dammit, Beth! Why won't you leave?" He slumped into a seat and placed his head in his hands, muttering, "I'm not worth it."

"You're not worth it? What we had together is not worth fighting for? You're not worth fighting for?" She took a breath. "I'm not into disposable relationships, Chad. I learned from losing Paul that life is too short. I know other people disappointed you, hurt you, but I'm not going anywhere."

"But Beth, look at all the pain I've put you through. Can't you see? I'm no good for you."

"I know your father said horrible things to you, Chad," she breathed, "but he was wrong. You are a good man. You have some problems, sure. But we all do." Beth crouched next to him. "You brought joy back into my life. Please don't take it from me." She placed her hand on his back, and it was his undoing. He turned to face her. Beth gazed into his eyes. "I know you think you are doing what's best for me. Everybody thinks they're doing what's best for me. But you are what's best for me. I love you, please don't push me away."

Unable to bear it any longer, he reached out and pulled her to him. The embrace awkward while seated, Chad rose, taking her with him. Having her in his arms again felt so right, the rocker felt his whole body relax as he exhaled out the anguish over the thought of losing her. "I'm sorry, Beth. I'm so sorry. I didn't mean any of those things." He pulled away to scrutinize her, to make her understand.

"I know."

Chad held her again. "I don't know what I did to deserve you."

"I DON'T EITHER," PETE muttered with a grin from outside the trailer. He shook his head as he ambled away, pleased with the way things turned out.

SOMEONE KNOCKED ON the door. "Chad. I don't want to bother you guys, but it's almost show time."

He and Beth stirred. They fell asleep in each other's arms, both exhausted by all the drama.

"All right. I'm up. Be right out."

David was waiting outside with a grin on his face. "Good to see you, Beth."

Her face relaxed into a smile. "Same here, David."

When they walked into the building it almost throbbed with the excitement of the fans waiting above. Chad nodded at Roger, whom he had not spoken to since their fight. Roger looked as if he wanted say something, but Stan came up to rush them on stage. At the beginning of the first set, things were a little tense on stage, but by the time they neared the end of it, the music that drew them together in the first place seemed to heal whatever was damaged between Roger and Chad.

They came off stage for a quick break before they started the next set, while Keith entertained the audience with a little drum solo.

"Are you ready, Beth?" Stan asked.

"Huh?" she asked confused.

"For your song?"

"Ooh, Stan. I don't think it is such a good idea after what happened."

"Nonsense. These guys are professionals. They're not gonna let a little tiff get in the way of entertaining all those good people out there, are ya fellas?"

Chad and Roger looked at each other.

After a pause, Chad spoke for them both. "No, it's okay."

"All right. Now get back out there and play some rock and roll."

"I've got a bad feeling about this," Beth murmured, but no one was listening.

Roger started off the song. At first, he was a little tentative, but soon the music and the crowd's reaction had him feeling good. He smiled at Beth and gave her a wink at the end of his lines.

Maybe I was wrong. Maybe this will be okay.

She belted out her part. Chad joined in and soon it felt like old times. Roger got up and started strutting toward Beth, as was scripted. Chad did the same. But somewhere along the line, whether it was a look or just seeing him close to Beth so soon after what he tried, Chad's angry lover act was no longer an act. Roger, seeing the fire in Chad's eyes, reacted the same way. By the end of the song, when it was supposed to end with Beth holding them apart, Beth was really holding them apart as they glared at one another. When the lights went down, Beth spoke to them both, "Boys! You have a concert to finish."

Chad lowered his chin a fraction then turned to stride back over to his mike stand. Roger followed suit. The audience cheered, thinking it was all part of the act. Beth exited and watched the rest of the concert from the footlights. Only those who knew them best could tell there was still some tension between them. After the second encore, Chad strode off stage and threw his arm over Beth's shoulder, intending to head directly to the bus to cool down.

"Chad. Beth. Wait!" Roger called after them.

Chad halted abruptly, gritting his teeth, and turned around.

He looked so angry, Roger almost backed away. "I'm sorry, man. I am. You, too, Beth. I was way, *way* out of line. For hitting you, Chad...for hitting on you, Beth..."

The way Roger phrased it made Beth laugh. Chad gaped at her for a second as if she was crazy, but then he started laughing, too. Roger looked from one to the other with a lopsided grin and a sigh of relief. Pretty soon the friends were strolling arm in arm, like the Mod Squad, out to the buses, the fight in the distant past.

CHAPTER TWENTY-SIX

"What do you mean, a 'special' date?" Beth inquired over the phone. "Just get yourself dressed to the nines. We're going out tonight."

It had been over a month since New York, and Chad had made some real progress with the therapist. Plus, appointments with her meant time together since she was located in Bloomington. "Umm! What did I do to deserve this? I want to know so I can do it again."

"You were just being you."

"Oh, is that all. Okay, Mr. Mystery Man, what time should I be ready?"

"Seven."

"All right. Seven it is. I'll be ready."

Chad rang the doorbell, nerves making him tug at his shirt sleeves to straighten his shirt. Everything had to go just right tonight. Beth opened the door, and light fell on the porch. "Damn!"

She laughed. "My, you do have a way with words."

"Let me see this." He whistled, stepping in and circling around her so he could get the full effect. Beth had on a longer emerald dress, with four straps crisscrossing her upper back before plunging downward and long slits gliding up her legs. Again, her hair was swept up, making her neck seem so much more inviting. He returned to face her, admiring her from the front. He laughed. "I'm sorry, it's just...damn." He shook his head.

"Oh stop," she mumbled, her face flushing as she hit him with her handbag.

"I love the way you blush." Chad touched her hot face and gave her a kiss.

When he pulled away, she blurted out, bubbling over, "I'm so excited. So where are we going?"

"Ah-ah-ah. Not yet. You need to wear this." He pulled a silky, black scarf from his suit pocket.

"Ooh. What kind of kinky thing am I in for?"

"You little vixen." Chad gave her a sharp swat on the derrière. He positioned himself behind his date again and brought the scarf over Beth's head to tie it behind her as a blindfold.

"What are you up to?" she asked coquettishly.

Chad leaned into that tantalizing neck, annunciating each word in her ear with a seductive whisper, "Try not to anticipate." Then, unable to resist, he kissed her there.

She squirmed with delight. "Ooh. That's so much better when I can't see you."

"Uhh...is that supposed to be a compliment? 'Cause, it doesn't sound like one."

"Oh, silly. You know what I mean." She tried to reach for him. "I can't find you to kiss you," she whined in frustration.

"That's part of the fun," he teased, now in front of her. "Okay," he continued, leading the way, "you need to take a step down onto the porch. Where's your key?"

"In my bag."

He took her handbag and locked the door. As he moved her toward the steps, another arm supported her on the right. "Wow, Beth. You look fantastic."

"Thank you, Pete. So, he roped you into this, too?"

"No rope needed. I wouldn't miss this for the world."

Chad shot his usually tightlipped bodyguard a warning look, which Beth, of course, could not see. After the two men got her safely in the limousine and closed the door, Pete commented, "If you don't propose to her, I will."

"Just you try it, old man," he returned with a grin.

Pete chuckled as he strolled around to the other side of the car with Chad to get in. Beth was running her hands over the leather upholstery with a huge smile on her face. "Is this a limo?"

"No. It's a '57 Chevy," he replied sarcastically.

"Ooh, I always wanted to do it in the back of a '57 Chevy. Oh gosh. The partition is closed, isn't it?"

He waited a heartbeat. "Yes, it's just you and me here, Beth," he promised softly.

She was able to bring her hands to Chad's face to guide her as she kissed him. "That's just how I like it. I've missed you, babe."

"Me, too." He ran his hand along the soft skin of her arm.

"You are the last of the great romantics, you know that?"

"We are a dying breed."

"Cali says you're extinct."

He laughed. "Cali would say that."

"Hey, how's Roger doing?"

"Better. Most of the time he's his old self. But every once in a while, I can tell he's thinking about Michelle. He really loved her."

They were quiet for a moment. "So, you agreed to let Pete tag along with us tonight. Did you think I might be a handful?"

He laughed. "You're always a handful. No, my little shadow is along with us tonight because of some hate mail I've been getting."

"What?" she cried out, concerned.

He instantly regretted telling her. "Oh, I get it all the time. 'Trapped Under Ice sucks,' 'You're a loser,' etc. No biggie."

"If you get it all the time, why is Pete here tonight when he hasn't been on other nights?"

"You know, Pete," he answered evasively. "He's overprotective."

"No. He's a bodyguard who's been in the business for over twenty years."

"Let's not talk about this tonight."

She hesitated. "Full disclosure in the morning?"

"Full disclosure, including all the evidence," Chad vowed, forgetting the letters were actually with a friend of Pete's who worked for the FBI.

The limo rolled to a stop. "We're here all ready?" she squealed.

"No. You've just completed the first leg of your journey," he answered mysteriously, kissing her on the tip of her nose. He got out and trotted around to help her out.

When Beth got out, she knew immediately where they were. "The airport? What are you up to?" she yelled over the sound of a jet taking off.

"You are so impatient."

They boarded the small jet taking them nearer to their secret destination. "I think we can take your blindfold off for a little while."

"Oh my gosh. This is beautiful." She took in the luxurious interior of the jet. There were leather seats set up around little tables, like conversation areas. A big-screen TV was recessed into one wall and lush carpeting covered the floor. He handed her a champagne flute.

"How did you do this?"

"The owner—"

"Is a big Trapped Under Ice fan."

He nodded. "It's amazing what a couple of concert tickets will do for you."

"I wouldn't know. You're the rock star recognized by thousands of people around the globe. I'm the lunch lady recognized by about three hundred children in a small, Catholic grade school."

"And a waitress in St. Louis. By the way, I finished *Abandon All Hope*. Great ending."

"You liked that, huh?"

"Yeah. And so did Roger."

She hurriedly swallowed her champagne. "Roger read it?" she blurted out.

"He read it. Keith finished it last week and David's in line next," he reported with a grin. "Roger said he's seeing a whole other side of you."

"I can't believe you guys are reading that trash."

"It's not trash. You need to quit saying that. And Cheri's read them all and keeps bugging me, wanting to know when the fourth one is going to be finished."

"I haven't gotten very far lately. Between work and Cassie's volleyball..."

"We're not going to talk about work tonight." He pulled her to her feet. He had other ideas about how she could find the time to finish the novel. "What we need is some music." He reached over and flipped on a built-in stereo system. The soft sounds of a saxophone filled the cabin in surround sound. "It's not Trapped Under Ice. I hope you don't mind."

Her lips turned up at the corners. "I can deal with it."

He came toward her, suddenly serious. "Beth, will you dance with me?" It was almost as if he were asking a crucial question.

"Of course." Beth took his extended hand. He pulled her close and all conversation stopped. They swayed easily together to the music, Beth laying her head on his chest, thinking she didn't ever want this to end. His hand was on the middle of her bare back, and he would occasionally trail it up and down, thrilling them both. At one point, she pulled away, gazing into his face, but saying nothing, for there were no words for what she was feeling.

"Beth, I love you, you know?" he told her, emphasizing his words with a kiss.

Strangely, there was a rap from the other side of the cockpit door. After a second or two, they realized whoever it was did not want to interrupt them. "Come in."

"Good evening, sir." The captain entered the cabin, tipping his hat. "Ms. Donovan. I just wanted to let you know we have almost reached your destination, and we'll need you to have a seat now and buckle in."

"And that destination would be...?" Beth asked innocently.

"Nice try," the captain commented, apparently aware of the mission's secrecy.

"Thank you," Chad responded, grinning at him. The singer led Beth to a seat. "You are a naughty girl."

She shrugged. "It was worth a try."

"The blindfold goes back on now."

"Aww."

"Just for a little longer."

IN REALITY, IT WAS more like a half hour before they arrived at their destination, but he entertained her with stories from the road, mostly involving Roger's latest antics.

"Okay, we're here." The limousine pulled up to the end of a drive. Her hands reached up to take her blindfold off, but he stopped her. "Not yet," he commanded.

He helped her out, and he and Pete guided her forward. She gave a contented sigh. "Man, is it a beautiful evening. Hey, I smell pine trees," she noted with a slow smile.

Chad smiled, too, thinking ahead to what was to come. "Okay," he said, "you can stop now." He inspected the grounds for the second time that day; everything was perfect.

"Are we there?"

"We're there." He removed her blindfold.

Before her lay a familiar terraced deck, one she knew to be situated on a cliff above the Missouri River, only this time it was night, and it looked like an enchanted fairy land. White lights were strung in the trees and along the top of the fence and intertwined in the railings leading down the many steps. The same bistro table they sat at before was candlelit and set with china, and in the grassy area between the deck and the fence, musicians in white tuxes began playing violin music. She gasped in surprise.

He watched her as she took it all in, feeling his love for her filling him completely. Her face glowed with delight and her eyes shone as she turned to him. "It's fantastic," she burst out with an air of breathlessness. "Chad, I don't know what to say. I'm utterly speechless."

"That's okay. You don't need to say anything. Would you like wine, or would you like to stick to champagne?" Mark waited in the wings with a tray.

"Champagne." She grabbed him by the lapels of his jacket. "I can't believe you."

Unable to resist any longer, he bent to kiss her, and it was as if all the others with them simply disappeared for an instant.

"God, I love you," she spoke as she pulled away.

Chad was flooded with joy. "Good." He grabbed two flutes off Mark's tray, handed one to Beth, and slipped his arm through hers, escorting her down to their table. After they sat, he grabbed her hand and brought it up to his lips. He hoped she would be overwhelmed by this evening; what he hadn't expected was the rush of feelings he was experiencing. As he gazed at her lovely face, he saw her tears shining in the candlelight. "Beth, you're not crying?"

She hung her head for a minute, taking her hand from his momentarily to brush away tears. "It's just, I can't believe you did all of this for me. Flew me up here—" Her voice cracked. "This is so incredibly special to me. But you know, don't you, I'd be happy just being with you at a fast-food joint. Well, maybe not just any fast-food joint, but an acceptable fast-food joint."

He laughed, holding her hand up to his lips again as he said, "I know, Beth. Sometimes I just have an urge to show you, in some way, how much you mean to me."

A tuxedoed waiter appeared out of nowhere with covered dishes of Rock Cornish game hens and wild rice. After they finished their scrumptious dinner, Chad asked, "Do you want to go down and find out if we can see the river?"

"Sure."

He led her down the stairs and to the fence, where the violinists were still playing. He wrapped his arms around her. She slipped a black shawl around her shoulders as the evening grew chillier, and the two stood, swaying together in the moonlight. Since the trail below was lit, they could make out just the currents of the river. Off to the left, the lights of the railroad bridge illuminated more of the landscaping on either bank.

She turned her head back to him slightly. "This couldn't be a more perfect evening."

"Oh, we're not done yet."

"We're not?" She turned to him with wonder in her eyes.

"Right this way," he instructed, ushering her over to the picnic table they sat on months before. It was covered in a white tablecloth, too. He offered her a hand to help her up as she put her—he couldn't help but notice—beautiful high-heeled foot, on the bench. The dress parted along the slit revealing even more of her shapely leg as she climbed to sit on top of the table.

SHE ADJUSTED HER DRESS and settled in, but to her surprise, he didn't join her. That was when she noticed the music had stopped. One of the musicians handed him a guitar, which they had hidden behind them, leaning against the fence. "What are you doing?" she inquired with a grin.

"I wrote you a song."

"Oh my gosh," she cried, her hands flying to her mouth. "This is too much."

"You haven't even heard it yet," he pointed out with a grin. "You might not even like it."

She laughed. "What do you think the odds are of that?"

His grin widened as he began to strum the first few chords of what was undoubtedly the most beautiful song she'd ever heard. When he sang, his voice sounded different from any of the other songs she'd heard him sing. The music really showcased his voice, which had a lot more depth than she ever realized.

MY LIFE WAS COLD AND black
> Before you came and fixed what was broken in me
> And now I just wish I could give back
> Just a little of what you've given to me

I THOUGHT THE POISON within me
> Had killed all the love I could give
> But loving you, Beth, is so simple
> Just being with you is to live

AND NOW I KNOW I LOVE you
> I no longer want to be on my own
> I want to have you by my side, Beth
> And for once I won't be so alone

MY LIFE WAS COLD AND black
> Before you came and fixed what was broken in me
> And now I just wish I could give back
> Just a little of what you have given to me

YOU CAME INTO MY LIFE, asking nothing of me
    You just loved me through all of my faults
    'Cause my heart was imprisoned and you held the key
    To release me from deep in my vaults

AND NOW I KNOW I LOVE you
    I no longer want to be on my own
    I want to make you my wife, Beth
    Say yes, and I won't be alone
    Say yes, and I'll love you alone
    Say yes, and I'll make you my own."

HE PLAYED THE LAST notes, but before taking off his guitar, she spotted him untying something suspended from its strings she had not noticed before. He handed the guitar back to one of the violinists and got down on one knee in the grass in front of her, taking her hand. "Beth, I love you, babe, and I don't ever want this to end. So—" he produced a ring, holding her hand "—will you marry me?"

"Chad, oh my gosh, it's beautiful. I can't believe you...oh...everything is so beautiful." She finally got so choked up, she couldn't talk.

He laughed, standing to turn to the members of the band. "I guess I did all right, fellas. The lady with all the words is speechless." They chuckled.

"Chad," she burst out finally, springing off the bench and into his arms, nearly knocking him over, "I love you, so much."

He laughed as she kissed him. Finally pulling away to say, "Well, don't leave a guy hanging? What's your answer?"

"Nothing would make me happier than to spend the rest of my life right here in your arms." She kissed him again, and there was applause from the musicians and from above, where Mark was clapping and Pete was whistling loudly.

CHAPTER TWENTY-SEVEN

They finally arrived back at Beth's house and Chad stood kissing her now-bejeweled hand on the porch. He was disappointed when he asked her whether they should go to his hotel or back to her house, but he was doing his best to hide it.

"Well, I guess I better go," he commented.

This is a twist. Usually, it's Beth leaving me.

"I don't want you to go."

"What? But isn't Cas home?"

"Yes. But—" she moved closer to him "—we're engaged now." She waved her hand at him.

"So, it's okay?" he asked happily.

"I think so. We are getting married, right?"

He smirked. "That's usually what being engaged means."

"All right, then. Send my carriage away," she declared grandly, turning to unlock the door.

He nearly skipped down the sidewalk to Pete's side. "I get to stay," he said, unable to mask his excitement.

"Good for you," Pete cracked.

He punched him in the arm. "I'll call you tomorrow." He turned to go, but Pete grabbed his arm.

"Congratulations, Chad," he stated sincerely.

"Thanks, Pete. And thanks for sticking with me. I know I don't make things easy for you all the time—"

"Yeah. But you're okay, kid," Pete reported, gripping his arm firmly.

He stood for a minute, stunned. It was the closest thing to a compliment he had ever received from the older man, and hearing so few from his elders in his life, it meant more than he could say. "Thanks, man," he sputtered, choked up.

Pete raised his eyes to catch Beth waiting on the porch and gave the singer a knowing grin. "Enjoy the rest of your evening."

Chad followed his gaze. "I plan on it."

But when they went inside, he began to feel uncomfortable.

"Cas is asleep," Beth whispered. "Are you okay? Is this all right with you?"

"Yeah. Yeah," he answered, finding his voice.

She led him without another word. The second floor, like the first, had an open layout. The hall at the top fanned out with doors to bedrooms and bathrooms along its perimeter. Beth moved forward into the master bedroom. She turned around to find Chad standing, still uncertain, in the doorway. She went back and drew him in, closing the door behind him. "Are you having second thoughts on the engagement already?"

"No, no way." When he was this close to her, everything else faded away. He ran his hands down her shoulders a couple of times, and then slid the sleeves off her shoulders, kissing her neck. She moaned, quickly shirking off her dress. She stood in a black and red, lacy bustier, with the straps buttoned in place to hold her stockings up.

"Damn!" he proclaimed for the third time that evening. He sat on the end of the bed running his hands along her sides and taking in every last detail.

Beth kicked a heel up on the bed next to him. "I may need some help with these," she commented, her eyes dancing as she indicated the buttons attached to the tops of her stockings.

"Okay," Chad returned, swallowing and trying to control his racing heart. He carefully unbuttoned one of the elastic straps and it snapped back. He gazed up into her face as his hands slid beneath her, to release the second strap. It was obvious she was into him being into her. He ran his hand down her leg a heartbeat at a time, letting his eyes follow their delicate curves, until he came to the strap of her shoe. He took a deep breath. This was going to be harder than he anticipated. As slowly as he could, he undid the strap and slid the shoe and stocking off. She took the leg away and kicked the other leg up on the opposite side of him. He repeated his movements, caressing her bare leg a little before she withdrew it.

She began to unbutton his shirt as he peered up at her face, his hands on the back of her legs. When she got to the bottom, she yanked his shirt out of his pants in one quick motion, nearly sending him over the edge. She brought her hands up under the cloth, along his bare skin, to his shoulders, pausing, totally in control of him and loving it. She jerked his shirt and jacket off. He sat contemplating the many, many directions that this could take now.

Beth kissed him once, stealing his breath away, and then climbed past him up the bed and onto the pillows. She leaned back, one leg bent, and waited for him to come to her. She reached over and turned off the bedside lamp, but she was still illuminated by the neighbor's security light beaming through the window, which had just been triggered by the wind. He lost the rest of his clothing and jumped on the bed next to her, making her laugh. He grabbed her and swallowed her up in kisses until she edged away and swung around to sit on top of him.

"You," he spoke, breathing hard, his hands running up and down her sides. "You are—" he searched for a word to finish his sentence "—incredible." He reached to grab her behind the neck and draw her to him, kissing her hard on the mouth. There was no mistaking it; he couldn't wait for her much longer.

In a short time, they were both completely naked, and he had his hands on her rear as she moved above him. He could not believe the exquisite ecstasy she gave him by just the way she moved her hips.

Afterward, she was lying in his arms, stretched out along his side languidly. They lay like that for several minutes, soaking in their happiness. She reached out her hand in the darkness, the engagement ring sparkling in the light from outside.

"Chad?" she spoke into the darkness around them.

He stirred. "Um-hum," he responded, his voice clouded by sleep.

"There's something I want to ask you," she began tentatively, "but I'm afraid it will hurt your feelings."

He woke more and pushed himself up on one elbow above her. He brushed the hair from her face. "You can ask me whatever you want. You can't hurt my feelings. Whatever you have to say, it can't be worse than what I've heard before." But even as he uttered it, he knew she had much more power than his father ever had to hurt him. The difference was he trusted her with that power.

"It's just, this ring is gorgeous. It's the most exquisite thing I've ever seen and I love it. Truly, I do. But...do you think we could get the jewelers to re-make it, the exact same design, just with smaller diamonds? It would make me too nervous to wear this," she ended. She held her breath, studying his face.

He laughed. "You are the only woman I know who would ask for fewer diamonds in her engagement ring." He lifted her hand to his lips and kissed it.

"You're not upset, are you? Because, really, everything was so perfect, all the work you put into it—"

The rest of what she was saying was smothered by his kisses. "You can have anything you want, Mrs. Almost-Evans." He paused, wondering if she would be willing to take his name after so many years as Beth Donovan. She seemed to be considering this new name. Would she be able to let go of the name her husband gave her on their wedding day?

He tried to read her face in the dim light offered by the alarm clock on her side of the bed. "Or, maybe you would rather keep the name Donovan. That would be all right with me, Beth."

WITH HIS WORDS, SHE knew it was time to let go. She would always love Paul, but there was room in her heart to love Chad, too. She reached up and caressed his face. "I would be so proud to be Mrs. Beth Evans."

"Good," he responded with satisfaction, lying back down.

Just as he was drifting off to sleep again, she whispered, "Chad?"

"What?" he mumbled, lying on his stomach.

"I was just wondering...oh, never mind."

His eyes opened in the dark. He flipped over to face her again. "What were you wondering?"

"Well, I'm not trying to push or anything, but I was just wondering...if you knew what your time frame would be? ...For the wedding, that is."

He smiled in the darkness. "We've been engaged a whole, what—" he squinted at the clock "—three hours, and you're already pressuring me, woman?"

"Well, no. I—"

"I'm kidding, Beth. If it were up to me, there would have been a preacher there tonight. But I know it's not easy for you."

"I want to get married right away."

"You do?"

"Yeah. I don't want to waste any more time not being together."

"Well, I don't really have any breaks in the schedule until—"

"Who needs a break in the schedule? Why don't we just have a small ceremony before a concert?"

"On stage?"

"Sure. Why not?"

"You don't want a big reception and the whole church thing?"

"Not unless you do. I've had all that before."

"Man. You are a cheap date. We'll look at the schedule and you can pick a date. Who do you want to come?" He sounded like he was getting excited.

"Well, Cas, of course, and Cali and the other lunch ladies. But that's it. Just an intimate kind of thing."

"That sounds fantastic!" He changed positions. "We should get some sleep, I guess. We'll talk about it more in the morning."

Ten minutes later it was Chad who broke the stillness. "Beth?"

"Mmm?"

"You know how you were saying earlier that you don't have enough time to write?"

"Yes."

"Well, I was thinking...when Cas goes to school in the fall, what would you think about giving up your lunch lady gig and touring with me? You could bring your laptop and have all the time you needed. You don't have to answer right away, just think about it. I know you like working with the girls and with the kids at the school. I just wanted you to know, traveling with the band would be an option, too. We can talk about it more in the morning if you want to. Go back to sleep."

"CHAD."

"Huh?"

"Cassie's awake."

He opened one eye. Beth was sitting, clutching her knees and listening for movement in the hall. He sat, too.

"I'm nervous about telling her," she confessed.

"You didn't seem nervous last night."

"Yeah, well that's 'cause I was all high on love and everything. This is reality."

"You don't think she'll like the idea?"

"I just don't know. She adores you, Chad, but the only man who's ever been in this house is her dad. I just don't know how she's going to take this."

"What do you want me to do? Do you want to offer to take her out to breakfast and I can call a cab and be gone before you get back?"

Her face scrunched up. "No. I shouldn't have said anything. I love you, Chad. And I want her to know it." She touched his face. "It's not something to hide. It's just...awkward, or something. Come on, let's get dressed and go tell her together."

"Are you sure that's how you want to handle it?"

"No. But let's do it anyway." Beth hopped out of bed and started opening drawers.

"Beth, all I have to wear is my suit from last night."

"Oh well, that's all you have to wear then, I guess."

Cassie was eating cereal when they walked hand in hand into the kitchen. She glanced up and froze, spoon halfway to her mouth. "You spent the night?"

"Uhh, yeah," he answered lamely.

Cassie continued eating. "Do you want some cereal or something?"

He exhaled and joined her at the table. "Thanks, that sounds great."

Beth reached into the cabinet for a bowl.

"Nice suit," Cassie teased.

He took an assessment of his wrinkled shirt and pants. "Yeah. Somehow I think it looked better last night."

Cassie snorted.

As Beth handed the bowl to Chad, Cassie's eyes got big, and she grabbed Beth's hand. "Umm, Cas—"

"You two are engaged?"

She searched her daughter's face. "Yes. That's what I wanted to talk to you about—"

Cassie jumped up and hugged Chad. "Way to go!" She ran over to hug a stunned Beth. "This is great! Congratulations! When's the wedding? How did you propose? Let me see that ring."

Beth laughed, pulling her daughter in for another hug. "I love you, Cas, you know that? But if you have any concerns, you can tell us..."

"Yeah, Cas. It wouldn't hurt my feelings. I'd understand if—"

"What? No. Chad's the best thing that ever happened to you, Mom. Anyone can see that. He made you laugh again, I mean, truly laugh. You get a certain glow every time he calls you, or you talk about him. This is fantastic news. I've got to go call Jessica. Can I tell Jessica?"

"Of course."

She ran out of the kitchen. They exchanged a smile. But before they could do anything else, Cassie ran back in and slid across the kitchen floor in her socks to give Chad a kiss on the cheek. "Welcome to the family."

He gave her arm a squeeze. "Thanks, Cas." She tore out of the room and ran up the stairs.

"Man," Beth commented, gliding over to his side. "You sure know how to charm the Donovan women."

"Do I?" he replied innocently, pulling her down into his lap and kissing her.

After a couple of minutes, she climbed out of his lap and sat adjacent from him at the table. As he was just shoveling his first bite of cereal in, she began. "Chad, we still need to talk about this hate mail you received."

"Oh, that." He hoped she would forget about it with all the excitement. "Really, Beth, it's no big deal."

"You promised 'full disclosure.'"

"All right." He set his spoon down. "I've been getting letters for a while. Ever since the first of the year, actually, and—"

"The first of the year? And you didn't tell me about them?"

"Well, I really didn't think it was a big deal. I receive hate mail all the time. As many crazy fans who love us, there's an equal amount of crazies who hate us for some reason. And as the face of the band, so to speak, things generally get addressed to me."

"So, why was this different?"

"I guess it was a little bit more personal."

"In what way?"

"They say stuff about the way I treat women."

Beth pondered this. "An old girlfriend?"

"That's a definite possibility, but I don't want you to worry about this. Pete will make sure nothing happens."

"I'd like to be able to put my trust in Pete, but it still makes me nervous to think someone is gunning for my man." She rose and kissed him on top of the head before heading up for a shower.

CHAPTER TWENTY-EIGHT

C had stood on stage, fiddling with his tie, alongside Roger, and Beth's uncle, who happened to be a priest. The men were joking around, when suddenly Roger's eyes got wide. Chad turned to see Beth approaching, wearing an off-white sleeveless dress, tied behind the neck.

"Holy shit! She's freaking gorgeous. You don't deserve her," Roger threw out, stepping forward. Chad simply swung his arm into his friend's midsection to stop him, a huge smile plastered on the lead singer's face. The couple met at mid-stage and immediately started kissing.

"Nah-ah-ah!" Keith yelled. "Not before the wedding."

"Dude, leave us alone," Beth told him between kisses, purposefully using the word "dude" as Keith seemed to employ it the way other people used "um." All of the band members cracked up.

"Mom, save it for the honeymoon," Cassie shouted.

"Oh yeah," Beth mumbled, coming up for air. "My daughter's here, ahem..." She scooted back to a more proper position. Throughout the short ceremony, the bride and groom never took their eyes off each other. Chad's hands circled her waist.

"You may kiss the bride," the priest finally announced.

As they kissed, ten-foot flames shot up on either side of them. "Nice touch," she murmured, her forehead resting against her new husband's.

"I thought you'd like that."

"Like those two need any more fireworks," Roger muttered out of the side of his mouth.

"No doubt," Cali responded.

He eyed her. "I like you. What are you doing after the reception?"

"If you're lucky," Cali answered with a wink, "you."

"I *really* like you." He trailed after her like a puppy.

WEEKS LATER, CHAD WAS back in Bloomington for a few days. Beth crawled out of bed, leaving him sleeping, to see Cassie off to school. She had just begun her workout DVD when he came down the stairs. Without saying anything, he sat on the couch, arms crossed, a grin on his face.

Beth, dressed in spandex shorts and a sports bra, eyed him skeptically over her shoulder. "What are you doing?" she asked with feigned annoyance. Because their schedules were so different from one another, she was secretly glad he was up; this would be the first day off she was able to spend with him.

"I'm just watching you work out." Latin music was playing and an overly smiley instructor named Carrie was counting off numbers as she sashayed across the screen. She didn't seem to sweat at all.

"Whyy?"

"I just wanted to see what you and Carrie had planned. Uum." He moaned as if in pain, watching Beth samba. "So, it's Carrie I have to thank for the way you move."

She turned to face him, dipping and moving her hips in an extremely inviting way. "I like to think I have a few moves of my own."

He sucked in his breath. "Uum-hum." He dove over the coffee table to grab his wife, but she dodged. She whirled and continued to follow Carrie's lead but cast a teasing smile over her shoulder from time to time. He bolted up and came around the coffee table, standing behind her.

"What are you doing now?"

"I want you to teach me how to samba." He stood directly behind her and ran his hands down her arms then grabbed her hands. He bent the left arm at the elbow and placed a hand on her bare stomach, just below her belly button, his large hand covering it. He left the right arm extended, bending his arm to compensate for her smaller arms. He bent his knees a little, to bring their hips more in line and pulled her in strongly against his body. "So, teach me," he whispered in her ear, letting his facial hair graze her skin.

They both knew this workout was going to end up in the bedroom, but they had to tempt each other first. She turned her head to the right to peer up at him, her lips parted, her eyes liquid. He bent in to kiss her, but she turned her head forward again at the last minute. He gave a throaty chuckle. She began to move her hips sensually, still keeping them a little distant from his.

After a few minutes she moved closer to him, so they flowed together, her hips moving backward and forward, up and down, left and right. She released his right hand, stretching her arm to bring it behind his neck, tightening her grip on him until they melted into one. He ran his hand slowly down her arm and across her right breast, before letting it join his other hand around her waist.

"I think I can give you a better work out than Carrie," he growled in her ear. "One that will get—" he punctuated each part of his sentence with a kiss and nuzzle on her neck "—your lungs going...and your heart beating...and will be good for a...number...of different parts...of your body." He used a hand to turn her head and kissed her hungrily. "Last one in bed is a rotten egg," he challenged, and tore off upstairs. She laughed. No one could leave her hanging better than he did.

But, in the end, he was as good as his word.

LATER IN THE DAY, AFTER Cassie got home from school, Chad was busy writing a song. He set down his pen as Beth entered the living room. "Hey, what's wrong with my girl?"

She came over and sat in his lap, crying.

"Sh-sh-sh. Come on now, Beth, what could be so wrong?"

"I'm sorry," she remarked, sniffling. "You know that guy who was supposed to take Cassie to prom? Well, some other girl asked him to go, so he dumped Cassie."

"You have got to be kidding me."

"Cassie's just devastated. She's been up in her room crying for an hour."

"What's the scum's name? Do you want me to go beat the shit out of him?"

"Well, yes." He made a move to get off the couch, but she held him back with her arm, looking at him with severity.

"Oh yeah," he mumbled contritely, looking unhappy. "This is supposed to be the new peace-loving Chad." He was referring to his visits to the therapist to deal with his scarred upbringing. "Peace, love, and rock and roll, see?" He held his fingers up in a peace sign.

She laughed. "Oh sure, right. I can just see you playing The Grateful Dead. I'd forgotten how much it sounds like 'Rip Your Heart Out,'" she joked, referring to one of Trapped Under Ice's singles, and bent his fingers back.

"Ouch, woman. That's not very peace-loving." Chad started nuzzling her and she giggled.

Cassie came around the corner. "Don't you two ever stop?" She shook her head at them.

Beth straightened. "Hey, Cas. Are you feeling a little better?"

"Yeah," the teen replied, flopping down on the couch next to Chad, her eyes still red. "Jason was a jerk, anyway." She blew her nose.

"Jason, huh? What's his last name?" he asked, putting his arm around Cassie confidentially.

Beth elbowed him. "Oh, you. Stop."

"Ouch. Your mom is violent."

"Tell me about it."

"Don't you two gang up on me," she cried, but she smiled. Seeing the two of them together made her feel good.

"Mom...you know what this calls for..."

"Ice cream!" they yelled in unison.

Beth jumped off the couch. "I'll get the spoons."

"I'll get the bowls," Cassie seconded, right behind her.

"We don't need bowls. We'll just eat out of the carton."

Their voices faded as they entered the kitchen. "What kind of weird ritual is this?" he asked no one in particular. He jumped up and followed them. "Wait for me."

A MONTH LATER, CHAD stood leaning against the mantle, tapping his foot impatiently, waiting for Beth and Cassie to come down. It was prom night, and they had been upstairs for hours, or so it seemed to him. The TV was on, but hearing footsteps on the stairs, he grabbed the remote to turn it off. He looked up as Cassie came into the room. "Wowww, Cas! You look beautiful."

She blushed. "Yeah, right." Before he could object, she asked, "What were you watching?"

"Oh, um...a documentary on the Great Wall of China. Very interesting stuff."

"You were watching your own concert DVD again, weren't you? You're so weird."

He hugged her, kissing her forehead. "You look just like your mother did on the night I proposed to her." Cassie did, in fact, have the same kind of glow. He gave her another squeeze.

"Uh, Chad. The 'do." The teen pointed to the mounds of curls cascading from a bun at the back of her head.

"Ohh. Not the 'do. How crass of me."

"Indeed," she returned regally, grinning at him. She decided to go to the dance with a girlfriend of hers who was similarly without a date, but he could tell she was nervous.

They both looked up as Beth descended the stairs. She wore a simple, flowing dress made out of a silky material. She told Chad she hated how some of the other mothers tried to show up the girls. "It is supposed to be their night, after all," she declared. But, with silver jewelry accenting her attire, she still looked stunning.

"Oh, honey," she scolded. "Watch the 'do."

He shuffled away from Cassie wearing a guilty expression. "That's already been covered."

"No, get back over there. I want to take your picture, just watch the 'do."

"Ah, Mom. I don't want any pictures." Cassie argued at the same time Chad protested, "But I just have jeans and a T-shirt on."

"Cas, this is your prom night," she ordered sternly. "You are going to want pictures. And you, you look hot in jeans and a T-shirt."

"Ick," Cassie squealed in mock-disgust. After the picture was taken, she rushed off. "I'm going to go get my purse."

"I still wish you'd signed me up as a chaperone too," Chad sulked.

"Honey, I said I was sorry. I didn't know you would want to."

"Not want to be at Cassie's senior prom with you?"

"I just thought it would be a mess with fans."

"All of her friends know we're married, but they haven't caused any problems."

"You're right. But Pete said it would be impossible to secure—" she stopped abruptly.

"You asked Pete about this?"

She sighed. "He didn't think it would be safe."

"What? Am I supposed to miss out on all the important things in yours and Cassie's lives because it 'may not be safe'? Give me a break." He turned his back to her and stalked over to the fireplace, leaning on the mantle.

She crossed to him, laying a hand on his back. "I'm sorry, Chad. I really am," she implored him. "It may take us some time to figure out how this whole being-married-to-a-celebrity thing works." She waited, but he didn't respond. "I should have asked you, though."

He could hear in her voice how badly she felt. This was a difficult transition for her, too. Being married to a rock star had some definite drawbacks.

He sighed. "No, Beth. It's all right. You were just trying to do what was best for all of us." He drew her into his arms. "We'll get it all figured out." He kissed the top of her head.

Cassie came down the stairs. "Are you ready, Mom?"

She glanced up again to see if he was okay. He gave her a small smile and a kiss. "Have fun." He turned to Cassie. "And you, don't do anything I wouldn't do."

"And what, exactly, does that eliminate?"

"Oh, go on and get out of here before I mess up your 'do."

"All right. I'm out of here," the excited teen announced. Cassie acted as if she was running out, then she turned around and came back and gave him a kiss on the cheek.

With one last long look, the two women in his life were gone.

AT FIRST BETH SMILED and chitchatted with people at the dance. The teens' enthusiasm was contagious. But after a while she drifted off by herself, thinking about Chad, and again scolding herself for leaving him out.

She scanned the room for a sign of Cassie. She saw her at a table with Jessica. As she watched, a young man came up and appeared to ask Jessica to dance. Cassie smiled at them as they left, but then she could see a shadow cross her face even from across the room. Or maybe it was just the expert eye of a mother who knew her daughter well. Her heart ached. This was one of the hardest parts of being a mother, watching your child in pain. Cassie fiddled with a napkin, turning it over in her hand, and then folding and unfolding it.

Should she cross the room and try to cheer her up? Or would Cassie prefer to handle this on her own? For the millionth time, she wished God provided her with a manual, so she knew exactly what to do for her daughter. She decided to move closer and try to pick up on some kind of signal from Cassie, when Mrs. Van Zandt accosted her.

"Beth. How are you?" She gave her one of those air kisses and stiff hugs that said, "I don't want you to wrinkle my dress," ever so politely. "I haven't seen you since your newest wedding—"

Like I've had five?

"How are things?"

"Wonderful. Thank you for asking." The doctor's wife wore a lime-green mermaid dress Beth would like to think seemed too young for her, but in reality, Botox and plastic surgery had her looking fantastic. Mrs. Van Zandt was one of the women she thought didn't mind stealing a little of her daughter's thunder on prom night.

"I saw your Cassie sitting by herself over there. Poor thing." Coming from anyone else, the comment might have seemed sympathetic, but the tone with which it was issued implied no such kindness. She stared at the woman with a blank expression for a second, but then her eyes automatically searched out Cassie again. Her daughter had just risen from the table with a very tall man dressed in black.

Her companion followed Beth's gaze. "Isn't that your husband?" the good doctor's wife was saying to her.

She beamed. "Yes. Yes, it is." As she watched, Chad steered Cassie out onto the floor and began to dance with her to a slower song. There was a ripple of recognition around the room as people started to watch the pair dance.

"My. He is a cool drink of water, isn't he?" Mrs. Van Zandt exclaimed, fanning herself with her handbag with obvious appreciation for Chad's body.

"Yes," she agreed with a smile. "He is at that."

Chad twirled Cassie gracefully around the dance floor. He peered down into her face, which was awash in happiness.

"I thought you weren't coming."

He leaned in and whispered in her ear, "Cas, I wouldn't miss this for the world." He pulled back again and smiled at her.

Her eyes scanned the room, catching all the looks of envy and admiration her peers were wearing. "I think having a rock star for a stepfather might not be that bad after all."

He laughed. "Glad to hear it."

When the song was over, he escorted her back to her table and pulled her chair out. "Now, if you would excuse me for a minute, I would love to dance with your mom."

He turned to search for Beth, and their eyes locked from across the room. An invisible electrical current seemed to pass between them. He strolled over to the DJ, pulling something from an inner pocket and handing it to him while holding a brief conversation with the young man.

"What is he up to?" Beth wondered out loud.

"I have no earthly idea. He's your husband."

Chad picked up the DJ's microphone. "Would Mrs. Beth Evans please report to the dance floor?" He handed the microphone back and moved to the middle of the dance floor.

The DJ announced, "Could everyone please clear the floor for just a moment, please?"

Forgetting to even excuse herself, she glided to the dance floor on air. As she approached, he extended his hand to her, and when she placed it in his, he walked around in a wide circle, never taking his eyes off her. Then, he pulled her into his arms so suddenly, she actually fell into them.

She laughed. "You're crazy."

"I never tried to hide that from you," he returned with a grin. The beginning notes to Jimmy Buffet's version of "Slow Boat to China" began playing over the sound system.

Her shock registered on her face as she began to sputter, "How did you...you remembered. I can't believe you..." Finally, she gave up on speech.

"We never got to dance at our wedding," he responded simply. He spun her around the dance floor, hoping she wouldn't ask where he'd learned, because it was Julie who had forced him to take lessons.

Although she never took a lesson in her life, Beth found it easy to match her husband's movements, their bodies so in tune with one another. At the end of their dance, he dipped her as the spectators who had gathered around the dance floor applauded.

The noise of the crowd seemed to awaken her from her dream. She laughed, a little embarrassed. As they left the dance floor, she took in the face of Marly Van Zandt. It was nearly as green as her dress. Beth's eyes were then drawn to a familiar figure at the back of the auditorium. Pete shrugged, as if to say, "Chad got his way again." But then, she noticed several big men who she didn't recognize as fathers of Cassie's classmates. They stood evenly spaced around the room, some with their hands conspicuously behind their backs in a guard pose.

"Pete bring some friends tonight?"

Chad glanced in his direction. "That was our compromise."

She turned toward him and toyed with his collar. "How would you like to go into the gym and make-out behind the bleachers?"

He chuckled lustily. "I'd like that." They snuck off together, noticed only by Pete and his men.

CHAPTER TWENTY-NINE

It was summer break, and Cas had gone to Myrtle Beach with her friend, Jessica's family. Beth was in the middle of enjoying a whole week touring with Trapped Under Ice, the last week of their tour before their own summer break of sorts. Cali, missing the opportunity to be with her friend at work, tagged along so they could spend some time together.

They were all returning from sound check on Friday night and being a bit boisterous; Roger was challenging Cali to a shot war after the concert. When they climbed into the bus, Pete, Dante, and a stranger dressed in a suit and tie were huddled around something on the coffee table.

"We got another one, Chad," Pete stated grimly.

"Another what?" Beth wondered aloud.

"Beth, it's just some business stuff," Chad answered, evading her eyes. "We'll go discuss it on David's bus, and you and Cali can just relax here for a while."

Chad seemed a little too nervous and Pete a little too concerned for Beth's liking. She stepped forward, her mouth set. "Another what, Pete?"

Pete stared at Chad.

"What the hell's going on, Chad?" Beth asked.

He sighed. "Go ahead and tell her," he muttered resolutely, sinking into a chair. "I know you want to."

"A death threat."

"What?" She turned to stare at Chad. "You said it was just hate mail. 'The usual stuff,' I thought you said."

He eyed her tensely, his jaw tight, but didn't respond.

"It's a little more serious than that, Beth," Pete answered for him. Chad shot him a look. "I've been against keeping her in the dark about this from the start," he countered, an edge to his voice. Chad stared at Pete stonily, but the bodyguard ignored him. "By the way, this here is Chief of Police Bernie Swallow."

"Nice to meet you all."

Everybody nodded uncomfortably.

Beth gestured to the note. "Can I see it?"

Pete and the police chief exchanged a look, and the latter nodded.

"Yes," Pete told her, "but try not to handle it too much. I'll send it to my buddy at the FBI, but it'll more than likely be clean like the others were."

Beth read the letter.

You haven't listened to my warnings, so this will be the last one...if you sing, "Beth's Song" tonight it will be the last time you sing or say her name. I'll be waiting for you in the audience, and I'm a pretty good shot. The two of you don't belong together, so it's simple: leave Beth or die.

SHE SUCKED IN HER BREATH. Who was this person, and why didn't they want Chad to be with her? It was so strange to see her name in print along with a threat on her husband's life. She handed the note back, her hands trembling.

She peered up at Chad, the fear evident in her eyes. This was just what he didn't want to happen.

"Babe, it's okay—"

"It's not okay." Her voice rose in pitch and volume. "Someone threatening your life is not 'okay' in my book." She took a deep breath to steady herself. "Why do you think this part is underlined, Pete?" she asked, pointing to the page.

"We both think," he replied, indicating the chief, "it means as soon as Chad sings your name in that song for the first time, the shooter would take his, or her, shot."

"What are we going to do?" she asked, ready to place her trust in him.

"Well, first of all, Chad's not going to sing that song. Then..." He paused to let Chief Swallow explain their plan.

"We'll channel everyone through a couple of entrances tonight, set up with metal detectors. I'll have several squads on hand, plus the security people the facility employs, and your own personal staff here."

"But," Pete interrupted, "in all honesty, if someone wants to get a gun in here, there are ways to get it done."

"Why don't we just cancel the concert?"

"Then what about the next concert, Beth? Are we going to let this person dictate our lives?" Chad questioned edgily.

"If it means keeping you alive and whole, yes," she returned, fire in her eyes. Everyone sat uneasily, looking from one to the other.

"Beth," Pete ventured, "I think Chad is right about this." They both turned and gawked at him. "We both do." The police chief nodded. "Let's face it; he is a walking target anywhere. We have a lot of things playing to our advantage tonight. For one thing, twenty thousand pairs of eyes. If someone tries anything in this crowd tonight, somebody's bound to see them. Two, we'll get cameras set up at the entrances and we'll know everyone who comes in and out of here. This will narrow down our suspects some."

"To one of twenty thousand people? Those aren't great odds."

"Well," Pete countered, "maybe you could help us with that. Up to this point we've been focusing on Chad's enemies, because we thought it was more likely someone would want to kill him, he being Chad and all," Pete added sarcastically, "than you, who I doubt has an enemy in the world."

"She doesn't," Cali stated loyally.

Chief Swallow spoke up. "Is there anyone you know of who would like to see you and Mr. Evans apart? An old boyfriend, perhaps?"

"No. My husband, Paul, and I were married for fourteen years. Before him, I only dated about a half-dozen guys in high school and college, none of whom I've kept in touch with."

"What about after your husband and before Chad? Anyone who had a crush on you? Asked you out, but you turned them down?"

She looked at Cali.

"Beth made it pretty clear she was not interested in seeing anyone. Any guy who liked her didn't get far enough to develop any real feelings for her. There were plenty of guys who were interested, but I sort of ran interference for her. I think you'd be looking in the wrong place there."

"Okay," Pete remarked, satisfied. "We're doing some checking on Julie Miles—excuse me, Julie Julien, now. I never liked that one," he mumbled under his breath. "It appears, however, she has been out of the country on some kind of photo shoot, but we're double-checking all the same. Right now, she is still our prime suspect. We need to go and set up the security measures I talked about. Dante will stay here with you all."

"And I'll have a squad car parked outside."

Pete looked at them each in turn. "From now on, I don't want any strays. You stay with the herd. Got it, everyone?"

They each nodded their heads solemnly.

As Pete passed Beth, he put his hand on her arm. "Beth, I've been in this business for a number of years. I've guarded diplomats and movie stars. I've foiled several attempts on my clients' lives. Chad is like a son to me." Chad stared at him in surprise. "Sure, we butt heads a lot, just like I did with my son before he was killed. He worked on the force, just like I did, until some two-bit crook killed him over a stereo system the owner later told us didn't even work." The bodyguard sighed, looking sad and older than usual for a minute. "I wasn't there that night to help my son. But I'm here now, Beth, and I'm not going to let anything happen to Chad. Trust me."

She nodded, squeezing his hand and giving him a weak smile. She knew Pete knew what he was doing. She just hoped it would be enough.

BETH WAS A NERVOUS wreck backstage with Pete and Cali. Cali convinced her to do a shot to calm her nerves, but it didn't seem to be working. Every camera flash seemed like a muzzle flash to her, and it was killing her to watch Chad on the big stage like a target in a carnival game.

Chad and Roger nixed her singing with them tonight on "I Just Had to Have You Last Night," although she put up an argument that if they could be a pair of idiots and put their necks on the line, she should be allowed to do the same. The band members stood firm, and Beth ended up having to back down. Now, she stood backstage, strung like piano wire, feeling useless.

Chad for his part seemed to be getting increasingly uptight on stage. The shot he downed to calm him seemed to be having the opposite effect. Halfway through the second set he called a powwow on stage.

"Change of plans. We're playing 'Beth's Song' next."

"Dude, are you crazy?"

"No way, Chad. We're not going to do it!"

"Listen, you guys, I'm not going to let anyone tell me not to sing that song. You guys can either accompany me, or sit back and listen, 'cause I'm singing that song!" Chad stormed away from them and started strumming the first notes.

Beth's face turned white. "Oh no. What is he doing?"

Pete didn't recognize the song at first, but Beth's reaction clued him in.

MY LIFE WAS COLD AND black
    Before you came and fixed what was broken in me
    And now I wish I could give back
    Just a little of what you've given to me
    I thought the poison within me
    Had killed all the love I could give..."

CHAD CLOSED HIS EYES and took a deep breath before continuing.

Beth's eyes were also squeezed shut.

Pete was scanning the audience frantically.

BUT LOVING YOU, BETH, is so simple...

NOTHING HAPPENED. CHAD felt no bullet tear through him. Beth heard no shot. Pete saw no flash.

Chad opened his eyes to find David standing in front of him, playing his bass guitar.

He stood, grabbing his microphone and striding out from behind the protection of David's body, glaring at him. When the song was over, Chad announced, "We're going to take a quick break while Keith entertains you on the drums."

Keith mumbled, "Why is it they all get to go off stage for a drink, and I always get stuck 'entertaining?'"

Chad stomped off stage. Pete and Beth saw him coming and, seeming to recognize his explosive mood, got out of his way.

As soon as they were all backstage, Chad turned on David. "What the hell are you doing?"

"Trying to save your life!" he yelled back.

Chad's eyes opened wider. It was the first time David had ever raised his voice to him. "You idiot! Don't you know you could have been killed?"

"I...know," he responded evenly. Everybody stood frozen for a minute, staring at the two.

Chad pushed his hair back from his forehead with both hands, flabbergasted. "It's my job to take care of you, Davy." His voice broke.

"Sorry, man. It was my turn."

Chad stared at him for a minute, stunned. Then, the two embraced and thumped each other on the back. "I love you, man."

"I love you, too, Chad."

When they drew apart, Chad searched for Beth. She ran the few feet to him, and he threw his arms around her, picking her up off the floor. He closed his eyes, holding her tight.

"You jerk," Beth choked out under her breath.

That was when everyone realized Keith was going into the fourth minute of his drum solo. "We'd better get back out there."

Beth let Chad go and squeezed David. "Thank you," she whispered to him.

Roger tapped her on the shoulder. "Beth, we kind of need him..."

She laughed and released him, slapping Roger on the tush as he turned to leave. "Yeah, right. Everyone else gets hugs..." Beth, feeling jubilant, ran after him and jumped on his back for a second before sliding back down to the ground. Roger turned to get a proper hug, kissing her on the head before leaving.

Pete didn't have the heart to tell her Chad still had an hour on stage, just as much a target as before.

CHAPTER THIRTY

B eth woke up to find the other side of the bed empty. Frantic, she pulled on her robe and left the bedroom. She rushed out to find Chad at his weight bench, which they set up in a little workout area just outside of Keith's door, pumping iron. She stood and watched him silently.

He wore jeans and a gray T-shirt that was soaked in sweat. His face was contorted as he extended the barbell overhead, his muscles bulging. His skin glistened, and she could see his face was angry as he dropped the barbell, and then pushed it back up in rapid succession, his breath coming out in loud huffs. A sort of fury seemed to fuel him, and she realized he was much more worried than he let on.

Cali abruptly came out of her bedroom wearing pajamas and yawning.

Chad shelved the barbell and sat on the end of the bench. He greeted Cali with a smile, grabbing a towel to mop his face with. "Hey!"

She glared at him. "Muscles don't stop bullets, you know, Chad," she answered callously, not seeming to realize Beth was there as well.

"Cali!" she shouted, shocked and angered.

"I'm so sorry," Cali stammered contritely. "I just have a raging headache. Maybe going toe-to-toe with Roger in a shot war wasn't my best idea."

Beth still frowned at her as she passed to get some orange juice out of the fridge. But then she thought about it.

I should be more tolerant. This death threat has us all on edge, even Cali.

She approached Chad.

He reached out and grabbed the back of her leg. "Hey, babe."

She touched his face then kissed him.

"I know we talked about this all night," he began earnestly, "but maybe now it's morning, you'll see things in a different light." He glanced down for a minute then met her eyes. "I want you to reconsider leaving here and going home."

"Chad," she uttered, exasperated, "we've been over this. I'm not leaving. We're husband and wife now. You're no longer a one-man show and you're just going to have to get used to that fact. What threatens you, threatens me."

Despite his concern for her, the words she spoke he took to heart. He was no longer the one-man show he had been all his life, especially when he had to grow up fast and take care of Davy when he was barely a teen. Beth came into his life and filled that void, choosing to become his wife. Sometimes he still couldn't believe it.

Chad stood and cupped her face in his hands, kissing her. "I need to take a shower. I'm all sweaty."

He turned to leave, and Beth took the opportunity to grab his rear. Even sweaty, he was a hunk. He smiled at her over his shoulder, removing his shirt as he walked.

WHEN IT CAME TIME FOR sound check, Cali was still "feeling a bit under the weather." She stayed in the bus to sleep it off while the others trudged into the stadium. Other than Roger suffering from "one hell of a headache," the check went well.

As they were coming back out to the buses, though, Roger was being given a pretty hard time by his friends.

"The Boss Lady thought Cali and I were a handful, but Cali and Roger are like an atomic explosion. I'm going to have to use the B.L.'s strategy and threaten to separate the two of you if this continues," Beth teased. Everyone laughed.

"Chad," Pete said in a low voice.

"Beth, why don't we go back and get my guitar."

But she recognized the warning tone in Pete's voice. Instead of turning back, she took a few steps forward, away from Chad. She stared ahead to the door of the bus, where she saw a note was attached with a knife. Red writing trailed down the page, looking as if it was made in blood.

"Oh, God, Chad. Cali's in there." Beth started running in the direction of the bus, but Chad and Roger lunged, grabbing her to hold her back.

"You stay here, Beth!" Pete yelled fiercely. "*You stay here!*"

He and Dante moved forward, hands ready to pull weapons from underneath their jackets. They signaled to a police car parked several yards beyond the buses, and two uniformed policemen scrambled out of their cars, hurrying toward them. When the group reached the bus, they stopped to listen. Hearing a noise inside, they drew their guns. Dante nodded to Pete, and Pete opened the door, stepping in just ahead of the rest. Noises were coming from Chad and Beth's bedroom. Creeping cautiously in the direction of the front of the bus, the two finally stood on either side of the doorway, the policemen flanking them. Mouthing a countdown, with his hand on the doorknob, Pete got to three and opened the door, springing through it with Dante. Cali, who sat on the edge of the bed, wrapped in a towel, jumped up with a scream, the motion causing her towel to fall to the floor.

Outside, they all heard the scream coming from the bus. Frozen for a second, Chad and Roger forgot to keep hold of Beth. She rushed forward a few steps, but they reached her and started dragging her backward. "Cali! Cali!" she screamed hysterically.

All at once, Pete appeared on the outside staircase. "Everything's okay, folks. Coast is clear."

"What about Cali?" Chad called.

"She's fine. We just surprised her is all. She'd just stepped out of the shower," he added, rather sheepishly.

Beth ran forward to check on her friend. By the time she got up the stairs and in the door, Cali was coming out of the bedroom with a T-shirt on, zipping up jeans, her hair still wet. She swallowed her friend up in a hug.

"You're sure you're all right?"

"Fine," Cali replied. "But you can tell your friends here, if they want to check out my goods, they just need to ask first."

Everyone laughed, lightening the mood a little bit, until they heard the twang of the knife as Pete pulled it out of the door. Beth scooted back over to Chad, and he put his arm around her as everyone gathered around the table where Pete was examining the note. It said: "You're going to get what you have coming to you, Chad." Pete felt the letters, which looked wet and dripping, but they were in fact dry. He brought the note up to his nose and smelled it.

"I think this is nail polish. Beth?" He handed the page to her, and she smelled it.

"Could be. Here, Cali, you smell it. You're the fingernail expert."

Cali held it up to her nose. "Ready, Set, Red #356, LePlume International." Everybody stared at her. "What? I was just trying to do my television crime scene investigator imitation. Yeah, I'd say it's a safe bet it's probably fingernail polish."

"Chad, do the words give you a clue? Has anyone ever said that to you before?"

He shook his head. "Only in jest. I haven't a clue."

Pete turned back to Cali. "And Cali, you didn't hear anything?"

"No. I wasn't feeling the greatest—" she slid an accusatory glance at Roger "—so I slept for...about twenty minutes or so, I guess. Then, I got up to take a shower. And then you know what happened next," she added pointedly.

Dante coughed in an effort to cover a chuckle. Pete's face turned red. "Yeah. Again, I'm sorry about that."

Cali snorted, as if not believing him.

"Don't you think all of us should stay in a hotel tonight?"

"I've been thinking about that, Roger, and I think we're better off staying here. A hotel would be difficult to secure with all the people in and out—"

"But whoever it is that is after Chad wouldn't know where we were."

"True. But let's face it, they obviously got around our security measures here. We're not dealing with any dodo." He paused to let this sink in. "If you all are here, we can limit access to you fairly easily. However, I would like to have Dante and I take turns sleeping on the couch and standing guard, if no one objects." Everyone looked at Cali.

"What? As long as you can resist the urge to climb into bed with me, I don't have a problem with it."

"I'll do my best," Pete retorted wryly.

EVERYBODY TURNED IN early, exhausted by the drama of the past few days. Sometime after midnight, Chad woke up. Beth was moaning in her sleep.

In her dreams, Beth received a phone call. It was a strange dream, voices shifting from clear to terribly distorted, and faces coming in and out of focus.

"Mrs. Evans?"

"Yes." The bottom of her stomach dropped out.

"This is Aurora Sinai Medical Center in Milwaukee, Wisconsin. We regret to inform you, your husband, Chad Evans, was shot and killed this evening. We did all that we could." The voice was mocking.

"Beth," Chad was shaking her.

She was breathing hard. "Oh. I'm sorry."

"No, it's okay. Was it a bad dream?" He pulled her closer.

"Yeah. But everything is okay now." His arms around her felt so reassuring.

"We'll catch whoever is doing this to us."

"I know."

"I love you."

"I know." Beth drifted off into a more peaceful slumber.

Having been awakened, Chad had a hard time falling back asleep. After tossing and turning for a while, he decided to get up. He crept out into the living room.

Pete's voice arrested him from the darkness. "Chad, what the hell are you doing?"

"I couldn't sleep. I thought I'd go into the building and get my guitar."

"What part of 'stay with the herd' don't you understand?" Even in the darkness Pete could see the stubborn set of his chin, silhouetted, as it was, by the parking lot's lights pouring in through the windows. The older man sat and buckled up his pants. "I couldn't sleep anyway. I'll go with you." Maybe getting Chad on his own, he'd be able to talk some sense into him about being more cautious and less headstrong, and ask him why he had the asinine idea to sing that damn song.

The two men left the bus, passing Dante outside and letting him know they'd be back in a little bit.

CHAPTER THIRTY-ONE

Beth woke up with a start after another nightmare. She reached for Chad and found his spot empty. A strong fear gripped her. She could see the light was off in the bathroom, and no light was coming in under the door to the living room either. She flew out of bed and pulled on a pair of jeans. She grabbed a sweat jacket and tried to zip it over her camisole as she moved toward the door. To her surprise, the couch Pete had been occupying was empty, and a quick glance out the door showed no signs of Dante either. What could have happened? Where was everybody? She decided to wake Cali so her friend could go with her to investigate.

"Cal?" she whispered after entering her bedroom. She could see a lump in the bed in the dark. She moved to sit on the edge of the bed, again calling out Cali's name. She reached over to switch the bedside lamp on. When she turned back, she screamed in terror and jumped out of the bed, stumbling back several feet. One flailing arm became wrapped up in the cord from the window shade. Lying next to her in the bed wasn't Cali; it was Roger's lifeless bodyguard.

Dante's eyes were open wide in shock, and blood saturated the sheets and mattress. Beth sat staring—her trembling hand over her mouth—as if she looked long enough, the scene would somehow change. Unable to tear her eyes away from the terrifying image before her, she staggered toward the door a few steps, then finally, turned and ran. She knocked hard into a chair bolted to the floor, sending pain shooting up her thigh and hip, but continued to charge toward the door of the bus.

Once outside, she ran straight to Roger's bus and pounded on the door, calling his name and Chad's. Lights came on immediately inside, and within seconds Roger opened the door. He stood inside with a pair of jeans on and no shirt.

"Beth, what's—"

"Is Chad here?" she panted, her eyes wild.

"Chad?"

"They're gone. Oh, Roger—" Beth was crying now "—someone killed Dante." She swayed and reached for the stair's railing to steady herself.

Roger, afraid she was going to topple down the stairs or pass out, grabbed her by the waist to support her. She clung to him, still trying to make sense of everything. "Beth, tell me exactly what happened."

She took a deep breath and tried to sort through the rapid-fire images in her head. "I woke up. Chad was gone and so was Pete." She started crying again. "I-I was going to get Cali, but it wasn't Cali." She peered up at him, unable to communicate the horror she had witnessed. Roger gazed into her deep green, horrified eyes and tried to comprehend her garbled statements. She glanced toward the other bus. "Dante...there was so much blood."

All of a sudden, they heard the sound of pounding feet. Roger, unsure of who was approaching, shifted so he was standing in front of Beth to protect her. Around the far side of Chad's bus, two police officers raced into view. "What's going on?" they yelled, recognizing Roger in the parking lot's lights.

"I'm not sure. I think someone may be hurt on that bus. Do you know where the others are?"

By this time, Keith and David stood just inside the door to the bus, looking on with confused expressions.

"Mr. Evans and Mr. Harris went into the stadium together. Shortly after that, the outside guard went inside the bus, and a woman came out, following the first two men into the stadium."

Beth was trying to scramble past Roger. "Chad's in there," she mumbled more to herself than to him.

He spun around and gripped her by the shoulders, bending to look in her eyes. "You can't go in there." Still watching Beth, he called back over his shoulder. "We need to go into the stadium and make sure everyone is safe."

"I'm afraid we can't do that until backup arrives. We called for another squad car. They should be arriving soon. We'll need to get some more information. Who's in charge here?"

Roger nodded at David, who slipped out of the door and put his arm around Beth while Roger stepped down to speak with the police officers.

One of the men was taking notes while the other one questioned him. After Beth reassured David that she was okay, the two ventured down the steps to stand behind him.

Beth's eyes kept sliding to the stadium door. There was a killer lose, Chad was behind those doors, and all these men were going to do was take notes. When she was certain David was distracted by the conversation, she inched away.

Roger relayed as much as he understood from Beth to the officers, then he turned around so she could confirm he pretty much got the gist of it, and found she was no longer by David's side. He immediately checked the door to the stadium and saw a glimpse of her before she disappeared behind it. David followed his gaze.

"Shit!" they said in unison.

CHAD AND PETE RETRIEVED the singer's guitar and were heading back to the buses. Chad tried to listen patiently to Pete's lecture about personal safety, but he was going to be glad to just sit outside with Dante and play some guitar. It was what he tended to do whenever he couldn't sleep.

"Hey, man, can I stop really fast before we go outside?" Chad said indicating a bathroom. "I had a lot of beer. You can stand outside and guard the door, and I'll be right out."

"Okay. But make it quick."

The door had no more closed behind Chad when Pete thought he heard a sound from the dressing room a couple of doors down. Cautiously, he crept forward, thinking it was probably a mouse or some other small animal, but you could never be too sure. When he got to the door, he saw it was open a crack. He pulled his gun and gave the door a push, letting it swing open of its own accord. Seeing nothing out of place, he entered the room.

Cali sat with her back to him on the couch. She turned when he entered. "Pete. Hey."

He holstered his weapon. "Cali, what the hell are you doing in here in the middle of the night?"

"Well, I thought I might have a little more privacy if I took a shower in here."

Pete strolled around to the other side of the couch. "Yeah, I'm really sorry about earlier—" His words caught in his throat as he saw what she held in her hand.

She smiled at him. "I'm sorry, too, Pete," she said sweetly, and shot him. He fell against the coffee table and slid down to the floor, staring at her with wide eyes.

CHAD CAME OUT OF THE bathroom. "Okay, I'm read—" He looked around confused—no Pete. He heard a noise from the dressing room. Was Pete just checking in there to make sure everything was safe? Or was something wrong?

He entered the dressing room. "Hi, Cali. What are you doing up?"

"Just couldn't sleep."

"You probably shouldn't be here by yourself. Pete and I will walk you back," he offered, coming around so she wouldn't have to stretch her neck to talk to him. "Have you seen Pete?"

"Yes, actually," she said just as Chad rounded the couch to see Pete slumped against the table, blood covering the front of his jacket. He was breathing with difficulty, and his eyes were open wide, but he didn't speak. Cali held a gun in her hand, which she now pointed at Chad. "I've been waiting for this for a while, Chad."

Cali? Cali was the one who wanted him dead? "Why?" was all he could manage to say.

"Why not?" she replied, laughing without joy. "Oh, you're serious. Because, Chad—" her voice turned harsh "—you just wouldn't listen. When you treated Beth so poorly, as I knew you would, and she came to me upset, I told you then you weren't good enough for her." She rose from the couch with lethal grace, keeping the gun trained on him. "She told me what you did to her was just an accident, but we all know it's not true. Even Pete here, right, Pete?" She kicked the bodyguard as she passed him, moving toward Chad.

Pete grunted, following her with his eyes, but he seemed to only be able to concentrate on his breathing.

"So, you want to kill me because you feel I'm not worthy of your friend."

"No. I'm going to kill you because I have to keep you from hurting Beth. She was there for me when Tony cheated on me, when I—" her voice broke for a minute "—when I was in the hospital. I'm going to make sure she never goes through that with you. She's not as strong as I am. It would kill her."

"But, I love Beth too. I would never do anything to hurt her."

"Yeah. Like Tony didn't feed me the same line of bullshit." Her eyes flashed.

Chad couldn't see how he was going to get out of this one. She stood between him and the door. He only knew, the longer he kept her talking, the longer he lived. And he wanted to live. Besides, it could buy some time for someone to come to his aid. Although, would anyone even be up right now?

"Yeah," he murmured. "Beth told me about that. He wasn't there for you when you lost your baby."

She seemed to falter for a moment, the gun in her hand wavering slightly, but then she pulled herself together. "That's right. Because he was too busy screwing my best friend." The bitterness seemed to ooze from her pores.

CHAD WASN'T THE ONLY one to see it. Out in the hall, Beth peeked into the room, hidden by the door. She heard voices as soon as she entered the building. She heard Cali speaking distinctly, but it wasn't her Cali. The voice was harsh, with an edge to it she had never heard. And now, as she peered in, she saw her friend holding a gun on Chad. She gasped involuntarily.

Both Cali and Chad turned toward the noise in the hall. "Who's there?" Cali called out. They both heard someone scurry away. "Damn it." She moved behind Chad, keeping him in her sights. "You go in front of me, Chad. Start walking." She jabbed the muzzle of the gun into his back and shoved him with her free hand. He stumbled forward but caught himself. He glanced at Pete again, their eyes locking for a moment, each wondering if they would ever see the other again, before he was pushed beyond the couch.

ROGER WAS IN THE BUS, putting a shirt on as he talked to David. A second squad car arrived, and the police searched Chad's bus, finding Dante's body. Beth's story proven true, they decided to wait and call for more backup before heading into a large stadium where a madman could be hiding anywhere.

"We can't just sit around and wait while Chad could be in there..." David didn't want to complete the thought. "And Beth. Someone has to look out for Beth. You guys need to keep the police occupied while I sneak in there."

"No way, man. It's my turn to do the stupid and foolhardy thing," Roger stated. "You already did that when you stood in front of Chad at the concert."

David looked like he wanted to argue the point, but a policeman stuck his head in the door. "We have a few more questions."

David and Roger stared at each other. "Okay," David finally backed down with an air of disgust. "I'll be right with you." The officer left the bus. David put his hand on Roger's shoulder. "Be careful, man."

"I intend to be."

CHAPTER THIRTY-TWO

C had entered the hall with Cali trailing him. Who had been outside the door? And where did they go?

Cali threw a glance to her left. Not far away was the door leading out of the stadium. But she didn't think they went that way. She hadn't heard a door close, so she pushed Chad to the right. When they came parallel to the men's bathroom door, she ordered Chad to stop. His guitar was propped against the wall where he had left it.

"Open that door."

He obeyed her and she leaned into the room, listening for the sound of someone breathing. Satisfied no one was hiding in there, she continued down the hallway in the same way, stopping to check on doors here and there, finding most of them locked. In a few minutes time, they covered the distance of the hall and came to the curtained area backstage. Her eyes continually scanned in all directions, but Cali could not find the person she heard in the hall. Coming to a lighting board, she switched on several rows of lights. In an instant, the stage was flooded with brightness.

"Come on." She alternately nudged and pushed Chad until she had him center stage. "Get on your knees," she ordered. He reluctantly did what he was told. He felt the gun pressed against his temple. "All right. No more games!" Cali shouted into the empty stadium, her voice pinging off the metal catwalks holding the lights. "Come out where I can see you, or you can watch me shoot this man."

Beth was crouching in front of the stage. She searched around for anything she could use as a weapon. All she saw were amplifiers, wires, and the pyro board.

"I'm going to start counting," the voice warned. "One, two—"

"Okay. Okay." She rose.

Chad's heart sunk when he saw her. What was she doing in here? Their eyes locked and he swallowed. All he could think about was how much he loved her.

Cali, too, was unhappy to see her. "Beth, I didn't want you to see this."

"Cali, what are you doing?" She studied her friend with a sad expression.

"I—" She started to move forward, forgetting momentarily about Chad. "Get up," she instructed him, her voice reclaiming its edge. He got to his feet. When she turned to Beth, her attitude changed again. "I know you don't understand this right now, Beth, but this is for your own good."

"Cali, you're right, I don't understand. Chad is the best thing to happen to me in a long time."

"You think that now, but he will break your heart. Trust me, Beth."

"Cal, he's not Tony. Can't you see how happy he's made me?"

"Yeah. And the bigger the height, the harder the fall, girlfriend. You'll thank me for this someday."

Beth blinked in disbelief. Could Cali really believe she would thank her for killing the man she loved?

"Cali, please, this doesn't make sense."

"Not now, maybe. But it will someday, I promise."

Beth stood with her mouth open, at a loss for words. She could see there was no way to talk her friend out of her madness, so she would simply have to find a way for them to escape. "Cali, you have always been such a good friend to me," she stalled for time, focusing on discovering a way out. "You always make me laugh." Cali smiled at her words. "You've been there with me when I cried. I don't know how I would have gotten through losing Paul without you. I'm pleading with you now, please, please, Cal, let him go."

Chad could see Beth clearly from his position in front of Cali. He saw now that her fingers were on the pyro board. She gazed at him intently, and all at once he realized what she wanted him to do.

"I'm afraid I can't do that, Beth," Cali remarked with sadness.

"Please, Cali, if you'd only listen to me and—now!"

Chad ran and jumped off the stage just as Beth ignited a ten-foot-high jet of fire a foot to their right. He grabbed her hand, and they ran as fast as they could up an aisle between sections of seats. Cali was temporarily blinded and almost knocked off her feet by the heat. They heard her scream with rage as they broke through the doors and emerged into a wide hallway.

He tried to circle back in the direction from which they came, to the left, but within seconds he heard Cali slamming open the metal doors that they had just come through. Without thinking, he ducked into the next door. They found themselves in a dark commercial kitchen, the only light emanating from a bank of glass-fronted refrigerators on the far side of the room. The light played across the stainless-steel tables dividing the room. Knowing she was seconds behind them, they hid behind a row of trash cans and tried to still their breathing.

She burst through the door. Sardonic laughter filled the room. "Now wouldn't this just be the ironies to end all ironies. Chad Evans shot by the lunch lady in the kitchen."

She flipped on a set of light switches to the left of the door. To the couple's relief, the lights were the fluorescent-type, which took a lengthy time to reach their full illumination. Chad tried to remember if there was a back way out of the kitchen. He had played this auditorium many times before, but all of the stadium kitchens seemed to blend into one another, and his anxiety over their safety didn't help his recall much either.

Cali inched farther into the room, checking behind tables as she did so. He decided the only sure way out was the way they came in, so slowly, trying not to make a sound, they duck-walked in the direction of the door they entered through.

"Chad, you might as well give up. You're only prolonging the inevitable. So why don't you save us all the trouble and just come—out!" She sprang forward behind the trash cans they had vacated seconds before. Chad took advantage of her distraction and bolted for the door. He heard the metallic ping of a bullet hitting the door as they whizzed back out in the hall.

With the pursuer on their heels, they had no choice but to cross and enter the concert hall again. Ducking low, they ran behind rows of seats, heading left again, toward the backstage area. This time, they got a bit of distance between themselves and Cali, who took too long to locate them upon entering the inner ring of the stadium. But as he was looking ahead, he realized, with dread, he had made a bad decision. The section of seats they were running along dead-ended before it reached the backstage area. Before them was a short concrete wall, beyond it, a forty-foot drop to the section below. Beth seemed to realize their predicament at the same time. They searched around for another way out.

"Chad. The catwalk."

Spanning the stadium was a huge, black catwalk supporting the numerous stage lights for the concerts. Beth reached it and immediately scrambled up the ladder, and out onto the skinny bridge. He followed behind her, glancing back to see their tormentor gaining on them. They ran, their feet banging on the metal, across the bridge, the stage lights that Cali turned on swinging crazily below them, shooting beams of light in a haphazard fashion. They reached the far end and started running down a zigzagging staircase just as Cali reached the top of the catwalk on the other side.

As she ran, Beth heard a zing, and then Chad cried out. She turned to see him slam hard into the far railing, his momentum carrying him over it.

"Chad!" she screamed in terror. She rushed to the edge and saw him sprawled on a lower landing of the staircase. As she watched, he struggled to pull himself up the railing to a standing position. Beth glanced up to see how close Cali was. She had stopped to take aim at Chad again. In desperation, she seized a microphone cable that was hanging down from the ceiling and tried to swing it at Cali. The cable was too heavy for her to actually hit Cali with at her distance, but the movement caught Cali's eye and might have been enough to throw her aim off. In any case, Beth saw Chad clear the last flight of steps and safely make it behind the thick curtains along the side of the stage.

Cali screamed in fury, her rage distorting her features, and took up her pursuit again as Beth continued to spiral down the stairs. When she reached the bottom, she took off in the direction she thought Chad took but couldn't find him. She came to a door and entered a hallway she didn't recognize. She stumbled onward, her legs beginning to tire, her breathing jagged. Somewhere behind her, she heard a door open. Blindly, she entered a wide set of doors on her left.

The room she entered was dim, but she could see the outlines of a large skating rink in front of her. Before she could make a move, someone grabbed her from behind, clapping a hand over her mouth.

"Beth, it's okay. It's me, Roger," a familiar voice whispered in her ear.

He let her go and she whirled around. Beth grabbed him and buried her head in his chest. "Oh, God, Roger. I've never been so glad to see someone."

"I know, Beth." He kissed her head. "Where's Chad?"

She gazed up at him, fear clouding her eyes. "I don't know."

They heard someone approaching in the hall. Roger pressed Beth back into the shadow provided by the wall just as the door opened. They both immediately recognized the figure in the doorway. Beth threw herself on him. "Chad! Chad!"

"Beth." He sighed in relief, but then hastened to add, "Come on. She's right behind me."

The three ran the short distance to the rink, although Beth saw Chad was dragging one of his legs. He opened the door to the ice, and Beth and Roger stepped through. He closed the door behind him, and the three ducked down behind the baseboard circling the rink.

"The first chance we get, we'll jump her and get the gun," Roger whispered.

Chad shook his head. "I can't hit her."

"Why not?" Roger and Beth asked incredulously.

"I can't hit a woman."

"Well, you sure picked one hell of a time to get all noble on us," Roger snapped in irritation.

They hushed their conversation, hearing a noise. They saw a line of light on the ice from the crack between the doors. It grew wider as someone opened the door. Huddled with their backs against the wall, they listened, all three faces tense, exchanging anxious looks as they waited in the semidarkness. Lights clicked on in quick succession all across the room.

"Next time you want to hide from somebody, Chad, don't leave a trail of blood." Cali's face appeared above them, her gun pointed at him. "Of course," she said dryly, "there won't be a next time. Get up. All of you."

The trio steadied themselves against the boards as they reluctantly stood. Cali motioned with the gun for them to come off the ice. They stepped out onto the concrete floor one at a time.

Beth could not believe this was happening. Could her best friend really be intending to shoot her husband? None of it made sense. It was like being in some surreal dream, and she kept hoping the alarm clock would go off. But images of Dante's face with his unseeing eyes kept reminding her, this was all too real.

"Beth, you need to go. You don't want to see this." Cali's voice was paradoxically kind.

"I'm not going anywhere, Cal," she shouted, catching everyone off guard. "If you're going to do this to him, you better be prepared to do it to me, too, 'cause I'm not going anywhere."

"Beth, you should go," Chad stated, his voice soft and resigned.

"No!" she screamed in shock.

Chad looked at Roger. He swallowed but put his hands on Beth's shoulders.

"No! No, Roger, no!" She looked at him, her eyes pleading.

"Beth..." His expression showed how much he dreaded the action he was about to take.

"No!" Beth started screaming. He grabbed her around the waist and half-dragged, half-lifted her toward the door. "Chad! Don't do this! Please!" She was crying hysterically and struggling against Roger.

Cali was staring at Chad, as if she were glad he'd finally came to his senses. Suddenly, Roger pushed Beth to one side and lunged at the madwoman. He grabbed her arm and brought her wrist crashing down on the top of the boards forming the wall of the rink. She cried out in pain, and the gun fell from her hand, sliding several feet across the ice. Chad immediately began to hobble over to the door of the rink. Cali snarled with rage, and catching Roger by surprise, grabbed his head and slammed it into the top of the boards beside her. With a groan, he slid to the ground.

She rushed onto the ice, pushing the injured Chad down before he could reach the gun. She put her heel on his leg, trying to determine by the amount of blood on his pant leg just where the bullet entered him. She put her weight down and was gratified when he screamed in agony.

The pain was so intense that Chad thought he was going to vomit. Discovering the location of his wound, Cali decided to drop to a knee on his leg with all her weight. Again, he cried out in anguish. He stretched his hand out toward the gun, but it was at least a foot away. As he watched with swimming eyes, somebody picked it up.

"Get off him, Cali." Beth eyed her steadily.

"Oh, come on, Beth. Like you would use that on me."

"I sure don't want to, Cal, but I will if I have to." Her face displayed a fierce determination.

"Like you even know how to work it," Cali responded, though her confidence was wavering.

"My dad taught me. Two-time State Champ."

Cali eyed her intently to determine whether or not she was telling the truth. In the end, she decided to give up, making sure to grind her knee in one more time as she stood. She backed up against the boards.

Chad rolled over on his back with a groan. He was panting with his eyes shut and his face pinched with pain.

"Are you okay, babe?" Beth asked, chancing a quick glance at him.

"Yeah," he mumbled, his eyes still closed.

"I'm going to check on Roger. Back up, Cali."

She did as she was told, stepping through the doorway and onto the concrete. Roger sat, shaking his head, a large gash open above his eyes. Beth bent to help him, and Cali took the opportunity to run from the room. They looked up just as the door closed behind her.

"It's okay, Beth. Let her go. The cops are probably out there in mass by now."

She helped him, shakily, to his feet. Glancing over the boards, she saw Chad was sitting. "Maybe I should leave you two here and go get you some medical help."

"No way!" Roger insisted. "We're not splitting up." He grinned through his pain.

"Okay," Beth said, grinning back. The two of them managed to get Chad on his feet, or one foot anyway, and they made their way slowly, but surely, out to the stage area, where they could hear a lot of commotion.

When they entered, they could see a lot of policemen standing in a circle. One of the men shifted his weight and Beth spotted a foot with a familiar shoe. She rushed forward, forgetting for a moment she was helping to support Chad. The men parted as she came up behind them, revealing her friend's broken body lying on the stage, limbs jutting out at unnatural angles.

Beth fell to her knees beside the lifeless body. "Oh, Cal," she whispered in despair. She reached out and held her hand, bringing it up as she sought to cover her eyes. Her shoulders began to shake as she cried for her friend. The men stood around respectfully, but after a while, exchanged uncomfortable looks with one another. Chad and Roger shuffled over. Chad put a hand on her head, wishing he could scoop her up in his arms, but his injured leg made it impossible. She placed Cali's hand across her friend's chest, then laid her head on top of it and started weeping anew. Her naked grief was about killing everyone in the room, especially those who loved her. Chad looked at Roger, a helpless expression on his face.

Roger signaled to a police officer to take his place supporting Chad. He squatted down beside Beth, rubbing her back. Two men arrived with a stretcher, but hung back, giving her time to say her goodbyes.

ROGER GAZED DOWN AT Cali's face, so pretty now that it wasn't disfigured with rage. He had really begun to like her and could not reconcile the fun-loving Cali of the night before with the murderous one of today. He couldn't even imagine what Beth must be going through with all the memories the two of them shared.

AFTER SEVERAL MINUTES, Beth finally pulled away from Cali, lifting her chest as if it was made of lead. She peered into Cali's face again and felt a fresh wave of grief push into her heart. She turned and sobbed as Roger wrapped his arms around her, placing his cheek against her temple. The stretcher attendants looked at him, and he nodded. They began to load the body and prepare to take it away. A second set of attendants arrived to take care of Chad.

"Sir, we need to get a look at your leg."

Chad seemed unwilling to leave Beth's side. "In a minute."

"Sir, I think we need to attend to it now. You don't look good."

It was true; he was as white as their shirts. Beth stirred and Roger helped her to her feet.

"We're going to need to treat that cut, too," they said to Roger.

Two EMTs helped Chad onto the stretcher and started to check his vital signs. The paramedics, who had finished loading Cali's body onto a gurney and covered it with a sheet, now turned to Roger to examine his wound.

"Come here, babe," Chad called out to Beth.

She plodded over to him, and when she saw his ashen face, worry replaced the pain in her eyes. She stroked his face. "Are you okay?"

"I'll be fine," he reassured her. "I'm sorry, Beth." His voice cracked.

She nodded without saying anything, tears dropping onto his arm. He reached up, forgetting the paramedic was trying to take his blood pressure, and put his fingers underneath the hair at the back of her neck, his thumb rubbing away the tears still coursing down her cheeks. He pulled her in gently to kiss her, the salt of her tears flavoring their kiss.

"Sir, we're going to need to take you to the hospital now."

She lifted her eyes to the paramedics.

"You can ride with us. I want the doctor to check you out, too. Just to make sure."

"Damn! That hurts!" Roger yelped. "Be careful!"

"I'm trying to, sir," a paramedic replied patiently. He looked up as the other team passed. "We'll be right behind you."

CHAPTER THIRTY-THREE

B eth sat without speaking beside Chad in the ambulance as the paramedics started an IV and continued to monitor him. Despite how worried he was about her, Chad eventually drifted off to sleep, worn out by his
ordeal and loss of blood.

In the hospital, he was whisked off to surgery to remove the bullet in his
thigh and repair the damage it caused. Across the hall from him, surgeons
had already been working for some time on Pete's wound. Roger arrived and
griped the entire time they were suturing the cut on his head. It turned out
he only had a mild concussion, and he was released after a few hours.

The doctor prescribed a sedative for Beth, but she refused to take it until
Chad was out of surgery. She sat with David, who held her hand for hours.
He resisted asking her questions about what happened in the stadium and
gave the detectives hovering around them dark looks whenever they seemed
about to approach. Instead, he sat and rubbed his thumb over Beth's hand
and simply waited with her. In the end, Roger joined them, sitting on her
other side, uncharacteristically quiet. It was as if what they went through together secretly bonded them, and they felt comforted only in each other's
presence.

Pete pulled through surgery, and it seemed as if the robust bodyguard
was well on his way to a full recovery. Chad was eventually rolled out of
surgery, weak, but without complications. When he woke up, Beth was so
overwhelmed with relief she started crying again. David convinced her to
take the sedative.

Chad gave her a feeble smile, lifting his arm so she could climb onto
the bed with him. His height required the staff to get a special bed for him,
which was also wider, providing them with ample room. The feel of his arm
around her served as a further sedative and soon the two were asleep. For

hours nurses came and went, checking his vitals while the two slept, oblivious.

After they woke up, Roger offered to call Cali's and Beth's boss, and she allowed him to, asking him to tell her boss she would call when she was feeling better in a couple of days. He struggled through the phone call. How did you tell someone their friend snapped and killed an innocent man and wounded three others and now was dead? The police told them she tried to escape over the catwalk, chased by several officers. When she saw more policemen approaching from the other end of the catwalk, she tried to slide down one of the many cables hanging from the ceiling but lost her grip and came crashing down onto the stage. She landed awkwardly, snapping her neck and killing her instantly.

Chad was released from the hospital, after raising hell, to attend Cali's funeral in a wheelchair. The rest of the band was there, too, to support Beth. She decided not to return to the kitchen in the fall, realizing it wouldn't be the same without Cali. Her boss would have the rest of the summer to replace them.

The summer seemed to drag on forever for Beth. She couldn't seem to shake herself from the funk that settled over her. Her days were full of physical therapy appointments for Chad and Pete, who came to live with them for the summer. Her nights were often full of frightening images of Dante's face on Cali's pillow, Chad's screams of pain at the ice rink, and Cali's body sprawled across the stage.

Her pain seemed to lighten some when they returned to the tour buses in the fall. In some ways it was difficult, because it reminded them of what took place the last time they were all on the buses, but on the whole, it helped to be back together. They seemed to draw strength from each other.

One day, Chad and Roger returned to the bus after a shorter-than-usual sound check. They found Beth staring aimlessly out the window, dressed only in a faded denim, button-down shirt of Chad's and panties, her laptop open on the table, reading glasses perched on her nose. She was so lost in thought that she didn't even hear them enter the bus.

"Ahem," Chad cleared his throat.

She looked over, startled out of her reverie, and realized she wasn't dressed in an appropriate way for company. She comically tried to stretch her shirt down to cover more of her legs.

"Oh. I'm sorry." She grabbed a throw from off the back of a couch and wrapped it around her lower half.

"No need to be," Roger answered lustily.

Chad wore a goofy smile, also affected by the sight of her in his shirt, wearing the glasses he found so sexy. They always reminded him of a teacher, and he desired to be her naughty student.

Beth hurriedly closed her laptop. "I'll just go get dressed."

"No need to on account of me," Roger teased, watching her as she left. She turned back at the last minute, her face red, but a smile playing on her lips, something they hadn't seen for some time.

"I'm glad you're here," Chad told him with a grin. "That's the first smile I've seen on Beth's face in a long time." He reached into the fridge and pulled out a couple of beers.

"She'll get better. It's just gonna take some time, is all."

"Yeah," Chad responded, looking wistfully over at the door she just vanished behind.

"How's the leg?"

"Not bad. Hurt a little when I was playing tonight, though. It was weird being in a stadium again," he added, his voice subdued.

Roger nodded, but didn't comment further, taking a chug of his beer.

"How's Cassie settling in at school?"

"Oh," he answered, brightening, "she's doing great. She worries about Beth some. Calls just about every night. She met some guy, though." He frowned. "I'm not sure if I like that."

Roger smiled at the thought of Chad, the overprotective stepfather; although the more he thought about it, the more it seemed to fit him, being an overprotective brother for so long. "I met someone, too," the guitarist slipped in.

"What?" Chad sat straighter. "Tell me about her."

He laughed. "Her name is Susie. She's a dental hygienist." He took a long pull on his beer, thinking. "Actually, she reminds me a lot of Cali," he murmured. Then, he chuckled. "Same irreverent sense of humor."

"Can't wait to meet her."

"Well—" he jumped up, draining his beer "—I guess I should get going."

"You're going back to your bus to call her, aren't you?" Chad asked, grinning.

"Shut up," he sniped, trying to evade his eyes. "See ya later."

Chad sat for a few minutes, thinking about how sad Beth appeared to be when they first came in. He finished his beer and ambled back to the bedroom. She sat at his desk, her laptop open, but he felt sure she hadn't written anything. He was glad to see she hadn't changed. He pulled his T-shirt off without saying anything, a little sweaty from playing guitar, and sat on the end of the bed.

"Come here," he suggested, unable to keep the need out of his voice. As of late, the times that they'd made love had been few and far between, what with the soreness in his thigh and her lingering grief. He was patient with her, although it was difficult. Now, he was rewarded with a smile.

She untangled her legs and walked over to him slowly, tantalizingly. He could tell by the look on her face she wanted him, too, and it made his desire sharp. When she reached him, he ran his hands up the back of her smooth thighs, breathing in through his teeth, his anticipation heightening his senses. She let her eyes and hands explore his body. He carefully removed her glasses then tossed them aside without care. She giggled, and he relished the sound of it, his heart soaring with the memory of her as she used to be.

She brought a knee up on the side of the bed, and then on his other side, straddling him as he supported her with his hands under her tight tush. That simple movement made him feel as if he were losing his mind. Her hands were on either side of his face leading her as she leaned in to kiss him. His hands slid up her sides, surprised and pleased to find she had nothing on underneath the shirt besides the panties. He swung her around onto the bed and let himself go, burying his face in her neck, running his tongue along the sweet curve there, sucking her flesh into his mouth and applying pressure with his teeth. She moaned and undulated beneath him, her hips rising to press against his groin. His hands worked on shirt buttons, pulling the cloth away, exposing more flesh. Their lovemaking was furious and animalistic, their need driving them beyond their control.

Finally, with an explosion of bliss, they quieted, lying in each other's arms, their sweat commingling, breathing heavily, but with satisfaction, finally sated. They lay without speaking as the sky outside began to darken. He twined his fingers in hers, squeezing them gently, and broke the silence.

"I've missed you."

She sat on her side hurriedly. "I'm sorry. I—"

"No. I didn't mean to make you feel bad."

"I know. I've missed you, too," she avowed. Beth ran her hand back and forth over his chest rhythmically, contemplating something. "Do you think it's strange I miss her?" She didn't need to explain who she was talking about, as it was the person who consumed her thoughts of late.

"No, of course not. She was a very important part of your life."

"But...she tried to kill you."

He frowned, trying to explain the unexplainable. "But that was not the Cali we loved. It was not the Cali who made you laugh, who was always by your side when you needed her. What happened to her really wasn't her fault in a lot of ways."

"Do you have any idea how much I love you?"

"No. And I think you need to go to great measures to show me," he commented suggestively.

Beth laughed and slapped him lightly on the chest. She sighed with contentment. "This is the best I've felt in a long time."

"I'm glad." He kissed her hair.

Pete pounded on the outside of the bus. "You have a half hour."

"Slave-driver!" he called out, disgruntled. He kissed Beth once more, rolling out of bed to jump in the shower. When he came out of the bathroom, to his surprise, he found Beth fixing herself up. He looked at her quizzically.

"Do you think we could work in a little 'I Just Had to Have You Last Night'?"

"Damn straight!"

IT WAS THANKSGIVING and Beth and Chad were at her sister, Dana's house. Roger and Susie joined them, wanting to spend time together, but not quite ready for the whole meet-the-parents thing. Beth liked Susie, even though the hygienist reminded her a lot of Cali. She had the same off-beat sense of humor.

"Uncle Chad! Uncle Chad!" her nephews, Sean and Patty, called, barreling into the room.

"Whoa! Whoa, there. What's all the excitement?" Chad held out his hands to keep them from slamming into the couch.

"Will you play Guitar Hero with us?"

"Guitar Hero? Sure." Then, he remembered his wife. "That is, if it's all right with you, Beth?"

"Sure," she answered dryly. "Go ahead."

Not taking the hint, he was off the couch and scampering away, a nephew grabbing each hand and pulling him toward the basement door.

"Well, that's the last I'll see of him tonight," Beth commented, getting up to get another drink. "More wine, Suz?"

"Why not?"

"Pete?"

"Sure. Let me help you," he offered, starting to rise from his chair.

"No. You relax. I've got it."

Beth refilled her glass of Riesling and wrestled the Shiraz away from her Uncle John, to refill Pete's and Susie's. Giving her uncle a kiss on the cheek, she returned to the living room with the three glasses. "I'm going to go down and see how Chad's doing on Guitar Hero."

As soon as she thought Beth was out of earshot, Dana turned to the group. "They're on the road together day in and day out. Don't they ever get sick of each other?"

"Never," Roger, Pete, and Susie answered simultaneously.

Quite a crowd, mostly her nieces and nephews, were gathered around the TV downstairs as Chad took Patty on in Guitar Hero. Kids wriggled on the floor, slouched in chairs, and a few even sat on the foosball table—something Beth was pretty sure Dana would not approve of. The song finished, and Patty hollered, "Ha. I beat you again, Uncle Chad. And it's your own song!"

"Yeah, well..." Chad growled.

Beth came up behind him. "Honey," she whispered in his ear, among the hooting and hollering and general hubbub, "you have nothing to prove here.

You are a three-time platinum record holder. This isn't even a real guitar. You know you'd smoke him with a real guitar."

"Yeah, I know," he groused. "Just let me try one more time?" he begged her, sounding just like the ten-year-old he was challenging.

"Sure, go ahead. Just remember, rock star," she whispered flirtatiously, "you're going home with me tonight." She flashed her eyes at him in that way, making his heart do the rumba as she left with a come-hither smile. He just about put his guitar down and followed her, but Patty taunted him again.

"Maybe I should just go get my baby brother. Maybe he'd give me some competition."

"You're going down, Chump," Chad countered, adjusting the strap of his guitar.

An hour and a half later, Beth and Roger and the gang noticed it being perceptively quieter in the living room. "I wonder where everyone went," Beth mused out loud.

All of a sudden, they heard a roar go up from downstairs.

"What the hell?" Roger exclaimed. He looked at her with a smile, and they both took off, climbing over the coffee table to beat each other to the door to the basement. A hip-check putting her in the lead, Beth reached the bottom of the stairs with Roger, Susie, and Pete bringing up the rear.

They couldn't even step down on the floor because her whole family was gathered wall-to-wall, standing room only, watching Chad rock out on Guitar Hero. Finally getting a hang of the timing, he wasn't even really watching the notes any more as they flew across the screen on expert mode. Patty stood with his mouth agape, but his eyes gazing in awe at the rock god his uncle turned out to be.

"Wait till I tell the guys about this!" he shouted jubilantly.

"Has he always been this much fun?" Susie asked Beth.

"No," Roger answered for her. "Before he met Beth, he was a real ass."

"A real ass," Pete seconded.

"Oh no, he wasn't," Beth chided.

"Yes, he was!" the two argued in unison.

Chad glanced up and caught sight of Beth on the bottom step. RREERT. An off-note sounded. "Okay, show's over," he announced, his expression guilty. "I need to spend some time with your Aunt Beth."

"Aww. Come on, Uncle Chad. One more."

"Yeah," came a general murmur, "one more."

He looked at Beth and shrugged, a huge grin on his face.

"Yeah, babe," she shouted over the crowd, "one more." She smiled at him with a mixture of fondness and pride.

Without need for further urging, he ripped into another song.

An hour later, Beth was on her way to the bathroom when a pair of strong arms reached out and pulled her into a bedroom. Chad saw her coming before she spotted him and ducked into the bedroom where coats of various sizes and designs lay in a colorful heap on the bed. Once in the room, he pressed her against the wall with his body, hands on either side of her on the wall, kissing her until she was breathless.

"Umm," she moaned, "what are you doing to me?"

He grinned. "Being Thanksgiving and all, I just wanted to show you how thankful I was for you."

"Oh really?" she said, kissing him back and smiling.

"Seriously," he pulled away and regarded her in earnest. Touching her hair, he began singing, without accompaniment, his newest song, which she hadn't yet heard. He sang to her, his face still inches from hers, his eyes never leaving her face.

BEFORE YOU, I WAS A lost soul
    Wandering around, my heart with a hole
    I'd have fun with my friends
    But when it came to an end
    I had no one to rehash the day with
    No one just to lie with

MAKING OUR MUSIC IN the dark
    Just you and me
    Making our music in the dark

BEFORE YOU, I LIVED, my life barren
 No one to take joy or to share in
 The good times I had with my friends
 But when it all came to an end
 I had no one to rehash the day with
 No one just to lie with

MAKING OUR MUSIC IN the dark
 Just you and me
 Making our music in the dark

WITH YOU I CAN SHARE my private thoughts
 And get into trouble just to get caught
 You're the insider to all my inside jokes
 And you fix whatever inside of me is broke

BEFORE YOU I HAD NO one to wink at
 No one to even make me think that
 My life could be more than just empty
 Because now you're here you just tempt me

MAKING OUR MUSIC IN the dark
 Just you and me
 Making our music in the dark

AND NOW I'VE FOUND my home in you
 No one else will do

I'll spend my whole life through
Making love to you
Making our music in the dark
Just you and me
Making our music in the dark.

CHAD DRANK IN HER FACE as he sang, ending with his heart in his throat. Beth shattered the ice that held his heart for so long, and he was never more thankful to have her to love.

AS HE SANG, HE TURNED Beth inside out. He had the curious ability to be a goof one minute and to set her heart racing the next. She never thought she could have a second chance at love, or that someone would be able to break through the guard she put around her heart when Paul died, but she was so incredibly thankful Chad did.

NOTE FROM THE AUTHOR

THANK YOU FOR READING TRAPPED UNDER ICE, the first book in my ROCKING ROMANCE COLLECTION. I hope you enjoyed it. Now that you've read the book, won't you please consider writing a review? Reviews are one of the best ways readers discover great new books. They don't need to be fancy or long, just a sentence or two honestly describing your opinion of/experience with the book. I would sincerely appreciate it.

Want more from M.J. Schiller?

Page forward for an excerpt from ~

SING A SONG OF SIXPENCE

ROMANTIC REALMS COLLECTION

SING A SONG OF SIXPENCE

The birds began to sing. Or rather, shriek. The high-pitched noise was followed by the loud whir of wings as they lifted into the air. Isadore crooked her neck and watched them rise into the sky, obliterating the sun for a second, then she was forced to shade her eyes from its glare. Subtly, another noise replaced the first, coming from the same direction as the birds had and getting louder and louder with each passing moment.

What is...horses!

A chill washed over her that had nothing to do with the frigid water she was standing in. She had come with a dozen others to wash clothing in this stream. The water wasn't as deep as their normal creek bed, but it was closer to home, which is why they had chosen it. Nearby villages had been raided lately, and parents wanted their daughters close. She scanned the horizon and saw it. The wisp of smoke that meant others had been to their village.

Her warning burst from her mouth at the same time the mounts erupted from the tree line surrounding the watering hole.

"Riders!"

She moved as quickly as she could in the waist-deep water, releasing the shift she had been washing, letting it slowly drift away as the quiet idyllic scene of moments before changed into a nightmare. Horses came charging into the water from the banks, and women screamed as they attempted to flee but were caught up in the hands of riders. She searched for her sister, Ysmay, and caught sight of her red dress. A man had his arm around her neck and shoulders as he dragged her out of the water, kicking and screaming.

"No! Ysmay!" She began to wade in that direction, frustrated by the resistance of the water and the weight of her dress. All she could do was cry out and watch as the man managed to haul her sister onto his mount and plop her in front of him. He laughed and pulled on his horse's reins, turning its head back to the bank. "No. Let her go." Ysmay, at sixteen, was two years her senior, but, as she was smaller framed, people often mistook them for twins.

Ysmay turned back. Isadore couldn't hear her but read her lips. "Run, Izzy!"

Her view of Ysmay was cut off when a soldier and his steed sliced between them, a yard in front of her. The man grabbed a younger girl, who couldn't have been more than ten, and she cried out. With dismay, Izzy realized that it was too late to help Ysmay, but maybe she could at least save this one girl. Isadore struggled forward and lunged at the last second to latch onto the girl's leg before she could be plucked from the stream. Getting her feet under her, Isadore reached up farther to try to claw the girl from the man's grasp and almost succeeded. But she was so focused on prying his fingers from the girl's arm that she didn't see the sword in his other hand until it was too late.

She managed to turn so the broadside of the sword didn't connect with her face, but the solid blow to the temple area knocked her several feet. The fury of noise about her was drowned out as she sank under the surface of the water. Everything was muffled, save for the ringing in her ear, but she was unable to determine if that was a sound or simply a sensation. Her head was heavy, and she would have slipped into unconsciousness and drowned had she not, in flailing around, cut her foot on a rock. The sharp pain kept the blackness at bay. She blinked, looking up as a splotch of crimson floated eerily by. Something knocked against her, and she spun around to find herself face to face with a corpse. Mistress Blackny drifted past, her eyes wide but unseeing, her throat slashed and a steady stream of blood coloring the water around them. The mistress was her best friend Thea's grandmother and was more of a grandmother to Isadore than her own. In her horror, Isadore scrambled upright again, breaking the water's surface and sputtering, disconcerted by the return of the noise and action all around her, and the fact that the girl she'd been trying to save and the rider who had been trying to steal her away were nowhere in sight. Had she lost her senses after all?

She didn't have much time to consider it as a new agony assaulted her when her single braid was yanked, dragging her back against a boot and stirrup. As the rider bent over his horse, his voice was near, although she couldn't see him with her head forced down by his grip on her hair. She could, however, see the sword he threatened her with.

"Get on this horse or I'll run you through."

The blade was at eye level, giving her an idea. She took a breath and dove underwater. The sudden movement threatened to drag her captor from his saddle, so, like she'd hoped, he reflexively brought his sword hand in to brace himself against the side of the horse. The blade sliced through her hair freeing her and leaving him with her limp braid in his hand.

If she tried to swim away from the ruckus, he would no doubt catch her. Her only choice was to make her way back into the middle of the fray.

When she came up for air, she was in much shallower water and able to move more quickly than before. She heard the man with her braid cursing behind her and trying to turn his horse around.

"Get her!" he screamed, but everyone else was involved in their own skirmish and she was able to make it ashore.

Some of the raiders had hung back, out of the water, but the nearest was several yards off. Hearing the shouts, though, he twisted in his saddle and spotted her. He pulled on the reins and spurred his horse to pursue her. Trying to pull her wet skirts up to free her feet, Isadore ran as fast as she could, knowing he would be upon her in seconds and that all hope would be lost. But luck was with her, and the horse slid on the muddy bank, giving her precious time to get away.

Looking over her shoulder she saw her neighbor, Avalon, who had also managed to make her way to shore, snatched up by the man who had earlier been chasing Isadore and another from the group on shore. Izzy's gaze connected with Avalon's, and a stab of despair cut through her. She shut her eyes, internalizing the scream that begged to be released from her lips. Then, forcing the ache away, she turned away and kept running.

SING A SONG OF SIXPENCE coming soon!

ALSO FROM M.J. SCHILLER

ROMANTIC REALMS COLLECTION:
    TAKEN BY STORM
    AN UNCOMMON LOVE
    LEAP INTO THE KNIGHT
    LADY OF THE KNIGHT
    A KNIGHT TO REMEMBER

ROCKING ROMANCE COLLECTION:
    TRAPPED UNDER ICE
    ABANDON ALL HOPE
    BETWEEN ROCK AND A HARD PLACE
    ROCK ME, GENTLY
    MIDNIGHT MELODY

LOVE AND CHAOS SERIES:
    ROCKED BY GRACE
    ROCKED BY LOVE
    ROCK IT TO THE MOON
    ROCK OF SALVATION

REAL ROMANCE COLLECTION:
    UPON A MIDNIGHT CLEAR
    THE HEART TEACHES BEST
    DAMAGE DONE
    BLACKOUT
    HOMETOWN HEARTACHE
    TAKE A CHANCE ON ME

DEVILISH DESIRES SERIES:

TO HELL IN A COACH BAG
DAMNED IF I DO
THE DEVIL YOU KNOW
SATAN, LINE ONE
PITCHFORK IN THE ROAD
SIN WORTH THE PENANCE
HELL HATH NO FURY
TEN MINUTES IN THE SIN BIN
DEVIL'S IN THE DETAILS
DEVIL'S ADVOCATE (Coming soon!)
HADE'S NIGHT (Coming soon!)

INSATIABLE FIRE SERIES:

BEATING IN TIME
LEAD ME ON
ROCK WITH THE RHYTHM
BASSIST'S INSTINCTS

OTHERS:

HEARTS FLUSH (Pre-order now!)

ABOUT THE AUTHOR

BESTSELLING AUTHOR M.J. Schiller is a retired lunch lady/romance-romantic suspense writer. She enjoys writing novels whose characters include rock stars, desert princes, teachers, futuristic Knights, construction workers, cops, and a wide variety of others. In her mind everybody has a romance. She is the mother of a twenty-seven-year-old and three twenty-five-year-olds. That's right, triplets! So having recently taught four children to drive, she likes to escape from life on occasion by pretending to be a rock star at karaoke. However...you won't be seeing her name on any record labels soon.